the game plan

kristen callihan

The Game On Series

The Game Plan

A beard-related dare and one hot-as-hell kiss changes everything.

NFL center Ethan Dexter's focus has always been on playing football and little else. Except when it comes to one particular woman. The lovely Fiona Mackenzie might not care about his fame, but she's also never looked at him as anything more than one of her brother-in-law's best friends. That ends now.

Fi doesn't know what to make of Dex. The bearded, tattooed, mountain of man-muscle looks more like a biker than a football player. Rumor has it he's a virgin, but she finds that hard to believe. Because from the moment he decides to turn his quiet intensity on her she's left weak at the knees and aching to see his famous control fully unleashed.

Fi ought to guard her heart and walk away; they live vastly different lives in separate cities. And Dex is looking for a forever girl. But Dex has upped his game and is using all his considerable charm to convince Fi he's her forever man.

Game On

To the readers who demanded "The Wise One's" story. I thank you, Dex thanks you, and I know Fi certainly thanks you.

PROLOGUE

Dex

SWEAT TRICKLES DOWN MY SPINE. My bones ache, and my legs are wobbly jelly as I slowly walk over the bright green turf, now marred by long gashes and deep divots.

Around me other guys amble, their uniforms streaked with sweat, blood, and chalk. Thousands of cheering spectators create a dull rumble that I feel in the pit of my belly.

Welcome to Monday Night Football. Prime time sports at its finest. And my team has just won. I've done my job, and now that the adrenaline is wearing off, my high is crashing down. I want a shower, a hot meal, and devote a few hours to painting in the small studio I've made in my townhouse. But I have a dinner date and houseguest to meet.

Teammates slap my pads, tell me "good game" as I make my way across the field. A few of the guys from the other team seek me out, shaking my hand. But I'm looking for one guy in particular.

I see him, his head above most others. He catches my eye and grins. But his face is wan, deep circles marring his eyes. I know it's not because his team lost. We weave through the crowd to come together.

"Dex!" Gray Grayson, my former college teammate and one of my best friends on Earth, catches me up in a bear hug. It's awkward with both of us in pads, helmets in hand. "Good game, man. But we're totally gonna kick your ass next time."

"Better tell your D to get their heads out of their asses, then," I say, giving his head a light tap. "Good to see you, Gray-Gray."

God, I miss playing with him. He's the best tight end I've seen in years. And our college team had been a well-oiled machine.

The NFL isn't the same as college. Ego, money, high stakes, all of it is just more. It's a job now. I love it, but the carefree joy is gone.

We walk toward the sideline together.

"How's Ivy and the baby?" I ask. They had a baby about a month ago and named him Leo, after Leonhard Euler, one of Gray's favorite mathematicians.

"Man," Gray says with a slow shake of his head as he grins wide. "I must have done something really right in another life."

"That good, huh?" I'm happy for him. Even if his exuberant happiness reminds me I have no one.

"Best family a man could ask for." Gray runs a hand over the back of his neck and squeezes. Despite his declaration, he sounds worn out.

"Not that I don't believe you, Gray, but you kind of look like shit. What's going on?"

His smile is tight. "Only you would notice that."

We're almost at the sideline, and he'll be going to the guest locker rooms. So we slow down.

"Leo hasn't learned to sleep through the night. Ivy and I are feeling it." He grimaces. "Mostly Ivy, unfortunately, because I'm on the road a lot."

If Gray is admitting he's losing sleep, it must be bad.

I brace his shoulder with my hand. "You got a bye week after this, right?"

"Yeah."

"Me too. Mind me coming over for a visit?"

Gray lives in San Francisco, and though I've been meaning to go out there, I haven't yet done it. While I'm happy to actually visit Gray,

I also know I can help him out. Not that I can tell him as much or he'd insist he has everything covered.

Gray's smile is wide. "I'd love to have you. I know Ivy would too."

"You sure about that? Ivy might not want visitors when she has a new baby." It has to be said, because Gray also tends to react before he thinks.

"Naw, she's been kind of lonely." His brows gather. "Neither of us likes solitude very much."

Tell me something I don't know. I give his shoulder another squeeze. "Great. Let's get something to eat."

Gray gives a long groan. "Oh, man, I've been looking forward to this. We're hitting up Cochon, right?" His eyes gleam at the prospect of eating at one of New Orleans' best restaurants. And, frankly, my stomach growls too.

"Yep. I told them we're coming, and they're planning something good for us. I believe I heard mention of the *whole hog.*"

Gray groans again. "I might cry."

He often gets weepy over food, so I don't blink an eye. "Meet me outside the locker rooms in thirty?"

Gray is staying at my place tonight before he heads back home with his team.

He gives a nod and starts to trot off, but then turns back. "Oh, hey, Fi's also gonna be staying the week with us. That cool with you?"

Everything inside of me stops—my heart, my breath. Then it all kicks up again, hard and insistent.

Fiona Mackenzie. Ivy's little sister. And I do mean little. Five foot three if she's an inch, her frame is petite but curvy. She caught my attention and kept it from the first time I laid eyes on her two years ago.

Bright green eyes, wild blond hair, smiling full lips, and a lilting laugh that, whenever I hear it, makes my dick hard. This is how I picture Fi—when I allow myself to picture her in the lonely hours of the night.

I haven't allowed myself in quite some time. Dreaming of Fi is a special type of torture. Sure, she's beautiful, but more than that, she's one of the most direct people I've ever met.

As someone whose career depends on analyzing false plays and misdirection, being around her is like stepping out of the stifling darkness and into a fresh, sunny day. Every time I'm in her presence I can breathe easier, see clearer. And I crave that more than I'd like to admit.

I'd say she was the girl who got away, but we were never that close. Fi has failed to notice me past the casual friendliness of an acquaintance.

Fiona Mackenzie. In the same house. For a week.

Gray is waiting for me to respond. I give him a nod. "Looking forward to it."

And suddenly I am. More than I've ever anticipated anything in my life.

CHAPTER 1

Fiona

TRUTH? I LIKE MEN. Scratch that. I *love* men. I love their strength, their deeper voices, the simple way they come at a problem. I love their loyalty. I love the way their wrist bones are wide and solid, and that their hips are straight and narrow. Hell, I even love watching their Adam's apple bob when they swallow.

And, yeah, I'm talking in generalities. Because I've met my share of shitty men. But, on the whole, I am a big fan of the male gender.

Which is why I'm slightly bummed to be man-free at the moment. I had a great boyfriend during college. Jake. He was hot and easygoing. Maybe too easy. He basically loved everyone. Sure, I was his girlfriend, but if I wasn't around? No problem. Plenty of other people to hang with.

He didn't cheat. He just didn't really care enough. And after seeing what my sister, Ivy, has with her guy? That kind of all-encompassing, I-have-to-be-with-you devotion? I want more than casual dating. I want to be someone's necessity, and for them to be mine.

Of course, I'm not going to find that at this tiny little club on a Tuesday night. But I'm not here for the men—most of whom are clearly on the prowl for a quick hookup. I'm here for the music. The band has a funky trip-hop sound that I love, and the atmosphere is mellow.

Since busting my ass to finish college and starting a job now plagued by a sneaky, idea-stealing co-worker, who I want to kill, I need mellow.

I slouch down in the bench seat—nestled at a far corner table, drink my Manhattan, and enjoy the moment.

I've decided I also love San Francisco, which is where I am now, using my vacation time to visit my sister and her husband. Unfortunately, Ivy and Gray had no desire to come out with me tonight because they have a new baby who wakes up every two hours. Yeah, not going to say I love the sleeping habits of babies, no matter how cute and awesome said baby is.

I suppress a shudder. My life might be frustrating at the moment, and I might be a tinge lonely, but at least I'm not walking around sleep-deprived. Instead I'm listening to a singer crooning about stars, her voice smooth as poured syrup. The cocktail is smoky-sweet on my tongue and warm in my veins. I'm so relaxed at this point that I almost miss the man sitting to my right.

I really don't know what prompts me to turn and look his way. Maybe it's because the set ends and my attention diverts from the stage. Or maybe I feel his gaze, because it's on me, steady and unblinking.

Not one to shy away, I stare back and take him in.

He's not my type.

First off, he's huge, as in built like a brick house, with shoulders so wide I'm fairly certain I could perch on one of them and have room to spare. He's slouched in his chair, so I don't know how tall he is, but I'm thinking he's at least six foot four or more, which would make him over a foot taller than me. I hate feeling tiny; I get that enough already without standing next to a super-tall man.

And he has a beard. Not a wild, bushy one, but thick and full, framing the square edge of his jaw. It's kind of hot. Even so, I am not into beards. I like smooth skin, dimples—a boyish look.

Nothing is boyish about this dude. He's a strange mix of lumber-sexual and pure, broody male. His hair is pulled into a knot at the back of his head, samurai style, which highlights the sharp crests of his cheeks and the blade of his nose.

He might not be my type, but his eyes are gorgeous. I have no idea what color they are, but they're deep-set beneath strong, dark brows. And even from here, his thick lashes are visible, almost feminine in their length. God, those eyes are beautiful. And powerful. I feel his stare between my legs like a slow, hot stroke.

He stares at me like he knows me. Like I should know him too. Weirdly, he *is* familiar. But my mind is muzzy with one too many cocktails to figure out why.

Apparently, he gets this because the corner of his wide, lush mouth twitches as if I amuse him. Or maybe it's because I'm sitting here staring back at him.

He's a cheeky one, isn't he? Just as blatant in his appraisal.

So I decide to glare, raising one brow in the same way my dad does when he's displeased. Having been on the receiving end of that look, I know it's effective. On most people. This guy? His amusement grows. Though he really only smiles with his eyes and lifts a brow as if to mock me.

And then it hits me: That quietly amused, slightly contemplative expression, I've seen it before. I've seen *him* before. I do know him. He's Gray's friend and old college teammate.

As if he reads my thoughts, he gives me a slow nod of hello.

I find myself laughing. At myself. He wasn't checking me out at all. He was waiting for me to recognize him. My fuzzy brain searches for a name.

Dex. He's Dex.

I give him a nod, inclining my chin. And he rises. Up. Up. Up.

Yep. Tall as a tree.

I remember that he now plays center in the NFL. And though a lot of centers sport a big barrel belly, Dex doesn't. No, he's just pure, hard muscle. All of it visible beneath the black tee and faded jeans he's wearing. All of it moving with the natural grace of a professional athlete as he strides toward me.

"Fiona Mackenzie." His voice is low, steady, and kind.

I don't know why I think *kind* but it sticks in my head and relaxes me in a way I ordinarily wouldn't if some guy I barely knew approached me when I was on my own in a club.

"Hi, Dex. Sorry it took me a minute. I'm usually quicker than that." I nod at the chair in front of me. "Care to join me?"

He glances at my nearly empty glass. "Want another drink first?"

"Yeah. Thanks." If only to have something to do with my hands. Because, while he doesn't threaten me, he has a presence that's potent.

My stomach tightens when he leans close as if he might embrace me, his massive frame shadowing the small table. But he merely sticks his nose to my glass and takes a sniff. With a nod, he straightens and turns toward the bar.

I do *not* admire his ass as he walks away. Okay, maybe a little. Because *damn*.

He returns soon enough, another Manhattan in one hand, a bottled water in the other. A memory hits me—of how he usually drinks water, almost never any liquor.

Before he can sit, a girl comes up to our table, her eyes pleading.

"Are you using this chair?" She puts a hand on the only chair at the table. The other side is pulled up against the bench seat I'm using that runs along the wall. Technically, Dex could sit next to me.

We all are clearly aware of this. The girl looks between us as if to drive this point home. It would be petulant for me to say no. So I nod. And she whisks it away before I can change my mind.

That amused look doesn't leave Dex as he settles next to me, his thigh close enough to mine that I feel his body heat. Not that I think he's doing this on purpose—he's just that big, and the space is just that small.

Smiling a bit, I take a sip of my drink. "You knew I was drinking a Manhattan based on smell alone?"

Dex sets his water on the table, calling attention to the tattoo sleeves he has on both arms. "My uncle owns a bar. I've helped out over the years." He glances at my glass. "That and the cherry gave it away."

And it's like my brain turns off, because I pull that cherry out of my drink and put it between my lips to suck it. Like some damn porn star. His gaze snaps to my mouth, and his eyes narrow.

Damn, but I feel it again. That slow, hot stroke between my legs. This guy makes me wet with just one look.

Flushed, and cursing myself an idiot for putting on a display, I yank the stem from the cherry and eat the fruit with brisk efficiency before taking a hasty sip of my cocktail. "So, Dex," I say quickly—as if I didn't just try to call attention to my mouth. "It's been a while."

He blinks, his gaze dragging from my lips to my eyes. "Ethan."

"What?"

"My name," he says. "It's Ethan." The corners of his eyes crinkle. "Ethan Dexter."

"Ah." I take another sip. "So I'm not allowed to call you Dex? That only apply to friends or something?"

He doesn't laugh or fidget, just keeps his gaze steady on my face. "Didn't mean it as an insult. You can call me Dex, if you like."

Before I can ask him why he'd insisted on Ethan if that's the case, he speaks again. "I haven't seen you since the wedding."

Gray and Ivy's wedding. Now *that* was a drunken blur. Good times.

Truly, I don't drink often. But when I do… Ahem. Which is why I try to avoid reaching the point of maximum craziness.

Memories of the wedding are a strain, but hazy edges of them remind me that I danced with Gray's boys—Dex included. Ivy danced too, which is always a show. My sister, who I love more than anyone on Earth, is a horrible, scary dancer. So mainly I'd concentrated on helping Gray run interference, making sure she didn't accidentally clock anyone on the head while she convulsed—*danced*.

"I remember you mostly holding one of the walls up all night," I tell Dex now. He'd danced a few songs, sure, then had taken a bottled water and leaned against the wall to watch the rest of us.

He grips his current bottled water. It's too dark to see what his tattoos are, but I can tell they're colorful, vintage looking. And he has more of them than he did a year ago.

"Sometimes it's more fun to watch." His gaze doesn't move from my face, but it feels like it does. My breasts swell heavy against my bra, more so when he continues. "You ripped your dress off and flung it in a tree."

A flush works over my cheeks. It was a tropical resort. And I'd wanted to swim. Everyone did. I lean forward. "Are you saying you liked watching me strip, Ethan Dexter?"

His chuckle is a gentle rumble. "I'm saying it was memorable." He glances down, those long lashes hiding his eyes. "And entertaining."

"I aim to please." Crossing one leg over the other, I study him. I'm enjoying myself, which is a surprise because I never pegged Dex as much of a talker. "What are you doing in San Francisco? I don't recall you playing for Gray's team."

"I have a week off, and so does Gray…" His broad shoulders lift in a shrug. "I thought I'd visit him and Ivy."

"Wait. What?" A bad thought rises in my head, and I find myself leaning toward him. "You're staying with them too?"

He nods, wariness creeping over his features.

"Did they send you here to babysit me?" I snap. I cannot believe he just happens to be at the same club. Not after both Gray and Ivy had complained about me going out on my own tonight.

"Yes and no." Dex takes a long pull of his water. "Yes, they said you were here. Yes, they were worried. But I happen to like this band, so I thought I'd come listen and say hello in the process."

"Oh, how convenient," I drawl, sitting back against the wall.

"Isn't it," he agrees in a dry voice.

I snort, the temptation to chuck my cherry stem at him riding high. I don't think he'll care if I do. Dex seems too unflappable to be offended by flying fruit bits.

"You don't have to stay," I tell him. "You can inform the wardens that you saw me, and I was fine, and be on your way."

He doesn't flinch. "I want to sit with you."

Okay. Right. The big football player wants to listen to moody music all night. Sure.

My expression must be skeptical because he gives me a half smile and hands me his phone. "Check my music selection."

He doesn't have a password—not smart—so it's easy to look. Flunk, Goldfrapp, Massive Attack, Portishead, Groove Armada, even some Morcheeba... He's got a veritable trip-hop library going.

I grin up at him. "You know, before this, I'd have taken you for a hard rock, or maybe even a bluegrass fan."

"It's the beard, isn't it," he asks.

"And the man-bun."

He laughs, a short rumble of sound. "Want me to let it down?"

Yes. Maybe.

"Not necessary. Man-buns are hot. I blame Jason Momoa. There was only so much watching him bang Khaleesi the female population could take before they wanted their own Khal Drogo."

Shit. I really don't know what the hell I'm doing. Because it sounds a lot like flirting to me. Instinct tells me flirting with Ethan Dexter isn't something to do lightly. And there's the fact that I don't go for athletes. At all. I don't care how fit they are. Or how confident. I don't like sports. Football bores me. Oh, I know tons about the sport—kind of impossible not to in my family—but I don't want to pretend that I care when I'd rather talk about other things.

Dex's eyes crinkle again, and he turns toward me, leaning an elbow on the table. "Doesn't Momoa have a beard?"

I wave my hand. "Who has time to look at his beard when his muscles are on display?"

I most certainly do not look at Dex's phenomenal arms.

"So your stance on beards is?" His gaze so strong I feel it in my toes.

My breathing picks up. "Don't particularly like them."

It's the truth. And yet I can't help but look at his. It's dark, framing his mouth, which should be a turnoff for me. Only it draws all my attention there. To the shape of his mouth—the upper lip a gentle curve, the lower lip fuller, almost a pout. There's something slightly illicit about the whole effect.

I clear my throat, glance up, and find him watching me through lowered lids. He doesn't seem particularly put out by my frankness.

"What don't you like about them?"

Is he serious?

He stares at me.

I guess he is.

Taking a quick sip of my drink, I search for an answer. "They're just so…fuzzy. Prickly."

He moves in, not crowding me, but putting himself at arms' reach. He smells faintly of cloves and oranges. It must be his aftershave or cologne, but it works for me.

I'm distracted by it and almost jump when he speaks again. "Do you know this based on experience, or are you making an assumption?"

My gaze narrows. "Aren't you the philosopher."

"You didn't answer the question."

"Fine. Assumption."

His lips quirk. "You should find out if your assumption is true before you condemn the beard."

"Is this some sort of creepy way to get me to touch your beard?"

A challenge flashes in his eyes. "There are a few guys at the bar sporting beards. You could go ask them. But I figure since we know each other…"

"Not *that* well."

"You'd rather ask a stranger?"

"You're assuming I care enough to ask, Slick."

His teeth shine white in the shadows of the club. "I know you're curious. You're fairly twitching with wanting to know."

I flatten my hands against the table and glare. Is it just me, or is he closer? Close enough that I can see his eyes are hazel, lighter around his cornea with a starburst pattern. I wish I could see the colors, but he's painted in shades of blue and gray right now.

And he's watching me. Patient. Calculating. Tempting.

"It's always the quiet ones," I mutter before taking a breath. "Okay, I'll pet your fuzzy face."

"Hold up." Without hesitation, he reaches for my drink and takes a sip. "Liquid courage."

A strangled laugh leaves me. "Because I'm *sooo* scary."

"You have no idea, Cherry."

I think I growl at him. I definitely want to give his precious beard a good, hard tug. But he simply lifts his brows at me. "Get on with it, then."

This cheeky bastard is totally playing me. And here I am falling into his trap. Because I cannot look away from his beard now. More specifically, his lips, which are parted just slightly. An invitation. A dare.

Shit. I've never been very good at ignoring a dare.

I hate that my hand trembles as I reach up to touch him. He stays perfectly still, his arm casually slung on the edge of the booth behind me, his body turned toward mine. But I don't miss the way his breathing has kicked up just slightly.

I hesitate, shy almost. Hells bells, I'm only going to touch a bit of facial hair. Why does it feel like we're two kids tucked in a dark corner, playing a game of "I'll show you mine"?

Annoyed with myself, I close the distance between us.

Soft. His beard is soft. And springy. I didn't expect that.

Gently I press my fingertips into all that springy-soft mass, stroke it a little. His nostrils flare on an indrawn breath.

I glance at him, search his eyes. He gives me nothing back. So I keep going, running my fingers up his jaw, against the grain. There's the prickle I expected. Only it feels good, sending little tingles of awareness over my skin, up my thighs.

I swallow hard, press my legs together. Can he tell? I'm too chicken to check. I keep my focus on his face, on his lips, which look so smooth in comparison to his beard.

My own lips part, suddenly sensitive. Somehow I've moved closer. I can't help myself. I trace the bottom edge of his lower lip with my thumb.

Sweet Mary Jane Watson, that was a mistake. The contrast between his soft yet firm mouth and the thick, crinkly beard sends a bolt of sheer, shocking *want* straight to my clit.

In a daze, I stroke his lips again, following the gentle upper curve, keeping contact with his beard while I do. Fuck, but I can't stop imagining his mouth moving over my skin. Would I feel his beard when he sucked my nipples?

I'm throbbing now. Said nipples aching for relief. Dex's warmth is a wall against my chest. I've moved onto my knees before him without realizing it, my free hand clutching his shoulder as if I'm afraid he'll back away.

But he won't. Not when his big, heavy hand has landed on my hip, bracing me, his fingers clutching in a way that's a little possessive and a little protective.

I should stop. I tell myself this even as I keep tracing his mouth, the corners of it, his chin. Dex breathes lightly through his parted lips, and each exhale sends a little gust of soft warmth over me.

I want—no, I *need*—to feel more. And that need has a mind of its own. I feel his shocked intake of breath a second before my lips graze his. God. *God,* that's good. Silky-firm, prickly-smooth. I do it again, touching the corner of his mouth, his beard tickling my lips.

A small whimper sounds between us. I don't know if I made it or he did. Doesn't matter. I've become obsessed with his mouth, taking kiss after kiss, just feeling it.

Jesus, there's something downright dirty about beards. Fucking naughty. All I can think about now is sex. About other places with hair that's both soft and wiry. My mind fills with images of this thick, full beard running over my clit and how it would tickle and tease. And it makes me frantic.

I lick into his mouth, greedy, needy, my thumbs bracketing the corners to feel him as I taste him.

Dex's groan vibrates through his body. A heavy hand cradles the back of my head, his long fingers twisting into my hair. Then he's angling his head, kissing me back, deeply and thoroughly, as if I've woken him from a long sleep, and he's starving.

Lust rushes through me harder and faster than I've ever experienced. It takes my breath, my reason. I can only stroke the sides of his face, press my tender breasts against his chest, and give him what we both want.

He tastes of whisky and sweet vermouth, candied cherries and some mouthwatering flavor I can only assume is his own. I slide my tongue along his to get more of it.

Dex's chest heaves on a breath, his mouth opening wider to let me in. His large hands cup my ass. Suddenly I'm weightless, dizzy. I land on his lap, straddling his hips. He's big enough that it's a stretch. I wrap my arms around his head, grind my center against a rock hard erection that's truly impressive. Perfection.

He reacts with a grunt and squeezes my ass, spreading my cheeks apart in a way that's downright lewd and so hot that I whimper, rock into him again.

That we're basically dry-humping and fucking each other's mouths is all I care about. Until I hear a catcall, loud and unmistakable.

"Fuck yeah, man. Give it to her."

We freeze, our lips still touching. My heartbeat thunders in my ears.

Putting a protective hand at the nape of my neck, Dex turns his head and glares over my shoulder. I can't help but look too, and find a table of three guys watching us with unabashed interest.

One loudmouth hoots again. "Fucking nice, honey."

Shit. It isn't really my style to give a public show.

Dex's muscles bunch. God, but he's solid. A veritable wall to lean on. His voice comes out deep and hard. "Enough."

That's it. One word. And the odd thing is, the guys listen. Immediately they turn away and busy themselves in their drinks.

I glance back at Dex to witness the tail end of his scary glare before it fades to his usual neutral expression.

Some guys are alpha dogs, snarling and snapping. Dex is more like a silverback gorilla, quietly going about his business until something pisses him off and he gives a warning.

I wonder what would happen if he truly lost his temper. He could easily pound the shit out of most people. Something those guys obviously understand.

But I no longer care about them. Now that we're not mauling each other, I'm slightly mortified over the way I outright jumped Dex.

His expression isn't smug, though. It's thoughtful and a bit tender. "So, still not a fan of the beard?"

Sign me up and call me a convert. "Tell the truth. Did you do all this just to get me to kiss you?"

"No." He gives my hair—now fisted in his hand—a tug, holding me a little away so he can study my lips. "I just wanted you to touch me."

Then he takes my mouth again. One more time in a slow, exploring kiss before letting me go.

Breathless and more than a bit befuddled, it takes me a moment to gather my wits and climb off of him. I don't even know what to do with myself. Don't get me wrong, I love sex and am not ashamed to go after it. But I don't do this. I don't make out with guys who aren't remotely my type. And I certainly don't hit on a friend of my family; that's just asking for awkward when things go south.

"Let's go home," Dex says quietly.

My gaze snaps to his, and he winces.

"I'm not implying to bed. Just back to Ivy and Gray's." He glances at his watch—a thick, black leather one that looks more like a cuff. "It's coming on two in the morning. Bar's going to close down soon anyway."

"Okay, sure." Home sounds like a good plan. Only I want to go alone and not have to face Dex anymore. Hottest kiss of my life or not, it's not something I can do again. Ethan Dexter could become an addiction if I take another taste of him.

CHAPTER 2

Dex

I N THE COURSE OF MY LIFE, I've done stupid things. Who hasn't? But kissing Fiona Mackenzie comes close to the top of the list. Ironically, it is definitely one of the *best* things I've done in my life as well. Painfully good.

Painful now. I've a hard-on that won't go away and is bent awkwardly down the leg of my jeans. I'd adjust, but I know Fiona would notice. Not much gets by her.

Then again, she's making a valiant effort to ignore me now, her gaze set on the window at her side as we drive Gray's old pickup back to his house.

I love Grayson. The man is worth over 25 million dollars, and he still drives his high school truck. But now I'm thinking about the fact that I had my tongue in his baby sister-in-law's mouth, and I have to resist the urge to wince.

I shouldn't have done it. But my brain took a vacation. I know how good I am at manipulating a situation, and I saw the curiosity in Fi's bright green eyes. So I cajoled, enticed, all but dared her to get up close and personal with my face. Had I expected her to kiss me? Hell no.

But I'd taken one look at her in that club and wanted her to touch me, to fucking *see* me more than my next breath. I've wanted that from the moment I laid eyes on her two years ago at her sister's Christmas party.

Even then I knew Fiona wasn't for me. I'm quiet, like to keep to myself. Fiona is life—bouncy, bubbly, snarky life. All wrapped up in a tiny, perfect package.

I've often heard Ivy compare Fi to Tinker Bell. I suppose that's accurate. Only I've always found the little cartoon fairy annoying, and I could watch Fi all day. Just the lilting sound of her voice entrances me. And when her nose wrinkles and she glares? Hard as a fucking pike.

Yeah, I've got it bad. Which is not good. I know full well she doesn't want anything to do with professional athletes. I'd heard her say that much outright at the wedding. A girl I was interested in during college ditched me for the same reason, and I've no interest in getting my heart stomped on again.

Which is why I shouldn't have touched, much less kissed, Fi. Because I can't stop replaying it in my mind. I know what she tastes like now. And she tastes like addiction.

Gripping the wheel, I turn us into Gray and Ivy's driveway. They bought a massive townhouse in Pacific Heights. I have to admit, I'm envious. It's the kind of place I'd love to call home. My place is a nice but fairly empty townhouse in New Orleans. I love its high ceilings, old wood floors, and natural light. But it doesn't feel like a home. Then again, maybe it's because I'm the only one ever in it.

We're silent as we pull into the garage and climb the back steps to the main floor. I'm only vaguely surprised when Gray comes shuffling out of the kitchen holding a bottle in one hand and a pot in the other. He's a mess, his blond hair flattened on the side, his sweats inside out and backwards. Deep circles shadow his eyes.

"Hey," he mutters. "Have fun?"

He doesn't look as though he cares much about anything other than sleep at the moment.

"What's the pot for, man-mountain?" Fi asks him before gently taking it from his hand.

He blinks down at it. "Right. I was going to put that in the sink."

From a flight above comes the irate squall of a baby.

"The tiny overlord demands his due," Gray says. But he stops to kiss Fi on the cheek. His expression lightens a bit as he pulls back. "You smell like cologne, Fi-Fi."

Hot pink washes over Fiona's cheeks. "I smell like a nightclub."

"Cologne," Gray counters as he trudges toward the stairs. His gaze lands on me. "Dex's cologne. And don't bother denying it. I roomed with the guy for years."

So much for keeping things from Gray. The guy might love to joke, but he's an outright genius, so I'm not really surprised he caught me.

He doesn't say anything more about it, though. His shoulders slump as he starts up the stairs. "I swear to God, I'd give someone five—no ten—million dollars right now if Ivy and I could just get one solid night's sleep."

Fi and I exchange a sympathetic look. It might be awkward between us, but at least we can escape to our beds and sleep.

"I'm going to go earn ten million dollars," I say to her and head for the stairs.

She follows behind. "This I have to see."

We find Gray in a nursery that would fit right into a design catalog. I know Fi decorated it, and she's clearly talented. Gray's slumped in a glider trying to give his agitated son a bottle. But the little guy is screaming, his tiny fists beating against Gray's arm.

"It's my turn to feed him," Gray says without looking up. "So bottled breast milk it is. He hates it. I know, little dude," he says to the baby. "I love Mommy's boobs too, but she needs to sleep."

From the far room, a muffled groan rings out. "Mother guilt has killed my sleep," says Ivy's disembodied voice. "And don't discuss my boobs with my son, Cupcake."

I glance through a connecting door and see her long legs sprawled over a massive bed. Fi is short, but Ivy is a good six feet tall. At the moment, she's totally wiped.

"Hand him over, Grayson," I say.

Gray looks at me as if I'm nuts, then shakes his head and offers me his son. His trust is something I will never take for granted. And guilt hits me anew for touching Fi. But now I have a wiggling, screaming one month old in my hands.

Walking over to the changing table, I pull out one of the many swaddling blankets they have stacked—unused—on the shelves. Leo turns a nice shade of angry red as I wrap him up tight, tucking his arms against his body. The result is a securely swaddled baby with only his head sticking out.

Gray and Fi come to watch, clearly curious. But when I pick Little G up and loudly shush him, they both flinch.

"Dex, dude, what—"

I give Gray a quelling look and shush the crying baby again, right in his ear. Finally he hears me and abruptly quiets as I gently jiggle his little body, all the while shushing.

Ivy's head pops around the doorway. Her dark eyes are wide with shock.

"What—"

Gray waves a frantic hand to quiet her, but I shake my head and walk back to the glider. "Don't be afraid of noise," I tell them. "Little man has been hearing it his entire existence. Well, until he was born and you guys started going silent on him."

I give the baby his bottle, and he begins to drink as I rock.

Fi comes to stand next to me. "And how do you know so much about babies?"

"My little brother was a surprise. My parents had him when I was seventeen. I know about babies."

I glance at Ivy and Gray, who are both gaping at me. "If you have a white-noise machine, I suggest you turn it on now and keep it on high."

Gray scrambles to get it, and Ivy comes closer. "Dex, I'm this close to crying at your feet right now. Don't ever leave me."

"Can we share him?" Gray asks as he turns on the machine.

I get up and hand Gray the baby. "Keep him swaddled. Do the shushing and jiggling thing if he wakes. I'm going to send you some video links in the meantime."

Ivy flings herself at me. "I love you, Dex."

"He's half mine," Gray reminds her. His bleary eyes meet mine. "I'll send you a check when I can see straight, man."

"I took your X-Box into my room. That's payment enough."

Gray waves a hand as he tucks his son close to his chest. "You can have the damn thing. I still might kiss you."

"Promises, promises." I do give the top of Ivy's head a kiss. She smells of breast milk and baby. But deep beneath that, there's a strange similarity to Fi. Nothing as potent, but enough to make me aware that she's Fi's sister.

I am aware of Fi as well, following me out of the room. We're quiet as we walk up the next flight of stairs to the guest level. Together. Alone.

Every touch, every slow glide of lips, tongue, fingertips. Every breathy sigh. All of what she did to me plays through my head like a footage reel.

Her cheeks are flushed now, her nipples pointing through the thin, silky ivory top she's wearing. I want to push my thumb against one of those buds. Pull her shirt over her head and…

I clear my throat as we reach our doors, one on each side of the small landing. She hesitates, obviously searching for something to say.

I know what I'd like to say. *Kiss me again. Let me in. Just…let me.* I keep my mouth shut. Fiona Mackenzie isn't for me. Hell, I can't even tell her that what we did tonight was the single most erotic experience of my life. I'm sure it was just a strange encounter with a guy and a beard on her part.

I run a hand over my mouth, my fingers digging into my scruff. I suddenly resent my beard. It's as if she wanted it more than she wanted me, and I can't stand that. "Well," I say before she can speak. "Goodnight."

"Dex," she says as I open my door.

I pause, my heart thudding against my ribs. But I don't turn. I don't want her to see my expression. "Yep."

"Thanks." She takes an audible breath. "For helping my sister and Gray. It means so much to them."

Disappointment punches through my chest with the force of a lineman. I manage a nod. "It was nothing." Which I guess sums up my entire night.

CHAPTER 3

Fiona

B REAKFAST AT IVY AND GRAY'S HOUSE starts at 11 a.m. Which is fine by me. After I went to bed last night, I tossed and turned far too long, the ache in my nipples and slick throb between my legs demanding attention I wasn't willing to give. Not with Dex across the hall. Not when I'd have thought of Dex while doing it. That would only have made things worse.

As it is, I'm grumpy and chomping on a slice of buttered whole grain bread like I'm trying to annihilate it. Worse? Ivy is watching me.

Her dark eyes track my movements as I pick up my coffee and take a bracing drink. "You're staring."

"Well, duh."

"Are you asking for me to ping you with this bread?" I say before taking another bite and talking with my mouth full. "Because I totally will."

She looks semi-rested now. Her hair, at least, is washed and combed. And she smirks before drinking her orange juice. "Gray says you smelled like you'd rubbed yourself all over Dex last night."

"Gray can sit on it and spin." I swear, these two are the worst gossips.

She snorts into her glass. "Colorful. Now tell the truth, Fi-Fi. Were you rubbing yourself all over Dex?"

Like a cheap suit on a sultry day.

As if reading my thoughts, she leans her elbows on the table and gives me a sly smile. "He's totally hot, in a bad-boy rocker kind of way. Which is weird considering his job."

"Bashing into people?" I laugh without humor. "Yeah, totally bizarre that he looks like a bad boy."

"Sarcastic is not a good look on you."

I stick my tongue out at her.

"Spill, Fiona May."

"Shit," I drawl. "You pulled out the middle name. That's harsh."

She crosses her arms over her chest and waits.

"There's nothing to tell."

Unlike Ivy, I actually have a poker face. That's one thing I learned from our dad. Never let them see you flinch.

But Ivy knows me well, so maybe I'm not fooling her. Or maybe she simply decides to give me a break, because she suddenly shrugs and grabs a slice of bread, slathering on blackberry jam.

"Dex is kind of…" She pauses, knife in mid-air. "Different."

"Different?" Okay, I know he's quiet. And obviously whip smart; he managed me with a deftness that scares me. But different?

Ivy sets her bread down, and her voice lowers. "He's really sensitive. In a good way, but…Gray thinks he might be a Tebow."

"What the fuck do you mean 'a Tebow'?" And why am I so annoyed? "You mean that whole kneeling and praying thing?"

She leans forward. "No. A virgin."

I swear all the blood rushes out of my face. "What? No way. He's…well, he's fucking hot." Okay, that slipped. "And he…" I bite my lip to keep from saying he sure as hell didn't kiss like a virgin.

Only it's been so long since I kissed a virgin, I'm not sure how one kisses, or if the way someone kisses is even a marker of sexual experience. I mean, sex is a lot more than inserting peg A into slot B—at least it should be.

I cover my slip with another truth. "He's got to be twenty-four. How on earth could he be a virgin? Is it for religious reasons?"

She shakes her head. "I don't think he's at all religious. Honestly, I don't know why he'd be a virgin either. And it's not something that Gray or his college teammates ever openly talked about, which is saying something."

"Then maybe we shouldn't be gossiping about it now." I know I sound snappish, which is unfair to Ivy; we gossip about everything. But it feels wrong talking about Dex this way.

Ivy blinks as though I hurt her, and I feel worse. But then she gives a small nod as if she understands. "Look," she says in a low voice. "I'm only mentioning it because... Hell. If you *did* fool around with him last night, or whatever, just be careful with him."

I can't help but laugh, though it hurts my throat. "What? Am I some sort of man-eater now?"

"No. Of course not. But Dex isn't hookup material."

"I think you should let Dex decide that for himself, seeing as he's a grown man and all. And before you start in on me again, I'm not going to do anything with him. Jesus. We only hung out an hour at most." And kissed like we were dying for it. "That's all."

Liar, liar, liar.

Ivy knows I am. I can see it in her eyes. Maybe motherhood has softened her, because she doesn't push, only takes a sip of her coffee and goes silent.

For a long moment, I sit there, silent as well. Then my fingers start to tap on the table.

"How do you stand it?" I blurt out.

"What? Your weak little innocent act?" she asks with cheek.

I stick out my tongue. "Funny, bunny. I meant, well... How do you stand being left behind while Gray travels to all his games?"

We grew up with a dad who left his family to play professional basketball, then later as a sports agent. And we've dealt with it differently. Ivy is the fixer, always trying to soothe ruffled feathers.

Me? I went out and partied, cracked stupid jokes, and shut down any and all deeper connections. It's worked so far, but seeing Ivy so gone on Gray and still she has to live this life? I don't understand it.

Ivy's long fingers wrap tight around her mug. "It was better when I could go with him. It sucks when we're apart. I won't lie about that, but…" She worries her bottom lip with her teeth. "I don't know how else to explain it except to say that Gray is my heart. Life simply doesn't work without him in it so…" She shrugs. "We do what we have to do during his season."

"And that's really enough?"

Her smile is almost secretive. "Yeah," she says softly. "Gray is more than enough."

The way she says it, like he's the joy that begins and ends her day, hits me square in the chest, and I have trouble breathing. Loneliness is this cold, drafty thing blowing over me, making me want to hug myself tight.

How must it feel? To be a part of someone else? And they're a part of you? Someone to have your back no matter what?

My knuckles press against the table. *I* should be enough for me. I shouldn't feel lonely. Fuck. Maybe I'm getting hormonal or something.

Thankfully, I don't have to wallow in my weird maudlin mood because the front door opens, and Dex and Gray amble in. My heart rate kicks up, seeing Dex's massive frame outlined in the doorway.

Gray zeroes in on Ivy. "Is he sleeping?"

"I put him down twenty minutes ago."

Baby G might not sleep at night, but he naps like a champ, a good two hours at a stretch. Something Gray knows better than I do.

He grins. "Shenanigans are go."

Yeah, I don't even want to know what that means, though I can guess.

Especially when Ivy blushes. "Seriously?"

"As a Hail Mary on Super Bowl Sunday. On your feet, woman. Time's a wasting."

Ivy grumbles under her breath about perverted cupcakes—again, don't want or need to know—and then gets to her feet. She's hauled off by Gray a second later. He carries her up the stairs, taking them two at a time.

"I got to give it to him," I say to Dex, who hasn't left the kitchen. "His stamina is impressive."

"Motivation helps," he answers dryly. God, he has a nice voice. Smooth, deep, even. "But, then, you know, we do train for stamina."

There's a gleam in his eyes that goes straight to my sex, gives it a teasing tweak.

I lurch up from my seat and refill my coffee cup because I'm not falling for that one. "You want a cup?" I ask.

Dex still hasn't moved from the entrance to the kitchen. Steady as always, I suppose. While I'm fluttering around like a fool.

He nods and walks to the heavy pine farm table that sits beneath a wall of windows. The table fills me with pride because I made it. I never intended to make furniture, but my two friends Jackson and Hal are furniture designers and cajoled me to give it a try. I love creating something with my own hands, going from concept to completion.

This table was my first try, and while I see where I could improve things, the design works well here, counterbalancing the modern, gleaming white cabinets and copper-covered appliances—because Ivy thought steel was boring.

And because veritable giants live in this house, the seats are large and sturdy. Even so, Dex's frame swallows up the chair as he sits in it.

I bring him a cup, and then I notice: he's wearing his hair down. Holy hell. It falls in thick, brown waves to the top of his collar. The sun has left streaks of gold running through it. And while the combination of full beard and flowing hair should be too much—call to mind an iconic Jesus or something—it isn't. It just looks hot. Wild.

Touchable.

I sit and curl my fingers around my mug.

He does the same, and the late-morning sun shines through the window, illuminating his tattoos. Black and red roses, a clock, a sugar skull, an indigo dragon, a 1940s battleship—there's a lot to look at. They run up his arms and under his sleeves, making me wonder if his chest and torso are covered too.

"Do they have meaning?" I ask, because I'm clearly looking.

"Some do." His rich voice is almost a shock to my system, as if by speaking, he's flicked my senses into overload. But he doesn't notice. "Some of them just came to me while I was drawing."

"You drew these?"

He nods, takes a sip of his coffee. "It relaxes me."

"I like to draw too. Mostly room designs nowadays."

"You did a great job with the house," he says, not bothering to look around. I have no doubt he's already made a study of the entire place.

"Thanks."

I'd like to think we're just making chit-chat. That we're just like any other casual acquaintances who happen to be houseguests at the same time and place. But that's not what's happening. Because Dex's gaze never leaves mine.

It's unnerving. Hot. As if behind his light conversation, what he's really saying is, *You loved it, didn't you? Sucking on my tongue, grinding on my cock. You want it again, don't you?*

Heat washes over me, and I struggle not to shift in my seat.

I realize we've stopped talking and are simply staring at each other. Every place he didn't touch last night—every place I want him to touch—is hot and achy.

I take a deep breath. Watch him do the same.

I'm about to bolt when he leans forward, his muscled forearms sliding a bit closer. "Go out with me. On a date."

"What?" I push back from the table. But I can't make my legs lift me. "I thought last night was…"

"A mistake?" He slowly shakes his head. "Not for me."

I know I'm gaping. I can't seem to stop. "But, but…"

His eyes crinkle. In the full sun, I see that they're a striking blend of colors—blue, green, gold, and brown—like polished agate. "Speechless?" he says. "I like it."

My mouth snaps shut. Then promptly opens. "You like me speechless. Well, there's a great motivator for going out with you."

"Like that I made you speechless. That I flustered you." He tilts his head as he looks me over. "You do the same to me. Get me all worked up. Only it seems to make me talk more than usual, not less."

A fresh wave of heat washes through me.

"Dex—"

"Ethan," he interjects softly. "Will you call me Ethan? At least some of the time?"

"Ethan," I say quietly, and it feels intimate. Especially when his lids lower as though I've stroked his skin just by saying his name. I swallow hard. "Don't take this the wrong way, but you don't seem like the hookup type."

"I'm not." He clenches his mug again. "I don't think you really are either."

"No," I admit with a small smile. "Not really. I'm looking for more now."

Dex—Ethan—nods. "Thing is, we're both here for the week. Ivy and Gray are in no condition to entertain. I like you. A lot. Why don't we go out together?"

"Erm…that's not what your proposition sounded like to me. You said on a date."

His lush lips curl. *No, do not look at his mouth.* I watch his lips move.

"I did. I want to kiss you again, Fiona. I couldn't sleep last night because I wanted that so badly."

Shit. Shit. Shit.

"So, yeah, I said date. Because if you let me, I'm going to kiss you again, as much as I can."

It's a struggle to find my voice. "Neither of us is looking for casual. We don't even live in the same city. I don't date athletes. Or friends of my sister. Or—"

"Why don't we start with what you *do*," he cuts in, his gaze direct, firm. It lowers to my mouth before sliding back up to my eyes. "Do you want to kiss me again, Fiona?"

Why does he have to say my name that way? As if it's a dare. And why is he so damn perceptive?

His eyes bore into me. "Did you think about me last night? In your bed?"

No one has ever been so blunt with me. Ever. It does my head in, giving me no place to hide.

"All I'm asking is for the truth," he says, his big, strong body rock solid in his chair.

Licking my lips, I try to breathe. Truth? I can do truth. It's not so hard. Right?

"Yes."

One of his dark brows rises. "Yes to what?"

If I have to elaborate, I might expire on the spot. "Does it matter when the answer is yes?"

He smiles, and it's like the dawn cresting over the sea. "When it comes to you, Fiona, the answer always matters. But I'll take that as a yes to all of the above."

The chair scrapes as he rises, and my heart threatens to pound right out of my chest. But he doesn't approach me. No, the smug bastard just finishes off his coffee in one gulp and puts the mug in the dishwasher.

He glances at me over his shoulder before he goes. "Can you be ready in an hour?"

"Hello? What about everything that I said?"

He doesn't blink. "Those are all fears. I respect that. But let's take things as they come and see what happens. Okay?"

"Okay." That's all I manage. This guy makes my head spin. He's just so *reasonable.* I don't have any defense against it. Against him and his damn sexy self. Damn it.

"Good." He gives me that smile once again. "Dress warmly. It's cold out today."

"You're kind of bossy," I call after him. "You know that?"

He stops and looks back at me. "Apparently only with you, Cherry."

I don't say another word, just watch his tight ass move beneath his jeans as he walks away.

"Well, fuck me," I mutter. I've been played. Again.

———————

Dex

IT'S OFFICIAL: I've lost my fucking mind. After spending the night basically staring up at the ceiling, I'd decided to leave Fiona alone. Be polite. Retreat into my shell. A safe and solid plan.

One that crumbled like sun-dried turf the second I saw her sitting in the kitchen, the morning light glowing like a nimbus around her golden hair. She was so beautiful she made my heart hurt.

Sharing a cup of coffee with her, watching those lovely full lips of hers move as she made idle small talk with me was more than I could take.

I want Fiona.

Badly.

Enough to ignore certain fears and go after her. But I'm so out of my element that a tremor goes through my fingers as I run them through my hair and gather it up in a knot.

Frowning, I comb my beard and stare into the mirror. My beard is a part of me now. How everyone sees me. Hell, it's why Fiona kissed me. And I have the urge to shave it off. Shave my hair off too. I honestly don't even know what I'd see reflected back at me if I did.

The door opens, and Gray saunters in as if he owns the place. Which he does. But still.

"Knocking, Gray-Gray, is a valuable skill."

"I'm too tired to knock." He flops onto the armchair by the window and leans his head back with a groan.

"Shouldn't you be satisfying your wife?"

"I satisfied the fuck out of her." He drags a hand over his face. "And then she fell asleep."

I snort, and he glares.

"Fell asleep on a wave of extreme post-coital bliss," he assures before looking me over. "Going out, big guy?"

In truth, Gray is two inches taller than me. But he's built for speed while I'm built for blocking, which means I carry more bulk muscle.

"I'm taking Fiona to the Japanese Garden."

Silence follows.

"So…Fiona, huh?" Gray sounds thoughtful.

Setting my hands on the dresser, I brace for a fight. "I want her."

More silence. I turn. He studies me with a blank look.

"Are you pissed?" I ask. I won't blame him. Hell, I expect it.

"If you were Johnson? Or Thompson? Or Marshal? Or any of those sharks, I'd punch your throat. But you? You think I wouldn't trust you with Fi? I'd take a bullet for you, man."

Damn. My throat closes, and I have to clear it to talk. "You should get some sleep. You look like shit."

He lets his head roll back on the chair. "What's the point? Little Man will be up any second now."

"I'm taking him with us," I say, putting my wallet in my back pocket.

Gray makes a strangled noise. "Seriously?"

My lips twitch. "Why do you think I'm here?"

"Uh, to hang out with us?"

"That. And you sounded like you could use a break. So here I am."

"You came to help us out?" His voice is creaky, raw.

"I told you I know babies. So let me give you a break today."

I swear Grayson goes weepy. He blinks rapidly before taking a breath. "I love you, man. I'm one step away from kissing you right now."

"You keep saying that, but I've yet to see any follow-through."

Slowly, he shakes his head. "I love my kid. Like, seriously love him. But I confess, I'm dreaming of some sort of sleep drug for babies right about now."

I reach for my boots. "He'll figure the sleep thing out soon. Then you will too. Go on and get his things ready."

Gray kind of falls-crawls out of the chair before righting. He really is dead on his feet. I feel for the guy.

He's halfway out the door before he halts. "Dex, man…just… watch yourself with Fi."

"You said you didn't mind."

"Not you." He winces and pushes a fist against the doorframe. "She's kind of capricious. And I've never seen you go after a girl, so…"

He doesn't want me getting hurt. Well, I don't either. But it's a risk I'll have to take. Besides… "I think there's more solidity to Fi than you're giving her credit for."

He nods, but it's clear he doesn't agree. Thankfully, an irate squawk sounds downstairs. Little Leo is awake. Gray inclines his head. "You sure about this?"

I know he's asking about more than babysitting. And I should be thinking about my sanity. But I can only think of Fiona and how her lips explored mine. Best feeling ever.

"As I am of anything."

CHAPTER 4

Fiona

"I WONDER WHAT IT IS that you're thinking," Dex says from his casual slouch on the bench across from me. He's taken me to the Japanese Tea Garden, a place so utterly beautiful and tranquil I blinked back tears as soon as we'd entered.

Now we're sitting in the Tea House, me at the railing, idly gazing at the glass-like reflecting pool that surrounds us, and Dex with sketch pad and pencil in hand. His expression is relaxed, a smile in his hazel eyes.

I can't help but smile back. "I was thinking you're a brave man, Ethan Dexter."

His chuckle is low and easy. "Now why would you say that?" He doesn't look down at the tiny baby nestled in the carrier against his chest.

"I'm sure I don't know," I drawl.

I admit, when he met me in the front hall earlier, carrying Leo in his car seat, I was shocked. I love my nephew. Fiercely. But I don't know anything about babies. I've never done a babysitting gig, didn't have friends who did. So the idea of taking care of Leo is daunting.

But Dex? I know he wouldn't have offered if he wasn't confident he could do the job. Not many men would be willing give up an afternoon to look after a one-month-old baby. It gave me the instant warm-fuzzies.

And my ovaries damn near burst into song when Dex pulled out one of those baby swaddlers and tucked my nephew into it to carry him against his massive chest.

I wasn't the only one. We couldn't go more than a few steps through the garden without some woman commenting, *how sweet, oh, such a lovely baby! Such a dear man*—that from an octogenarian who gave Dex a sly pat on his ass, causing him to blush beet red.

Now he's sketching me as I drink my green tea and Leo snoozes on.

"I swear, you've got this whole seduction thing down pat," I tell him, fighting the urge to fidget. I hadn't realized he was drawing me until he'd already started. I feel exposed. Naked. And slightly turned on by the way his gorgeous eyes study every inch of me.

Dex's lips twitch, but his pencil doesn't stop making those little scratching noises across the pad. "Seduction thing?"

"You know, the baby, beautiful garden, drawing me. Are you going to pull out a guitar next and serenade me?"

He laughs at that. "No guitar. I may or may not have a harmonica in my pocket to use for later. But I prefer to keep you in suspense."

"So you aren't just happy to see me. Good to know."

"Cute."

"It was terrible and cheesy." I lean forward. "Are you really drawing me? You aren't, are you? There's really just a stick figure giving me an obscene gesture on that page, isn't there?"

His low bass rumble makes something in my lower belly just hum with pleasure. I love that I can make him laugh. I don't think he does it often, so each time feels like a reward.

He turns the pad to show me his efforts. And my breath catches.

What he's drawn isn't sweet or sentimental. He's done a close up of my face, my head tilted, my smile almost secretive.

He didn't sugarcoat me. My chin-length blond hair shoots out in all directions. He's drawn the small bump on the bridge of my nose—a female replica of my dad's nose, unfortunately—and the tiny crescent-shaped scar on my jawline from when Ivy and I were jumping on my parents bed when we were eight and six, and I crashed into a dresser.

My attention goes back to my expression. It's seductive and covet-ous, as if I'm hungry. Heat fills my cheeks. God, have I been looking at Dex like that?

I glance back at him. He's patiently waiting.

"Okay," I say, my voice a little husky. "So you actually can draw."

He runs a hand over his beard as he regards me, then flips the sketch book back onto his bent knee and starts up again. "I told you I could." His gaze flicks up to mine. "Do you find it hard to trust men?"

"Do you often hide behind exposing other people's insecurities?"

He freezes. A frown pulls at his mouth. I don't want to look at his mouth. It gets to me every time.

For a moment we're silent, and then Leo makes a small snirddling sound. Dex goes back to drawing. "Touché," he says in a low voice, his body tense in his seat.

I take a sip of my now-cold tea. "I don't trust men in general."

His hand makes a short stroke across the page, but his shoulders visibly relax. "When I analyze others, I find it easier to figure out my own bullshit as well."

"So you're sitting there figuring out my weaknesses while simulta-neously thinking about your own?"

"Something like that."

Finishing my tea, I stand. "Come on, Ethan. Let's walk."

CHAPTER 5

Dex

W HAT IS IT ABOUT Fiona Mackenzie that makes me say things I shouldn't? Do things I wouldn't? She sees right through me with her grass-green eyes.

Five-foot-three and the tiny terror intimidates the hell out of me. That it's also a turn on is kind of disturbing.

We're walking through maple trees, now scarlet and carnelian with their fall foliage. Fi's head barely reaches my shoulder. I'm a giant next to her, my feet hitting the walkway with dull thuds. Against my chest, Leo snuggles, a warm but light weight. I rest a hand against his little butt as we walk over a footbridge.

"Why do you play football?" Fi asks, her voice soft in the quiet of the garden.

"The pain," I answer without thinking, and then wince. Shit. Again, she has me confessing.

Her doe eyes peer up at me as her lips twist in a frown.

"Aggression, release," I feel compelled to add, somehow struck with verbal diarrhea after one glance from Fi. "It's a way to go outside of my usual self. To perform on a physical level."

I hold a hand out to guide her over the stepping stones dotting a pond. She takes my hand—though I know she doesn't need the help—and I don't let it go once we're back on the path.

"A center doesn't just cover the quarterback and create lanes. A good one reads the game, what each player, both offensive and defensive, is planning. He anticipates, adapts, protects."

"Perfect for you," she murmurs.

New warmth floods my chest. "Yeah."

Most girls I've been around are divided into two camps: those who want me because I'm a football player. I could be ugly as a mole and a total asshole, and they'd still want to fuck me. Then there are ones I'm interested in who, ironically, don't get what I do and don't really want to.

Amy was like that. A fellow fine arts major, I'd fallen hard for her during the beginning of my junior year. She hadn't reciprocated. To her, I was a big oaf obsessed with a violent sport.

Fi has outright told me she doesn't date athletes. But she's here now. And she gets me. I *like* her. Always have. She's honest in a way that's never cruel, only pure and unfiltered. It's so refreshing. I find I can truly breathe easy around her.

Her hand in mine is slim, the bones delicate and so easily breakable. I hold onto her carefully, let my thumb stroke her wrist. And though I'm the one stroking her, a shiver of awareness runs along my arm and straight down into my cock. Because I'm touching her. She's letting me.

I want to run my fingers all over her small, curvy body. My gut tightens with that need, my heart pounding against my chest, because I'm royally fucked up. I don't know what the fuck to do with women—I've avoided getting close to them for years.

Which flat-out sucks for me now.

Fi notices I've gone quiet, and glances up at me. "Get out of your head, Ethan."

"I live there," I say, trying for lightness. "Not that easy to escape."

She gets me enough to understand that about me, but I'm happy she doesn't know *why* I'm stuck in my head.

"Last night," she says in a conversational tone, "I went to sleep wondering how your beard would feel between my legs."

I stumble over a paver. The baby snorts, but I right quickly.

Fi isn't even looking. She's walking a few steps in front of me, her voice light and unaffected. "I wondered, would I feel its tickle if you sucked on my nipples?"

Heat floods my lungs. I can't breathe. My cock is a throbbing shaft in my jeans. Maybe I make a sound because she turns, glances at me over her shoulder. Whatever she sees in my expression has her smile fading and pink washing over her cheeks.

Her steps slow, but mine don't. I stalk forward, keeping my eyes pinned to hers. Still flushing, she backs up. I think I grin. I'm not sure. My goal is clear.

I shepherd her toward the bench set beneath the curtain of a weeping willow. My hands easily span her waist, and it's nothing to lift her up. She stands before me on the seat. Her breath comes in soft, audible pants, her pert breasts at my eye level.

She doesn't say a word as my hand slips beneath her sweater. Satin-smooth skin greets my palm. I slide it up, over her flat belly, past her ribs—watching her eyes the whole time. I love the way those eyes grow wide, the shock and the heat that glow in them.

She doesn't say a word when I run my fingers over the swell of her breast and catch hold of her lace bra, tugging it down. A small sound escapes her, though, as I slowly lift one side of her top.

"The baby—"

"Is asleep. Don't wake him." I'm so close that I can see the flutter of her pulse against her neck. Her warm scent floods my nostrils, woman and sweet, green tea.

The soft cashmere slips over her breast, freeing it with a little bounce, and my dick surges against my jeans. I swallow a groan. God, she's beautiful. Creamy, firm flesh, a rosy-brown nipple the size of a quarter.

"Hold your top." My voice sounds guttural.

But she does what I demand, her breast shaking a little with each quick breath.

My hand shakes too as I cup her warm skin, plump her sweet tit for the taking. Then I kiss her nipple, grazing the tip, tickling it with my lips and beard.

"Ethan…" Her hand lands on my shoulder, holding tight.

I'm so hot, my skin burns. I kiss her breast like I would her mouth, licking and sucking, nipping the stiff bud, brushing my lips over it. And do it all over again. I get lost in the act, fucking worshiping her breast the way it ought to be.

Small, needy whimpers leave her mouth as she clutches my shoulders with both hands now, her sweater sliding a little and falling onto the bridge of my nose. I don't care. I drag the flat of my tongue slowly over her nipple, savoring it, and she groans. Long and loud. The sound is a hard tug on my cock.

My free hand finds her hip, pulls her forward.

And Leo wakes with a squeak and a little cry of protest.

Instant bone kill. I yank my head out from under her sweater and take a step back, careful to keep my hands on her hips so she doesn't fall.

Closing my eyes, I take a breath, then another. Jesus, I've never done anything like that, never let myself *not* think and just take what I want. And I want to do it again, and again, lose my fucking mind on pleasuring Fiona Mackenzie.

I'm almost breathing normally as I turn to sit on the bench so I can see what Little Man wants.

Next to me, Fiona rights her clothes and jumps down. Keeping her back to me, she runs a hand through her hair. When she finally turns, she doesn't look embarrassed or regretful. She simply helps me change the baby's diaper as if nothing happened.

I don't know if I should be grateful or disappointed. Right now, I'm going with disappointment.

CHAPTER 6

Fiona

"IS IT WRONG THAT I'm thinking of hiring a mother's helper?" Ivy picks up a perfume bottle, sniffs it, then wrinkles her nose and sets the bottle down.

"I'm inclined to say it's wrong you haven't already," I say.

She sighs and runs a hand through her dark hair. It's longer than I've seen it in years, spilling over her shoulders, her ubiquitous bangs grown out to frame her face. "Mother guilt blows. I feel like I should be ashamed for wanting some time to myself. And with Gray."

"Ivy Weed, I've been at your house for all of two days, and I want to cry for you. Babies are tough work. You have the means to hire help, so do it. Happy mommy and daddy, happy baby."

I don't mention our childhood. I don't need to. Our mom stayed at home and refused to seek any form of help, even though she had the means. She was a walking stress basket. There's kid guilt too. And it sucks.

I glance in the small mirror set up on the glass countertop and smear a bit of poppy red sample lipstick on my lips. The shade is too strong for my light coloring. "Here, this would look better on you."

After Dex and I had returned home, Ivy had all but attacked him with hugs of gratitude. Fairly well-rested after a few hours off baby duty, she'd been itching to go out, and called a sitter. So here we are, having sister time and idly shopping. And I'm fighting the good fight to not think about what happened in the Tea Garden.

Ivy shakes her head. "Gray doesn't like lipstick. Says it tastes bad."

I snicker and move on.

"Speaking of jobs," she says as we leave the store. "How's yours going? Bob Sugar still giving you grief?"

I laugh at the nickname Ivy and Gray gave Elena Ford, my little shithead co-worker. At least Bob Sugar was upfront about stealing Jerry Maguire's clients. Elena is far more insidious. About two months ago she started at the design firm where I work in NYC.

At first, I thought I'd made a friend. Elena was sweet, slightly clueless, and immediately came to me for guidance.

"You've been here six months," she'd said in her sweet, pleading voice. *"And you're so talented. Me? I'm terrified I'll get everything wrong and be out on my ass."*

I know all about fear of failure. I am the family fuckup, always flitting from this thing to that. So I helped Elena, showing her my designs, talking about what inspired me, what I thought the client was looking for.

How was I to know she'd waltz into our Monday mockup meeting with designs for the Greenberg condo that looked almost exactly like mine?

Sure, there were differences. Just enough that it didn't look like a complete copy. But the overall style and themes were exactly the same. I'd felt sick. But, hey, it could have been a coincidence. And Elena was still so nice, thanking me for all my help. Cracking jokes in the staff lounge.

Except our boss, Felix, chose Elena to assist him with the condo. She'd won. And I'd been *okay* with that. Only it happened again.

Ivy's arm links through mine, pulling me back to the present. "You've gone quiet."

I sigh and lean into her shoulder as we head for the Embarcadero.

43

"I don't want to dislike anyone, but I'm beginning to actively hate this woman."

"What did she do now?" Ivy asks darkly.

"It's my fault," I mutter, my stomach twisting. "I told her what I had planned for 44 Park—"

"Fi," Ivy cries. "You didn't!"

"Give me a break. It was before I realized that she was, you know, thieving scum—"

"A creative leech," Ivy puts in helpfully. We have another name for her too; it rhymes with hunt. "Argh, that bitch is totally gaslighting you."

"Yeah." I sigh. "I feel so stupid." And sick. Heartsick. "She did it again. This time it was worse. Same use of Art Deco touches mixed with raw woods and industrial framework. Same fucking color scheme."

"How in the hell does Felix not notice?" Ivy's dark brows are nearly touching now, she's scowling so hard.

"He made a comment once on the similarity. Elena just grinned and said some bullshit about great minds thinking alike."

Ivy snorts. "Brilliant."

"Yes, wasn't it? Her mother is a creative editor for *Elle Decor*. She has numerous and powerful contacts. Why should Felix care when it's good business?"

As usual, I vacillate between rage and sorrow. Working with Felix is my dream job come to life. He's a major player in the NYC design community. And I'd been his star apprentice. Until Elena came.

Now I'm second fiddle, watching as she climbs the ladder on the rungs of my work. It blows. Especially since she makes it her business to stop by my desk and fill me in on all the cool shit she gets to do with Felix. Evil hag.

"Well," Ivy says. "Now you know. Don't give her any more fodder, and she'll have to come up with something on her own."

"I guess. I just keep thinking, I'm here and she's there, working her witchy voodoo." Part of me hadn't wanted to go on vacation. But I'd already been granted the days; the flight was booked.

"Do you want to go back?" Ivy asks, sympathy making her eyes wide.

"Naw." I give her arm a squeeze. "I need the break. And I've missed you, Gray-Gray, and little Leo so much."

"We've missed you too." She kisses my cheek.

"And I guess it could be worse." I smile. "I could be working with dad." Ivy is his partner-apprentice.

"Har!" She rolls her eyes. "Though he really isn't that bad."

"I bet living on opposite coasts helps."

"You know it. Let's go eat. I'm starving."

We end up at a Spanish tapas restaurant on the Embarcadero and basically order our weight in food. I pop a cube of Manchego cheese in my mouth and sigh.

"Maybe I should move to San Francisco," I tell Ivy. "I love it here."

Her nose wrinkles. "Don't tease. It isn't nice."

"I'm serious. I've been living in Dad's apartment like a mooch. NYC is exhausting. Maybe I should move out here."

Even as I say the words, I know what I'm doing. Dreaming of running away. Shit gets hard, I bail. I'm not proud of it. But I can't seem to stop.

Ivy gives me a sad little smile, as if she too is aware. But she doesn't say that; her attention is diverted by someone behind me, and she waves whoever it is over.

I glance back to see a very large, very hot guy making his way toward us. He's dressed in smoke gray slacks and a pale pink cashmere sweater that would look horrible on most guys but works with his dark skin and bulging muscles.

"Hey, hey, Mrs. Grayson, I thought that was you." He leans down and gives her a kiss on the cheek.

"Hey, Jaden." Ivy glances at me. "Fiona, my sister. Jaden Willing-ham."

He gives me a grin. "Best defensive lineman in the business."

"Modest too," I say, well aware of athlete egos. And though I really don't get into sports, it's impossible not to be aware of things with Ivy and Dad in the family. So I know Jaden is a player with Gray's team.

"You know it," he agrees happily.

"Have lunch with us," Ivy says, gesturing to the unoccupied seat between us.

"Cool." Once he sits, he turns to me. "So, Fiona…Ivy's sister."

"Wait." I hold up a hand. "Don't say it. You knew the moment you saw us. We could be twins."

He chuckles and gives me a long, appreciative look. "Gorgeous identical twins."

Ivy and I are like a yin and yang sign. But it's fun to tease.

Jaden takes the plate Ivy has made up for him. "So where's your lazy half?"

"Working out," she says with a smirk.

After the sitter arrived, Gray and Dex have gone to train. You know, for fun. *Shudder.* I get my ass on a treadmill three times a week. But what they do? No, thanks. Although I can appreciate the results.

I take a sip of sangria and take my mind off of Dex. But it's hard. I swear I still feel his mouth on my breast.

Answer to the question about whether I'd feel his beard if he sucked my nipple? Yes. Hell yes. To my toes.

I'm still experiencing aftershocks from what he did to me in the form of random clenching between my thighs and painful throbs of need.

Fuck. That man is too sexy for his own good.

"What you up to on your week off?" Ivy asks Jaden. "All play?"

He takes a drink of water that our waiter has set down for him, then leans my way. "This is what I love about your sister; she's like a den mother and coach all rolled into one."

I know he means it. Ivy has a way with guys. They always end up a little in love with her.

She laughs when Jaden gives her a friendly half-hug and exaggerated kiss on the cheek, but then she frowns, her gaze shooting across the restaurant. "Damn," she mutters.

Jaden follows her gaze. "What? That dude with the camera?" He shakes his head. "Little pests, man."

Paparazzi. Ivy and I grew up with them. Though they're nowhere near as annoying toward athletes—or most of them—as they are with actors and singers. Even so, we've always regarded them as the enemy.

Since I'm not really news, I've grown lazy about spotting them. But Gray is a huge star here. Already one of the best tight ends in the NFL, and ridiculously hot to boot, he has his fair share of attention. Ivy, as an agent, daughter of my dad, and Gray's wife, gets a lot as well.

"I think they took a picture of us kissing," Ivy says to Jaden.

"And tomorrow they'll be saying we're having a wild affair," he says with an annoyed sigh. "Don't let it bother you, Ivy."

"I don't." She shrugs. "It just pisses me off. Gray deserves better than that shit."

"Well." I toss down my napkin and turn to Jaden. "Let's give them something else to talk about. Smack one on me, lineman."

A glint lights his eyes. "I like your style, Fiona."

I know Jaden can tell we're just messing around to help Ivy. I've always been a flirt. Pretending to kiss a guy is nothing to me. But some small part of me wonders why I offered to do this, because it suddenly feels very wrong.

It's too late to back out. Jaden cups a hand at the back of my neck and leans in. His kiss is brief—hell, he's practically laughing as he does it—but it's just long enough to make certain the photographer will see and take a picture. And though Jaden is good-looking, I don't feel anything other than mild satisfaction that we're taking attention away from Ivy and Gray's relationship.

Jaden pulls back and smiles wide. Ivy is laughing and shaking her head. But her smile fractures, turning into dismay as she glances over my shoulder.

And I feel cold to the pit of my stomach. Because I know. I turn and Dex's gaze clashes with mine. The cold within me turns to hot, painful lead. His expression is unreadable. Gray's isn't; he's pissed.

Together, they make their way to us.

"Ivy Mac," Gray says softly as he bends to kiss his wife. He snags a chair from an empty table behind him and sits close to her. Dex takes the empty seat at my side.

Shit. Fuck. Shit.

My throat clenches tight but some sullen, childish part of me wants to rebel. We've only exchanged one kiss and, okay, some seriously hot boob action, but we aren't in a relationship. We don't even live in the same city. Then I think of how I'd react if I saw Dex kissing someone else. I'd want to punch him in the junk.

Guilt and embarrassment grow painful as I feel Dex beside me, his arm resting on the table near enough to touch.

"Gray, my man." Jaden and Gray exchange a dude shake, and then Jaden looks at Dex. "Dexter. Last time I saw you, I took your QB down at the thirty."

Dex's mouth twitches in a shadow of a smile. "Yeah, that two-point conversion we made on the next play for the win must have chafed."

Gray starts laughing. "That loss fucking sucked. Way to bring it up, J." He gives Jaden's back a hearty slap.

The guys laugh.

"Forgot about that part," Jaden admits with a head shake.

"Happens to defensive linemen all the time," Dex says as if in sympathy. "They're easily confused."

Annoyance rises within me. Here I am feeling guilty as hell for exchanging a fake kiss with a stranger, and Dex is acting as if nothing happened. Well, it didn't. But *he* doesn't know that. He's ignoring me.

As if he hears my thoughts, his hazel eyes meet mine. Still nothing. No emotion other than casual friendliness.

"So you're lunching with my girl," Gray says to Jaden.

"Naw," Jaden answers easily before slinging an arm over my shoulders to give me a friendly squeeze. "I'm lunching with my girl, Fiona."

Great. Lovely. Perfect.

If looks could kill, I'd be dead. Speared through the heart by Gray's glare.

I force a laugh and give Jaden a light shove. "Then you can pick up the check."

He sets his attention back on Gray and Dex, both of whom I'm ignoring in favor of *patatas bravas*.

"I got a poker game going tonight," Jaden tells Gray. "Dean, Jamal, and Monroe will be there. Even pretty boy James is in. You coming?"

Gray doesn't even blink. "No way. I'm staying at home and sleeping if I can."

"That's right. I forgot you're on baby duty. How's the little man?"

I drift away from the conversation and glance at Dex. He's focused on Jaden and Gray, his profile to me. The slant of his nose and the jut of his chin are like the stamp of a Roman coin. I could totally see him as a centurion, slashing his way through armies.

I really have to stop crushing on him. I know myself. I'm not good at flings. One-night hookups I can walk away from without a problem. But if I start to like the guy, I need more. I'm not going to get more with Dex.

His deep voice breaks me out of my fog.

"Yeah, sure, I'll go," he says to Jaden.

I'm guessing he's in for poker.

"Cool." Jaden makes as if to rise. "It starts up in an hour. Why don't you come with me now?"

"Sure."

So Dex is leaving. Never once having said a word to me. He stands, his chair legs scraping over the floorboards. And a sense of loss plummets to my stomach.

I want to apologize. I want to yell at him for ignoring me.

I say nothing. Dex and Jaden exchange goodbyes with Ivy and Gray.

I get a kiss on the cheek from Jaden.

"Good to meet you, Fiona." His dark eyes twinkle. "If you want to hang, give me a call. Gray's got my number."

I give him a tight smile. But my attention is on Dex. "That's sweet, but I'm spending my time with Ivy and Gray and Dex."

At the mention of his name, Dex finally looks my way. "Night, Fi." That's all.

I manage a nod, determined not to let this bother me anymore. We weren't meant to be anyway. But then, as he walks past my chair, the tips of his fingers run along the back of my neck.

A shiver goes through me, a smile tugging at my lips. And then he's gone.

———————————

Fiona

THE MOMENT DEX IS OUT of the restaurant, Gray turns on me. "What the hell was that, Fi?"

"Oh, would you relax," I snap. "It was just a joke."

"I guess I missed the punch line." Gray scowls at me before stealing my water and taking a drink—while glaring over the rim of the glass.

"A pap took a picture of Jaden kissing my cheek," Ivy explains. "Fi and Jaden were just giving him something else to gossip about."

"I guess." Gray shrugs but then gives me another hard look. "Still,

Fi, that was not cool. Dex likes you and—" He flinches, rearing back as an olive bounces off his forehead. "Did you just ping me with that?"

"Did you miss the part where I threw it at your big head?" I ask sweetly before frowning. "Do not lecture me like I'm an idiot, Gray. I had no idea you guys were coming here." I give Ivy a pointed look, because she could have warned me. "And I feel shitty enough as it is."

"Well…" Gray starts.

I cut him off. "That said, Dex and I aren't…" I wave a hand. "I don't know what the hell we are. We went on one date. I'm leaving in a week."

He pouts, crossing his arms over his massive chest. "Then maybe you should stay away from him."

Hurt caves in on my chest. "Wow. Thanks. It means so much to me that you feel the need to rush me off Dex's front porch."

Gray's tight mouth eases a little. "I didn't mean it like that. Okay, maybe a little. Shit."

"No, no." I hold up a hand. "I get it. And maybe you're right. But that's my call, not yours."

Tense silence falls over the table.

Ivy sets a hand on Gray's arm. "We have one hour before the sitter needs us to return. Let's not waste it arguing, Cupcake."

He looks at her for a long moment, then nods. His blue eyes are wide and serious as they seek me out. "Sorry, Fi. I shouldn't have gone off on you."

"Sorry about the olive. That shit can stain," I say, grudgingly. "Next time I'll throw a nut."

I get a napkin to the face in return. And we both laugh. But my insides are heavy, restless. As annoyed as I am with Gray, I know he's right. And doesn't that just suck the big one?

CHAPTER 7

Fiona

DEX DOESN'T COME HOME. Not when Ivy and Gray head up to bed. Not after I've read in bed for a few hours. It's nearly two in the morning when I give up the ghost and turn off my e-reader.

In the silence of my cozy guest room, tucked under the eaves, I stare at the window, now blocked by heavy pink silk curtains. I decorated this room. My first project. I'd gone for white walls, a gold-leaf Rococo dresser, a white Louis XVI-style bed trimmed in lime green satin, and a set of vibrant Warhol Queen Elizabeth prints hanging on one wall. I call it shabby Brit chic. It's in honor of my mom, who's British and uses this room when she visits.

The room across the hall, where Dex is staying, I decorated for Dad, the color scheme dark and masculine. Gray flannel on the walls, ebony wood bed, bold photo prints, and pinstriped gray curtains. It's empty now. Something I'm painfully aware of.

Is Dex avoiding me? Is he angry? Hurt?

I replay the brush of his fingers against my skin when he'd left me. It had felt like a conversation. A promise, maybe.

But what the hell do I know?

Why does it matter so much? And so fast? Just last night I'd told myself he wasn't my type. Then I had to go and kiss the hell out of him.

Huffing, I kick the covers free, my skin hot and itchy as though I have ants crawling over it.

Maybe I should listen to Gray and nip this thing—whatever the hell it is—in the bud. Dex is out for the night? Good. I'll avoid him in the morning. And that will be that. We'll politely go our own ways, and I'll leave next week.

An hour later I am still wide fucking awake. Damn it.

Dex

ONE THING ABOUT LIVING ALONE, you don't have to sneak into your house. Being a guest, however, I try my best to get up the stairs without waking anyone—a certain baby, to be specific.

I'm bone-tired and smell like cigar smoke. Some of the guys insisted on lighting up. Swear to God, those dogs playing poker paintings have a lot to answer for. Because I can see no good reason why filling up a room with vile blue smoke is conducive to winning poker.

I certainly didn't need any aid to win. Defensive linemen are shit at keeping a neutral face. I could read them like a book and am a few grand richer for it. A smile pulls at my mouth at the memory of Jaden cursing as he lost again and again.

My smile fades. I took sick pleasure in beating his ass. I tell myself it didn't have anything to do with that little scene I witnessed at the restaurant, that it was all about being a good center and not letting a lineman get one over on me. But I'm only lying to myself.

Suppressing a sigh, I creep into my room. And halt.

The small, bronze bedside lamp is on, casting a soft, warm glow over the room. Not much light, but enough to see perfectly clear.

Curled up under the covers, an e-reader still in hand, is Fi. She's fast asleep, her golden hair spread out over my pillow.

For a second I look back at the door. Did I go into Fi's room by accident? No. I've seen her room. It's light and colorful and feminine.

Besides, my boots are in one corner, a pair of my jeans hanging off the back of the leather armchair next to the window.

My gaze wanders back to Fi, who looks tiny in the big bed. And I'm having a Goldilocks moment here, because I definitely feel like the bear who's found his bed invaded.

Hell.

I tried to avoid thinking of her all night. She kissed Jaden. I don't know why. It hadn't looked involved. They'd been laughing, clearly goofing around. Still didn't stop me from feeling as though a pole had been punched through my chest.

But her big, green eyes had held guilt and regret when she looked at me. So what could I say?

I don't own Fi. I want her. I fear wanting her. But I don't have a claim.

A soft snore leaves Fi's lips, and she snuggles down farther in the bed.

Fi. In my bed.

Maybe I do have a claim.

I unbuckle my belt and slide my jeans off as quietly as possible. I'd wanted to take a shower. Now, I'm not risking leaving, only to find her gone when I return. I keep my shirt and underwear on, not trusting myself to be naked in a bed with Fi.

Turning off the light, I approach the empty side of the bed and slip beneath the covers.

Fi doesn't wake up, but she turns my way, as if seeking me. Fuck it. I pull her against me, tucking her back to my front. And she settles in with a sleepy sigh. I let myself soak in her warm body, breathe the scent of her skin. She feels so damn good, my heart hurts.

I hold her closer, my arm around her narrow waist, my hand cupping her soft breast. It feels so right, everything in me relaxes. Yeah, I'm now horny, but exhaustion and the relief that Fi sought me out have the greater claim. I fall asleep before I even know it.

CHAPTER 8

Fiona

IT'S AN AWKWARD THING, waking up in a man's bed when you don't remember falling asleep, much less sleeping with the man. It's even more awkward when you wake up alone.

Sunlight streams across my face, and I stretch my arms over my head. There's a crick in my neck from reading too long in bed. I don't know what crazy impulse pushed me to sneak into Dex's room to wait for him. Clearly that didn't go well.

Glancing at the rumpled spot beside me, I can tell he slept next to me. Damn if I can remember it though. It stings that he isn't here now.

But that's probably a good thing. I have morning breath, and my hair feels matted on one side. Skulking back to my room is like the walk of shame without the benefits of having enjoyed the night before. Yay hay.

A hot shower and cup of coffee don't relieve my pissy mood. The house is utterly silent and empty, which kind of freaks me out. You'd think somebody would leave a note.

I'm back in my room, scrolling through social media on my phone and having visions of being stuck in some bad *Twilight Zone* episode where I find out every person I know has disappeared from the face of the Earth, when Dex appears at my door.

Just the sight of him has my skin tightening and my heart beating faster. And it doesn't matter that I'm wearing an old t-shirt and yoga pants, or that I haven't yet put makeup on. He looks at me, and I feel beautiful.

"Hey." He leans against the doorway, his arms crossed over his broad chest. He offers me nothing more.

I slap my phone down on the bed. "Where the hell have you been? Where the hell is everyone else? And what the general hell?"

His wide mouth quirks, making his beard twitch. Yet those golden-green-blue eyes of his remain steady as ever, as if he can look straight into me. "I see someone is in a good mood."

"Just peachy. I'd like to see how happy you'd be to wake up alone and wondering—" I snap my mouth shut. *Stinking Dex, always making me say more than I want to say.*

His smile grows, a slow curl of smoky heat. He pushes off from the door. His stride is measured, stalking, and it sets off a reaction in me, clenching my lower belly, igniting heat and an insistent throb between my legs.

The mattress creaks as he places a knee on it, crawling toward me. And, though I've been annoyed, I start to smile, even as my breathing goes light and fast. He smiles too, his eyes crinkling at the corners.

He doesn't pause, just kisses me—soft, melting, and thorough. My hands touch his cheeks, the springy hairs of his beard brushing my palms. God, he tastes good, feels good. I slide my tongue over his and shiver.

Dex grunts deep in his throat and nips my lower lip, suckling it a little as if he's hungry. Then he pulls back to look me in the eyes. "I left you alone this morning so I wouldn't do that."

My thumb glides over his lower lip, now slightly swollen from my kiss. "Do you honestly think I'd have minded?"

His lids lower a fraction as he studies my mouth, and the soft brush of his fingertips along my jaw follows. "I brought you bagels. Probably not as good as New York bagels, but they're fresh."

"Ethan," I say softly. "You're avoiding the question."

He eases down next to me, resting his head on his hand. "Gray told me you kissed Jaden to help Ivy out."

My shoulders tense. "I swear Gray gossips more than a flock of old ladies at a cotillion. Where are he and Ivy anyway?"

"Took the baby and drove to Muir Woods to walk around the redwoods."

"Those shits. I wanted to go there."

"I'll take you." His expression is calm, but his gaze is sharp on my face.

I snuggle into my pillow. "Gray was right. It was just a peck, a stupid joke, really."

"I didn't like it." A wrinkle forms between his brows. "Seeing that, I mean."

"I know." My fingers curl into the covers to keep from reaching for him. I don't feel like I have the right to now. "I'm sorry. I wouldn't want to see you kissing another woman."

"I don't want to kiss another woman."

We stare at each other, nearly nose to nose now. And it feels…comfortable, tentative, new, strange. "I don't know what to make of this," I whisper. "I didn't expect you, Ethan."

His eyes search my face. "I've been waiting two years for you to see me."

He says the words clearly, without hesitation, and still I can't believe them.

A lump rises in my throat. "We've only interacted twice before in all that time."

"Four times, not counting the wedding. You were there when Gray and I graduated. And at Draft Day."

"You went high in the first round," I say, remembering now. "That's rare for a center."

"You wore a white sundress with cherries on it for graduation, and a gray knit dress with black knee-high boots for Draft Day."

My chest feels too tight, and I have to clear my throat to speak. "Why didn't I notice you before?" Because he was right in front of me the whole time. This big, beautiful man who doesn't shy away from honesty.

With a caress of his thumb, he eases a lock of hair behind my ear. "I didn't exactly make myself known."

"Why not? And why now?"

He frowns, watching his thumb glide over the edge of my jaw toward my lips. "Couldn't stay away from you this time."

Before I can ask what he means, Dex slides his large hand to my nape and hauls me close. His mouth claims mine—needy, demanding, a complete counterpoint to the careful way he holds me. Hot mouth, gentle hands.

It drives me crazy, and I press up against his solid frame, thread my fingers through his hair as I meet him kiss for kiss.

A grunt of contentment rumbles in his chest as he rolls me back and rises over me. He's huge, his shoulders so wide they blot out the light. Flowing hair and full beard, he also looks a bit wild—pure man when I've only ever been with boys.

On the outside, Dex comes off as reserved, maybe even shy, but he doesn't act that way when he's with me. Right now, he's in total control. He angles his head and kisses me deeper, exploring with a steady thoroughness that leaves me restless and desperate for more.

Dex is too perceptive not to notice. With slow, sure strokes, he runs his hands down my sides, back up to my cheeks, soothing me, slowing me down. And still he kisses me as if it's the most absorbing thing in the world.

His touch, the way he tastes me like fine wine or sweet cream, settles into my bones, makes my flesh hot and heavy. I grow languid under his care.

The tip of his tongue traces the corner of my mouth, the edge of my lips. I'm so sensitive there now, the touch shimmers over my skin, down to my sex. Breathing hard, I turn my face toward his, open my lips wider, silently begging for more of his torture. Large hands frame my face, hold me still while he sips at my mouth.

The rough of his beard tickles my throat as he moves downward, stopping to suck the spot where my neck meets my shoulders.

"You taste so good, Cherry." He licks me again. "Like wet dreams."

His muscles shift and bunch under my grip. I clutch him close, open my thighs to him so he can lie between them. Dex grunts, grinding his massive cock against me as if he can't help it.

More. I need more.

He does too. His hands gather up my shirt, pulling it over my head with an impatient tug. "Let me see you." His finger flicks open the front clasp of my bra before he smoothes his rough palm under the cup and along my breast. "Let me touch you."

I groan, arching up, desperate to wiggle out of the bra. He helps pull it free.

Dex kisses me once, almost distracted, then his gaze moves to my chest, a lock of hair falling over his brow as he looks down. "Mmm," he hums, rubbing the flat of his palm in a circle over my chest. "There they are."

He captures the stiff tip of my nipple between his fingers and gives it a tweak, tugging a little. And I moan, the action sending heat punching straight to my clit.

"You like that?" He does it again, lingering longer before swooping down to suck my abused nipple deep into his warm mouth.

God. My hands grip his hair, holding him there as he sucks and tugs, his wet tongue flickering over me. He plumps my breast with his fingers, sucks me again. The way he goes at me is almost single-minded, as if the world could fall apart around us and he wouldn't stop. It is so fucking hot I can barely breathe.

Big hands cup my breasts, kneading and playing with them. And all the while he licks my nipples. Sucks and nips at them until I'm writhing beneath him, desperate for some relief, for him to sink his cock into me. I make a sound of impatience but he simply lifts his head and stares, rapt, at my chest.

"God, you're so fucking gorgeous," he rasps. "Look at you, all pretty and flushed and panting." He presses the tip of his thumb against my nipple, making me whimper. "Will you come like this? From me playing with your tits?"

I just might.

"Dex—"

"Ethan," he says. "When I have my mouth on you, it's Ethan."

Then he puts his mouth on mine, claims it like he already owns it. I shiver, lick my way across his upper lip before kissing him long, deep. He shivers then too.

"Ethan," I say, just to give him what he wants. "Ethan."

He kisses me, a rhythmic undulation, his tongue slowly thrusting in and out of my mouth, his fingers worrying my nipple, plucking at it, flicking it in a way that's almost crude.

It's too much.

"Touch my pussy," I demand against his lips. I'm almost halfway to coming as it is. "Touch it."

I feel his smile.

"Is it wet?" His hand slides down my bare stomach.

"Fucking dripping," I pant, kissing his cheek, the corner of his eye, his mouth again.

He slips beneath my panties, and I'm so worked up, so hot, that I arch off the bed, a strangled groan tearing from me as his blunt fingers ease over my slick flesh.

The world tilts on its axis. Dizzy, I grab onto his rock-hard shoulders.

His breath fans my face, his lips just grazing mine as he watches me. I stare back, unable to move—to fucking breathe—as his fingers slip-slide and circle my sex. His touch is messy. No finesse, just pure, methodical greed.

"I think you're a closet sadist," I say through gritted teeth, my hips jerking against his hand.

Though he's shaking, sweat dotting his brow, his eyes smile at me. "Why?"

"You're enjoying this. Driving me crazy—" A strangled moan tears out of me and his thick, long finger plunges in deep. "Oh, fuck."

With an answering groan, he drags that finger out, pushes in again. I strain into his palm, my arms stretching overhead to claw at the pillows.

"Ethan…" I want to fuck him. I need to. My teeth grind with impatience.

He pushes another finger into me. So thick. So good.

"Cherry," he whispers, licking my breast. "Give it to me, Cherry."

My orgasm rides through me so hard, I come back to myself in stages—the warmth of his hard body, the sheets wrinkled beneath my sweaty skin, my breath slowly leveling out.

Slightly dazed, I blink up at him. He looks slightly dazed as well, his eyes wide, his lips parted.

"You're beautiful," he says.

"So are you." I mean it. I want to strip him bare, lick my way over every inch of his big body. But he's moving away, pressing a soft kiss on my belly before standing.

He's fully dressed, and here I am, shirt off, nipples wet and tight, my pants halfway down my ass. I'm not one to be shy about my body, but I sit up and tug my shirt on. Because he's clearly not getting undressed, even though the bulge in jeans is enough to stretch them tight.

"I'll go toast the bagels," he says. Right before he bolts.

CHAPTER 9

Dex

THERE'S A SLIGHT TREMOR in my hand as I saw the knife through a sesame bagel. I grip the handle tighter when really I want to chuck it, bagel and all, across the kitchen. Because I left Fi—gorgeous, delicious Fi—alone in the bedroom.

Jesus Christ, I'm an idiot. She'd been lying there, flushed and panting, the rosy tips of her nipples glistening from my mouth. And I left her like that.

The sweet sounds of her coming, those breathy whimpers, ring through my head.

The bagel splits in two, and I set the knife down, take a slow breath. I made Fiona Mackenzie come. Hard.

She doesn't know hers is the first pussy I've fingered. I had no idea she'd be so slick and warm, so tight. My teeth grind at the memory.

I want to fuck her so bad it hurts. My dick fucking *aches*. And though I'm familiar with repressed need, this is a new level. I'm so jacked up now, my hips push against the edge of the counter like they have a mind of their own.

"Fuck."

But that's the problem, isn't it? She was ready for me to fuck her, practically panting for it. And so was I. Only I can't do it. So I left her like a coward.

I don't expect Fi to come down. She's probably pissed. Maybe even disgusted with me. And for good reason.

My eyes squeeze shut, and I draw another slow breath through my clenched teeth. Such a fuck up.

"So what kind of bagels did you get?"

I nearly jump out of my skin at the sound of her cheerful voice. She breezes into the kitchen, her hips swaying. She's dressed in tight black jeans and a fitted gray sweater that reaches mid-thigh and looks soft, touchable.

It's all I can do not to stare at her pink, kiss-swollen lips. Because I've completely lost my voice.

Fi stops at my side and picks up the halved bagel before moving away to pop it into the toaster. "You get any good cream cheese?"

She looks up at me with wide eyes the color of new leaves. No judgment, no anger. Waiting, it seems, for me to hand her cream cheese.

"Fi…" My voice cracks, and I swallow hard. "I…uh…."

The front door opens. Gray and Ivy are home.

"Hey," Ivy calls as she sets the baby car seat down on the kitchen table. "Did you get bagels? Thank God. I'm starving." She leans down to unhook Leo. "A certain evil husband thinks it's cool to hike at freaking 7 a.m."

Gray ambles in looking better-rested than I've seen him since before the baby. "We were up anyway, and I was going stir crazy in this house. Ooh…is that poppy seed?"

I try to catch Fi's eye over Gray's head, but she's already taking her nephew from Ivy's hands and kissing the top of his fuzzy little head.

A weight settles on my chest. I feel like I've lost my chance. Like she's slipping away.

But then her head lifts. Bright eyes look straight at me. "Let's go for a ride after we eat."

I TAKE HER TO POINT REYES, find a spot where we can park, and we walk along the cliffs. The mountainside, covered in a blanket of browns, greens, and soft purples, rolls toward the Pacific. Sunlight glints off the deep blue ocean. Yet all I can focus on is the girl at my side.

She's taking it all in with wide eyes, the sea breeze whipping at her hair. The top of her head reaches my shoulder. And even though we're nowhere near the edge of the cliffs, I have the overwhelming urge to haul her close and hold on tight—to protect her from any potential harm.

Shit, didn't a hiker die in a landslide a few years ago? Has it been raining? I'm ready to tell her we should go when she gives a happy little sigh.

"God, it's beautiful here."

"Yep." I keep a sharp eye on the path.

She turns, and the soft California sunlight sets her skin aglow. "You've been to San Francisco many times before?"

I snap a sage leaf off a nearby patch, rubbing the velvety leaf between my fingers. "Grew up in Santa Cruz."

"Really?" She smiles. "California, huh? So you were one of those dudes who hung out under the boardwalk and surfed all day?" She's grinning as if the idea amuses her.

"Well, not all day. Mostly before practice or when I had some free time."

Her green eyes go round with surprise. I'm guessing I don't really look like a surfer. I silently laugh at what she'd make of my dread-wearing phase.

I tap the tip of her little nose. "It's great for balance, strength, focus, and stamina. Kind of like football training. Only more fun."

"Athletes," she mutters, shaking her head, then looks me over again. "I did not have you pegged for a California boy."

I laugh at that. "Where did you think I was from?"

"I don't know." She shrugs. "Somewhere rugged where dudes rope steers. Montana or Wyoming or Texas maybe."

I laugh again. "The only bullshit I'm familiar with is trash-talking on the field."

Fi grins wide and picks a sage leaf as well, bringing it up to her nose to draw in its scent. "Somehow I can't imagine you talking shit."

"No. But I'm well versed in it from defensive linemen trying to get into my head."

"And you just let it roll off you like oil on a duck's back, don't you?"

"Pisses dudes off more than any words can."

I love the sound of Fiona's laugh. It's loud, free, and unashamed. Her entire face lights up when she laughs. And I have to clench my hands not to grab hold of her, capture that sound with my lips, and swallow it down. I imagine that laugh might fill me up, warm all the cold places in my chest.

She comes to stand beside me, and her slim hand finds mine. Instantly, I thread my fingers with hers.

"So your parents live pretty nearby, then?" Her fingers tighten just a bit. "Or are they divorced?"

"They're still together. The house is about an hour's drive down the coast. But they're in Europe right now with my little brother, doing a group tour."

"But he's got to be…what? Eight?"

"Yep. They homeschool him so they can all travel the world." The corners of my mouth twitch. "They're probably sampling bratwurst in Germany about now. Dylan, my brother, is probably whining for an American hot dog."

"I think that's lovely." There's a sigh in her voice.

From Ivy, I know their parents are divorced and have been for years. Sean Mackenzie spends most of his time in New York or Atlanta, and their mother lives in London.

"Do you miss your mom?" I ask.

She squints into the sun-dappled ocean. "Yeah, sometimes. I spent most of my summers with her, either in London or traveling. But it's become forced over the years." Her blond hair whips in the breeze, and she brushes it back with her free hand. "I don't know…we're just not very much alike. She's focused, organized. I'm…"

Fi doesn't finish.

I give her hand a squeeze, tug her against my side. "Creative. Full of life."

"Sweet talker," she scoffs, but her head rests against my shoulder.

We're silent for a minute, just watching the ocean, my hand in hers. I run my thumb along her palm and find a callus. She notices and gives me wry smile. "Not very soft, I know."

Taking my time, I follow a path of small, new scars and rough patches. Her hands are torn up. "What have you been doing to yourself?"

She moves to pull away but I hold fast, catch her gaze with mine.

"Nothing bad," she says, giving up on the little tug of war we've got going. "I've been…" Her plump cheeks flush. "I've been making furniture. I wear gloves for some things, but you have to have a feel for the wood."

"Furniture?" I find myself smiling. "That's… Well, it's fucking cool."

Her color rises. "I haven't really talked about it with anyone. It's just something I do to relax. But I like it."

"So those are hard-earned scars." I hold up my own hand, knuckles swollen, nails cut to the quick so they won't tear out during a scuffle.

She leans in closer to me. "Yeah. I guess they are." Fi pauses. "I made Ivy and Gray's kitchen table."

I hadn't been paying attention to the table then because Fi had been in the room, but I can recall it well enough. "That's a substantial piece. Beautiful." I look down at her, my chin resting near her cheek. "You should be proud."

"Thanks." Her voice is quiet, almost shy as she stares out at the sea.

She's shared a confidence with me. One she obviously has trouble embracing. I don't know if she did it to let me know I could trust her, or she simply found herself exposing a truth. Either way, it humbles me.

Fi's soft, feminine warmth at my side is like nothing I've ever experienced. And I know I need to tell her everything if I have any chance of making her mine. I take a breath, smell the sweet mix of sage, eucalyptus, salt, and sun. "Fi…"

But she cuts me off. "I've heard there's a creamery around here that sells cheese."

I frown, my eyes staying on the scene before us. People are easy for me to read. Fi is no exception. I get her on a bone-deep level. The problem is, she reads me easily as well. I'm not used to that. No one ever really bothered before.

All day I've been expecting her to demand an explanation. But never once has she made mention of my cut-and-run. At first, I didn't know what to make of it. Now I'm thinking she's purposely avoiding it because she knows I'm struggling.

She moves to go, but I tug her back. "I know I fucked up, leaving you this morning." A cold sweat breaks out over my skin, and I swallow hard, run a hand through my hair, only to have my fingers snag because I have it all bound tight.

Cursing, I look out over the ocean. "I…"

"Hey." She touches my arm, and I feel it at the base of my spine. "You don't have to say anything."

"Yeah, I do." I force myself to face her.

"Is it the virgin thing?"

My breath halts.

But she doesn't notice and keeps talking. "Because I don't mind that. At all."

Fuck if my cheeks aren't burning. "You're right, Gray does gossip more than a flock of old ladies." I squeeze the back of my neck. "Yeah, technically, I guess I am. It's not like I'm going around hiding it. I just don't really mention it either."

"Well, why should you? Your sex life isn't anyone's business."

I look down at her. "I'd like it to be your business."

She blushes at that. Sweet Fi who, by all accounts, doesn't fluster easily. I love that I can make her blush, can leave her tongue-tied.

"Look," I say, "I didn't want to make this a big deal, but I thought I should tell you because I know there are guys who freak out when a girl doesn't have experience and they weren't informed, and—"

Fi's mouth shuts me up. Her kiss is firm, as if she's trying to tell me it's okay, yet it's also tender, which makes my entire body clench with some weird, uncomfortable emotion.

She lowers from her tiptoes and looks up at me with solemn eyes. Her slim, warm hand takes mine again. "I meant what I said; you don't have to talk about it if you don't want to. But I can see that it bothers you. So if you want to tell me, Ethan, I'll listen."

The last thing I want to do is talk. But I take a deep breath and try. For her.

CHAPTER 10

Fiona

B ABBLING, BLUSHING DEX IS NEW. It's almost cute, the way this big, burly guy who could easily lift me over his head and spin me with one hand becomes all flustered. Except I don't like that he's obviously upset. So I don't smile. I simply hold his hand and wait for him to talk.

Because I know he will. Though he's a virgin—which, holy hell, I cannot believe this gorgeous giant is untouched—and he might be quiet, Ethan Dexter is the most forthright man I've ever known. I'm used to guys who fake their way through life with false bravado and grand boasts. Ones that, when cornered, lash out. Or guys who lie about uncomfortable truths.

But Dex? No, he just takes a breath and admits that he's a twenty-four-year-old virgin. Again, the thought ripples over me, and I find myself more than a little turned on over the prospect of being the only girl to have him, to see him come. Hot damn, I want to witness strong, silent Ethan break apart and lose his mind.

Suppressing a shiver of lust, I lean in closer under the pretense of letting his big body block the wind, when really, I just want to surround myself in his warmth and delicious scent.

Dex tugs my hand, and we sit on a wide, flat boulder that's tucked a little crook on the hillside. Tall, fragrant grasses buffet some of the wind, and the sunlight grows warm on my skin.

The corners of Dex's eyes crease in a frown as he stares at his hands on his massive thighs. Then he reaches into his back pocket and pulls out his wallet to remove an old, laminated photo. He doesn't look at the picture he hands to me.

"I met Drew and Gray at a football summer camp during my junior year in high school." He clears his throat. "I'm the one on the left."

He doesn't need to clarify. There are three guys in the picture. Wearing dirt-stained uniforms, they have their arms slung over each other and are smiling for the camera.

I notice Gray straight away. He's the tallest, his hair bleached pale blond by the sun, and he's grinning extra wide as if he's on top of the world. Drew, the one in the middle, is a quarterback and Ivy's client now. I got to know him well when she and Gray married. He was Gray's best man, and I was maid of honor. He's model cute—even then—with light brown hair and eyes and a crooked, almost sly smile. Then there's Dex.

If it weren't for those serious, beautiful hazel eyes of his, I might not have recognized him. He isn't wearing a beard—not surprising, given that this is high school—and his smooth cheeks are plump and round. Dex is plump and round. Oh, you can see the beginnings of the massive muscles he has now, but high school Dex had yet to shed his baby fat.

His smile is more reserved than his two friends', cautious almost, but I see the joy in his eyes. He loved being at this camp. Clearly loved his two friends as well.

"I was always a chubby kid," he says in a low voice. "You know, the big guy who looked like he'd been held back a couple of grades when he stood next to the rest of the class."

Lump in my throat, I nod.

"Girls never noticed me." Dex takes back the photo when I offer it to him and puts it away. "Not until junior high when I started to play football, and then only in a, 'Hey, good game, Dexter,' sort of way."

He stares out at the ocean. "They noticed me in high school, though. Made the varsity team freshman year. Went All-American senior year." He shrugs. "I was still more fat than muscle, but the cheerleaders were all about giving players the love. And that included me."

Well, why wouldn't they? Dex is awesome. And I seriously doubt he's changed much since his childhood.

"I fooled around some. Thing is, I knew they were only into me because I was on the team."

"Why would you think that?" I can't help asking.

He gives me a look that says, *get real*. "Outside of my high school circle, not one girl gave me the time of day. Ever. And…" He scratches his beard. "One of them admitted it. Lisa Unger told me, 'Don't worry, Dexter, we'll take care of you. You're on the team, after all.'"

"Bitch."

His mouth quirks. "Just honest, I guess. Anyway, after that, I didn't want to mess around. I kept to myself. Hell if I was going to be with a girl who wanted me just because I played football."

"Okay, but what about college? There are lots of girls in college who *aren't* shitty little shits."

Dex snorts at that, and his eyes crinkle. But it quickly fades, and he grows pale beneath his tan. "By the second year of college, I'd lost the fat and felt a bit more…confident. But then…" He blows out a breath and braces his elbows on his knees.

"Ethan." I touch his back and find his long-sleeve shirt damp with sweat. "What happened?"

His large hands clench into fists. "I'm not proud of this part."

My stomach tightens, but I keep my palm firm against his body. "It's okay."

I really don't know if it is, but don't know what else to say to reassure him.

"So…I…uh… Spring Break sophomore year, a bunch of us from the team headed down to Mexico. It was wild. Girls everywhere. Sex everywhere. I'd never seen anything like it. Our season was over, we'd won our first National Championship, and we were treated like gods."

His shoulders go so tense, his body is like granite beneath my hand. A fine shiver works over him, and I rub his back, desperate to calm him down. When he speaks, his voice is rough and rusty.

"First night out, we all got completely drunk, smoked some pot. I'd never tried it before, and it hit me hard. We're at this party, and two girls come up to me. They're wearing nothing but these tiny little bikinis and are so fucking eager to please me. That's not even it. These girls, it's like they want to outdo each other by being as wild and willing as they can."

Yeah, I know the type well. Growing up around athletes, I knew those women even when I was too young to understand what sex was. My dad, who was an NBA star before he was an agent, fucked those types of women and ruined his marriage.

The feminist in me wants to say it's the men taking advantage and using woman like disposable sex toys. But the truth is far more muddy, because some women are more than willing to play that role. In fact, they compete for the chance to be used.

"I was drunk and high enough not to care," Dex says slowly, as if every word is being dragged out of him. "Next thing I know, all three of us are in a back room, one of them is sucking on my cock—though I'm so far gone I can barely feel it—and the other has her tits in my face. And I'm thinking *finally, finally*. But it also feels kind of off.

"Then one of them starts begging me to get down and dirty with her, says she loves it 'dirty.' Fuck if I know what that means, but then she's on all fours, telling me to fuck her in the ass."

Dex pauses, runs a hand over his face. He looks so ravaged, I don't want him to go on. And yet I do, because if he trusts me enough to tell me his secrets, I'm going to listen to them.

"I was a virgin. What the fuck did I know about doing that? But the other one is coaxing me, 'Do it to her. Let me see you fuck her. Oh, that would be so hot, baby.'" He shudders. "We were all wasted, stupid. I don't... I remember trying to get inside her, and it chafed, wasn't comfortable. But the one chick watching was kind of chanting, 'Give it to her good.' And the other, the one I'm, you know, trying to... She's shouting, 'Come on, get it in already.' But my mind's wondering, isn't she supposed to be wet and slick?"

I feel sick, hearing his tale, twisted and sad. When he lowers his head and clears his throat, I want to cry and hold him tight. But I don't move, don't want to break whatever spell he's under that's allowing him to talk—because he clearly needs to get this out.

"Then it was kind of slick. I looked down and...there was blood...on my..." A ragged breath tears out of him. "I saw that, and everything just kind began to spin. I threw up. They left, shouting names at me, saying I was a bad fuck even for a football player...shit like that. But the girl I'd..."

Wide eyes the colors of earth and sea look up at me. "She acted as though she liked it. Wanted me to do that to her. Why? I made her bleed. Why would she want that? Because she wanted to claim a football player did that with her?"

"Ethan." I don't hesitate now to pull him close. He's stiff with resistance, but his head rests on my shoulder, his breath coming out in agitated puffs.

"I couldn't do it after that. It felt so ugly. Tainted. What I did, it wasn't right."

"No." My palms cup his cheeks, and I lift his head to look into his eyes. "You got pulled into a bad scene. People do stupid things when they're wasted."

He tries to shake his head. "If I'd been more experienced, I'd have known enough to say no. Or get some..." His cheeks pink. "Lube or something."

"Yeah? And what about that girl? If I asked a guy to do that, you better believe I'd demand some lube."

Not that I've done anal before. But facts are facts.

"Look," I say when it's clear he's going to argue, "you were stupid. She was stupid."

His hands wrap around my wrists as he looks me in the eye. "I didn't mean it to come out as a sob story. Logically, I know all this. But I remember, and I feel ashamed. After that, I just couldn't tune out those thoughts. I couldn't do casual sex. A relationship would be all right. But I don't want someone who wants me because of what I do instead of who I am."

My heart sinks a little. "Dex, we can't have a relationship. You live in New Orleans, and I live in New York."

His eyes drill into me. "I've wanted you from the moment I saw you, Cherry. You say what you mean and don't filter it…"

I wince. "I've been working on my filters."

He flashes a quick, tender smile. "It's a good quality. I trust you. I'm insanely attracted to you. I want to fuck you. I want to know you. I want to be with you. If you want all that from me too, I won't let something as small as inconvenient living locations get in the way."

Holy hell. I can't even speak.

Letting my wrists go, he searches my face, his expression almost stern. "I want you badly enough to put my all cards on the table, show who I really am. So I guess it's your play now. I'll understand if what I said turns you off and you'd rather end this."

His lips press tight, as if he's forcing himself to say no more, but his eyes never leave mine.

My fingers reach out, trace the corner of his mouth where his beard frames it, just like the first time I touched him. "I think, Ethan, I want you more now than before. But a relationship? I have to think about it.

Okay?"

He blinks. Then the corner of his luscious mouth curls upward, his gaze going hot as melted chocolate. "Just say the word and you can have me, Fiona."

CHAPTER 11

Dex

Patience. I have it in spades. I've trained myself to use patience as a tool, knowing that the right moment will come, and when it does, I'll take it. But right now, patience is wearing thin. Because Fiona has yet to give me an answer.

Back at Point Reyes, she kissed my cheek and told me she'd have to think about being with me. Not because of my past, she was quick to reassure, but because she's afraid to start something that has a clear expiration date.

Frustration rolls through me. I don't see an end to us, just how good we could be together. I should have stated my case all those years ago, when I first wanted her. When we lived in the same damn town. Only she had a boyfriend then. And I was too wary to step in between that. Stupid of me.

Maybe we'll always be off with our timing. But, fuck it, I'm not giving this up. No fucking way. Not when I've gotten a taste of her. Not when she's heard my ugliest truths and accepted them without judgment. We can be real together, which is something rare and precious in my world. So I'm regrouping.

First step: we go out with Ivy and Gray. If I can't get a date, a double date will do for now. One of Gray's teammate's nanny is watching Leo.

We go out for dinner first.

Ivy and Fi entertain us with stories of their childhood and how their dad brought home athletes who are now our heroes.

"Tell them how you won a bet with Jordan when you were six," Ivy says to Fi.

My girl's green eyes sparkle as she laughs. "Oh, God." She takes a drink of her cocktail. "I bet him I could jump higher than he could."

"No way did you beat Jordan," Gray insists, shaking his head.

"I did so!" Her cheeks flush a pretty, soft pink. "The stakes were a dozen donuts. He went first. And man, he has ups."

We all nod at that. Fi leans in closer, her voice dropping. "I acknowledged his awesome skills, then took my turn."

Ivy cuts in. "The little stinker waltzed into our kitchen, so we all followed. And as bold as you please, Fi climbed on the counter, looked Jordan in the eye, and jumped."

"What?" Gray exclaims. "That's totally cheating."

"That's what Jordan said." Fi shrugs. "I pointed out that we never said the jump had to start on the floor, and since I did technically jump to a higher point, I won."

I laugh at that. "And you call me slick."

She grins, unrepentant. "Hey, he conceded defeat and brought me donuts. Said he could respect my determination to win at all costs."

And so it goes, talking and eating and having more fun than I've had in as long as I can remember. Whenever I grow too silent, Fi pulls me into the conversation, sometimes by touching my elbow and looking my way to ask my opinion. Sometimes by saying something so outrageous, I can't help but comment.

And I have the strange sensation of something deep inside me clicking into place, as though I'm becoming the person I was meant to be. It's both a relief and kind of unnerving.

Sitting next to Fi, close enough to catch the fragrant scent of her hair, feel the brush of her arm against mine whenever she turns to say something to Gray who's on her other side, settles me and makes me crave more.

I want the right to put my arm across the back of her chair the way Gray does with his wife. To lean in and kiss her smiling lips whenever she says something cute, which is pretty much all the time.

We end up going to a bar, and it's karaoke night. Which means it's crammed full of slightly drunk and extremely exuberant off-key singers. We've managed to get a table up front and center. I'm thinking it's because the owner is a huge football fan; I'm pretty sure the table was occupied when we walked in.

But the hostess insists we sit here and hurries off to get us drinks.

"Excellent," says Gray, rubbing his hands together, a gleam in his eye. "The last person to sing gets to buy the drinks."

Ivy grins wide. "You're on, Cupcake. I'm going to sing the house down."

We all pause, our gazes darting back and forth as a certain sense of terror falls over the table.

Ivy sees us and slaps her palm onto the table. "Oh, for fuck's sake. I know what you twats are thinking! If I suck at dancing, I'll suck at singing? Well, I don't. I'm awesome."

Awkward silence ensues, and she snorts.

"What? You think I don't know I suck at dancing? I just don't give a shit." She glares at Gray, though there really isn't any anger in the look. "So you can stop dancing like an ass now."

A strangled sound leaves him. "You knew?"

"Of course." She tosses a lock of her hair over her shoulder. "You're too coordinated on the field, and you kind of forget to suck when you do those victory dances."

He gapes at her for a long second, then gives a bark of laughter. "I fucking love you, Special Sauce." With that, he hauls Ivy into his lap and kisses her.

Fi, however, finally snaps out of the trance she's been in since Ivy confessed. "You sneaky shithead," she shouts over the music. "All these years I've been covering for your craptacular dancing, and you knew!" She shakes a fist. "I swear to God, Ivy Weed…"

"Oh, please," Ivy counters. "You pretend you suck at baking so you don't have to cook for family holidays."

Fi sniffs, looking guilty as hell. "I don't know what you're talking about."

Ivy leans in, her eyes narrowed. "Midnight cookie baking ring a bell, Tink?"

Fi's cheeks flush, and she studies her nails with undue interest while muttering something about traitor sisters under her breath. "Those are for PMS cravings and nothing more. I was baking under duress."

"Right then," Gray says, smart enough to interrupt before they can go down the dark road that is discussion of their periods. "We're going to do a duet, Mac."

Ivy bounces up. "I get to pick the song!"

She runs off, and Gray shoots out of his seat. "No chance in hell, Ivy Mac. Mac!"

Fi rolls her eyes. "She's going to go all Beyoncé-Jay Z on him."

I laugh hard at the thought of them singing "Drunk in Love." "I'm filming the whole thing." I pull out my phone and get it ready.

They don't sing "Drunk in Love." It's worse. Much, much worse. Or maybe equally horrific.

"Oh. My. God." Fi's eyes go wide before she bursts out laughing.

Gray and Ivy have decided on "You're the One That I Want" from *Grease*. Oh, they own it, belting out the lyrics just slightly off-key— well, completely off-key in Gray's case—and totally working the crowd, who are all shouting and lifting their phones to film them. It's clear Gray has been recognized.

But still, it's terrible.

Fi and I howl with laughter until my sides hurt and I have to gulp down half my bottled water.

"I can't believe she knew she sucked at dancing," Fi mutters watching them, a smile still pulling at her lips.

"Well, when you think about it, she'd have to be blind not to know," I counter. "I mean, the arm flailing alone…" I shudder dramatically, and Fi snickers, just as I'd hoped.

"Watch it," she says, her gaze on the stage and a smile in her eyes. "That's my sister you're talking about."

"Hey, I love her like a sister too. Does that count?"

Fi turns, and her green eyes hold me captive. "As long as that doesn't make us like brother and sister."

I lean in until my lips nearly brush hers. "Not even close, Cherry." I steal a quick, soft kiss and have the satisfaction of hearing her breath hitch.

My satisfaction grows when I pull back and she gazes up at me with a slightly dazed expression. I run the pad of my thumb over the smooth curve of her lower lip. My groin tightens with heat and want.

"You gonna give me an answer soon?"

Her lashes sweep down, and she reaches for her drink. "We're out now, right?" Green eyes peer up at me. "This is a double date, isn't it?"

"Yep."

Her lips purse like she's trying not to smile. "Slick."

"Not really." I lean closer, pressing my arm against hers. "Look, I know I'm asking you to go out of your comfort zone—"

"Yes, how about that?" Fi counters. "I mean, do you often do the same? Because, from where I sit, you seem to play it safe."

My brows lift. "I'm pretty sure there's nothing safe about going after you."

She smiles, shaking her head. "But you know I'm attracted to you."

Love hearing that. I sit back and watch Gray get on his knees in a sad John Travolta parody. Running my hand over my beard, I turn back to Fi. "Okay. How about this? I hate being the center of attention. If I get up there and sing my ass off, will you give us a go?"

She laughs. "You're serious? Are you bribing me for sex?"

"First off, I'm not talking about sex. I'll never withhold that from you." I grin, touching my forehead to hers. "We can go home right now and fuck, Cherry, if that's what you want."

Hell, tell me that's what you want. I can take it. I'm a big boy. Part of me is growing bigger by the second at the thought of finally having Fiona.

She goes so pink, I can see it in the dim of the club.

"I'm asking for a relationship," I say. "Or at least taking a leap of faith."

Fi looks me over as if she's trying to figure out if I'm crazy or not.

I let her look, sitting back, my hips low in the seat. Her slow inspection has my skin tingling. I have the mad urge to haul her on my lap and kiss her into compliance, lose myself in that sweet, plump mouth of hers. But I stay still.

"You're really going to go up there?" She nods toward the stage where Ivy and Gray are now bowing—the hams.

"And sing my ass off," I add. My gut rolls at the idea of performing in front of all these people. It's not something I want to do. But I will.

I ignore the small twinge of guilt that follows when she gives me an evil grin. I know she's looking forward to seeing me make an ass of myself, just as we laughed at Ivy and Gray.

"Before you answer," I say above the applause that follows our friends' performance, "I'll warn you now. I will never lie to you, Fiona. But I don't intend to fight fair either."

Her cheeky grin just grows. "Playing me again, are you, Slick?"

"Maybe."

She cups the back of my neck and gives me a quick, hard kiss. "Bring it, Dexter."

CHAPTER 12

Fiona

HO-BOY, I'M IN TROUBLE with this man. He gives me a quick, impish grin as he rises from his seat, that big, bold body flexing and stretching beneath his worn jeans and tight gray t-shirt. He's completely unaware of how sexy he is, which only makes him hotter.

But he isn't stupid. He knows his boldness is irresistible to me. His fist raps once against the table top. "Game on, Cherry."

Gray and Ivy are sauntering back, their faces aglow with sweat and happiness. "We were fucking awesome," Gray announces just as Dex walks off.

My attention is on Dex's taut ass. I kind of want to follow him and smack it. Seriously, his ass is a work of art. I'm pretty sure if I ever see it bare I'll spontaneously combust.

Heat rises up my thighs. I want to see it bare. I want him. Badly enough to risk a reckless, long distance relationship?

Gray finally notices Dex by the stage. "No fucking way!" He glances at me, his eyes wide. "He's not, is he?"

My cheeks hurt from the stretch of my smile. "He is."

Ivy plops down next to me and takes a long drink of her beer. "Someone should check outside and see if pigs are flying."

Gray is still wide-eyed and gaping as he sits next to her. "No shit. What gives, Fi-Fi?"

"Why are you looking at me?" I blink with all the innocence I can muster.

"It has to be about you when it comes to Dex."

I'm not going to acknowledge how that sentiment warms me. Instead I watch Dex make his selection and say a few words to the karaoke operator. A flutter of nerves goes through my middle. He looks relaxed enough, but his shoulders are definitely tight.

Shit. I made him go up there.

Well, not *made*. It was his idea.

To impress you.

Color me impressed. He has more guts than I do. No way would I sing in public. Cats fighting under a full moon sound better than me.

I shift in my seat, leaning forward, then plopping back, as Gray pulls out his phone and gets ready to film, all the while going on about hell freezing over and Dex leaping into the deep end of the crazy pool.

Maybe I should put a stop to this?

Dex takes the mic and slowly walks up the stairs to the stage.

There's a ripple running through the audience. They've recognized him too.

Shit on a popsicle stick. He's going to hate this.

My fists clench as he takes center stage, his head bent, his hand clutching the mic tight.

Shit. Shit. Shit.

I'm halfway out of my chair to stop him when the music starts. I recognize the opening notes. He's picked "Gold on the Ceiling" by The Black Keys.

"Bold choice," Gray mutters.

My heart is pounding so hard, I can barely breathe.

Then Dex starts to sing. And I swear my jaw hits the table.

Gray's and Ivy's do too.

"Holy shit," Gray says before he leaps to his feet, his fists punching in the air with a loud whoop. "Dex!" He shouts, jumping up and down as the music thrums.

Because Ethan Dexter is bringing the house down, singing the song like he fucking owns it.

His deep, raw voice rolls over me, and my nipples go so tight they hurt. I get on top of my chair and holler my approval, dancing along to the music, singing the refrain with the rest of the crowd.

As for Dex? He holds the mic with two hands, his eyes closed, his thick thighs parted. One leg bounces in time to the beat. Tatted and bearded, muscles flexing, he's so damn hot, the women in the crowd scream for him.

He doesn't seem to notice.

Then his eyes snap open, and he zeroes in on me. That smug bastard grins as he belts out the lyrics, telling us all it's all right if we want to steal from him, that there's no guard in his house. But I know he's talking to me. Waiting for my answer.

I grin back, my body swaying, my hips snapping. I've been to countless parties, clubs, and concerts. I've had boyfriends and one-night stands. I've grown up around fame. And it isn't until now that I truly realize how bored I've been, going through the motions. Maybe that's how life is; you kind of just plod along, fall into a nice little rut until something comes along to shake things up.

Dex doesn't bore me. Not even close. Life is never a slogging road when he's around.

He ends the song with a sweeping bow, tosses the mic to the operator, then hops down, headed straight for me.

Sweat gleams on his brow, plasters his shirt to his chest. People slap his shoulders and back, try to give him high-fives, including Gray, who is beside himself with glee. Dex doesn't slow, doesn't break his stare.

Every cell in my body seems to zing, making me twitchy with want and joy.

When he's a couple of steps away, I launch myself at him, and he catches me. My legs wrap around his waist as I cling to him, find his mouth, and take it.

Cupping my ass, he holds me tight against him as his tongue slides deep.

We're both breathless when we part.

"I knew you were playing me," I say against his mouth.

He's laughs, low and unrepentant. "I never said I sucked, just that I didn't like the attention. Told you I wouldn't fight fair, Cherry."

I nip his lower lip. "Take me home, and let's get to popping yours, Big Guy." He stills, and I lean back to look up at him. "That was lame, wasn't it?"

Dex shakes himself as if waking up. His grip on me tightens. "Not sure. Is that a yes to my question?"

My fingers thread through his hair, still knotted at the back of his head. "I won't lie to you either, Ethan. Despite my…er…outspoken ways, I don't actually like being in the public eye. I had too much of that growing up."

His gaze is steady on mine. "I won't put you in the public eye, Fi. Ever."

I nod, because I know he'll protect me. That's his nature. Unfortunately, I know my nature too. "And I don't know if I'll be satisfied with a long-distance relationship." He opens his mouth to talk. I kiss it, quieting him before speaking again. "But I'll try, Ethan. For you."

His response is to walk us straight out of the club.

CHAPTER 13

Dex

DESPITE WANTING TO LEAVE the club as fast as humanly possible and find a bed where I can take my time with Fi, we drive home with Gray and Ivy, sitting in the backseat of Ivy's cavernous SUV.

Gray is a bundle of effusive energy. "Dude, you were like a rock star up there," he shouts over his shoulder as he drives, making Ivy wince.

"Inside voice, Cupcake."

He ignores Ivy's request and keeps on. "You never told me you could sing like that! Jesus, I don't know what to think about anymore. My honey knows she's the worst dancer in the world, and Dex is like a fucking rock god."

That earns him a slap on the head from Ivy and an eye roll from me.

"I'm not that good."

I'm all too aware of Fi at my side. She's warm and soft and leaning against my shoulder in total trust.

I'm going to fuck her. The thought is a stark declaration splashed across my mind. It's all I can do not to burst out of my skin. My heart is beating a frantic, anxious pace, and my dick is throbbing against my leg with impatient need. He wants out and in. I take a breath, ignore his demands.

"I'm just a mimic."

"A mimic?" Fi asks. Her face flashes in and out of view as we speed past light posts.

"Yeah. I can sing all right, but I basically pretended to be Dan Auerbach up there, used his style and intonations." I shrug. It was no big deal. So I sounded a bit like the lead singer of The Black Keys. It was fun. "It's easy being someone else up there."

Fi looks me over, her gaze penetrating. "And yet you loved it, didn't you?"

I find myself grinning, remembering the powerful surge of energy and joy that had gone through me, knowing I was entertaining her. "Yeah," I say quietly, "I did."

And because I suddenly feel exposed, the car too quiet, I call up to Ivy, "Hey, what happened to the Fiat?"

Ivy and Gray met when Gray borrowed her tiny *pink* Fiat. The guys had gotten a lot of laughs and given him endless shit when he squeezed his ass into that car.

Ivy's nose wrinkles with her grin. "Still have her. I don't think I'll ever let her go."

"You'd better not," Gray says. "That's our car of love."

Beside me, Fi makes a gagging face, sticking her finger in her mouth as if she wants to vomit. I chuckle and settle down closer to her, taking her slim hand in mine.

"Anyway," Ivy drawls, her smile still in place. "When Leo was born I thought it better to have a family car."

"And I told her it would be over my left nut that we'd get a minivan." Gray makes a face.

Ivy pats his knee. "And because I like his nuts—"

"*Aaand* we're done," Fi cuts in. Thank God. The word "nuts" calls attention to my own. They're aching now.

The car's gone quiet again. Gray turns up the stereo and drives. Which leaves me cocooned in darkness next to Fi. The lazy tones of

Flunk drift over us, and my awareness becomes the soft breaths she takes. Her faint scent grows stronger—girly shampoo and a faint musk I realize, with a kick to the gut, is arousal.

I'm going to fuck her. I probably should phrase it nicer—make love to her or worship her body with my dick. Something like that. But I'm fairly certain my first time will be straight-up hard and frantic fucking. I just pray I can last more than a minute. That I can satisfy her.

The fear that I won't makes my chest clench. I want to please Fi. More than please her. I want her to forget every guy who came before me. But aside from watching porn and reading up on certain techniques, I have all but zero applied experience, which vastly lowers my chances of giving her maximum satisfaction.

Why did I wait all this time? I know full well how important it is to practice. I should have just stopped overthinking and done it in college. Fucked my way past ignorance and accumulated some skills to do her right.

Fi's thumb glides over my palm, barely a touch, but every nerve in my body seems to be tracking it. That tiny caress feels better than anything I've known. I turn into that touch, burrow my nose in her hair. No one on Earth smells like Fi. No one else makes that particular sound when she breathes. And the fact is, I'm glad I haven't been with anyone else. I don't want to touch anyone but her.

The tips of her fingers wander up my inner arm. Up and down. I feel the stroke like a phantom touch along the shaft of my cock. The weight of her stare has me realizing I've had my eyes squeezed shut, my teeth clenched so I don't grab her here and now, haul her onto my hard dick.

Releasing a breath, I meet her gaze. In the darkness of the car, her wide eyes gleam. My breaths slow until I'm aware of every inhale, the way it stretches the muscles along my chest, how every measured exhale tightens my lower abs.

And still she strokes me, her touch feather light over my biceps, lingering at the knobby bone of my wrist. Jesus. She gives my index finger a little tug and it's like she's grabbed my dick. I grunt, swallow a louder moan.

And Fi watches it all, her expression rapt. I'm so under her spell that when she speaks, a low murmur meant for my ears only, I nearly jump out of my skin. "I can't stop touching you," she says.

"You hear me complaining?"

Her pretty lips curl. But the smile dies just as quickly, and she releases a soft breath. "This is the longest car ride ever."

I can't help it. I have to touch her. My hand slides up her thigh. I know beneath those tight jeans she's smoother than silk, soft and lush. She trembles under my touch, and when I cup her heat, those plump thighs clench over my hand. I give her a squeeze. She's damp, even through the thickness of her jeans. Fuck me.

"You aching here, Cherry?" I whisper, watching her eyes glaze over, her lids fluttering down.

Little white teeth bite down on her plush bottom lip as she gives the barest nod. My chest hitches. I push just a little harder and am rewarded with the sight of her lips parting, her brow knitting as if she's fighting a whimper.

She grips my wrist, and I think she might push me away, but she holds me fast. Slowly, I grind my fingers in a circle. "Here is the only place I want to be," I tell her, my voice a ghost in the dark.

She slumps against me, her open lips on my shoulder, her breath, humid and panting. Beneath her soft sweater, her nipples peak, hard buds that I want to test with my teeth, suck in my mouth.

I'm drifting downward, intent on doing just that, when the car halts, snapping the spell. Gray throws the interior into harsh light 'hen he opens his door. Fi catches my eye. Her cheeks flush pink.

"'e're here. And it's going to happen.

Fiona

I SWEAR MY HEART IS trying to pound its way out of my chest as I take Dex by the hand and silently head up the stairs, aware of my sister's and Gray's stare but not caring. Dex follows me, his grip secure, his steps steady.

Truth is, I might be the one walking up those stairs first, but he's the one leading me with that intense gaze of his, all hot and wanting. It prompts me to put one foot in front of the other. To rise higher and higher.

I tremble climbing the stairs. This is going to be Dex's first time. And he's giving that honor to me.

What surprises me is how much that matters. How much *he* matters.

When I'm with Dex, I'm not worrying if I'm good enough. Instead, I'm aware of my body, the way it feels, moves, and reacts to his. He puts me in a state of euphoria mixed with tight anticipation. He's addicting, and I want all of him.

By the time we enter his room and close the door behind us, my knees are weak. I turn to face him, maybe to reassure him—I'm not even sure of what—and he's on me. His mouth is hot and open, assured and taking what he wants. My pulse leaps. I suck in a breath and kiss him back, jumping up into his arms when he grabs my ass and lifts me high.

The room spins, and then I'm in Dex's bed, straddling his thick thighs as he leans against the headboard. As if being in the bed somehow grounds him, he slows us down, caressing my shoulders, murmuring a sound of contentment.

"I love the way you kiss me," I say against Dex's lips. We exchange air, a gusty sigh, and he angles his head, flicks his tongue along my upper lip.

"I love the way you taste," he murmurs before taking a slow, languid taste of me again.

I shudder, feeling it down my spine, up my legs. "You don't kiss like a virgin, Ethan."

He kisses me again, a little deeper, nipping my lower lip. With a grunt, he grips my ass and tugs me closer.

"And you sure don't act like one," I whisper breathlessly.

"Guess I forgot to read the virgin handbook." His voice is husky against my skin. "I've had a lot of time to think about what I'd do with you once I got my chance. Vivid, detailed plans, Cherry."

His hand cups the back of my head, completely engulfing it, and he kisses his way down my neck. I shiver in response, wrapping my arms around him, pulling myself a little closer—because there's no way I'm moving *him*. He's too big.

Had I snubbed big guys before? A mistake. There's so much to explore. My hands coast over his shoulders, the muscles there liked honed granite.

"Take this off." I pluck at his sleeve. I want to see him, feel his hot skin.

Dex sucks a sensitive spot at the base of my throat before pulling back. He reaches behind him, grabs hold of his shirt, and tugs it over his head in one swift motion. His hair flows wild around his face as he sits back and looks at me with eyes like smoke-quartz in the lamplight.

"Sweet hot peppers," I say on a gasp.

He grins, even teeth flashing white in the frame of his dark beard. "Never heard that one before."

I can't even answer. I'm too busy just *looking*. Because Ethan Dexter without a shirt on is breathtaking. I knew he was built—kind of hard to hide that. But seeing him in the flesh is so much more.

There is nothing lean or sinewy about him. He's simply solid, defined bulk. A body designed to take a hard impact and not cave. To endure. Broad shoulders like mini boulders, pecs as big as dinner plates. His abdomen is a veritable slab, a wispy little happy trail of golden brown hair starting a few inches below his navel.

Tattoo sleeves run from his wrists to the caps of his shoulders. Elegant script the width of my palm spans his collarbones.

"'Here be dragons,'" I read out loud. "Are you the dragon?"

The corner of his mouth quirks. His hands rest on my hips, holding on with just enough tension to tell me he isn't quite comfortable with the inspection but is letting me look anyway.

"Map makers used to put the saying along the borders, for places where they hadn't yet charted. It's in reference to the unknown, to be mindful of the unexplored."

I peer closer and see the faint latitude and longitude lines drawn beneath the words. The map stretches to his shoulders where twin sea serpents play.

I trace the words, and he shivers, his nipples drawing tight and—

"Holy hell." His left nipple is pierced. "I did not expect that."

The tops of his cheeks pink. "I…ah…have sensitive skin. Tattoos, piercing—getting them hurts like a motherfucker. But pain helps me focus when I get too…" His color grows deeper.

"Horny?" I supply, my finger running gently over his skin, because I can't stop touching him.

"Yeah."

"Got a lot of tattoos, Ethan."

His eyes burn into mine. "Yeah."

It's almost too much, thinking about all that suppressed lust and need, and how it's now focused on me. I touch the small silver barbell. Dex grunts, his hips shifting against mine. He gazes at me though lowered lids, his lips parted.

"You like that?" I whisper, doing it again, tweaking a bit.

His fingers clench my thighs, the thick erection in his jeans rocking me forward. I brace my hands on his shoulders, caress his smooth skin.

"Have you any idea how fucking hot you are?" I press a soft, lingering kiss on the hollow of his throat.

He swallows hard. "Whatever you say now, I'll believe."

Humming in response, I kiss him again, between his pecs, moving down to that tempting little nipple.

A groan tears from him as I suck the hard, cool barbell into my mouth, worrying the nub of his nipple with the tip of my tongue. He's so tight his body trembles, his fingers kneading my shoulders as if he can't decide to hold on or let go.

It spurs me on, makes me take that delicious nub between my teeth and bite, pulling at the metal.

"Oh, fuck, Cherry." He practically bucks me off with the thrust of his hips, his back arching off the pillows. And I haven't even gotten to his cock.

Which is all I want to do now. I smile against his skin and nibble my way down the divot that divides his abdomen.

Dex pants beneath me, and I know he's watching. I come up on my knees, angling my body so he has a better view. My tongue flicks out, licking into his small belly button.

"You're trying to kill me," he rasps.

"In the best possible way." I nuzzle his happy trail, my fingers working the fly of his jeans. They're stretched tight over his cock, and the zipper makes a loud buzz as I force it down.

I love the way he sucks in a breath, his abs retreating as if he's almost afraid to feel my touch, but then he cants his hips as if to say, *please, please, go lower.*

The flat of my tongue drags across thin, tight skin, the muscle beneath quivering, and I slowly part his jeans. Crinkly brown hairs greet me. Hell, there's nothing under these here but Dex.

His cock slides out, standing up for attention.

"Jesus," I rasp.

"What?" His hoarse whisper drifts down to me, and I glance up, see his flushed cheeks, his dazed expression. He's panting now, a sheen of sweat glistening over his chest.

"Give me a moment," I say, my hand reaching out to stroke his hot skin. He's so fucking hard he pulses. He swallows, his cock jumping under my touch.

I have to take a breath and calm myself. Some girls don't like cocks—or at least the look of them. I do. I love everything about the male anatomy. Dex's is beautiful—big enough that I know it's going to be work getting him in, and long enough that I know I'll feel each thrust he makes. The thought alone has my thighs pressing together in anticipation.

But that's not what holds my attention now. No.

He's pierced. Silver studs glint at the base of his wide cock head. One on the top and one on the bottom. I've never been with a guy who's pierced, but I've heard stories. I know those little nubs will hit all the right spots inside of me.

My thumb rubs the larger of the balls on the top, and Dex sucks in a sharp breath. But he doesn't move. He's waiting to see what I'll say.

"Now, this," I rub him again, loving the way it makes him twitch with pleasure, "had to hurt going in."

"You have no idea," he says in a raw voice.

"When?" And why?

Dex licks his lower lip. "After the wedding. You stripping down to that pretty green bra and those tiny panties. My wet dream walking. Should have gone for you then."

I wasn't ready for him then. I was still all about wild parties and dragging myself through college. I wouldn't have appreciated Ethan the way he deserves.

I stroke along the underside of the flared head, finding the smaller steel piercing. His hips shift, and he hisses, but he lets me play.

"You could have found someone else," I murmur. "Do you know how many women would kill to have you?"

"Didn't seem to want anyone else," he whispers. "It had to be you."

God, the thought of him wanting me so badly. All that pent-up need hiding behind such a calm façade. It terrifies me. And it makes me want to take him hard and keep him forever.

His solemn eyes, framed by thick lashes, are open wide and trained on my face as his broad chest lifts and falls with each heavy breath.

"They have no fucking idea, do they?" My voice is barely a whisper.

He stills, the muscles along his torso going tight as he stares back at me. I don't have to explain myself; he knows exactly what I mean, and he gives me the barest shake of the head, his throat working on a hard swallow.

No. No one sees him the way I do. Because he doesn't let them. Content to stay in the shadows, provide support when needed, never demanding anything for himself. Until me.

I see Ethan Dexter; he shines for me. And I burn hotter than the sun when I'm in his orbit.

I take a deep breath, and the air feels hot and dry going down, I'm so needy for him. But this isn't about me. Not right now.

My hand glides over his length, barely touching his silky skin. Even so, his whole body shivers, his expression pinching tight as though it's both torture and ecstasy.

"No more thinking, Ethan. Show me how you want it." I give the rounded tip of his cock a kiss, and it jumps against my lips. Eager, so unbelievably eager. My eyes stay on his. "I need you to show me."

His nostrils flare on an indrawn breath, and then he reaches for me, his big hand spanning the back of my head. Long fingers twine in my hair, gathering it in his grasp. He holds me just tight enough that I feel it in my scalp. Hell, I feel it down my thighs.

They clench when he slowly guides my head back to his cock. Those serious eyes peer down at me. His voice is a low rumble.

"Open."

God.

My lips part, my breath coming in a soft pant. But he doesn't shove himself in. No, he's fucking deviant because he wraps his free hand around the wide base of his cock and slowly runs the fat, swollen crown over my upper lip.

The cool, metal ball runs along the seam of my lips, such a strong contrast to all that hot flesh, that a moan breaks from deep within me. Without bidding, I open wider, wanting him on my tongue.

His eyes burn into mine. "Give it a lick."

And I do, a teasing flick along the tiny slit of his dick.

His nostrils flare. "More, Cherry. Lick it good and slow."

"Like this?" I run the flat of my tongue around the crown, licking him up like he's an ice cream cone.

Ethan bites his bottom lip, his lashes fluttering down, and manages to give me a nod. So I do it again, earning a moan from him.

"Oh, Jesus, Fi… Maybe…ah…God, Cherry, do whatever you want to me. I'm yours. I'm all yours."

He's sprawled back, his long body taking up all of the bed, one arm thrown over his forehead, his lip caught between his teeth as if in pain. He gazes down at me so full of lust and need, he seems almost helpless, this massive guy.

Mine.

Kissing the tip, I smile up at him, and then suck him deep.

He grunts loud and long, a garbled "*unf*" that tears from his throat as his back leaves the bed, almost dislodging him from my mouth. I wrap my fingers around his base, my free hand smoothing up and down his thigh, soothing as I work my tongue over his piercing.

"Fuck, fuck, fuck." He fists the sheets, pulling them from the mattress, as his hips shift and twitch.

I smile around his cock. Soon.

Torturing Ethan tortures me as well. I'm so hot my thighs quiver and my nipples ache. I curl over him, my palms braced on his thick thighs. He's so big and hard in my mouth, my jaw hurts. I don't care. I could do this every day.

I take my time, explore every substantial, glorious inch of him, cup his heavy balls and gently roll them in my palm. Oh, but he loves that.

"Give them a tug," he whispers, sounding desperate.

When I do, his whole body shudders.

"Fi, Fi, I'm gonna…" He licks his lips and gazes down at me as if he's lost the power of speech.

Oh, but I know. I want him to come spectacularly. The power in his body moves under my touch. It's heady. And when he comes with an agonized groan, giving himself fully over to me, I fall completely under his spell.

CHAPTER 14

Dex

FANTASY AND REALITY are never the same. I've fantasized about Fiona Mackenzie's mouth sucking on my dick more times that I should admit. Never once did I get it right.

I didn't want to recall those vague, fractured memories I had of the only other girl who'd performed that service for me those many years ago. They had no place being anywhere near the vicinity of Fi. So I'd only had my imagination to go on.

My imagination is a weak bitch compared to the reality of Fi's warm, silken mouth, the way her delicate hands glide over me, stroking and petting as if my pleasure, *my need*, is all that matters.

It cuts me off at the knees. I want to fall at her feet and confess my undying devotion. If this is what a blowjob reduces me to, I can't even think of what finally sinking into her sweet body will do. I'll probably have a fucking aneurysm or something.

As it is, I'm panting as if I've run thirty drills in a row. Sweat slicks my skin, makes my jeans damp and clingy around my thighs. I want them off. Everything off. Nothing between us now.

Truth is, I'm a fucking mess. My hands are clumsy and shaking as I reach for Fi, haul her up my chest so I can kiss her. She comes willingly, her lips parting, her tongue tangling with mine. She tastes of me, of herself, of us.

That we've become an *us* has my fingers threading through her hair, holding on tight. My kiss has no skill now. Just need. "I need you bare. I need to touch you."

She nods, takes another kiss, fumbles to reach the hem of her sweater. I'm holding her too close, but I don't want to let go. I whip off her shirt, then sit back to shimmy out of my jeans.

"I didn't want to come," I tell her. It sounds like an accusation, but it really isn't. Coming in her mouth. Jesus fuck. Just fuck. She'd sucked me down, her hot mouth tugging at my dick as if she needed it to survive. It made me feel weak as hell and like a god among men. Because Fi had chosen me. Out of all prospects, she wanted me.

"You'll come again," she assures, nibbling at my neck. "I just took the edge off."

More like unleashed my primitive side that says, *claim her now and do it hard*. Only I can't seem to control my limbs. Hell, my cock is rising again. I'm pretty sure hard and ready is going to be its go-to state for days.

She's laughing now, her voice all soft and husky. I know it's because I'm stuck in my jeans, the fabric snagged on my ankles. Fi reaches out and pulls me free. I'm naked, and she's not. This needs to be rectified.

"Off." One, swift tug and her skinny little jeans are sailing across the room.

"Whoa, Big Guy," she says with another laugh, her green eyes dancing. "Hold on a sec."

I've been holding on for twenty-four years. But I take a breath, make myself calm. Whatever Fi wants, I'll give her.

Swallowing with difficulty, I sit up, pressing my fists against my thighs so I don't reach for her. Because she's lovely, sitting there in her lacy pink bra and panties.

She ducks her head, tucking a lock of hair behind her ear. "I have an IUD."

"Really?" I probably shouldn't say it like that, all shocked and shit, but I'm distracted, and it slips out. That sounds like something a girl in a committed relationship gets. I hate the idea of Fi having been in a heavy relationship before me.

She gives me a look. "I know it sounds…extreme. But after Ivy…" She bites her lip and shrugs. "I just wanted to be extra careful."

I nod because now I get it. Ivy and Gray got pregnant their senior year of college. It wasn't planned, and then Ivy miscarried. It tore Gray up, and I spent many a night with him and Drew playing video games and basically distracting the guy. Later, when they were married and became pregnant again, Gray was a nervous wreck until Ivy reached her second trimester and he could actually see a sonogram of a live and healthy baby kicking around in her womb. I can imagine Fi witnessed a lot of Ivy's pain as well.

Gently, I rest my hand on her bare thigh and rub it. "Okay."

Fi puts her hand on mine. "I'm clean. Got tested after my last boyfriend. I have an email of my results." She moves to reach for her phone but I stop her with a touch to her shoulder.

"I believe you."

Oddly, she frowns. "You shouldn't. Don't believe what any girl tells you out of hand. There are too many liars and cheats gunning for professional athletes. Hell, you should check to make sure I have an IUD—"

I kiss her. No tongue, just a pressing of my lips to hers to stop her word spew. She blinks up at me when I pull away.

"Cherry, it's just you and me. So stop talking crazy about other girls. I trust you, and I don't really give a shit if you think I shouldn't."

Her lips purse, but she's fighting a smile. "So touchy."

"Yeah, well, it pisses me off when you imagine me with other women."

"The thought pisses me off too, Big Guy."

"Good." I caress the tight little corner of her mouth with my thumb. "Now, is all this your way of saying you don't want to use a condom?"

The thought does funny things to my insides. Makes me think about forever and exclusivity and finally being inside Fi.

"You're grinning," she points out.

"I am." I grin some more, kiss the fragrant curve of her neck.

Fi tilts her head to give me room. "It's your first time, Ethan. You ought to get the full experience."

Delicately as I can, I run the tip of my tongue up her neck, loving the way she shivers. When I reach her mouth, I dip in to snatch a taste, and she moans, opening up wider. God, she's delicious.

Mine. All mine.

My fingers thread through her hair, holding on tight. "Can I have the full experience now?"

She chuckles, the sound muffled against my lips, and her arms wrap around my neck to bring me closer. "You can have it all, Ethan."

"Be warned, Cherry, I'm going to take it." With that, I swing her onto my lap. A flick of her bra snap and it slips off. I palm her breasts, graze my lips over the stiff bud of her nipple before sucking it deep, taking as much of her breast into my mouth as I can. Greedy, so greedy, for her.

I love the way she moans and pushes into my touch. I want more of her sounds. My teeth bite down, just enough to make her feel it, make her squirm. Pain and pleasure.

I know how my confession must have sounded, how I'd pierced myself in the most painful place possible for the want of her. But it wasn't entirely impulsive. I'd known that eventually the pain would fade and there would be only pleasure. Added pleasure for me and for whoever I was with.

Yeah, I'd been picturing Fi. Didn't matter if I tried to move on. Eventually, my mind returned to Fiona. She's my One, whether I want her to be or not. But want her I do. And now I'm going to have her.

Like that, any lingering nerves about having sex for the first time dissipate like fog in the sun.

Easing her back on the bed, I take hold of her panties. The journey that small scrap of silk takes down her legs seems endless. Torture.

Fi only chuckles, kicks her panties aside. I've never met a girl like her. She isn't shy, yet she doesn't preen. She knows I'm dying to see her. It's clear in the way she lays back, one arm draped over her head, the other resting on my shoulder. In the way she looks up at me as if to say, *I'm yours, do as you wish.*

A breath gusts out of my mouth. I'm shaking like a leaf. Sweat covers my skin, makes me shiver even more. And yet I'm so fucking hot I can barely breathe.

I can't stop stroking her curves, her skin so smooth and soft I could touch her forever. Can't stop staring at the deep rose tips of her nipples, at pert, creamy breasts that fit perfectly in the palm of my hand. At the dip of her waist and wide swells of her hips. The little triangle of golden curls, the exact shade of spun sugar.

She is so gorgeous, so perfect, my chest feels like it might cave in.

Her plump lips curl in a smile. "Now I know even a virgin football player has to have seen his share of naked women."

She's right. Girls aren't shy around star athletes. I've seen plenty of them. In all sorts of shapes, sizes, and colors.

"I can't be that different," she says.

My hand stills on the curve of her hip, at the spot where it sweeps down to her luscious ass. "You are." A little furrow works between her brows, and I lean down to press my lips there. "You're mine. That makes all the difference in the world."

I can feel her smile. She cups the back of my neck, runs her fingers down my skin, sending lightning strikes of heat along my back. "Take me, Ethan."

I'm not even conscious of moving, but I'm kissing her, deep and hard, like I need her to breathe. Soft lips, warm, wet mouth. My tongue dips in again, again, needing more. I move over her, my hips settling between her legs.

Hell, she's so much smaller than me, delicate and breakable. I don't want to crush her, but she spreads her thighs wider, sighing into my mouth as she does it, and I just want to press into her until every inch of my skin covers hers.

My cock is so hard it hurts, nestled along the slick channel between her legs. I can't help but move my hips, slip-slide and grind against her sweet pussy. But it's not enough. I want in. It's pure aggression, this need.

Gritting my teeth, I rest my weight on my elbows and peer down at her. "Okay?" I don't know if I'm asking her or asking myself. I'm shaking again. Always shaking with this girl. She could slash me in two with a word, a look, and she doesn't know it.

Or maybe she does. Her smile is tender as she brushes back the tangle of my damp hair hanging around my face. "Perfect, Ethan."

I force a breath into my lungs, then cant my hips, lifting back enough that the aching tip of my cock finds her opening. So warm and slick. I swallow convulsively, my heart threatening to pound its way out of my chest.

"Fi," I whisper, searching her eyes.

Her hand glides down my spine to my ass, clutches tight, urging me to move. And then I'm pushing in and in. And in.

A groan tears from me, so ragged it sounds like I'm in pain, when really I'm in Heaven. Tight, wet, hot Heaven. I think I sob. I don't know. My only thought is *more*. And *now*.

I push until she's too tight to get any farther. Then pull back.

Holy sweet hell. The glide out is almost as good. Only, fuck, I need to thrust again. And harder. Get deeper. So I do, working my way in, fighting for every inch and loving every fucking second of it.

Beneath me, Fi's eyes flutter closed, her slim back arching up toward me. She's fragile beneath me. And yet, God, the way she spreads her legs wider, the little whimpers and gasps for air, like she's desperate for me to give it to her hard. It takes all my will not to pound into her like a beast. Because I need to know for sure.

"Good?" I whisper, my voice raw in my throat as I pant, my arms braced at her sides and shaking.

"So...very..." She swallows hard, rocks her hips, working herself on to me.

Tight, so tight. Slick walls squeeze me. My dick throbbing and stiff, nudges just a bit deeper. "You like being stuffed full of my cock?"

"Fuck yes." The hard points of her nipples brush against my chest. "More," she says. "More."

So I give it to her. Pumping through the perfect clench of her pussy. Until I bottom out. For a second I hold perfectly still, my entire body straining against hers. I close my eyes, clench my teeth. Shivering heat licks along my skin. My dick pulses so hard, I feel the shock waves in my ass, down my thighs.

Don't come. Don't you fucking come.

I take a breath, and it burns through my lungs.

Then she touches me, the brush of her fingers tracing my cheek. "Ethan."

I find her gazing up at me, her cheeks flushed and dewy with sweat. So beautiful I can't speak. Her thumb caresses my skin. "Now, baby."

A groan rips from me. I lose myself, thrusting with blind need. And it feels so good, so fucking good, my entire body ignites. I can't help glancing down, watching myself—harder than I've ever been and glistening with her sweet slickness—tunnel in and out of her tight clasp.

The sight sends my awareness into overdrive, has me pushing harder, loving her with my entire body.

But I need to do right by her. "Tell me what to do," I rasp against her mouth. "Tell me how to please you."

She's breathing light and fast, her arms limp around my shoulders.

"What you're doing now…" She shifts a little beneath me, her brow furrowing in concentration. So fucking beautiful. "Push upward when you thrust. Right…" Her breath hitches when I comply. "Yes. Right there. There, Ethan."

I do it again. Watching her. Loving the way her pretty face twists with pleasure, how she whimpers and pleads when I hit that spot within her. And each time I do, my metal piercing shifts and pulls, sending ripples of pure feeling down my cock.

I fuck her until my balls draw up, pleasure coiling them so tight my spine tingles. "Cherry, I'm close. I don't want to…" I thrust again and groan. Lust is like a thunderclap within me. "I don't want to go without you."

Her eyes are wide, dazed. "Suck my nipple and fuck me hard, Ethan."

Jesus. I nearly come there and then.

Panting, I crane my neck, find the stiff bud of her nipple and pull it in deep. She moans, writhes against me like she wants to get away. Only she's grabbing my hair and tugging me closer as if she's afraid I'll stop. Not a chance.

I pound into her. Giving her more. Taking more.

Until Fi utters a cry, her slim body straining against mine. The walls of her sex clamp down tight, beginning to tug at my dick in rhythmic pulses. And I lose it.

So good. So good, I can't think. Her nipple pops free and my face burrows into the sweat-slick crook of her neck as I cry out and pound into her until I come so hard, I can't even remember my name.

Just hers.

"Fi."

CHAPTER 15

Fiona

I WAKE UP LATE. Again. Okay, earlier I woke up to Dex sliding into me and fucking me with a languid, almost lazy pace. I was sore, and so was he. Not enough to stop either of us. Not until I lost my ever-loving mind, which I do every time he slides into me.

Because his piercing? Hallelujah and praise the brave soul who first thought, *I'm gonna adorn my man-crown*. Nothing, *nothing*, on this green Earth is as good as the feeling of Dex's thick, studded cock pushing in and out of me.

Well, perhaps one thing: witnessing Ethan Dexter come. I swear, I could have an orgasm just watching him, the way his big body starts to quiver, his brows drawing up tight as though he's in actual pain. But it's mostly the way he gives himself over to it, pounding into me like he'd die if he stopped, the almost desperate sounds he makes, somewhere between a whimper and a groan.

That this big, strong, normally self-contained man falls apart for me makes me fall a little deeper every time. And I'd wanted him to stay in bed with me. Possibly never leave it.

But annoying Gray began texting and then calling up the stairs, nagging Dex to get his ass up and get ready.

"He's not going to let this go," Dex had muttered.

"This is some sort of sick payback, isn't it?" I flopped onto my back.

"Guys are kind of assholes that way." He sat up with a groan.

So while he showered and went to work out, I slipped back into sleep, a boneless bliss known only to those who have been thoroughly worked over.

As soon as I wake, I want him here. He's been gone for two hours, and I miss him with a terrible ache that swims through my bones. My stomach should be in knots over my work mess, but instead it's fluttery with anticipation. I can't wait to hear his voice, see all those deeply weighted thoughts going on in his agate eyes. I want to feel his solid warmth, touch his body.

God, my hands twitch with the need to wrap themselves around that thick, strong cock of his, to play with the silver piercing and hear him make those low, needy groans.

I have to press my legs together to ease the emptiness there.

All this and it's only been a few days with him. Already I'm addicted. One hit and he is my drug of choice. And what good will this do when I have to go back to New York?

The ringing of my phone pulls me out of my thoughts.

The caller ID says it's my co-worker Alice. Which is weird enough that I answer.

"Hey," Alice's voice is thin, the sound of traffic loud in the background. "You having fun in San Fran?"

Fun isn't the word for what I'm having. Super happy lust tornado? Pleasure palace experience of a lifetime?

"No complaints," I say casually. Which is also a gross understatement. "What's up?"

I don't usually get calls from Alice.

"Felix pulled us all into a meeting today. Said he was planning on naming his new assistant designer on Friday morning."

I bolt upright, my spine so stiff it hurts. "Friday? But I'm not back in until Monday."

Alice makes a noise that sounds a lot like *duh* although she's too nice to say it outright. She's already a junior designer, so she's got nothing to worry about. I, on the other hand, am clearly up shit creek without a paddle.

"And since when did he plan on having a new assistant?" I practically squeal.

"Probably after the millionth time Elena mentioned how good it would be for him to have one. She's been getting really cozy with him this week."

Alice is one of the few people in the office who sees Elena for what she is, and who vocally disapproves. At least to me. Which makes us comrades of a sort.

"Of course she is," I say, my blood rising hot over my chest and face. "I knew I shouldn't have gone on vacation. Shit."

"Look, normally I wouldn't say this, but you might want to consider cutting your vacay short. Get in here and show Felix what you've got. Something new and not tainted by Elena."

I'm already up, hurrying to my room as fast as my short legs can carry me. I refuse to look back at the bed I've just left. But it doesn't matter. It haunts me still, like a cold fist grinding down my spine. "Thanks for the head's up."

She makes a noise of disgust. "If that little bitch gets a promotion, there will be no living with her. I'm likely to take a walk into rush-hour traffic."

"I'll join you."

"Besides, it's only a matter of time before she starts copying someone else, and I'm not going to be her next victim."

"There's the Alice I know." I laugh without much humor. "Keep calm; I'm on it."

But I have the horrible, sinking feeling that it's already a done deal. So why am I frantically packing my bag? Why am I online cashing in precious air miles so I can get a ticket back to NYC today?

With each decisive action, my jaw grows a little stiffer, my heart a little colder.

You're running away. You're just using this as an excuse.

No. I need to protect my job. I'm not running.

Thirty minutes later, when I finally stop moving and planning, I sit in the quiet of the guest room I decorated and think of Dex.

I'll be leaving him regardless. If not today, then definitely on Sunday. A few days more will only make this worse. I've had boyfriends before; I know when I'm in danger of losing my head over a guy. And I know it's never been as strong as this. Usually the start of a relationship is the best part for me. Attraction is a heady rush, a kind of giddy high—like going out and dancing all night. You know it will end eventually. It's just part of the process, a little built in fail-safe to keep me from getting too attached.

Only with Dex? I don't like the idea of us having an end date. At all.

I struggle to swallow past the panic. I'm so deep in my own fear that I don't hear him until he's walking into my room.

Fresh from a shower at the gym, his sun-streaked hair is damp and neatly swept back in that Samurai bun. He's wearing a navy t-shirt with a graphic of a big, green Hulk fist smashing through cinder blocks. I'm betting Gray gave it to him.

I'm also betting Dex is wearing it now *because* Gray gave it to him. Dex is like that—the big papa bear who makes sure those in his circle know they're loved and appreciated.

The pain in my throat grows. I have to slip my hands between my knees and press hard to keep from reaching for him.

There's a smile in his eyes. But he clearly sees that something is wrong, and he halts. Instantly his gaze scans the room as if he knows he needs to search out any possible threat.

His eyes cut to the packed suitcase on the floor and a line forms between his thick brows. "You're leaving?"

He sounds so incredulous, his voice lighter with shock, his body visibly recoiling like I've slapped him. I did that to him. I hate myself for that.

Talking proves harder than expected. "Work emergency."

The line between his brows gets deeper, and he puts his hands low on his hips in the way guys do, his stance wide. His fists are clenched tight enough to make his knuckles white, and I get the feeling he's trying not to grab my bag and hurl it back into the closet.

I want to do the same. But I'm cutting and running like a coward instead.

Dex's eyes meet mine. Already he has such power over me. One look and I want to walk into his embrace, beg him to fuck me, make me forget about everything and everyone. It would be so easy. I know he'd do it.

His low voice slides over the distance between us. "Why are you really leaving?"

Am I that obvious? Apparently so.

"I… Shit." Standing, I take a deep breath and blurt it out. "I think we made a mistake." My voice is overloud and desperate.

"Why?" His question is stark, as if ripped from him. "It was good. I know it was better than good—"

"Oh, God." I hold up my hand to stop him from saying more. "It's not that. Ethan…" I run hand through my hair. I'm so clammy, my skin snags along the strands. "It was too good."

He takes a step forward, his head tilting as he peers at me. "I'm not sure I get why *too good* is a mistake."

"Because I'm going to want so-fucking-fantastic-my-knees-are-still-weak every day." At this, his lips quirk, a gleam lighting his eyes, and I fight a smile. "I'm kind of selfish like that."

Another step and he's almost within touching distance, but he comes no farther. "Still not seeing the problem, Cherry." His voice goes dark. "I'll give it to you every day. Several times a day, if I have a say in the matter."

He's slowly coming closer, as if he's afraid I'll bolt. I want to. As it is, I press a hand to his solid chest. The instant I touch him, all my happy parts clench tight and hot. But I hold his gaze, don't let him duck down to kiss me. "That's the problem, Big Guy. You can't. You won't be where I am. And I…"

Dex's soft lips brush against mine, stealing the breath from me.

"And I…" I say again. "I'll miss it too much."

Again he kisses me, a slow, melting nuzzle of lips. Soothing, tempting. Despite myself, I cup his cheek, stroke along his beard. His big, warm hand holds the back of my neck, keeping me steady as he gives me another kiss. No tongue, just mouth to mouth, an exchange of air. Just enough to let me feel.

"I'm kissing you," he whispers against my lips, "and already I miss you."

A ragged breath leaves me, and I break away from him. Not that he lets me go far. He holds my cheeks and presses his forehead to mine. With his great height, the action makes it seem as though he's sheltering me, his broad shoulders hunched, his thick arms surrounding me.

With another man it might be intimidating. I simply feel protected with Dex. Which makes all of this so much harder.

"That's the point. I hate being left behind, Ethan. I hated it when my dad did it. I hated it when my mom decided to live in another country. I hate the idea of it now. I tried to tell you this before. But you're…*you*, all sexy and sweet and strong and beautiful… God, I'm babbling. You make me babble, Ethan. No guy has ever made me do that. How am I supposed to resist you?"

"You don't." The corners of his eyes crinkle, but it doesn't look like amusement; it looks like pain. Perhaps the same pain I'm feeling.

"Last night," I tell him, "was… I've never felt that before. Not just the sex, although…Hell, Ethan Dexter, you rock my world." My fingers tighten on his jaw. "I know I said I'd try but… Shit…now I know it will slowly kill me not to have all of you."

"You have me," he rasps as though I'm killing him now. "You fucking have all of me."

His declaration rips through my heart. We've only had a few days together. Already he knows as well as I do that the connection we made altered us. But I'm afraid I can only bend so far before I break. My throat swells tight.

"That's the thing. I don't have you. I will never have you with me all of the time."

His body jerks, and I'm the one holding tight, afraid he'll pull away.

"Ethan, I wouldn't change you for the world. Football is part of who you are. Take that away, and I take away an essential component of you. But it doesn't change the fact that if I don't pull back now, I'll regret it."

He steps away, shoving his fisted hands deep in his jeans pockets. Massive muscles bunch along his shoulders and down his arms. His expression is like stone, but Dex was never very good with hiding emotion in his eyes. Maybe he doesn't want to be. So much pain there. Anger too.

"I never want to be a regret to you, Fiona." His throat works on a swallow, and he glances away, giving me his strong profile. "I don't want to let you go. But if that's what you want, I'll respect your decision."

So fucking grown up. I don't feel like one. I'm the stupid kid who makes all the wrong choices. Is this one of them? I'm trying to do the right thing, and I know my usual self would toss caution to the wind and screw the consequences. But that's led me down too many bad roads.

This is the smart choice. End it now before I turn into a whining, nagging leech girlfriend.

An unsteady breath leaves me. "I—"

He holds up a hand, his eyes still not meeting mine. "I can't. Whatever it is you want to say just…" He moves then, faster than I'd have ever imagined.

Before I can even blink, he has me, his hands fisting my hair, his mouth on mine. It's hard—his grip, his touch. He takes me, parting my lips with his, plunging his tongue in deep.

My knees do that weak thing again as he kisses the ever-loving fuck out of me. I can't even hold on, I'm too dizzy with the feel of him just taking what he wants.

When my air runs out, his lips leave mine on a soft gasp. Dex rests his forehead against my heated cheek. The tips of his thumbs run along my skin. And when he talks, his voice is so rough, I almost don't recognize it.

"Goodbye, Fiona Mackenzie. You rock my world too."

And then he's gone, walking out of the room and not turning back to see me fall.

CHAPTER 16

Dex

USUALLY I DO MY RUNNING up and down stadium stairs, or towing a weighted sled while doing relays—brutal workouts designed to increase my strength and mental toughness or develop intense bursts of speed. Jogging along a flat trail is more of a luxury than a workout. Out here, I can soak up the scenery, get some much-needed fresh air.

Unfortunately, I'm not as fast as Gray, and the little shit catches up with me about a mile in. How he found me is some sort of Houdini magic because I sure as shit didn't tell him where I was going.

"Hey," he says as he comes alongside me.

I think I grunt. I'm not really in a talking mood.

"I'm guessing you know Fi left," he says carefully.

I glance his way before facing forward again. "Say what you're going to say, Grayson, and let me get on with my run."

"Do you know how long I've waiting to have a heart-to-heart with you? Shit, Drew's gonna be so jealous he wasn't here."

So glad my pain is such an event.

He must read this on my face because he winces. "Sorry. I suck at this. I'm not you."

"Yeah, usually I lead in with a thought-provoking question, then wander away to let you work it out on your own." I nod toward the path behind us. "Feel free to skip to the wandering part."

"Nice try, Big D."

At our side, the Golden Gate Bridge rises out of the morning fog. It's beautiful. Almost peaceful. Only Gray won't let me have any peace.

"You're just going to let her go?"

For a hot second I actually want to hit him. Did he think it didn't kill me to watch her walk away? I pull in a calming breath. Calm. I'm always calm. "She threw down an argument I had no solution for."

Short of quitting my job, there is nothing I can do to solve the problem of me always leaving Fi.

The dull pain in my chest spreads down my arms. All I can do is run, listen to the sound of my feet hitting the pavement, the rasp of my breath going in and out.

"Man," Gray finally says. "I'm sorry. I thought she'd be different with you. That she wouldn't flake—"

"Grayson," I cut in, because I really can't handle pity right now. "There's nothing to be sorry about. You might be a parent, but you're not mine or Fi's. I knew what I was risking."

He manages to keep quiet for a few beats, but Gray's a talker, incapable of prolonged silence. "Still," he mutters, "fucking sucks balls."

I couldn't agree more.

He gives me a sidelong look. "So what are you going to do about it?" He knows me too well.

I fight to keep my face neutral. "What I do best. Assess the defense, find another angle." Because I've had a taste of Fiona, and I can't give her up without a fight. Unfortunately, until inspiration strikes, I have to retreat, give her space, or risk acting like a stalker, which no guy in his right mind should do.

Gray gives my arm a nudge. "Hey. Last one to Fisherman's Wharf buys breakfast."

Little fucker. We both are good for quick bursts of speed. But Gray is better at longer distances. So I do what any self-respecting competitor would. I shove him into the grass and take off.

Fiona

AIRPORTS SUCK. As soon as I step into one, I get tense. Someone is always watching you somewhere. You're treated as cattle. Annoying cattle at that. And all you have to look forward to is a cramped seat and paying for a crap meal wrapped in plastic. Yay-hay.

My eyes are gritty, and I have a sore throat. Maybe I'm coming down with something. Because I'm finding it really hard to breathe too.

I've been this way pretty much since I left Ivy's house. Ivy who looked at me with such disappointment, I felt lower than shit on a shoe. Gray didn't even bother to look my way. He shut down completely and muttered something about taking a run.

The ticket agent informs me that I have a seat on the last row of the plane. Another bonus: all the people waiting to use the bathroom will stand there, shoving their asses in my face.

If you weren't such a chickenshit, you'd still be in bed with Dex. Which is now officially the best place in the entire world.

I tell myself to shut up.

Boarding pass in hand, I turn, pulling my carryon bag behind me, and nearly smack into a couple kissing.

Fuck a duck.

They're going at it. Not in a gross, slobbering way, but…shit, in a romantic, you're-my-air way. Dude holds his girl's cheeks with care as he tilts his head and goes in deeper. She clutches his back as if she'll never let him go.

And here I am, staring like a perv. I can't help it. I now know how it feels to kiss like that. The consuming fire of it, the way your entire body sways into your lover's with the need to sink into his flesh and bones and become part of him.

The pain in my throat swells outward, lodging hard in my chest. I stalk around the couple and blindly race for the TSA line.

But it's no use. I can't stop my thoughts. Or the pain.

Like a zombie, I wait at the gate. Like a zombie, I board the plane, find my seat. It isn't until yet another couple settles into the row in front of me—the guy helping his girl put her bag in the overhead before giving her cheek a kiss—that I break.

Biting back a sob, I fumble for my bag and search for my phone.

I call up the wrong number twice, my finger shakes so badly. *Stupid. I was so stupid.* The thought that I've ruined everything has my entire chest clenching tight. Around me passengers are finding their seats, a toddler is whining for Cheerios.

And the phone keeps ringing. Dex's gruff message starts up. I have to blink hard. Just hearing his voice gets to me. But is it a bad sign that I've gone straight to voice mail? Is he avoiding my call? I wouldn't blame him.

I hate leaving a message. But part of me is relieved that I can say what I have to say and then hang up, without the threat of him telling me he's done.

Please don't be done with me

"Hey, it's me. Fi. Shit, that rhymes. I hate it when I inadvertently rhyme. I mean, if you're going to do a rhyme, own it, right?" *Shut up, Fi.* I take a breath, my palm slipping on the case of my phone. "I…ah…There was this couple kissing. By the ticket counter. I don't know if they were leaving each other or reconnecting. But they were so into each other, you know? And it hit me. I'll never kiss you again. Never feel your arms holding me close. And…"

Shit, I'm about to blubber. My hand wipes so hard at my eyes it hurts. I swallow hard. "It hurt, Ethan. Too much. How can that be? How can it be that you already feel like a part of me? But I guess you are because the idea of never being with you again… Fuck. I'm babbling. Again. But Ethan—"

The loudspeaker blares, announcing that it's time to cut off all electronics.

I hunch over, turning my body toward the window. "Ethan, forget what I said, okay? I'm sorry. I was being a coward. I want you. Just you. I don't care about the rest. Please say it isn't too late. That I didn't fuck us up before we really began."

"Miss?" The flight attendant is hovering. "You have to turn off your phone now."

I glance at her, tears in my eyes, holding up a hand. "I've got to go," I say into the phone. "I'll be in New York tonight. I…just… I'm sorry, okay? Call me?" I lick my dry lips. "Okay, then. Bye."

Ending the call, I sit back and stare out the small window. And hope he still wants me too.

CHAPTER 17

Dex

I DON'T SEE THE MESSAGE waiting for me until I'm out of the shower and scrubbing a towel over my dripping hair. I don't know how long I stand there, phone in my hand, deliberating over whether I want to hear what Fiona has to say now or later.

The room is cool, prickling my bare skin. I should get dressed, go down to dinner with Ivy and Gray. I'd rather not talk to them or anyone. Just go back to my empty-ass town house in NOLA and paint until my eyes blur.

But Fi called. Which means I'm going to listen; I'll never ignore her.

My heart thuds hard against my ribs as I hit the play button and put the phone to my ear. Her slightly husky, lilting voice is a kick in the guts. God, I miss her.

Then I listen, really listen. And slowly sink to the floor. My lips wobble on a grin as I lean my head back against the edge of the bed.

I listen to her rambling, breathy message again and again. I want her so badly my muscles tighten with the need to move. A low laugh leaves me. I can't help it. I'm happy. Truly happy. I still have no idea how to make this work. But I know one thing: I have a chance with Fiona Mackenzie. Protecting that has now become my number-one priority.

Fiona

"HEY. I GOT YOUR MESSAGE." Even though it's through the phone, Dex's voice sinks into my heart and warms it all up.

"Yeah?" It's all I can think to say, I'm so nervous. Me. Nervous over a guy. Over a football player. Next thing you know, I'll be buying his jersey. Although, really, I probably should show a little Dexter support.

"Yeah," he says back to me softly.

I lean my head against the stinky cab seat and just smile. "So…we're good?"

"Cherry, let me lay this down for you. I'm all in. I want you. I always have." That voice of his goes deeper. "You going to let me have you?"

Jesus. I cross my legs tightly, heat pulsing through me. "You've already had me."

"That was only a taste." It's a rumble in my ear, all his need and impatience a driving force that leaves me breathless and thrumming. "I want more."

"Ethan. You're killing me."

He curses under his breath, and I hear him sigh. "I'm killing myself. I know this isn't ideal. Just…" He's clearly struggling to give me some word of comfort. "Can you place your trust in me? That I'll find a way for us to be together?"

My hand cradles the phone to my cheek, a weak substitute for touching him. But it's all I have. "I can do that."

Again he sighs. This time it sounds relieved. "Thank you. Look, I'm going to go. I…" He stalls out. It's like I can actually hear his mind switching gears, so the sudden lightness in his voice isn't even a surprise, though his words are. "Found your panties balled up at the bottom of my bed, Cherry."

I choke out a laugh. "God. Give them to Ivy and she'll mail them back to me."

He makes a noise of disbelief. "You want me to give your underwear to your sister? Hell no."

"Dex! Those are Myla."

They'd been a very expensive birthday present from Ivy, who knew I always shopped at their boutique when I went to London to visit our mom.

"I have no idea what Myla is, darlin', but they're soon to be wrapped around my cock. If I can't have you, I'm fucking the panties."

With that, the big bastard hangs up. And I just know he did it with a smile on his face.

————————

FearTheBeard: I suppose you think sending me this pic of you wearing the top half of your lingerie set and nothing else is some sort of payback. You're right. My hand is tired, but your beloved Myla and I are well acquainted now.

CherryBomb: I don't know if I should be disturbed or turned on. I'm going with a little of both.

FearTheBeard: No more pics, Cherry. I'm in enough danger of developing tendonitis of the elbow as it is.

CherryBomb: Remember RICE: rest, ice, compress, elevate.

FearTheBeard: You're kind of evil, you know that?

CherryBomb: I am sweetness personified. And seems only fair that I get a sexy man pic in return.

FearTheBeard: Yeah, no.

CherryBomb: ETHAN!

CherryBomb: GIMME, GIMME, GIMME!

CherryBomb: A picture of you glaring is NOT what I had in mind.

FearTheBeard: Payback's a bitch, sweetheart.

CherryBomb: I'll keep that in mind as I go without underwear until I see you again.

FearTheBeard: Fuck.

CHAPTER 18

Fiona

RETURNING TO WORK SUCKS. The realization slaps me across the face hard enough to make me come to a halt. I actively hate walking into this office. I shouldn't. It's a beautiful space—a light and airy loft, all brilliant white. White to relax the eye and let us show sample colors in their purest state.

There's an energy here, as if each person is so grateful to be part of this place that they exude anticipation. Every person but me, apparently. My steps shuffle with clear reluctance, a pit of ugly feeling lodged low in my belly.

No one seems particularly surprised to see me. I get a few sympathetic nods in my direction as I head to my desk.

"Brilliant," I mutter under my breath. I can handle a lot, but being pitied burns me.

My desk sits in front of a massive Palladian window that starts at the floor and rises over ten feet above me. Outside, traffic is a flowing river, people darting to and fro. I want to be out there with them.

I'm just turning my computer on when Elena appears. Honestly, for someone who's caused me so much grief, she ought to look the part. I don't know, maybe have black-and-white hair and long, red nails or something. It would feel so much better if she was also in hot pursuit of a Dalmatian puppy coat.

But she looks…normal. Dark blond hair, snub features, medium height. She looks like the girl who'll be your best pal—the happy, if not slightly ditzy, sidekick.

It's a good disguise.

I'm tempted to ask her if she's Kaiser Soze. But I doubt she'd get the reference. Elena once told a group of us that the only time she was willing to watch a movie was if a date took her to one, and then she'd be moving on—because no way was she going to see a man who thought a movie date was acceptable.

Then again, not a week later, when Felix had mentioned his deep lust for all things Loki, Elena had waxed on about The Avengers and who was the hottest.

I lost points for picking The Hulk. They can look at me as though I'm crazy all they want; when Bruce Banner loses control and fucking roars? My nipples go tight.

For some reason this makes me think of Dex. And I do not want to think about him when Elena is perched on my desk. He's my happy place. She is not.

"What can I do for you, Elena?"

It doesn't escape me that she's tilting her head to catch a glimpse of my computer screen. I don't know what she expects to find there since I do most of my work on sketch pads.

She gives me a bright smile. The same easy, friendly smile that messes with my head and has me wondering if I'm making more of her than I should.

"Just getting in?"

Considering my bag is on my desk and I'm carrying a takeout coffee cup? "Yep. Just getting in." I also don't miss the implication that she's been here for a while. I still can't decide if she plays dumb or really is. It's hard to tell.

"Look, Fiona…" She places her warm, slightly moist hand on top of mine. "I know things have been strained between us lately. And I'm really sorry for it."

Some of the stiffness eases out of my shoulders. But she keeps talking.

"I know it's hard for you when we have such similar tastes, yet Felix keeps choosing me. I'd be upset too."

Right. There's the Elena I know. My eyes narrow as she leans closer.

"Maybe we can work together."

I stand abruptly. "We already do."

"You know what I mean, silly. Maybe we can collaborate on a project."

My smile actually hurts, I'm pressing my lips together so hard. When I manage to talk, it's through my teeth. "If we collaborate any further, we're going to have to share a brain."

She frowns as she follows me to the conference room for our morning meeting.

Tom, Alice, and Nathan are already sitting around the spotless glass table. I don't know how it manages to escape basic handprints and smudges, but it does, as if it dare not defy the exacting expectations of our boss.

Felix glides in a moment later, tiny espresso cup in his hand, gold Prada sunglasses perched on his nose. "Someone please tell me whose idea it was to paint this entire office white. It's fucking blinding."

"It was your idea," Nathan deadpans. "Hangover, oh fearless leader?"

Lucky for Nathan, he's one of Felix's best designers. And he knows it. Felix glares but does not reply.

With exaggerated care, Felix sets down his cup and sits back in his chair, folding one thin leg over the other. Dressed like an Italian film star from the 1950s, his ink black hair immaculately combed and glossy, he could be from another era. Through the gray tint of his glasses, his dark gaze finds mine. "Well, hello, Fiona. I didn't expect you back so soon."

"Oh, you know, San Francisco can't compare with New York City." Lame. So fucking lame.

His expression says much the same, and I fight not to cringe. Thankfully, he moves on. "Now then, where are we with the Meyer project?"

Nathan sits back, looking bored. "Ms. Meyer decided she wanted her bedroom candy apple red. The entire room."

"Then let her haul her ass down to Home Depot and paint it herself." Felix sighs and pinches the bridge of his nose. "What did you tell her?"

"That a glossy red powder room would have more impact, and all her friends would be able to see it."

A sniff tells us Felix is pleased. His head turns my way. Or Elena's. I can't be sure because she's hovering at my side as usual. "Mrs. Peyton has decided that the cerulean blue silk drapes remind her of her first husband, Clyde. As she divorced him after finding him riding his hot little PA, Jonathan, that 'simply won't do'."

"Go, Clyde," Nathan murmurs with a cheeky click of his tongue.

Felix's nose wrinkles. "Having seen Clyde, my sympathies go to Jonathan. Elena, what would you suggest?"

"About Clyde and Jonathan?" she squeaks.

I manage to hold in a wince. Felix simply sniffs, this one annoyed. "About the drapery."

A test. Felix loves to pop these little questions on us. Elena's mouth opens, her gaze darting around the table as if one of us will mime the answer and save her.

As tests go, it isn't a difficult one. The rest of Mrs. Peyton's living room color scheme is set: deep, glossy mink-colored walls, low-slung ebony furniture covered in gold mohair, and dusky blue satin.

The silence stretches as Elena starts sputtering. "Um, well…"

Felix sighs and turns to me. "Fiona? Thoughts?"

My mind turns as I tap my pen on my sketch pad. This is my chance to gain ground and remind Felix what I can do. "I'm thinking of that Jonathan Alder chain-link print you fell in love with. The gold and cream—"

"Cream one," Elena cuts in. She has her phone out and is frantically tapping on it as she beams at Felix. "Fiona and I were talking about it this morning, if you can believe it. I was saying how timeless that pattern was."

My mouth is stuck open. Frozen in shock. Inside my head, I scream at myself to snap out of it, say something. She's already holding up her phone. "If you like that idea, I've got a supplier on thirty-first who has it in stock."

The air leaves my lungs in a whoosh, and I turn back to Felix, who is smiling.

"I do love that fabric," he says, swiveling his chair back and forth. "And it would work well…" He sits up. "Great work, Elena."

Across from me, Alice lifts a brow, her gaze hard. Because I'm still sitting here like a boob. Only, what am I supposed to say? This is real life. Shouting, "You lying hag!" will only result in me looking like a bitter nut.

My back teeth meet as I turn my chair and stare at Elena. She doesn't flinch and gives me a big smile. Mine grows as well, so hard my cheeks hurt. "You know, it occurs to me that the master is also cerulean blue. Surely Mrs. Peyton will object to the color in her bedroom too."

"Chances are," Felix agrees from the head of the table.

I keep my stare on Little Miss Steal It. "What do you suggest for that, Elena? Or have I forgotten one of the many conversations we had this morning?"

She flushes. "Well…I…we could…" She nibbles on her bottom lip.

"That's all right," Felix says. "I'm sure you can work it out with

Fiona. Bring me a color scheme after lunch." And as if he hadn't just metaphorically punched me in the gut, he stands. "Now I'm going to lie down. Unless the office is on fire, I do not want to be disturbed."

At my desk, I allow myself a moment to slump over, press my forehead against the cold glass surface. So coming back to work early was a bust. But I've got time. Or I could just walk out. I picture it, how good it would feel. And then… What? What would I do?

Thankfully, my cell ringing distracts me. My voice is muffled when I answer because I don't pick up my head. "Hello?"

"Fi, darling girl, how are you?"

My mother. Her cultured, crisp English voice is both soothing and annoying. Soothing because it's mom, the woman who held me when I cried, tucked me into bed every night until I was fourteen. Annoying because she is never frazzled. She is perfect. Oh, I know she has her failings, but to me, she'll always be stunning and cool, not a blond hair ever out of place.

"Hey, mum. I'm fine."

"You sound like you're face down in bed."

Close enough. I sit up and smooth my hair back from my face. "Bad connection. I'm at work."

"Lovely. I've been meaning to tell you how proud I am of you for landing that position. I couldn't be happier, Fiona."

Right. A ragged breath gets caught in my chest. "Thanks."

"And you know, if you keep at it, soon you'll have your own design firm."

She's being encouraging. But I know her enough to hear the slightly desperate tone under it all: *Please, Fiona, keep at it. Don't quit this time.*

I heard the same tone every time I changed my major. Every time I asked to learn an instrument or join a dance class. I can't even blame her, because I quit all of those classes and camps, usually just a few days into them.

Grimacing, I turn my chair away from the open office space and face the window.

My mom keeps chattering. "And how were Ivy and Gray? And my little poppet?"

"All fine and well. Leo is getting bigger." And louder.

"He's beautiful, isn't he?" Mom had been there for the birth and instantly became a doting grandmum—as she insists on being called. "I tell you, he has my eyes."

I can't help but laugh. "Mom, his eyes are blue."

Hers are green like mine.

"All babies' eyes are blue. His will turn. And they look like mine."

Anyone can see that Leo has Gray's eyes. Down to the exact shade of blue. But I don't argue. "How's the business?" I ask instead. My mom owns a chain of bakeries. Ivy was supposed to go into partnership with her but chose to be an agent like our dad instead.

I don't know who was more shocked by that—Mom, Dad, or me. Ivy hated how Dad's business pulled him away from our family almost as much as I did. Yet here we are, Ivy as an agent and, hell, me falling for a football player.

As my mom talks about her shops, the image of Dex's grin—so rare but so gorgeous, framed by his lush, dark beard—pops into my mind. My palms tingle with the need to run over it, to smooth over the massive swell of his hard, hot chest.

I swallow and focus on Mom. She's telling me about a yeast delivery gone bad, her voice breathy with exasperation, and I blink hard. I miss her. I miss Dex. I miss everyone.

I clutch my phone, feeling lost and abandoned, which is ridiculous. No one has left me behind. I'm here because it's where I chose to be. This is life. Like some messed-up game of Boggle, it shakes us all up, and we land where we fall.

This isn't even close to the first time I've felt this way. But usually

I'm able to distract myself with friends and parties and laughter. Only I can't find it in me to laugh anymore. And I wonder if this is the only way life can be. Because I want some fucking control back.

CHAPTER 19

Dex

"**L**OOK, IT'S SINATRA!" Delgado, my fellow lineman, shouts when I walk into the locker room.

I'm greeted with a rousing chorus of "Gold on the Ceiling," all of it off-key and loud. I'd been informed by a cackling Gray that video of my karaoke performance had gone viral. If that hadn't been enough, the ESPN highlight, complete with accompanying jokes, made it clear I'd get my fair share of shit come Monday morning.

"Yeah, yeah," I wave an idle hand. "Laugh it up, fuzzballs."

Sampson, a nose tackle, makes an attempt to roar like Chewbacca but ends up choking, which cracks the guys up even more.

Grinning, I sit down and kick off my shoes. Finn Mannus, my QB, saunters over, a smile wide on his face. He gives my shoulder a hearty slap. "So, Dexter, have a good week off?"

"Say what you're gonna say, Manny, and fuck off," I tell him lightly.

He's still grinning at me like a smug fuck. "I must say, I enjoy seeing you hang your balls out, Dex. I didn't know you had it in you."

"Pretty sure there's a lot you don't know about me." I've stripped down to get in my gear when I catch his eye. He's no longer smug but serious.

"That's kind of the point," he says. "You're my center."

His words give me pause. I like Finn. He's a rookie, which especial-ly sucks for him because he has to carry the team without the freedom to ease into his job. But he's also a good quarterback, and it's *my* job to protect him. But I don't know him like I know Drew. I haven't taken the time. Guilt tilts in my belly.

"Come out for a beer with me later," I suggest. "And I'll tell you all about my wild week."

He looks at me with those famous baby blues that have women all over America sighing and throwing their panties in his direction. Doesn't do anything for me, but I'm comfortable enough in my manhood to see what chicks dig about him. I guess I'm doomed to always cover pretty boys.

"Yeah," he says. "Sounds good." He moves to go but then halts. "Hell. We've got that photo shoot at four."

A scowl works across his face, and now I'm the one who's laughing. "Ah, the charity calendar. Thought that would be right up your alley, GQ."

Apparently not, if his disgusted look is anything to go by. "Charity, yes. I'd just rather do it talking to a bunch of kids or something, not offering my ass up like a side of beef."

"Aw, Manny," says Sampson, walking past, "but it's such a big ass. Almost as big as your head." With that, he snaps a towel at said ass and takes off as Mannus lunges for him.

"Keep running, dickhead," Mannus calls.

I suit up, more than happy for the attention to slide off of me and back to Mannus, where it belongs. Only that isn't the case. For the rest of practice, guys serenade me. On the sidelines, when I'm gulping down Gatorade and stretching out my burning quads, Dean Calloway, the offensive line coach stands beside me, his gaze on the other players, but his mouth twitching.

"Guess I know who'll be the lead in our annual team musical, Dexter."

"Didn't know we had a musical, Coach." I toss my empty bottle into the trash.

He turns to me. "Maybe we should start one now." Giving me a slap on the back, he ambles off with a, "Good work, Dex."

I watch him go, and it occurs to me that although I've played for this team for going on two years, I haven't really engaged. It's too easy for me to hide away from the world. But laughing with my team, not taking shit too seriously, it feels good.

I could be happy, genuinely happy. There's only one thing missing, and she's over a thousand miles away.

Fiona

I'M HEADED OUT FOR DRINKS when Dex calls. Which has me grinning even before I answer the phone. "Hey."

"Hey, Cherry." His deep voice gives me a little thrill. Every single time. "What you up to?"

"Going out for drinks with Anna." I dart across 5th and weave past a slow-strolling tourist family.

"Drew's Anna?" Dex asks in obvious surprise.

"Yep. We've gotten to know each other over the years. Gray always invites her and Drew to spend Christmas with us."

Drew lost both his parents when he was in high school, and Gray lost his mother to cancer around the same time. Gray has made it a priority never to let Drew go a holiday without family. "Family" being him, and now Ivy and me.

"Right, I forgot about that. Kind of kicking myself for going home to my parents' instead of to Gray's Christmas party last year," Dex says with a wry laugh.

Because he'd been invited too. Every year.

"You were being a good son," I say.

"I was avoiding the temptation of you," he answers.

It makes me stumble. Frowning, I quicken my step. "Why did you avoid me?"

He sighs, and I can imagine him rubbing a hand along his beard the way he does when he doesn't want to admit something. "Well, last year you were still in college, and I was a rookie in the NFL. There was absolutely no hope of us ever seeing each other. And, besides, you were Gray's baby sister-in-law."

"I'm still that. Although I object to the term *baby*."

"Fine, *younger* sister." There's a smile in his voice before his tone goes serious. "I asked him, you know. If he objected to me making a play for you."

"What?" I practically shriek.

"He's one of my best friends, Fi. It's man code. And you don't mess with the code."

"And what if he'd said no?" The idea of Gray lording over my sex life does not sit well with me.

"Then I'd have laid out a perfectly logical and irrefutable argument for him to change his mind," Dex says. "Or I'd have pounded on him until he said uncle."

I laugh. "So much for the man code."

"Punching out an argument is an accepted form of conflict resolution in the man code. It's part of our bylaws."

"And you say women are confusing." I laugh and hurry along so I'm not late. "So what about you? What are you doing tonight?"

"Same thing. Going out with my QB."

"Finn Mannus?" I give a little sigh. "He's dreamy."

Okay, I'm still a little irked by Dex's archaic "man code" thing with Gray, and payback is a bitch.

Predictably, Dex makes a noise of disdain. "Thought you didn't follow football."

"There's a difference between following the sport and following a hot player," I tease.

"Never thought I'd be the jealous type," he drawls. "But I guess I am because I have the sudden urge to punch the little shit in the face right about now."

"Don't do that! You'll ruin the pretty!"

"Fi." Dex sounds ominous. And pained.

Laughing, I put him out of his misery. "Baby, you know I only have eyes for one guy. And he is way sexier than some skinny quarterback."

"Yeah?" He's practically purring now.

All my pleasure points stir. "Yeah."

I hear him sigh, and his voice lowers. "I want to look at that pic you sent me. I want that so badly my dick hurts. But I know if I do, it'll hurt more. I can't beat off to thoughts of you anymore, Fi."

My breath hitches. "Why?"

"I've had the real thing. Imagination no longer cuts it."

"Have you… You used to think of me when you touched yourself?"

I swear I hear him swallow down a groan. "You know I did."

"We could…" I sidestep a woman running toward the subway. "We could talk through it."

Another groan from Dex. "No," he says. "It'll kill me, Cherry. Not being able to touch you."

"I can touch myself. Pretend it's you." I don't know why I'm pushing this. I'm in the middle of Manhattan and can't do a thing. But teasing Dex is fast becoming one of my favorite things. Only because I know he likes it. Even more, he *needs* it. Dex is too closed off. Which wouldn't really matter, but I've seen that spark of life in him that's aching to come out and play.

I can hear it now when he gives me a dark chuckle. "Babe, the thought of you touching yourself is even worse. That's something I need to see, not hear."

"We could Skype."

"Fi."

"Ethan."

The smile in his voice remains, but he sounds tight. "I don't have smooth words. I'd fuck it up by saying the wrong thing. You don't need to hear how today I thought of backing you into a quiet corner of my locker room so I could shove my hand up your skirt and fuck you with my fingers, knowing my guys walked around a few feet away. I'd tell you to be nice and quiet while I did it, not make a sound, even though you were dying to.

"Of how I'd pinch one of your perky little pink nipples with my other hand. Nice and firm the way you like it."

I've slowed to a complete stop, my skin on fire, my breath short and rasping, as the world passes me by. Jesus. My nipple throbs as if he were here now, tweaking it with a rough touch; my sex aches, the ghost of Dex's thick, long fingers pumping into it.

I clear my throat. "I think you got the talking down pat, Big Guy."

He pauses and takes an audible breath. "I never got to taste you, Fi. I regret that. I have no idea what a pussy tastes like, and all I can think about is yours. God, I want to spread you wide and take my time, savor every inch, see if your flavor changes when you come."

"Ethan," my voice cracks.

"See? It's too much, isn't it?"

Somehow I manage to laugh. "Any more and I'm going to spontaneously combust right here on Fifth Avenue."

"Yeah?" He sounds surprised. Poor, deluded, sexy center.

"I think you're right," I say, forcing myself to walk again. "No more sex talk. It's killing me too."

A sad sort of half-chuckle rumbles through my phone. "I know. So…" His voice strains as if he's reaching for lightness. "Tell me something else to take my mind out from under your skirt. How's work?"

Yeah, right there is an immediate buzz kill.

Fuck, my throat hurts again. I want to tell him everything, right down to the bone-deep agony I feel in failing once again. But I don't want him to see that side of me. Flighty Fi who can't keep her shit together. I can't stand the thought of being diminished in his eyes.

"It's fine."

He's silent for a moment, and for the first time, I'm grateful for the physical distance between us. He can't see my face.

"I thought you had to leave because of a work issue," he says carefully.

Great. Either I'm lying about work or I lied about why I left him. Silently cursing, I grind my teeth and search for an answer. "It's all settled. Not as big a deal as I'd thought."

"Well," he says. "That's good."

He doesn't sound like he buys my story. God, I'm fucking up already, building this house-of-cards relationship on a shifty set of lies. But I can't tell him. I can't. I'll start crying here and now.

"I'm at the bar," I tell him with false levity. "Call you later?"

"Always, Cherry," he says softly. I hear him take a breath. "Fi?"

My heart pounds as I grip the phone like a life line. "Yeah?"

"Just know I'm with you. Even when I'm far away, I'm with you."

It's all I can do not to sob. I stand on the corner of 5th and 25th, the world flowing by me like rippling water, and feel such loneliness I have to hug myself around my middle. "Thank you, Ethan."

I hang up then, because I can't say anything more without breaking my heart wide open.

CHAPTER 20

Fiona

Anna and I end up not drinking but buying sandwiches at Eataly and claiming a table in the Flatiron Plaza, the little pedestrian triangle of concrete between Broadway and 5th. The weather is gorgeous in the way of New York in the fall—crisp breezes cutting through sun-warmed air.

I don't talk about my job issues. I'd rather enjoy the evening than ruin my appetite.

"So, Dex?" Anna grins before taking a sip of her latte.

I don't know if she found out from Ivy, or if Gray blabbed to Drew—though my money is on Gray. Regardless, I can't help but grin back. "Yeah. Dex."

I hold in a dreamy sigh, because that would be overkill. But Anna's too quick. My satisfaction doesn't escape her notice.

"That good, eh?" Her cheeks plump, and the breeze sends her red curls spiraling around her head.

"Let's just say fauxgasms are unnecessary."

"Fauxgasms?" Anna asks with a laugh.

"Fake orgasms." I give her a look. "God, please don't tell me you've never had to fake it. I think I'll die of envy."

My sex life hasn't been horrible or anything, but college boys, by and large, are pretty much pump and dump, lather, rinse, repeat.

Dex had been a virgin, and yet he'd put his entire body and soul into the act. I'd felt cherished and my body worshiped. Never mind that Dex is so freaking sexy, all he has to do is look at me and I'm a hot mess.

Anna swallows a bite before shaking her head. "Of course I've faked it. Never with Drew, though."

I roll my eyes at that but laugh. "I hope not since you're marrying the guy."

"Oh, he leaves me quite satisfied. Quite."

We give each other an immature fist bump and dissolve into laughter.

"I have to admit, I'm surprised," Anna says.

"Why? Because of the athlete thing?"

"Well, partially that. I mean you've shrugged off every friend of Drew's who's hit on you."

More than a few guys on Drew's team have made passes whenever I hang out with him and Anna. And, yes, my refusals were mainly because they were football players. But some were also total meatheads.

"But really," Anna continues, "it's more that Dex is so quiet. I mean, I love the guy, but you're not exactly shy."

I have to laugh. "He's not quiet when we're together. Anyway, I'm pretty sure I'd kill someone who was exactly like me. Imagine all the noise, noise, noise!" I fake a shudder.

Anna gives me an obligatory smile, but then it fades. "So why do you look so sad, Fi?"

Like that I wilt. I could tell her about my job. But that's not what's hurting my heart at the moment. "Because I don't think I'm cut out for a long-distance relationship. I miss him already." I don't just miss him. I need him. Here. Now. "I've got all this fluttery anticipation and nowhere for it to go until we see each other again. Won't it get worse the more attached I get?"

Reaching out, she takes my hand and gives it a squeeze. "Shit, I wish I was better at this. I don't know. I fucking hate it when Drew is gone. But what can you do? We love who we love."

"I thought falling for someone was supposed to be awesome."

"Ha." Anna leans back, her eyes bright. "Best and worst time of your life, kid."

Dex

THE PHOTOGRAPHER'S STUDIO IS IN New Orleans' Warehouse District. We've been scheduled in small groups. I'm here with Rolondo, Finn, and Jake Ryder, our other wide out.

Aside from Ryder, none of us are particularly comfortable with the idea of modeling for the next few hours, but it's for charity, so we'll make due.

No one is here to greet us, which is odd. When ringing the bell fails to get a reply, Finn pounds on the metal door with the side of his fist.

"We get the time wrong?" he asks over his shoulder.

"Nope. In fact, we're a few minutes late."

"The photographer had better not be having some sort of artistic huff."

Finn is the one who appears to be five seconds away from a huff, but I shrug. "Maybe he's on the can or something."

"Great," drawls Ryder. "We've gotta wait for a shit? That could be half an hour at least."

Rolondo bends his head back and looks at the ceiling. "Lord, these boys keep leaving themselves wide open for a smack down. It's almost too easy."

Ryder smirks, then reaches past me and slams on the door as well. "Dude! Nip it off and open up!"

"Jesus," I say, my ears ringing. "Have some class."

He just grins.

The door whips open, ending the conversation. A tall young woman with long, straight hair a saturated shade of magenta gives us a dark scowl that takes our measure. I'm guessing we're found lacking.

"Nip what off, do tell?" she asks, her voice so husky I wonder if she's a smoker.

We all kind of shuffle, then Finn steps forward. "Er…we're here for the calendar shoot."

"Well, I certainly didn't think you were here for the little league group shot I have scheduled later."

"You're the photographer?" Finn's eyes widen in obvious shock.

"Let's not be a cliché, eh, pretty boy?"

Ryder snickers. "She's got your number, sweet cheeks."

Finn is a pretty boy. We all love to tease him about it. But he doesn't seem to like it now. "Hey now, we were told our photographer's name was Chester Copper. Excuse me if I assumed it was a man."

Her lips pinch. "I go by Chess. I've no idea how your PR manager got my full name."

"Probably because they do background checks to weed out the freaks." Finn's dubious expression clearly states that PR failed in this case.

Chess gives a bored roll of her eyes.

"Chester Copper… That's kind of like Chester Copperpot from *The Goonies*," Ryder adds helpfully. "Remember that movie?"

Our photographer utters a ripe curse.

"Yeah, that's a cool flick." says Rolondo to Ryder. "Little dude who played the lead grew up and played Samwise Gamgee. Man, talk about a sad sap. As if I'm gonna toss myself into the fires of Mount Doom cuz I gotta boner for a hobbit."

"He was on a quest to save Middle-Earth from Sauron, chuckle-head," I tell him.

"Naw, he wanted Frodo bad."

Ryder makes a noise of annoyance. "Hello? Can we please get back to *The Goonies* and Chester Copperpot? You know, that old dude they find all shriveled and crushed by a boulder?"

Chess goes full-on red. "Yes, I know," she grinds out. "My parents met at a draft house viewing of the movie. They expected a boy, and since my grandmama had already embroidered all my baby blankets..." She shrugs as if to say, *what can you do?*

"And they actually named you after a *Goonies* character?" I ask, kind of horrified. It's worse than Gray's mom naming him after a John Grisham character.

"Yes." Her voice is tight, and none of us says a word, though I hear Rolondo murmur something about crazy white people under his breath.

With that she turns and walks briskly into the studio. After exchanging looks, we follow. Lights are set up around a large canvas. To the side, a long table holds football equipment: pads, footballs, our team helmets, even some shin guards and tape.

A slim guy wearing a fedora and a lime green skinny-pants suit straight out of the 1960s appears. Like me, he has a beard, though his is red and scraggly.

"I'm James," he tells us. "Chess's assistant. Sorry about the delay. We were on the balcony having a smoke." He grins, giving Ryder a onceover. That makes Ry shift his feet and frown in confusion. "Or I was. Chess was just keeping me company."

Chess goes to a table and picks up a large camera. "They don't need a play-by-play excuse, James." She doesn't glance our way as she adjusts her equipment. "Changing room is to the left. Strip down, and James will get you oiled up."

She might as well have dropped a stink bomb in the center of the room. I swear we all take a step back, our faces twisting with various levels of shock.

"Oiled up?" Finn sounds like he's sucked a lemon through his teeth. "You fucking with us?"

"When I fuck with someone, he knows it, Mr. Mannus."

Ryder laughs. "I love this chick."

"I am not a chick, Mr. Ryder. I am a woman."

Rolondo makes a faint, mock crowd-roar, and I elbow his side.

"Let me guess," Finn drawls. "You're obsessed with finally finding One-Eyed Willie."

Ryder chokes on a smothered laugh, and I have to run my hand over my beard to hold in mine.

"Man," Rolondo mutters. "You've gone and done it now."

Chess has the stare of death. Like, scary fierce. I'm pretty sure her closet is full of the skeletons of other smart-mouthed ball players who dared to cross her path. It's so bad we all stand there like recalcitrant boys who've been hauled up before the principal.

But my lips are twitching. I know in about ten minutes we're going to be bare, and Finn is going to hate every second of it. I itch to take out my phone and text Fi. My smile dies a swift death at the thought of her. Fi didn't sound right. She was hurting, and damn if I know why. The distance between us is like a cold hand gripping my spine. I don't like the feeling, or the fact that she didn't tell me the truth.

But I'm going to find out. The sooner I'm stripped and "oiled" the faster I can. I take a deep breath and step forward. "I'll go first."

CHAPTER 21

Fiona

IT IS A UNIVERSAL TRUTH that women like to talk their problems out. Unfortunately, all the talk in the world won't make a problem go away. Mine is waiting for me like a looming black cloud as soon as I get into work and see that Elena has moved to her own office at the end of the hall.

She waves, grinning broadly, as I walk past. I briefly wonder how a finger-wave back would go over but don't bother. Instead she gets a chin nod as if I'm channeling a bad biker cliché. It feels stupid and ineffectual, and I'm in a piss-poor mood by the time I get to my desk and find that Felix's to-do list includes ordering fabrics that I picked out but are now considered Elena's design contribution.

She comes to my desk just as I'm turning on my computer. "I thought you'd want to hear it from me. Felix just called me into his office this morning. He gave me the associate designer job." She squeezes my hand. "I hope we can still be friends. I've really enjoyed bouncing ideas off each other."

God, she says it so sincerely. And what can I do? I'm pretty sure punching her in the face won't help the situation. Though it might feel really fucking good.

I glare down at my hand, my fingers slowly curling into a fist. But for some odd reason, I start to think of Ethan's hand wrapping around mine, holding me down as he slides into me.

"You feel so good, Cherry." Brilliant eyes of green-gold and amber look at me with glazed wonder. *"Nothing better on Earth than this."*

"Fiona? You okay?"

I suck in a breath and glance up at Elena, who hovers. "Yep. All good." Not entirely true. But I'm calmer. Able to speak, anyway. "Anything else?"

She frowns a little. "Ah…no."

"Okay. Well, I'm getting some coffee then."

I leave her standing there. For now I'm calm. But every step I take hammers it in: I hate this. I hate this.

It occurs to me that I have to be a little more proactive. Take the bull by the horns. I am woman, hear me roar and all that.

I wait until the end of the day to make my move. Yes, I'm that brave.

"Felix? You have a moment?" I clutch my clammy hands behind the folds of my skirt.

Felix looks up from his laptop. A tiny white espresso cup sits beside it, which means he's probably reading up on celebrity gossip. "Sure, sweetie."

Sweetie? I want to gag. And now that I've worked up the nerve to approach him, I actually have to talk. Part of me really wants to laugh. I have absolutely no trouble talking to people. I don't think I could go a day without saying something to someone, even if it's just to tell a person they have on cute shoes.

But now a golf-ball-sized lump of panic is lodged in my throat, and it's all I can do just to get my ass in the chair opposite Felix.

"Want an espresso?" He gives me an overly friendly smile, the one he uses on clients he fears might be difficult. So I know he isn't exactly unaware of why I'm here.

"No. I'm good." I focus on his eyes. Always look them in the eye. Reminds you that you're talking to another human. Nothing more.

"You…ah…made Elena associate designer?"

Everything inside of me wants to scream, maybe throw Felix's coffee onto his pristine white leather Corbusier lounge chair.

With an expansive sigh, he sits back in his chair, crossing one leg over the other. "Yes, I did, hon."

"I thought you weren't going to make that decision until next month."

"Fiona, I understand that you're disappointed." His tone is so patronizing, I have to dig my nails into my palms to keep from twitching. "But you and I both know it was coming to this." He takes a dainty sip of his macchiato. "I simply sped up the process."

"Is it…" I suck back a sobbing breath. "Is it because I went on vacation?"

His cup clinks on the glass desktop. "God, no." He regards me for a moment, his dark eyes almost sad. "Elena simply has an edge that you do not. Namely, contacts."

This time a sob does escape me, only it sounds kind of a like a laugh. "You promoted her because of her mother?"

"No, because of her mother's friends. She has lots and lots of friends with lots and lots of cash." He smiles slyly. "Her designs aren't bad either. Fresh and lovely without being too daring. Just what the bored, rich Manhattanite wants."

I swear to God, my entire body wants to dry heave. Somehow I manage not to. "Her designs are—"

"Copies of yours?" he supplies. "Yes, I know."

I think I gape. I don't know anymore because I've gone numb. "You know?"

Felix shrugs, takes another sip of his drink. "You'd have to be blind not to notice, honey. Yours are a bit more risky, however. You push yourself where she plays it safe."

Okay, now I know I'm gaping. "I can't believe this. Mine are more daring, and you're rewarding her?"

"Honey, safe sells more. And you've really got to applaud her ingenuity." He sighs again, resting his elbows on the desk. "First client I scored was done using José, my lover's, designs. I lost a good lay but gained a business."

"That's horrible."

"That's business. Calculated risks, use what you know will work." He gives me a reproachful look. "You should understand this."

"Don't remember taking that course in college," I snap.

"I'm talking about your dad, sweetie. Sports agents aren't exactly known for being above board. Frankly, I assumed you'd be more hardened. More cutthroat."

"My dad," I grind out, "never stabbed his colleagues in the back."

Felix gives me a disbelieving look. I ignore it and stand. I want to quit, to tell him he can go fuck himself with one of his precious Ferragamo slippers. I want that so badly I can taste it. But just the mention of my dad has me holding my tongue. He thinks I quit at everything. Flighty Fi, always running at the first sign of trouble.

And maybe Felix will fire me now. But I'm not going to stomp off in a dramatic rage first. Straightening my skirt, I manage to collect my temper.

"I'll be in late tomorrow. I'm picking up those fabric samples on my way," I tell him.

"All right." He turns his attention back to his online gossip mag. "Take your time. Oh, that lovely little sandwich shop is next door to them. See if anyone wants sandwiches. Not me. I'm skipping lunch this week."

The faint hum of the city seeps in through the windows. Somewhere down the hall, a telephone rings. It's nothing compared to the ringing in my ears.

Sandwiches? I'm expected to go to Elena and ask if she wants a fucking sandwich for lunch tomorrow?

"Yeah," I croak. "Sure."

Except I'm not asking anyone a damn thing. My hands shake by the time I've pulled my purse from my desk drawer and grabbed my coat off the hook.

It's a struggle not to cry. With every step I take, the spike of my heel connects with the raw-wood floorboard and thuds in my heart. My throat is closing, a lump rising.

Get it together, Mackenzie. Deep breaths.

I want to scream so badly my stomach clenches. I swear to all that's holy, if I see Elena's fuckity-fuck face I will fucking lose my shit.

Keeping my head down so I don't accidentally make eye contact with anyone, I move toward the lobby.

The elevator dings before I'm close enough. I lift my head, ready to run for it, because I need *out*. But my steps stutter to a halt, shock buzzing along my skin.

Don't cry. Don't cry.

Dex stands ten feet away, his big hands stuffed into his jeans' pockets, his broad shoulders covered by a dark blue Henley. That steady, powerful gaze of his meets mine.

My lip wobbles, emotion pushing up past the lump in my throat. He must see my distress—the smile that'd been blooming drops.

My chest heaves as I struggle to keep my breathing normal. If I can just get to Dex, everything will be okay.

I walk straight to him, not stopping until I wrap my arms around his waist and bury my face against his solid chest. The scent of cloves and oranges is stronger now that I haven't been near him in a while. He's warm, strong, safe. His arms surround me, hold me secure. I sag into his embrace.

"Hey," I say to his chest.

Dex presses his lips to my crown. "Cherry. You all right?"

No. Not at all. My eyes burn and prickle. I hug him tighter, breathe him in. "I'm just…really glad to see you, Ethan."

His chest lifts and falls on a breath, and his husky voice rumbles over me. "I missed you too, Fiona."

Dex

DESPITE THE FACT THAT I play professional football for a living, I'm not a violent man. I solve problems with my mind, not my fists. I tell myself this as I tuck Fi against my side while we take a cab to her apartment. She's trembling, her delicate hand roaming over my torso as if she needs to pet me to keep herself grounded.

And it slays me. The need to pound into someone, something, *anything*, surges through me in waves that I tap down by burrowing my nose in Fi's fragrant hair and breathing in deep.

Women have nice-smelling hair, that's a given. But something about Fi's scent just does it for me. Pheromones. A basic biological lure that hooks one person to another. One whiff of Fi, and I'm both hard and utterly content.

"You're here," she whispers. "I can't believe you're really here."

I take another deep breath before I speak in a low voice, trying to coax her out. "What happened, Cherry?"

She stiffens against me, and I have to grind my teeth. If someone hurt her… Yeah, I'll be resorting to violence. But then she sighs and her fingers drift over my chest, finding my nipple and stroking it over the thin fabric of my shirt. I try to ignore that touch as she tells me the whole tale.

The heartbreak in her voice tears at my own heart. She bleeds, I bleed. That's just how it is now. Worse, I can't fight this for her. I can't go and pummel her shallow boss or her conniving co-worker. I can only hold her tight, press my lips against her head, and let her talk.

"I just feel so…" She waves a hand as she struggles to find a word. "Angry. Hurt. Dejected. Yeah, that's the prevalent emotion right now."

With a sign, she presses her nose against my chest. Her warm breath seeps through my shirt. Still she plays with my nipple, twisting the little barbell I wear just enough to make me feel it in my balls.

My hips shift in reaction, but my mind is on trying to make this right. "Baby, I—"

She silences me with a look, her big green eyes luminous with unshed tears. "Ethan, I know you want to fix this." She gives me a watery smile. "Don't look so shocked. I know you better than you think."

"I'm not shocked." *I kind of love how easily she reads me.* "I admit it. I want to take your pain and make it better."

Stretching up, Fi kisses my jaw. My beard makes it impossible for me to feel more than the pressure of her lips. I want more. I want to imprint her on my skin. I turn toward her and lower my head.

I kiss her softly, tenderly, wanting her to know how precious she is.

Fi smiles against my lips. "You want to make it better, Big Guy? When we get upstairs, make me forget the world for a little while."

The cab pulls up in front of her apartment. I thread my fingers through her hair, holding it secure. "Cherry, that was always part of the plan."

CHAPTER 22

Fiona

BORN OF THE DESPERATE NEED to keep our hands off each other, Dex and I stand on opposite sides of the elevator going up to my apartment. The main deterrent to any shenanigans is the fact that Mrs. Flannery, my sixty-something widowed neighbor, stands between us.

She stares straight ahead, her crimson-painted lips twitching. It's as if she knows exactly how much Dex and I are itching to touch each other, which wouldn't surprise me since her sex life is far more active than mine has been until now. I've caught her in many an elevator embrace. Honestly, the woman is my sexcapade hero.

Over her head, Dex's eyes meet mine. The heated look he sends makes my breath quicken. But then he pushes it over the edge; he makes a total goofball—crossed eyes, pointed tongue—face at me.

It's gone in a flash, but so very un-Dex-like that I snort down a laugh. My eyes water as I try to contain it.

Mrs. Flannery glances at me. "You coming down with a cold, dear?"

Coughing over a snicker, I clear my throat and stand straight. "I might be."

Her smile is serene. "I'm sure your young man here will take good care of you."

Dex waggles his brows behind her back. *Ass.*

Mrs. Flannery leans toward me, her voice dropping into a pseudo-whisper. "It's always the big, quiet ones, isn't it?"

Ha. Solemnly, I nod. "Yes, ma'am, it is."

The elevator reaches her floor. As soon as the doors close behind her, I launch myself at Dex, poking his ribs as he laughs and tries to get away from my marauding finger.

"She totally knows we're going to have sex," I tell him, laughing but trying to be outraged.

His arms circle me, bands of steel that lean me onto his hard chest. "Of course she does." He kisses my temple. "Considering that she groped my ass right before we got on the elevator, I'd say she approves of your choice."

"What? That little sneak."

He grins wide. "You actually look pissed."

"Of course I am." I'm not really, but still. My hand drifts down to his awesome ass. Seriously, his butt is like warm granite. "Your ass is mine, Ethan Dexter."

"I promise you can play with it later."

Because I want "later" to happen sooner, I all but push him down the hall when the elevator doors open on my floor.

When we reach my apartment door, Dex presses against me from behind, his forearms braced on either side of my head. "Tell me you live alone."

A smile tugs at my lips. "I live alone."

He lets out a gusty breath, and his lips trail along the sensitive skin of my neck, his beard tickling. "Good." The hard length of his cock nudges my ass. "Open the door, Cherry."

My hands fumble with the key, and then I'm stumbling into my apartment—oh, so graceful of me. Laughing a bit, I turn, expecting Dex to grab me, give me the kiss I know we both want.

But he doesn't.

He stalks me instead, his steps steady, his gaze hot. And it sets my pulse racing as I walk backwards, keeping my eyes on him.

A slow, evil smile spreads across his lips. "Keep going."

The low, drawling command works like a band around my middle, constricting my breath, clenching my belly. I edge away until my butt hits the dining table. Trapped.

My inner thighs draw up in anticipation. My clit is so swollen I feel it there, this hot button of need that craves his touch.

He stops in front of me, so tall it's almost overwhelming, and yet comforting because I know he'll use his size and strength to protect me. Without saying a word, he sinks to his knees, then sits back on his heels. But his gaze never leaves mine. His voice turns deep. "Show me where it hurts, Cherry."

A breath puffs out of me, my nipples going tight. Oh, holy hell. His words make the aching emptiness between my legs clench with sweet pain. Never looking away from him, I find the flaring edge of my wool skirt and raise it high, bunching it around my hips.

His attention flicks to my panties, and his entire body seems to sway. With utter care, he grasps the sides and slowly lowers them. I watch them go, watch his rapt expression as he exposes me. His nostrils flare, as if he's breathing me in.

It should unnerve me, but the strong flush that rises over his cheeks and the way his chest moves with every panting breath sends a wave of heat through me. I spread my legs, wanting more of his all-consuming attention.

He swallows hard, his gaze growing fierce. The heat of his hands covers my thighs, his fingers curling around them, pressing gently as he parts my legs further.

"Most beautiful fucking thing I've ever seen," he rasps.

I can only stand there, my sweaty palms clutching my skirt, my thighs trembling beneath his grasp. I'm so wet now, the air on my sex feels cool, makes me shiver.

Then he lifts one hand and those big, brutish fingers delicately part my folds. My knees go weak. I think I whimper. I can't tell because my attention is all on Ethan, on the way he slowly leans forward, his lush lips parted and his brows knitted in utter concentration.

God, he looks gorgeous, all the bold lines of his face taut and flushed. His lips press against my clit, and a groan tears from him, his whole body trembling. My breath leaves in a whoosh, but I don't get to recover because he's licking my sex with long, lingering strokes, his lips sucking and nuzzling.

"Oh, fucking hell, Cherry." He licks deeper, slower.

So intent. But never frantic.

He's savoring me. That, more than anything, has me so hot I break out in a sweat, struggle to find my breath. The low, almost helpless moans he makes, the soft gasps when he has to take a breath before coming at me again, eating me out like I'm the best thing he's ever tasted—it's almost better than what he's doing to me.

Almost, because, *damn.* He might be a novice at this, but he's making up for lost time. Strong lips, warm tongue, and that beard. Holy fuck, that beard. Soft, prickly, it adds another level of sensation, so good—so naughty-good—that I circle my hips, chasing the feel of it brushing my clit, tickling my inner thighs.

It's too much. I lean against my dining room table, afraid I'll fall or maybe pass out. I don't know. I can't think straight.

And then I see his arm moving. Oh, God. Somewhere along the way, he's undone his jeans and pulled his cock free. His erection is enormous, ruddy and angry. He palms his dick, tugging at it with rough, rude jerks.

When he runs his thumb over the glistening crown of his cock, toying with the sliver piercing, the sight is so illicit, I come without warning, my knees giving out. A little wail leaves my lips as I sink into the sensation. "Ethan."

He's rising, gathering me up.

I wrap my legs around his waist, rub my aching sex against the crinkly hairs at the base of his cock. "Ethan." My lips find his. He tastes of sex. My kiss is frantic, little gasps still leaving me. "Now. Ethan. Now."

Big hands palm my ass. He lifts me high and then thrusts, going in deep. He groans into my mouth. "Oh, fuck yes."

I can only hold, my arms wrapped around his thick neck, as he pumps hard and fast, bouncing me on his cock. Every time his hips impact with mine, I feel a shockwave through my body, a flare of pleasure-pain in my clit. Every stroke of that little metal ball on his cock sends a rush of bliss through me.

"More," I tell him. "Give me more." *Give me everything.*

And he does, driving into me until I scream his name, my body arching tight against his as I come again—so hard my vision dims.

He comes with me, his teeth clamping on my shoulder as he gushes, hot and wet within my body. The aftermath leaves us both shaking and panting. I rest my head on his big shoulder, shivering so hard my stomach aches.

He walks us to the bedroom with lumbering steps, weaving a bit as if he's drunk.

Oddly, I feel like crying. My throat hurts and my eyes prickle. The feeling only intensifies when he lays me down in my bed, his softening cock still deep within me, his hard arms holding me close against him. I don't know which way is up or down anymore. The only thing that feels real and true is Ethan—the man I can only have in stolen moments of time.

CHAPTER 23

Fiona

"**S**MILE FOR THE CAMERA." My grin is goofy and wide. Dex makes a laughing noise of protest and tries to wave me off. "Get away from me with that thing. I'm all pictured out."

We're lying in bed, having a well-earned rest, and I've been amusing myself taking multiple shots of Dex. He pretends to be annoyed, but I know better. He can't hide the smile in his eyes or the curve of his lips.

"If you don't want me messing with the phone, put a password on this sucker, babe." I take yet another photo. The image of his big, wide hand fills the screen. "Aw, man. You messed it up."

He sighs. "Cherry, I do not need naked pictures of myself on my phone."

With a move so quick I don't have time to blink, he snatches the phone away and hauls me close. "Here," he says, holding the phone high with an outstretched arm. "If we're doing this, you're going to be in them."

"You say that like I'd protest."

We take more pictures, laughing over the results. I pause at a shot of me licking Dex's tight little nipple. "Here's one for my wallet."

"Did you just quote *Parenthood*?" His smile is relaxed and happy. I love seeing him this way, without walls, just being himself.

"I didn't take you for an eighties' movie buff."

Dex shrugs. "The guys watch a lot of cable on the road."

"Well, bonus points for noticing, Big Guy."

"Mmm… And what do I get as my prize?" He rolls over, taking me with him.

Much, much later, I relax against him with a sigh. "Do you think we ever truly figure out who we are?" My voice is soft.

At my side he moves, lifting his head to rest it in the cradle of his palm. "Well, now," he drawls, "let me see if I can help you out. I'm Ethan, and you are Fiona."

"Har." I give his chest a lazy smack. "You know what I mean. Or maybe you don't." I stroke the edge of his collarbone. "I don't think I've met anyone who knows their own mind as well as you do."

He rolls his eyes, but sets his hand on my hip, caressing and edging me closer. "Babe, I hate every fucking second of getting tatted. I hate needles with a passion, yet I get a cortisone shot after nearly every practice and game. The ones in the hands skeeve me out so badly I have to look away or risk fainting."

At this I take his hand in mine. It isn't pretty: battered, swollen knuckles; scrapes and callouses; the middle finger crooking inward as if it's been broken one too many times. A warrior's hand.

Those long, scarred fingers wrap over my smaller ones with a gentle hold, and I lift his hand to my lips to kiss his reddened knuckles.

Behind the veil of his lashes, he watches me do it. "I hate those things, and yet look at me. Tatted, pierced, and a pro football player. Fact is, I run to the pain. Part of me gets off on it. So while I might know my mind, I've clearly got my own issues."

He doesn't look embarrassed by this. No, his eyes shine in good humor. Which makes all the difference and only proves my point. He knows himself in a way I don't know myself; I envy that.

The blunt tip of his thumb, the one with a bruised nail, brushes the crest of my cheek. "Why do you ask about knowing yourself, Fi?"

With a sigh, I fall back against the pillows and stare up at my ceiling. "I don't want to go back to work."

"So don't."

A loud snort blows through my lips. "It isn't that simple."

"Course it is. You're miserable there. So leave."

A glance his way reveals that he's absolutely serious.

"This from a football player? I thought you guys were always about never giving up. Mental and physical endurance is key, blah, blah, blah."

He flashes a quick smile. "Blah, blah, blah? Nice to know we players are so eloquent." His smile falls. "You also forgot 'Don't play the game unless you're one-hundred-percent commented.' Which really just means, if you don't love it, get out. It isn't worth the pain, otherwise."

"If I leave, she wins."

Dex looks at me for a moment with that stare of his that I always feel down to my bones. When he speaks, his voice is steady, thoughtful. "Winning is a subjective thing, Fi."

"Again, I can't believe a professional football player would say that."

He chuckles. "If anyone is an expert on the subject of winning and losing, it's an athlete. Last year we lost out on the NFC championship based on one loss. On a fucked-up foul that the refs got wrong, made a bad call. That shit burned, Fi." His expression stays calm, but his eyes fill with ire. "Even now, when I think about it I want to punch something. And you better believe those fuckers on the other team taunted us without shame. Didn't matter that they won on a technicality. Scoreboard was all they needed."

Slowly, he reaches out and cups my jaw. "Darlin', that shit happens all the time. I know from personal, painful experience that winning doesn't necessarily make a person the best. Sometimes, it just makes them lucky."

"Well," I say, still full of petulance and resentment, "that bitch will get even luckier if I leave."

"Nope. Hell, one day she might become the most successful designer in New York—"

"Not helping."

"But it will be based on nothing but her own insecurity. While you?" He leans in and gives me a soft, lingering kiss. "Have true talent and will be happily serviced by yours truly."

I have to laugh at that. But it dies quickly, and I flop an arm over my hot forehead. "You don't understand."

"So educate me."

"I'm a fuck-up."

"Fi…"

"It's true. Almost every plan I start—and believe me, I always have a plan—goes off the rails at some point."

"You're describing the majority of the population, Cherry."

"Do your plans fail?"

Dex's wide mouth goes tight as if he's annoyed at me. But the look he gives me is tender. The bed creaks as he pulls me into his embrace, tucking me against his side. "I planned to stay away from you." The rough tip of his thumb caresses my lower lip. "Best failed plan of my life."

"Ethan." His heart beats strong against the wide wall of his chest, and I give him a soft kiss there. Sighing, I rest my cheek on his shoulder. "It's just…I've always dreamed big and have never been afraid to tell anyone and everyone about my big dreams. Except my dreams often change—here one day, alive and bright with all these possibilities, then dead and on to the next something new."

I glance up at his solemn eyes. "Unfortunately my exuberance has made me into the Girl Who Cried Dreams. And my friends and family no longer believe me when I latch on to a new passion. I don't blame them, but I'm tired of seeing people give me that tight, slightly patronizing, slightly irritated smile. I don't want to be viewed as a quitter anymore."

"Fuck what other people believe. Do you think you're a quitter?"

"I told you. I never stick to anything." My fingertip traces a longitude line on his collarbone. I love the way his skin pebbles under my touch. "I changed my major three times before I settled on art and design, and even then, my eye was always roving."

Dex shifts a bit, his hip canting as my nail scrapes his tight nipple. His voice is gruff, a sure sign of him being turned on. But he runs his hand over my shoulder, stroking me. "Why did you keep changing?"

For a second, I simply play with his nipple, worrying it this way and that, because it turns me on too, the way he reacts, his breath growing heavier, his cock getting thick again. "I don't know."

In a blink, I'm on my back, my wrists held overhead in Dex's massive hand. With a low grunt, he settles between my legs and hovers over me, the long strands of his hair tickling my cheeks. "Now ordinarily," he says in a low, smooth voice, "I love your particular method of avoiding hard questions."

"Oh, really?" I challenge, opening my legs wider so that his hard cock notches between the slick lips of my sex. A low hum of pleasure runs through me.

"Really." He shifts his hip slightly, rubbing his hardness over my sensitive flesh just enough to tease. "Thing is, I want an answer before I fuck you."

God. He's a wall around me, unrelenting, hot. I want all that strength pounding into me. I think I whimper. I know I wiggle my hips, trying to seek him out. "Why is it so important to you?"

His eyes are dark now, seeing more than he should. "It's important to you." He rocks against me, sending little shivers of sweet lust rippling outward. "Answer the question, Cherry. Why…" He slides up, "…did you…" A down stroke. "…keep changing majors?"

I lick my dry lips. "They never felt right."

"Mmm…" He moves again, the rounded crown of his meaty cock stretching my opening. Slowly, with a smooth glide, he sinks in.

And I lift my hips, my legs parting wider, as if this can somehow give him more room. He fills me so good, I can barely focus. But Dex's eyes are on me, his lips hovering just over mine. "You wanted to be happy."

"Uh-huh…" I can't really concentrate, not when he's gently easing in and out of my swollen flesh, his lips taking mine with soft, slow kisses.

He nuzzles me as he talks and fucks. "You seek joy in your life, don't you, Cherry?"

I shudder, my fingers curling around his hand. He still has me pinned. "Yes."

He smiles against my mouth. "You were never quitting. You were searching."

Despite what he's doing to me, my attention snares on his words. He pauses, his cock deep inside me, his brilliant eyes wide open. Searching for joy.

A laugh bubbles up within me, and I crane my neck to reach his mouth. I kiss him as deeply as I can while I'm still laughing. And he grins against my lips, our breath mingling.

"Fuck me, Ethan," I tell him, not letting him go. "And give me some more of that joy."

He nips my lower lip, his grin still wide. "Yes, ma'am."

And he does. He does it so well, I'm limp and breathless when we finish. I should move, get cleaned up, offer him dinner, something. But I can only lie against him, draped over his solid body like a sweaty girl blanket, and just drift.

"Aren't you scared?" I whisper after a time. "I flit from boyfriend to boyfriend too."

I don't know why I'm saying this. Maybe I want to test him. Maybe I just want to know he believes in me. All I know for sure is that trickles of ice-cold fear run down my spine at the thought of ever ending things with Dex.

Rolling me to his side, he peers down, those eyes of his searching my face. His teeth flash, framed by his pirate's beard. "Nope. That was just another search." He leans in, nips my ear. "The search is over, Cherry Pie."

"Ugh. Do not refer to me as pie!" When he just chuckles darkly, I have to smile. "You're kind of arrogant, you know that?"

"Mmm…" The calloused pad of his thumb strokes my nipple. "Think we covered that." I shiver. He does it again, slowly. "Abuse my character all you like; you know I'm right."

God, I love the way he touches me, love the dark, rumbly quality of his voice. I even love his unfailing confidence in all things Us.

My palm slides down his back to the hard swell of his ass. I really love his ass. It's massive, rock hard. The ass of a titan. Laughing a little at that thought, I give it a squeeze, earning a deep grunt from him.

"Yeah," I say with a small smile as I feel him up. "I think you just might be."

CHAPTER 24

Fiona

W E SLEEP WRAPPED UP IN each other, my smaller legs clinging to Dex's like vines. Dead to the world until sunlight slants across the bed and shines in our eyes. Dex tries to shield us by turning on his side and tucking me into the crook of his shoulder, but it's too late. I'm awake, and real life is upon us once more.

Grumbling about buying darker drapes, I crawl over him, earning a light slap on my butt as I go to get us some coffee.

When I return, Dex is on his back, his head propped up by pillows. The sight makes me pause at the threshold of my room. Sun-kissed, golden brown hair spilled over white linen; lush, dark beard and pouty mouth; colorful tattoos on swelling, rolling muscles. Good God, it's like a burly pirate landed in my bed and is waiting for another round of debauchery.

Ridiculous fantasies of me pillaging his willing flesh dance in my head, and I fight a snicker. The sound catches his attention, and his mouth slowly curls.

"Look your fill yet, darlin'?"

The silver barbell in his nipple winks in the light as he moves to take his cup.

"I don't think it's possible to get my fill." I slide in beside him, where it's warm and wonderful. "I'm thinking we get you a couple of chunky rings, maybe a do-rag and a cutlass, and we can play capture-the-pirate later."

Dex grunts, his hazel eyes gleaming in obvious pleasure. "Tell you what, you put on one of your sweet little lacy getups, I'll let you tie me to the bed, and you can work over my mast all you want."

He gives me an exaggerated leer, and we both burst out laughing.

I press my nose against his shoulder. "God, that was terrible."

"You started it." He chuckles, the sound deep and yet light with ease.

We drink coffee under the covers, then he puts the cups aside so I can snuggle in close once more.

Despite our goofiness, or maybe because of it, a heavy weight settles under my ribs and a lump lodges in my throat.

I run my hand over his chest, the dusting of hair between his pecs tickling my palm. "When is your flight?" We didn't get to the particulars last night. But I know he isn't here for long. And, as much as I hate it, I have to go to work soon.

His chest lifts on a sigh. "In a few hours."

"Oh." I'd hoped for more. At least one more night.

Dex swallows hard and glances toward the window. Sunlight lines the curve of his cheek and glints gold on the tips of his lashes. "I should have waited until I had more time freed up." He turns back to me. "But you were upset. I could hear it in your voice when we talked. So I jumped on a plane."

My fingers spread wide over the center of his chest. He came for me. I'm always being left behind, and Dex will do that too, but he also dropped everything and came here for me. No one has ever done that.

The lump within my throat grows. "Thank you," I whisper. "I…you…" I take a ragged breath and press my lips to the hard plane of his chest. "It means a lot, Ethan."

He doesn't answer, but I can feel him nod. The room goes silent, awkward and heavy with the weight of his eventual departure.

Dex takes a deep breath and rolls away from me, sitting up at the edge of the bed, his shoulders hunched and his head bent low. He doesn't say anything, just stays quiet, his profile drawn tight with a frown.

"What is it?" I ask, sitting up as well.

He doesn't stir, and for a second, I think he hasn't heard me. Then his frown deepens. "I don't want to tell you."

"What?" I squeak, shocked and offended. "So the whole, 'you can tell me anything' speech only applies to me baring my soul? Great. Lovely."

He winces. The thick muscles along his back bunch and flex as he runs his hands through his loose hair. "I don't feel like I have a right to, Fi." His voice lowers to a rumble. "I hate this."

The words send my heart thudding against my ribs. "Hate this?"

"Leaving you," he says, waving an arm toward the door. A sigh gusts from his lips. "I know I'm the one who pushed for a long-distance relationship. I asked you to trust me to make it work. But the thought of constantly leaving you eats at me. I don't want to."

The bed creaks as he half turns and his eyes find mine. His expression is sad, troubled. "I hate how I found you in pain. The idea that you have to face this shit alone just…" He bites his lower lip and shakes his head. "Fucking sucks, Fi."

A small smile tugs at the corners of my mouth as I crawl toward him. His skin is hot and smooth, and I press my breasts against his back, wrapping my arms around his waist to soak up all that wonderful heat.

Dex immediately puts his hand over mine, his touch almost needy.

"I know," I say, my lips gliding over his skin. "I don't want you to go either."

He shivers, as if his entire body is protesting the thought, and his grip on my hand tightens. But he doesn't say anything, simply holds on.

Sadness sinks into my bones, weighing me down. "This…" I clear my throat. "This is why I tried to stay away."

Dex stills, his body going rigid. I hear him swallow, feel the ripple of his muscles. "You want to call it quits?"

I can't breathe. My ribs actually hurt, as if they've clamped down over my heart. "Is that what you want?" I ask in a small voice.

I forget how quick Dex can be. I barely see him turn before I'm lifted up and hauled onto his lap. Thick arms band around me, crushing me against a solid, wide chest. A soft whisper of chest hairs tickles my nose.

"No," he nearly shouts, then calms. "No, Cherry." Gently he kisses the top of my head. "This is why I didn't want to say anything. I'm just feeling selfish and petulant."

I smile against his chest and snuggle in closer. "I'm feeling a little that way myself. It's okay, baby."

Dex grunts, but his hold turns softer, petting me now instead of clutching. His big, calloused hand runs down my back. "From the first moment I picked up a football, I've been dreaming about playing in the NFL. God, I wanted it so badly. The promise that one day I'd go pro kept me going through every dark hour." His hand slows, climbing back up to my nape to rest. "Now that I'm here…" He shakes his head. "It's a lonely life, Fi. They never tell you that."

"What?" I quip, my voice thick. "It isn't all fast cars and willing women?"

Women I will punt if I catch them touching my man.

I can almost feel him smile and wonder if he knows the direction of my thoughts.

"If you want only one woman, the rest is just noise."

He gets a kiss on his big pec for that, and his little nipple draws tight in response. I'm tempted to play with it, torture him a bit. But his words give me pause.

"I just…I thought I'd be happier at this point," he says. "Content, maybe."

Lifting my head, I meet his troubled gaze. It would be so easy to encourage him to quit. I can feel it in my skin. Part of him wants that prompt, for me to give him a reason.

The power I have over him hurts my heart. It might unnerve me except that I suspect he has a similar power over me.

I could do it, tell him to quit, to try something that doesn't put him at risk of concussions and spinal injuries, that doesn't send him away from me every week. I could have all of him without having to compete with football.

"Do you love the game?" I ask him.

"Always," he says without hesitation.

"Then, as you said, it's worth it." I kiss the crook of his neck, where his skin is smooth as fine satin. He loves that spot, and shivers now, pressing his cheek to the top of my head.

"Fi, I promised you honesty. Truth is, my desire to have you blinded me to the hard fact that these short moments are all we can have during the season. When I'm not playing, I'm practicing, reviewing footage, working out, eating, sleeping. Free time is a myth."

He looks down at me, and there's pain in his eyes. "I wanted to give you more. But I can't. And I don't know what to do about that."

I've always known this. It was what I expected when I let him into my life. I kiss him again, putting all my faith in him, in *us,* behind it. "Live your dream, Ethan. We'll find a way to make it less lonely."

But even as I make the promise, the fear that we're both lying to ourselves remains. Because it's clear this relationship isn't working the way we need it to, and something will have to give before it breaks.

CHAPTER 25

Fiona

SOME PEOPLE HATE NEW YORK. I get it—the place is loud, busy, dirty, swarming with activity. But I love it. The very second I step out onto its streets on Saturday morning, I feel energized, my pace picking up and my back getting straighter. Walking down Park to catch the subway downtown, I can almost pretend my time with Dex was a dream.

Except my nipples and thighs are sore. Every step I take sends a pleasurable little twinge through my sex, which aches as though I've been battered from the inside out with a large, blunt object.

I smile, remembering the thick length of Dex's cock pounding into me. And I almost want to stop walking and squeeze my thighs together, as if it will keep the feeling with me for just a bit longer.

I miss him. It's been less than a week, and I miss the sound of his voice, the warmth of his skin, the sly way he teases me. I miss teasing him. And I really just want to be back in that bed with Dex, tracing the lines of his tattoos, getting him to suck in a sharp breath when I play with his nipple ring.

None of this is good. He doesn't live here. We'll only see each other when he can fly into town. I need a distraction, and I aim to get it.

My steps grow quicker as I leave the Subway on 9th and make my way to Horatio Street. By the time I make it to Jackson's apartment, I'm in desperate need of a fix. Thankfully, he lets me in quickly and is waiting for me as soon as the industrial elevator rolls to a stop on his floor.

Handsome and fit, he gives me a smug grin. "Not back in the city for a day and already you're here. I told you you'd become addicted."

I give his sandy jaw a peck. "Yes, yes, you're very smart. Now shut up."

Jackson slings an arm around my shoulder. "Did you just quote *The Princess Bride* to me?"

"If you have to ask, you're not worthy, Jax."

The apartment is part of a vast, renovated warehouse. Astrid Gilberto croons about a girl from Ipanema, and the fragrance of fresh coffee and baked bread mixes with the prevalent scents of wood chips and varnish.

Jackson lets me go and calls out. "Would you stop playing that shit? You're going to turn us into a cliché."

Hal walks out of the kitchen, holding a tray and wearing a glare. "You keep that up and I'm going to Chinatown to buy us matching silk robes, asshole."

Then Hal grins at me, his blue eyes twinkling. "Fi-da-lee," he drawls as I give him a hug. "Jack's right; you're addicted."

"Maybe I just come here for the food." I grab a croissant and take a large, obnoxious bite.

Jackson leans against the steel kitchen countertop. "So then you don't want to see your table?"

"It's ready?" I say around a mouth of food, though I'm pretty sure it really sounded like, "Pits meddy?"

"Breakfast first," Hal insists, pouring me some coffee.

Which makes Jackson and me roll our eyes and head toward their workshop, Hal calling us barbarians as we go.

I've known Hal and Jackson since my senior year in high school when my mother stopped in their studio to look at some dining tables. Known as Jackson Hal Designs to the rest of the world, the couple creates some of the most beautiful modern furniture I've seen.

They work out of their apartment and have a studio on the ground floor, both of which Jackson inherited from his uncle, who bought the place in the '80s when the Meat Packing District was, as Jackson puts it, "The domain of queers and steers."

Now, it's a fashionable district, filled with couture, night clubs, and hot restaurants.

And there is my baby. I give a little happy sigh as I run over to the dining table I made. Sixty-six inches long, it features a butcher-block top of reclaimed wood, organized in a pattern to take advantage of the natural colors and grains of each slab of wood.

At the moment, it's all held together with massive clamps that have been in place while the glue dried.

"Want to do the honors?" Jackson asks.

I'm already unscrewing everything, eager to see the table unbound.

For the past five summers, I've been apprenticing with Jack and Hal, learning everything I can about furniture making. It's helped me become a better designer, and I like that I get to work with my hands instead of simply drawing out sketches of rooms.

We all stand back and check out the table. It's rough and needs sanding. I don't want to use a slick varnish but plan to rub on several coats of soft, subtle wax.

"I don't like that one dark piece," I say, pointing to a length of wood that catches my eye. "It looks off."

"You need a bit of imbalance," Hal argues. "Otherwise the thing becomes bland."

"Hal's right." Jackson walks around the table with a critical eye. "It works."

We discuss the merits of the table and what I can do to improve it for a while, but eventually, my friends drag my troubles out of me.

Curled up in the corner of one of their massive couches, I palm my second cup of coffee and finish up my tale of professional woe.

"So quit." Hal waves a hand as if this piece of advice solves everything in one fell swoop.

"And do what? I need to work. And I can't just run away whenever things get hard."

"Felix is a talentless hag," Hal says with a sneer. "And he knows how to manipulate. You want to stay in that toxic environment? For what? So you can lose your soul?"

"Very dramatic," Jackson deadpans before looking at me. "But he's right. Felix isn't going to teach you anything but how to succeed in business by being an ass. There are other ways. Do what you love, love who you do."

"Don't you mean 'love what you do'?" I ask with a laugh.

Jackson leers. "That too."

"I'll keep that in mind," I say, taking a sip of coffee. "I'll have lots to do while he and the-thief-who-shall-not-be-named have fun on the Robertson project."

"Robertson as in Cecelia?" Hal asks.

"Yep." Cecelia Robertson and her thirty-million-dollar penthouse.

"She bought a dining set from us last year." Hal crosses one leg over the other. "That bitch better not be ditching it in her redesign."

"That bitch," Jackson drawls, looking at me, "is in fierce competition with Janice Marks. I know because that's all she could talk about during our consultation. How she had to have bigger and better than Janice. How her table could *not* look anything like something Janice would purchase."

A slow, evil grin spreads over my face. "You don't say."

"Mmm…Janice is having a cocktail party at her house in two weeks. Want to be my date, sweet thing?"

Hal glances between us and grins as well. "You two…"

At that I stand. "Gentlemen, it's been a pleasure as always. But I'm suddenly feeling the need to go in search of a cocktail dress."

I've got a revenge to plan.

IT IS A SAD TRUTH THAT, yes, I do kill time on social media during work hours. A little lookie-loo over a coffee break, a little web surf at lunch. It's a bad habit. I'm trying to nix it. But I don't feel too guilty since I've caught Felix doing the same many times now. Who are we kidding? Our world is one of online addicts.

At lunch on the next Friday, I sit back with my chai tea and go to one of my favorite gossip sites, a total rag—my shame, my addiction.

My hand pauses over my tracking pad when Dex's picture pops up in the headline. At first it doesn't compute. Dex is in profile; his mouth—so nicely framed by his lush beard—is stern. Why the hell is he on a gossip site?

Leaning closer to my laptop, my heart pounding, I peer at the story. And the spiced tea I just sipped nearly chokes me.

"Mother fuck…."

The headline is large and ugly:

Pippa Bloom offers 1 Million Dollars for Proof of taking NFL Offensive Lineman Ethan Dexter's Virginity

Heat prickles my cheeks and tingles the tips of my fingers. I can't believe it. I read the article, a brief piece discussing how this private club called Pippa Bloom doesn't believe a prime bachelor such as Dex is still a virgin. They want to take him down.

Why? There's no explanation except for the fact that they've just gotten tons of free publicity by putting the public eye on my man.

I'm so angry, I can't move my eyes from the screen. My fingers shake as I hit link after link discussing the offer, discussing Dex as if he's some sort of sad case.

My first instinct is to call him. But no, I'll be all screechy, and that won't help the situation. I could call Ivy, but I'm guessing *she'll* be all screechy, and I can't handle that right now. So I call my friend Violet.

Violet and I were roommates freshman year, and though I quickly moved out to live in my dad's guesthouse from sophomore year on—because, despite being social, I loved my privacy—we remained close friends.

"What up, Fi-Fi?" she answers in her best bro imitation.

I roll my eyes but smile. "Ms. Day." Yes, her parents actually named her Violet Day. Then again, her mother's name is Sunny, so I'm thinking they were aiming for a theme.

"What can I do you for, Fi?"

"You know you really need to stop talking like your brother. It's getting uncomfortable." I laugh when she curses, but the ugly headline still on my screen sobers me. "So I met a guy."

"Ooh, tell me all."

I can imagine her now, legs pulled up on her massive office chair, her gray eyes wide as she twists a strand of her honey brown hair around her finger.

"His name is Ethan. He's a friend of Gray's. They used to play together in college. He's a center in the NFL now."

"A football player? Get the fuck out."

"I know. I'm surprised too."

Violet knows my thou-shall-not-date-an-athlete vow well.

"But he's kind of different. Unexpected. I just…I really like him."

"I can tell by your voice," she says softly.

"Yeah. Thing is…" I turn and scroll through the hideous article. "Have you read the news today?"

"Yeah…" Vi sucks in an audible breath. "Holy shit, are you talking about Ethan Dexter?"

I hate the scandal in her tone. I know she doesn't mean it, but my cheeks prickle in irritation. Not at her, but the whole ugly situation.

"That's him."

"You're dating a virgin?" she almost shrieks.

So much for avoiding high-pitched conversations.

"You know what," I snap. "I'm going hang up—"

"Sorry!" Violet interrupts. "That was totally rude. And not my business."

"No."

"But are you?" She rushes on as if she can't stop herself.

I make a face at the ceiling as my head rests on my chair. "Let's just say they're a little late in their hunt."

She snickers, but it's a happy sound. "Go you, because I'm looking at his picture and holy Moses, he's hot. Not your usual type. But hot. Much hotter, actually."

I can't help but smile. "Yes, he is. But right now I'm worried about this offer. And who the hell is Pippa Bloom?"

There's a moment of silence, and I know Violet's calmed down enough to actually get to the real point of the article.

"Pippa Bloom—" Violet all but sneers the words. "—is both the name of a club, and the scummy little shit who created it."

"Tell me more."

"Pippa Bloom, the woman, started off as a matchmaker for the rich and powerful. But it soon became clear that these *gentlemen* really wanted an easy hookup without all the stickiness of a relationship or the illegality of paying for sex."

"Isn't that how it's always been?"

"Yeah, but she's the one who made the connection and found a way to provide this easy, high-class hookup service. So she formed a club. It's like Tinder for the wealthy. Members are vetted; attractive men and women are procured. They all know the score."

"I don't really want to side with anyone who's out to hurt Dex, but I still don't see what's so bad about that."

Violet makes an annoyed sound. "The club promotes cheating.

They play up the taboo of fucking around on your spouse, marketing mostly to men. And they do cheap shit like this stunt with Dex to get publicity."

"Fine, Pippa Bloom is cockwomble—

"What?" Violet laughs.

My lips twitch. "A very bad person. A twat."

"I love when you break out the Brit."

I acquired quite the cursing education during my summers in London.

"It happens when I'm hella pissed. But to speak in good ol' American, she's a punk, sleezoid, insert rage-filled adjective here."

"Name-calling is well and good, but I'm going to bring that bitch and her club down." Violet's tone is hard and determined.

"I don't see how." I tap my pen on my desk and stare off. "It doesn't matter, anyway. Dex matters. I need to talk to him."

"It matters to me. This shit tore my parents apart. Now your man is a target? Hell no. Enough is enough. She's going down."

The thing with Violet is, I know she could do it. Behind her sunny smiles and foul mouth, Vi is a computer genius. From an early age she's lived and breathed computers. Now, at age twenty-one, she's a highly paid network securities consultant. Which means she also has the knowledge to go dark.

"Fine, go scorched-earth on her. Just be careful. I don't want to see your ass wearing orange. I don't care if it's the new black."

"I'd find a way out."

Her confidence is not comforting. I run a hand through my hair and sigh. "I gotta go…"

"Find your man and give him comfort, Fi-Fi. Let me worry about damage control."

I really don't want to imagine Violet's version of damage control. Better to remain ignorant in case of criminal proceedings. And right now, I have to concentrate on my own version of damage control.

CHAPTER 26

Dex

HAVING NEVER BEEN IN THE limelight before, I can say that it flat-out sucks to suddenly be thrust under its glare. At first, I don't know what's going on. Why are cameras aimed at me? I get the occasional picture taken, but I'm a center. I'm not news. I do my job and support the team.

This fucking flash-blitz that blinds me as I leave practice? Never happened before.

And then come the shouts.

"Dexter? Dexter? This way!"

"Dexter! What do you think about the virgin hunt?"

"Dexter! Are you really a virgin?"

For a long moment, I can only blink, try to get my sight back. One word hammers through all the ringing in my skull: *virgin*. It's like a hit to the ribs. I can't breathe.

They're talking about me being a virgin.

Shame surges hot over my skin, like I've been stripped of my clothes and placed in the desert. I duck my head and shoulder through the crowd, aware of my teammates at my back, looking at me. And then comes rage. I shouldn't be ashamed. My life is my own business.

It actually takes me five steps to realize I'm *not* a virgin. I'm so fucking blindsided that for a second, I forgot about Fi. Jesus. I'm not a virgin. But obviously the world thinks I am. And why?

"Dex." Someone touches my elbow. I flinch, ready to throw the guy off. But it's Rolondo, his dark eyes serious.

"Come on, man. I'll drive to dinner."

Dinner? People are still shouting, crowding. Cameras still in my face.

'Londo grips my upper arm and gives me a nudge toward his SUV. Right. We're supposed to go out to dinner with Drew and Johnson. We play their team tomorrow. Dinner. I don't think I can eat. I kind of want to throw up instead.

Numbly, I get in Rolondo's ride. The thud of the door shutting is a relief. It muffles the sounds from outside.

'Londo hops in the driver's seat. "We'll hang at my place until it's time to go. You don't need this shit."

He turns the ignition, and the car explodes into ear-ringing rap, his system set so loud my ass vibrates. He gives me a toothy grin and swerves out of the parking lot, leaving the press behind.

We drive a block before he turns the stereo down. "Damn, I didn't roll over any of those punk-ass fuckers." I know he's only half kidding. His expression turns grim as he reaches into his jeans pocket and finds his phone.

"Google yourself and find out what the fuck's going on, D."

Part of me doesn't want to. But knowledge is power, and I can't fight what I don't understand.

The headline immediately hits the top of the search page, and it's a punch to the gut all over again. Fuck. Fuck. Fuck. I'm a marked virgin? With a fucking bounty on my dick?

I could almost laugh, but my stomach turns instead. I have to choke out the story to Rolondo, who just whistles long and low.

"Shit, man. That's some…" He winces, rubs a hand over the short dreads he's wearing. "That's some shit, Dex."

"Who the fuck is Pippa Bloom?"

He gives me a look. "You never heard of it?"

"It? Sounds like a woman to me."

"Pippa Bloom is one of those hookup sites. Only they cater to rich dudes. You know, specialize in eccentric shit. Truth, I think there's much more to them than just sex. Their slogan is 'What's your pleasure?' It means anything. And I do mean *anything*."

"How do you know about them?"

Rolondo squirms in his seat. "It…uh… It isn't just guys looking for women."

"God, you're a member?"

"Not after this," he snaps. "Not after they messed with my boy."

"Thanks." I run a hand through my hair. "No judgment, by the way."

"Right, man. I didn't hear *any* judgment in your tone."

I can practically feel him rolling his eyes. I look over at him. When we graduated, Rolondo told our inner circle he was gay. I'd suspected it, but never said a thing. It's been hard for him, but we have his back. Always. He's yet to tell the media, which I know wears on him.

"I'm serious," I tell him. "Live and let live. But, yeah, okay, I'm judging the shit out this site now. The fucking bounty on my ass kind of killed my good will."

Rolondo laughs. "But, hey, you're gonna be infamous after this."

I know he's joking. It doesn't help, though. I can just hear the spew on ESPN now. The jokes. I'm stuck sitting here, feeling exposed, pissed, humiliated, then pissed again.

"Why the fuck did they decide to target me?" I'm not even aware that I've spoken until Rolondo shrugs.

"You got this whole man-bun, tattooed, broody big-guy thing going on. You know how many chicks dig that shit? And being a virgin on top of that? Fuck. It's like catnip."

My brows raise as I look at him. "Man-bun? You sound like an eighteen-year-old girl, you know that?"

I swear he blushes. But he shakes his head as if I'm the crazy one. "Man, I got younger sisters. It's impossible not to know this shit."

I squeeze the bridge of my nose. I feel a headache coming on.

"The real question is how did they figure out you were a virgin?"

"I'm not."

I know he gets what I'm saying. I shouldn't even mention it. But it fucking irritates me that this dating site has labeled me primary objective number one because they think I still am. "I mean, I was. Before… Shit, never mind."

"Well," Rolondo drawls, "at some point we all were virgins, D."

I don't want to smile. "You know what I mean. I'm saying it isn't out of left field that they assumed I was. I never hid it. But I didn't advertise it either. Doesn't matter because—"

"You're not anymore; I get it." He turns in to the driveway of his condo. "You don't gotta explain anything. But be prepared for some shit. This bitch-ass agency offered one million dollars for proof of getting into your pants?" A low, mirthless chuckle leaves him. "Man, shit. You're gonna have bitches coming out of the woodwork for your ass."

With a grunt, I slump in my seat, my heart clenching in my chest. "Fuck." I've got to talk to Fi, prepare her for what's coming. My insides roll. I promised her privacy, normalcy. This is far from fucking normal.

When I get inside Rolondo's place, I try to reach Fi, but my call goes straight to voice mail. It keeps going to voice mail until it's time to go out to dinner. And I'm left with this sinking feeling that everything has just fallen apart.

———————

DESPITE MY FOUL MOOD, dinner with the guys actually helps. Immediately they're giving me hearty slaps on the back and offering inane jokes as we're led to a quiet corner booth.

But once seated, Johnson leans in, wearing the fierce expression that has the press calling him The Viking, with his long yellow hair and slightly ruddy complexion. "Seriously, Dex, why the fuck did they start in on you? I mean…" He pinks a little. "We all kind of guessed you were—"

He slaps his mouth shut, unwilling to go there, which is kind of ironic considering he'll talk shit about everything else under the sun. And I wonder if they pity me, thinking I'm some sad case. It pisses me off. The base part of me wants to tell them what I told Rolondo, that I'm no longer a virgin, or that I don't give a shit about what I hadn't done before, because being with Fi is the best feeling in the world.

But what I do with Fi is private. And I'm not even going to think about it now, not when she's a thousand miles away and I miss her to the point of pain.

Yes, pain. It's lodged in my chest. I rub the spot, hating that it feels cold and empty. There's a pressure along my spine, like a hand pushing me toward wherever she might be. It's getting worse, this urge to just leave where I am and go to her. Why isn't she answering her phone?

I have dozens of voice mails right now. From Ivy and Sean Mackenzie, asking if I'm all right and wanting to discuss a game plan. Calls from my team's PR rep wanting the same thing. Calls from nearly everyone I know except Fi.

Johnson is waiting for an answer.

"I honestly don't know." I rub the back of my neck where it's stiff and sore. "I keep a low profile."

"Man, I don't think so," Rolondo says with a shake of his head. "Not with you singing in bars and shit."

Johnson laughs, hunching over. "Oh, man. I nearly pissed myself when I saw that video. Fucking crazy, D. I cannot believe you did that."

I can't either. But then Fi brings out parts of me I didn't know were there. I'd gone into it trying to win her, but ended up having fun. I'd let go in a way I've only ever done on the field.

"Thing is, that video has been out for a while. It had a run on social media, got a good laugh on ESPN, but that was it."

"It's your calendar. They've released the photos." Drew holds out his phone. There's a picture up on his browser, and we all make a swipe for the phone to see. I get there first, elbowing Johnson off as I look down at the screen.

"Shit. I forgot about this."

"Sexy Dexy," Rolondo sings out with a laugh, earning a shove from my other elbow.

My team's calendar photos. Nude photos. Yeah, I did it. Mainly because the photographer was a hot young woman who had a way of scaring the pants off all of us. Literally.

Thing is, she clearly had talent, and she didn't treat it as some gratuitous man show—not that most of the guys would have minded.

The photos were tasteful, done in full, saturated color so rich it appeared as though you were looking at an oil panting.

My photo was a side shot against a deep red background. I'm taking a knee, my helmet on the ground beside me, my head bent and my arm resting on my thigh. A sort of football-style "The Thinker," the photographer had insisted.

Aside from showing the side of my ass, none of my goods are on display, though I suspect there might be a little Photoshop at work—things hang and all that. I look weary yet undefeated, my expression thoughtful.

"It's a good pic," I say absently.

Drew smirks.

And I glare. "What? It has artistic merit."

"It's man candy," Johnson says. "Look at you, all thoughtfully flexing your muscles. Did you flex your ass too?"

"Nothing to flex. That's just my natural form." I give him a look.

"Jealous?"

Rolondo laughs. "Yeah, he is." He gestures to the screen. "I'm gonna have mine blown up and hung over my bed."

"Typical," Johnson says. "How'd you pose for yours? Doing one of your showboating dances?"

"Holding a football in front of his dick while he strikes one of his showboating poses," I deadpan.

"Fucking hot as hell," Rolondo assures.

"I'm not letting Anna see these." Drew shakes his head. "She'll be all over me to do one too. But, yeah, man. There's an article here." He hits the screen, and it goes back to another page. "They're calling you the hot, tatted, sensitive sentinel of football. Apparently your pic got the most hits."

"What? Sexy Dexy got more hits than me? Oh, hell no." Rolondo scowls and pulls out his phone, apparently checking all the articles himself.

I roll my eyes.

Drew's mouth turns down at the corners as he reads. "It was that fucker Randolph Norris who said you were a virgin."

Norris was a nose tackle who played for the rival college team we beat in our last two conference championships. He and I faced off several times, and he always came away looking like a chump. To say we dislike each other is putting it mildly.

And since he'd played for a college only ten miles from ours, he was privy to the local gossip.

"Fucking ass stain," Johnson mutters. "I hated that guy."

"He was drafted by New Orleans this year," I add. "But Coach cut him during the last round of training camp. Rumor was he didn't like Norris's attitude."

"Because it sucked," Rolondo mutters. "Nearly snapped Finn's head off during a light practice."

Putting the health of the starting QB in danger because you're showing off in practice isn't a smart move. Thank Christ I don't have him on my team anymore.

"So he's bitter and clearly hates Dex," Drew says. "He had loads to say—about how Dex never went out with any women, or dudes. How our college called him the patron saint of football. How people took bets on when he'd lose his V card."

"Did they?" I ask.

They all give me hesitant glances. I guess so. I'm not really pissed at them, but it fucking irks to realize people have been talking about me this whole time.

And now the world is too.

I sit back with a sigh. "Put it away. I'm going to get indigestion before I even have a chance to eat."

"And we all know you do not come between Dex and his meals." Johnson wags a finger.

"No, that's you," I say.

"True that." Rolondo grins wide.

"Man, you should, like, star in *The Bachelor*," Johnson says. "I can see it now." His voice drops. "This season, on a very special *NFL Bachelor*…"

"That's your favorite show, isn't it?" Drew asks with a grin. "I bet you watch it at night and just cry when he sends some poor girl home."

We all laugh as Johnson turns red, his fair skin unable to hide his flush. "Do not."

"Excellent come back," I tell him.

"Anyway," Drew says, "Dex can't go on that show. He's already got a girl."

"No shit?" Johnson looks at me like I've grown two heads.

"Yep," Drew answers for me. "Fiona Mackenzie. Ivy's little sister."

"The cute blonde who took her dress of at the wedding?" Johnson's expression borders on a leer.

"Hey," I warn. "Just wipe that right the fuck out of your memory."

Drew shakes his head. "See? Gone on her already."

I drink my water and endure a round of kissing noises. "You kids done?"

Johnson wags his tongue in a lewd manner. "Now I'm done."

"Bunch of juveniles," I mutter. But I'm not mad. I've missed this. I missed my guys.

Rolondo frowns. "If you're with Fiona now, this whole virgin-hunt thing goes out the door."

"No," I say with force. "I don't want Fi anywhere near this. The press does not get a piece of her."

"I respect that," Rolondo says. "But you gotta know that what you want and what the public takes are two different things, my friend."

Unfortunately, he's right. I hate the fear creeping over my shoulders. There are things I can't protect Fiona from, and it frustrates the hell out of me.

We eat dinner and gossip. I'm not afraid to admit it's pure gossip: who's done what knuckle-headed thing, which coaches suck, which don't.

And of course, war stories. How we've manned up in the face of pain and adversity and made spectacular plays, which are always ten times more impressive in the retelling, as if we don't all watch Sports Center highlights and know when one of us is lying out of his ass.

By the time the waiter slides a dessert that consists of chocolate in five different forms in front of me, I'm almost normal again.

Johnson scowls at his plate. "It's so tiny. Everything here is tiny."

"It's gourmet," Rolondo says, picking up his spoon.

"Who picked this place, anyway?" Johnson complains.

"I did." I slide a spoonful of dark chocolate mousse into my mouth and almost groan. Damn. Fi needs to come here with me. And like that, I'm missing her again. I ignore the emotion and glare at my guys. "It's delicious. Just order another one if you're still hungry."

Rolondo just laughs and eats while Johnson mutters about me

being some sort of metrosexual.

"Lumbersexual," I counter, getting a look of horror from Johnson. I shrug. "That's what Fi says, anyway."

"Why would she say you like having sex with lumberjacks?" Johnson asks with a confused frown.

Rolondo throws a napkin at his head. "Man, you don't know jack about jack."

"Lumberjacks?"

We all groan.

Except Drew, who doesn't say a word. He hasn't even noticed his dessert. He's way too fidgety and practically glued to his phone screen, which isn't like him.

"Why do you keep looking at your phone?" I ask him. "Shit, is there more bad press? Am I now up for grabs for both sexes?"

"I'd do you," Rolondo puts in with a grin.

"You're too high-maintenance for me."

"This is true." 'Londo nods and looks me over. "I'd most definitely make you shave that beard. I'm not into bears."

I shrug. "We were never meant to be."

Johnson rolls his eyes. "I don't care if I sound like a dick. This whole exchange is bizarre."

"You always sound like a dick," Rolondo says. "So we're used to it."

He ducks a chunk of bread Johnson pings at him. An older couple across the way turns to stare.

"Ladies," I say mildly, "mind your manners. This isn't the college bar."

"Yes, Mom." Johnson sits back and looks around. "Why is it that we aren't in a bar? I mean, yeah, we got money now. But this place is making my shoulders itch."

"I'm checking the place out," I tell them. "It's for sale, and Gray, Drew, and I are thinking about investing in restaurants."

"Seriously?" Johnson looks surprised.

"We need something to fall back on. We aren't going to play forever."

Since the three of us love to eat, we thought about the restaurant business. Gray and Drew have been looking at places on the west and east coasts, respectively.

I glance at Drew. "If a certain QB would get his face out of his phone and taste the food, it would be much easier to do."

Drew lifts his head. "The atmosphere is a little staid, but the food is good, and the place is packed."

"Agreed," I say. "It always is, but I'd make changes."

Drew nods, then drifts back to his phone.

Rolondo shrugs. "As long as we don't go to one of Johnson's strip bars, I'm cool with anything."

"You'd rather we go to one of your strip bars?" Johnson asks.

"Naw, wouldn't want you to develop a complex about your shortcomings, man."

"There ain't nothing short on me. And when I make a lady come, it takes all night."

"Takes all night to make her come? Yeah, I'd buy that."

As Rolondo and Johnson bait each other, I glance back at Drew, who is still eyeing his phone and being awfully quiet. "Seriously, Baylor, I'm about to confiscate that thing."

He raises a brow at me, and gives me his old, innocent grin—which I am not falling for. "You really are a mom, aren't you?"

"As I recall, you played the role of Mom. I was Dad."

"Doesn't that mean we're on a date now? And all I get is this lousy dinner?" Drew leans his arms on the table. "Where are my flowers?"

"I'll make it up to you with sweet talk later. Now answer the question, Battle. What the hell is up with the phone?"

As if I've activated it, the damn thing lights up, and Drew glances down. He fights to hide his smile. "What can I say? I'm totally pussy whipped by my wife to be. That's right, I'm replacing you with Anna." With that, he presses his palms to the tabletop. "Gentlemen, time to wrap this up. I have a phone date to get to."

Oddly, the guys don't go the obvious route and give Drew shit. They glance at me and then at each other—not exactly subtle, though I know they think they are.

"What now?" I ask, glaring around.

"Nothing, man," Rolondo assures. "Stop being so uptight. It isn't all about you, D."

His expression says different, but I let it slide.

Johnson pulls out some bills. "My treat this time, yeah?"

"Excuse me while I take in this moment," Rolondo says expansively, his arms open wide. "Johnson—punk ass, cheap motherfucker Johnson—is paying."

"Man, shut the fuck up," Johnson says with a laugh. "We meeting up for coffee in the morning?"

"Yeah, man," Rolondo says. "I'll pay that."

"Talk about cheap."

"Breakfast is the most important meal of the day, boy."

"And the cheapest."

"I'll pay every meal for the season's meet-ups if you two will shut up now," Drew says.

Since graduation, we've made it a point to meet up a few times a year. Sometimes there are more of us, sometimes less. Mostly we meet when we're playing a game against each other. But the Red Dog team will always be brothers.

Drew is hurrying us along, all but pushing Johnson toward the door.

I've always envied what Drew has with Anna. Not the sex, but the knowledge that there was someone he belonged to. Even when he was suffering when they first got together, I envied him. Because his emotions with her were real. Honest.

My whole life feels like one long fog of numbness, punctuated by manufactured pain. The tats, the piercing, hard hits on the field—all of them ways to make me feel something other than bland indifference.

But with Fi, I'm alive. I anticipate every single breath because it's another moment closer to getting back to her.

I follow the guys out, but my mind is on Fi, and the ache around my heart grows. I miss her so much that at first I think I'm imagining her leaning against the side of a black town car.

A balmy southern breeze drifts over the road, lifting the ends of her golden hair and making the skirt of her dress sway. She's wearing a white sundress dotted with brilliant red cherries. That dress with the little teasing red bow just below her breasts. That dress has haunted me for what seems like an eternity. I've dreamed of sinking to my knees and lifting its skirt to find the prize beneath. She's wearing that dress for me.

I'm frozen in place, surely gaping at her as the guys walk past. Out of the corner of my eye, I see their smug faces. Drew gives Fi a nod.

"Thank you, Drew Bee," she says to him, drawing out the initial in his last name with affection.

"Any time, Fi-Fi." His smile is wide and satisfied.

I remember that they know each other and live in the same town and hang out. I'm instantly jealous of Drew for that. But he clearly helped set up this meeting with my girl, so I can't hold it against him.

My attention is on Fi anyway. On her hesitant smile, the shine of happiness in her eyes. She lifts her arm, holding up a plastic produce bag full of something lumpy.

Her slightly husky voice drifts over the space between us. "I know guys bring girls flowers, but I figured you'd be more into food. So I brought you some cherries—"

Her words cut off with a squeak as I wrap my arms around her slim frame and lift her high. I kiss her without hesitation, opening her mouth with mine, my tongue sliding along hers. She tastes of cherries and Fi, and smells of joy.

My joy. My Fi.

Like that, I'm overwhelmed. Fuck, I'm almost weepy. And I'm all but mauling her on the street.

My voice is rough when I pull back and smile down at her. "Did you eat some of my cherries?"

Her nose wrinkles. "I had to see if they were okay. I'm not going to give you subpar cherries."

"You've got a whole theme going here."

"I'm not very subtle, Ethan," she says with a goofy grin. "Better get used to it now."

"Don't ever change."

She's still in my arms, her feet dangling around my shins, those sweet tits of hers pressed against my chest. I can't help kissing her again, on the warm spot just below her ear, the corner of her mouth, which always makes her shiver.

Hell, I can't stop kissing her period.

And she's running her fingers across my nape, massaging the tight muscles there as if she knows how badly I need it.

"Fi…" I can't even talk.

"Show me your home, Big Guy."

Problem is, I don't think I'll be able to let her go once she gets there.

CHAPTER 27

Fiona

E THAN INSISTS ON WALKING. It's a nice night; the air almost balmy. And though it's November, it's in the 70s—warm enough to wear this silly cherry sundress and a cardigan. But it was worth it to see Dex's wide smile unfurl when his gaze slid over me. Yeah, he knew I wore the dress for him. And it lit him up with happiness. So. Totally. Worth. It.

"Aren't you afraid of being spotted?" I ask as we amble along, his arm around me, my head resting against the warmth of his chest.

He stops and kisses me—soft, seeking, a smile on his lips as he pulls away. "Not really. No one's around. I got my cap on." He gives the brim of gray his newsboy cap a tug as he winks. "And I don't exactly look like myself."

No. He's not in his standard jeans and tee, but wearing soft black slacks and a light knit dress sweater that covers his trademark tats. He looks more dapper-New-Orleans gentleman than football player now.

Drew and his friends have driven off, making a lot of noise that I suspect was designed to bring attention to them and away from Ethan. They're good friends, loyal. I know they'll do anything to protect him. And yet I sense there's a wall between Ethan and, well, everyone but me.

"Your friends never call you Ethan. Always Dex or Dexter. Why?"

He shrugs. "I've always been Dex to them. I'm not even sure some of them know my first name. It's who I am."

The casual way he accepts that bothers me. I want to shout, wave my fist in the air, something. As it is, my voice comes out fierce and angry. "You're more than that. So much more."

"Only for you." He touches my face, runs the blunt tips of his fingers along my temple, as he looks at me with such tenderness my heart hurts. "No one else gets all of me, Cherry."

This man. I know he isn't trying to do it, but he always says the one thing guaranteed to turn my world on its head. My ire on his behalf dissipates, leaving behind the soft warmth of contentment.

Smiling, I rest my cheek in the palm of his hand. "Just so you know, no one else gets to call me silly fruit names."

The white of his teeth flashes in the shadow of his beard. "I know." His thumb caresses my cheek. "I've missed your face."

"I missed your…everything." It has been two weeks. An eternity when it comes to my need for him.

He kisses me again as we walk, and I grow lightheaded, giggling against his lips—drunk off Ethan.

And he seems that way too, the both of us laughing at nothing but the joy of being together, stopping every few feet to kiss, touch each other's faces, because we can.

It starts to rain, a gentle fall that brings out the scents of the city, the baking brick walkways, the warm scents of cooking, and underneath it all, a faint, murky odor of mildew and rot that gives the city a sense of age that New York refuses to acquire.

Around us drift lilting strains of jazz, hard beats of rock, the twang of country, disjointed notes of pop. It all melds together to make its own song. The rain feels soft, sluicing over our skin, warm and wet.

We pass Bourbon Street and move deeper into the French Quarter, away from the river. On a quiet street, Ethan backs me against a pair of glossy black French doors, protected from the rain by a stucco archway.

He cups my cheeks and kisses me like he aches for it. Slow, fevered, deep. Soft licks of my upper lip, hard nips of my lower lip. It feels so good, I shiver against him, my hands fisting his sweater.

He's so big, he blots out the light of the street entirely, and I know I'm hidden behind him in this damp little nook. His hands span the sides of my neck, his thumbs on my jaw, holding me where he wants me.

I can only whimper, cling to him, kiss him back for all I'm worth.

One big hand slides down my chest, covering my breast and giving it a possessive squeeze before gliding lower, past my ribs, my hip. He leans further into me, his chest against mine as he reaches down and gathers my skirt.

"Did you know," he murmurs almost conversationally against my lips, "that when you get all breathless and make those little whimpers…" His fingers brush the crease of my hip, tracing the edge of my panties. "I always find you…" He slips under my panties. "Wet." His body shudders as the rough pad of his finger rubs along my slick flesh. "Always so fucking wet for me."

"Yes."

"God, just feel you. You're dripping onto my fingers." A fine tremor works down his arm as his eyes flutter closed and he kisses me again. Again. Again.

He's spinning a spell over me, making my limbs heavy and hot. My sex pulses, loving the attention, wanting more of it.

His fingers find my opening, and I whimper. He dips in just enough for me to feel it, to want more, then drifts away, strokes and circles, a lazy, languid exploration.

"Ethan…" I wiggle my hips, desperate to get him deeper. "Stop playing with me."

He gives my upper lip a little lick, and still he gently fondles. "You love it."

I do. So much. But I'm incapable of speech right now. I can only whine and rock my hips, wanting more. He holds me fast, not relenting.

"Say it, Cherry. Tell me how much you love it, and I'll give you what you need."

Licking my swollen lips, I look up at him, his face a collection of shadows in the dim light. "I love it, Ethan. Fuck me with those long fingers, and then shove your fat cock into me."

His breath leaves with a gust. "Well played, darlin'." He plunges deep, hard, and there. That's all it takes to set me off. The orgasm rushes over me so fast, I suck in breaths like I'm drowning.

Ethan works his fingers slow and steady, his other hand cupping my neck, his lips coasting over mine as if he wants to drink up my pleasure.

And when I finally relax against him, my body limp and spent, he pulls his fingers out and lifts them to his lips to suck them clean. "Sweetest thing I've had in my mouth all night."

A weak laugh escapes me. "I've created a monster."

Ethan just grins wider before turning his attention to the little control panel beside my head. "Watch carefully now." He moves to punch in a number, but I stop him with a little cry.

"This is your house? We were going at it right in front of your house?"

He doesn't stop smiling. "You sound annoyed."

"Well…" I'm flustered. "Why didn't we go in? You know…" My cheeks heat. "Before." I don't even know why I'm being prudish. I certainly didn't mind.

A laugh rumbles in his chest, and he gives me a look as if he is thinking the same thing. "That was the plan. But then I felt your sweet body against mine, and it was all over."

Biting his lower lip as if to keep from smiling any longer, he punches in the code: 11-55-88. The door clicks open. "Did you get it?"

"Yes." I force myself to stand taller.

"Good." He nods toward the panel. "Remember it. Any time you want to come here, my house is open to you. *Any time*, Fi. For as long as you want."

The back of my throat tickles. I stare up at him, struck dumb and only able to squeeze his big hand with my much smaller one. It feels momentous, what he's done. Huge. The kind of commitment that speaks of permanence.

It's terrifying and wonderful all in one breath. So I say the only thing I can. "Am I wrong, or wasn't Gray's college jersey number eighty-eight?"

Ethan blinks, clearly expecting something else, but he nods. "Yep. Drew's was eleven. Mine was, and still is, fifty-five."

"Aww. Aren't you cute?" *He's perfect. And mine.*

"It's easy to remember," he says gruffly. "Now let's get inside."

Fiona

THE DOOR TO ETHAN'S HOUSE opens to a little carriage way, lit by an overhead wrought-iron lantern. We follow the path to a private courtyard.

"Wow," I say as we walk farther into it. "This is beautiful."

Frosted globe lanterns are hung across the yard. Little lights twinkle in the ivy-covered walls surrounding a garden of crepe myrtle and various palms. In the center, an ornate fountain runs.

"It came like this," Dex says at my elbow. He glances around as if seeing it from my eyes. A loggia covered in bougainvillea shelters a double-wide lounger. There's a massive tractor tire to one side of the courtyard. As in, it's as wide as I am tall. His lips quirk at the sight of it. "Well, except for the tire."

"You gonna tell me what's up with the tire?"

He ducks his head and scratches the back of his neck. "I whack it with a sledgehammer. Sometimes I flip it."

"Oh, sure. Because why not?"

"Does the job. But that's for off-season training." So nonchalant. But he can't really hide his smug grin.

"That's got to weigh, what?"

He shrugs his massive shoulders. "A thousand pounds."

Laughing, I shake my head. "Get the hell out."

Dex winks. "JJ Watt does it, so I do it too. No way am I going to be caught with my dick in the wind facing one of those defensive linemen coming at me like a tank."

As unassuming as Dex can be, he's also fiercely competitive.

I give his arm a squeeze. Not one ounce of give. "My big, strong man."

"Yes, I am," he says without hesitation, then surveys the courtyard. "The narrow building along the side is a guest house. The building at the back is an old carriage house, now a garage on the ground floor, and my painting studio is above it.

"You can look around tomorrow," he finishes, his voice soft, his hand warm in mine. He's pulling me toward the main house. We go up a flight of stairs, straight to the second floor. We walk past a large, open living room—exposed brick walls, wide, worn wooden floorboards—and through a gourmet kitchen. More exposed brick. Huge center island, stainless steel appliances, white marble counters.

I want to soak it all in, but Dex is on a mission, leading me along with purposeful steps.

"Not hungry?" I tease as we pass through.

He glances back at me, heat and need in his eyes. "Not for food." He wrinkles his nose. "Christ, that was cheesy, wasn't it?"

I laugh. "It was cute."

"Cute," he repeats. "Just what every guy wants to be called." He hesitates at the doorway leading out of the kitchen. "Are you hungry? I should have asked. I've—"

"Not for food," I tell him. Because I can be cheesy too.

That has him picking up his pace. We take a set of stairs to the top floor. His bedroom overlooks the courtyard. And the dim light from the outside lanterns slants through the massive paned windows, half covered by louvered shutters. There isn't much in here, just a big club chair, a dresser, and a king bed with a padded leather headboard.

I smell the pine of the floorboards, the spicy scent of Ethan's skin. It's warm and quiet in his room. Quiet enough to hear his soft breaths and the steady pounding of my heart. He stands before me, so big and present; I feel his warmth even though we're not yet touching.

Slowly he reaches up and slides off my damp cardigan. Gentle fingers ease the strap of my sundress down. When my breast pops free, he moves to the other side, pulling the strap until the other is exposed. Ethan has seen me naked, licked and sucked every inch of me, but standing here now, on display for him, makes me so hot. I struggle to catch my breath.

It grows erratic when he gives a little hum of satisfaction and runs the tips of his fingers across my nipples. Back and forth, barely touching them. God. I fight the urge to arch into his touch, because it's hotter to hold back, to let him fondle me while my nipples grow stiff and achy.

He circles them, worrying the tips with the rough pads of his fingers, and then, without warning, pinches—pulling until my breasts stretch—before letting go.

My breasts bob back into place, and I whimper, my knees going weak.

"I had this whole seduction thing planned," he whispers as he plays with me, stroking, tweaking. It's almost lewd the way he handles me as if I'm his plaything, except it's reverent too. "But I don't think I can wait."

I lick my dry lips. I'm close to coming now, and he's only touching my tits. "Don't wait," I say.

His gaze catches mine. In the shadows, he looks so serious, almost fierce. But I know that expression. It's need. Strong and pure. Just like him. I lift his damp sweater over his head and wrap my arms around his neck. The press of his warm skin against mine makes us both groan. With a sigh, I kiss the hollow of his throat. That's all it takes.

Soft bedding surrounds me and Ethan's hard body covers mine. There's no more talking.

CHAPTER 28

Fiona

SWEAT-SLICK AND LIMP WITH EXHAUSTION, I lie draped over Ethan's naked body. I love that he's so big not an inch of me hangs over the edges of him. Even so, his arm wraps loosely around my waist, holding me secure as if he's afraid I'll fall. His fingers trace random patterns on my back.

"How do you want to handle this?" I ask him.

His body tenses, so I know he understands my question. "Nothing to handle. I'll just make no comment, and it will go away."

I lift my head so I can rest my chin on his chest. "I hate to say this, but I'm not sure it will go away all that quickly. Maybe… Well, why don't you just tell them you're with me?"

"No." He practically shouts the word, his lips flattening. And my heart caves in as if it's been stomped.

"You don't want to tell people about us?"

Instantly, he cups my cheek, his eyes going wide. "Shit, Fi, I did *not* mean I was ashamed or wanted to hide it. I mean there is no way in hell I'm bringing you into a media shit show."

"That really should be my decision. Especially if it helps you. And I want to help you, Ethan."

With a sigh, he flops his head back on the pillows and stares up at the ceiling, his hand still stroking my cheek. "Thank you for that,

Cherry. But I can't…" He takes a ragged breath. "Don't ask me to agree to that. I couldn't take seeing them tear you apart." He glances down at me, his eyes now golden-green in the lamplight. "Please."

"All right," I say with reluctance. "For now. But, I swear, if a bunch of crazy women start stalking you, I'm stepping in."

A slow smile curls over his firm lips. "Kind of love you being all possessive, Fi."

I harrumph, but give his chest a little kiss. "I am sorry, though. That this is happening, I mean."

"Yeah," he says with a sigh. "Me too."

We grow quiet, lost in our own thoughts, Dex stroking my hair and me drifting in a strange half-sleep state.

"Six Underground" by the Sneaker Pimps plays softly from a set of bedside speakers.

"I never asked how you came to like trip-hop music," I murmur, too content to talk louder.

"Are you asking me now?" There's a smile in his voice.

"Smartass." I give his ribs a little nudge, loving the way he squirms as if it tickles. "And yes. I told you when we first kissed that I didn't expect you to like this music. It's still a surprise."

He takes a breath, and I lift along with his chest. "Okay, but don't laugh."

"That's basically assuring I'll laugh."

"Fine. Laugh it up," he says. "It was a car commercial. I kept hearing this song and…" He cranes his head to glare down at me, though there's a smile on his lips. "You're laughing already?"

I smother my laugh. "It was the same for me, is all."

His lips twitch, those hazel eyes of his gleaming more gold than blue now. "Which song?"

"It was two songs. Morcheeba's 'Crimson' and Massive Attack's 'Paradise Circus'. You?"

"Zero Seven's 'In the Waiting Line'."

"I love that song. They used it in *Sex and the City* too."

"I'll take your word for it." With a grunt, he turns, and suddenly I'm on the bed and he's over me, his warm body gently pressed to mine. His lips find my neck and suckle. "God, I love the way you smell."

My fingers comb back his loose hair. "And how do I smell?"

"Like happy dreams and well-fucked woman."

A shout of laughter leaves me, and I tug him closer as he works his way along my collarbone, his hand sliding up to my breast. The thick slab of his erection presses against my thigh, tempting me, but I let the anticipation build for now.

"I love the way you smell too."

He pauses, his lips brushing my shoulder, his beard tickling my breast. "How do I smell?"

"Like…" I smile up at the ceiling as I consider. "Pancakes and midnight."

"Oh?" His voice is muffled as he resumes exploring my neck and teasing my nipple with the blunt tip of his thumb.

I squirm, trying to open my legs wider to let him settle between them. He does with a low groan, but doesn't enter me. He's waiting for my answer.

My voice is breathless, distracted as I am by his roaming lips. "You know…" I kiss his temple, the crest of his cheek, "when you've had a night of sweaty, hot fucking…" I give the line of his jaw a little nuzzle. "Going at it until you can barely move. And you've worked up an appetite that only a stack of pancakes and more hot sex will satisfy?"

Ethan lifts his head then, his eyes slumberous but his expression careful. "You had a lot of those nights?"

It hits me what I've said, and my fingers tighten his hair as I tell him the absolute truth. "Only with you, Ethan. That's why it's your scent."

God, his smile, it unfurls like a spring leaf to the rain, spreading wide and open. "Good answer."

Unfortunately, my stomach also has an answer, and that's to make a God awful growl as if talk of food has released the hunger hounds.

Ethan grins wide, and a laugh rolls out of him. "What was that? I didn't quite catch that last bit there."

"Shut up." I slap his shoulder while blushing hot over my entire body. "We've been at it for hours."

"And hours," he confirms with a solemn nod, though the smug satisfaction in his expression grows.

Before I can say a word, he leaps up, hauling me with him. I squeal as he lifts me with one arm. "Ethan, what the hell?"

He strides out of the bedroom. So much for being depleted. His stamina awes me. "Where do you think? To go make you some pancakes. I need to keep up my girl's strength."

Dex

DESPITE MY GOOD INTENTIONS, my plan to feed Fi pancakes goes south as soon as she tells me we need flour to make them.

"Shit," I say, stopping in the middle of the kitchen. Fi's clinging to me like a little barnacle, her legs wrapped around my waist, her pussy pushed against my abs—which threatens to break my will and turn me back to the bedroom.

She smiles with sleepy but lust-filled eyes. "You've never made pancakes, have you?"

"I'm not much of a cook. Hang on." I walk us over to the fridge. Holding her tight with one arm, I open the door and bend to rummage through it.

Fi makes another of her adorable squeals as we tilt down. But I've got her. She isn't going to fall on my watch. She weighs next to nothing.

Vague fantasies of doing drills while carrying Fi on my back drift through my head as I grab a box of takeout and set her on the counter, earning another squeak.

"Shit, that's cold," she says with a laugh. But she leans back on one arm and gives me a cheeky grin, her golden hair sticking out wildly around her face.

Damn, but she's gorgeous. So fucking perfect for me, she takes my breath. Sweet, perky tits with puffy nipples that always seem to be begging for a suck. Tiny waist and wide hips. A butt that's more than a handful. A true Tinker Bell body.

Though I'd never call her Tink the way Ivy and Gray do. She might be diminutive, but to me, she's also larger than life.

Grasping her knees, I spread her thighs wide. Ah, and there's that pretty pink pussy, all glistening for me. My favorite spot in the entire world. I step between her legs and rub her gloriously curvy hips. "I'll warm you up."

"I'm sure you will," she murmurs, her gaze roaming over my chest in a possessive way that fills me with pride and gratitude.

"First, though, I promised to feed you." I grab the takeout box and pull out a Chinese dumpling.

Fi's brows lift. "Cold dumplings?"

"Best late-night snack ever." I hold the dumpling near her lips. "Trust me."

Her expression is dubious but she takes a bite and makes a little moan of contentment.

"Good, yeah?"

She swallows down her bite and opens her mouth for more.

Carefully, I feed her dumplings until she tells me she's done. Then I hand her some water. "All good?" I ask, kissing the sensitive little corner of her mouth.

"Yes."

Good. Licking my fingers to get the dumpling grease off, I step closer. "Sorry I couldn't give you pancakes at midnight."

I run my hands up her soft thighs. One tug and she's at the edge of the counter. Fi's eyes narrow, her plump lips curling in a sly smile.

I smile back, not saying a word but letting her know she's mine all the same. The tip of my cock brushes her entrance. She's slick and warm, and holds all my attention.

A light shiver runs over her body. "Dumplings are a pretty good alternative."

"Mmm." I nudge her just slightly, taking hold of her hips to keep her steady. "Dumplings and deep-dicking."

She laughs at that. "Deep-dick—Oh!"

I thrust without warning.

"Oh!" Fi gasps again, her back arching, as I push my way deeper inside. Her tits lift like an offering. Well, then… I swoop forward and capture one rosy tip with my mouth.

"Oh, shit," she whispers, her brows furrowed tight and her mouth open on a hot pant. "Oh, shit, Ethan."

I don't stop but pull her farther onto my dick, loving how she whimpers and wiggles as she struggles to accommodate me but clearly wants every inch I can give her.

It's a snug fit, the warm, wet clasp of her squeezing me so hard I feel it in my balls and down my thighs.

When I bottom out, I pause because it's just too good. But Fi is grasping my hair, shoving her tit in my mouth like she'll die if I don't suck harder, and writhing as if she needs more.

And I can't hold back. We both groan as I work her in an easy, undulating rhythm that has no pause, because it's heaven fucking Fi. Pure, perfect heaven. Every thrust I take grows a little harder, goes a little deeper, my piercing sliding over that spot within her that has her gasping a reedy "ah!" each time.

I mouth her nipple, my tongue sliding over it. Heat licks up my thighs and down my spine. I groan, slamming into her, again and again. And she loves it, her hands gripping my shoulders, her legs wrapping tight around my waist as she slumps against the marble countertop.

"Ethan. Ethan." It's a weak, needy cry.

I bend over her, practically crawling onto the counter with her, pumping with blind lust now. She's utterly beautiful spread out before me, her expression slack with pleasure.

"Don't stop," she says.

I won't. I can't.

This. This is what I want, what I need, this connection with Fiona in whatever variation I can get for as long as I can.

She comes on a sob, and it breaks me. How am I going to let her go again? My orgasm takes my breath, my voice. I empty myself into her, giving her everything I have, and it won't be enough to keep her here.

It's never enough.

CHAPTER 29

Fiona

Airport again. Why do they all smell the same? Dex walks me to the TSA line, and I feel like I'm going to my execution. My entire body wants to resist moving forward. Maybe Dex does too because he doesn't try to hurry me along, even though my sluggish pace causes him to take unnaturally short steps.

When we get within sight of the line, his fingertips press my lower back, as if he's entertaining ideas of grabbing hold and pulling me away. I wouldn't object.

With a soft sort of grunt, he turns me into his embrace. I get a glimpse of his eyes, serious and pained. His warm hands cradle my cheeks, and then he's kissing me.

It's deep, desperate, and savoring, as if he's putting his entire heart into each touch and taste, as if he's trying to memorize every second. And I'm lost. Utterly lost.

Sounds fade. There is only Ethan and how good he feels, how good he makes *me* feel. I'm on my toes, my arms wrapped around his neck, as I kiss him back, consumed by my need for him. I don't know how long we stand there, but when he moves his mouth from mine to explore my jaw, taking soft nibbles, my lips feel tender and swollen.

Big hands caress my back, my sides, sliding down to the crest of my butt and up to just under my breasts. Keeping it decent but driving me wild all the same.

"Be sure to drink water," he murmurs against my skin, kissing my neck, my chin, mouth, cheek.

"'Kay." My hands roam too, finding the hard rounds of his massive shoulders, sliding over his firm pecs.

He tugs me closer, his breath warm on my skin. "Some strange guy tries to talk to you, tell him to fuck off."

I laugh at that.

Ethan doesn't. He grazes the side of my neck with his teeth, his beard tickling. "Make an effort to stretch your legs."

"Ethan," I run my fingers through his silky hair. "It's not that long of a plane ride."

"It's too long," he grumps. And I know he isn't talking about time but distance. My breath hitches with a twinge of pain.

It breaks the spell between us. He takes a step back, his hands falling away as if holding me any longer hurts him.

He stares down at me with eyes suspiciously bright and glassy. "Safe flight, Fi."

"See you soon, Ethan."

His nod is a ghost of a movement.

It takes effort to move, to take the handle of my roll-on bag. I'm turning to go when he mutters an oath and grabs me. I'm engulfed by a wall of muscle and arms of steel. He hugs me tight, hunching over me, his nose buried in the crook of my neck.

My arms wrap around his waist, fingers digging into the loose fabric of his shirt.

He breathes in deep, then lets it go with a shaky gust. "I hate this. I hate it so much." His grip makes my ribs protest, and his voice goes rough. "I feel like some essential organ is being ripped from me."

My eyes burn, my throat locking up tight. I have to swallow hard to speak. "Ethan…"

But he shakes his head and sets me away from him. His expression is almost angry, jaw set beneath the blanket of his beard. "Time to go, Cherry. Just…don't look back, okay? Or I won't be able to let you go."

Fuck. My vision blurs. Sniffling, I nod. "All right."

But I can't move.

With a sad smile, he takes me by the shoulders and turns me toward the dreaded TSA line. "Go on now." His big hand slaps my butt. "Get."

I jump a little, glaring over my shoulder. "You sounded awfully Southern just now, mister."

That smile quirks. "Went to a Southern university. Guess I picked up a few things, ma'am." The smile falls. "Go on, Cherry. Don't look back."

"I won't." I can't. Or I'll never leave.

My rolling bag weighs a thousand pounds as I drag it behind me, every step taking me farther away from Ethan. I don't turn around, but I feel him watching. I know he won't go until I'm out of sight.

Tears threaten to fall, but I breathe through them. I can't let him see me cry.

When I'm through the line, my cell dings. Glancing down, I almost lose it again.

FearTheBeard: <3 <—mine goes with you. Always.

CHAPTER 30

Dex

MONDAY NIGHT FOOTBALL. The audience is not as rowdy as in college. Fans are more likely to shout "you suck" than give their undying love. Because it's about the win. Sure, we had that need to win in college. But school spirit trumped the team's record. Here? My job is on the line if I don't perform.

The stadium isn't as big. Doesn't need to be. Cameras are everywhere, taking in every fucking move we make for an audience that grows year by year—a big, voracious mass of unseen fans. Damn if I haven't begun to think if it not as a sport but theater. We're giving them a show, and it had better be good.

Right now, I'm facing off against a big bastard of a nose tackle. Emmet Sampson. We played against each other in college, and I know his ways well. He loves to talk shit. Excels, at it, actually. I'm pretty sure he makes a study of his opposition to find the worst dirt he can on them.

Emmet can't stand me because I've never once blinked in the face of his bullshit. Not that he doesn't keep trying.

"Lookie here," he says as we take the field. "It's old Paul Bunyan. Where's your big blue ox, boy?"

At your mamma's house having a smoke.

But I don't say it. Not speaking is much more effective.

I hunker down, my quads giving a nice stretch that brings me right back into the physical.

"So that shit true, Dexter?" he goes on. "You haven't busted your cherry? Damn, man." He shakes head. "Some sorry-ass shit right there."

I breathe in deep. Pay attention to my team. His team. Watch. Wait. Listen.

"Naw, I don't believe it. What's the matter, Dexter? Afraid of the pussy?"

Emmet is meowing like a cat. The sound fades as I focus on the line. The pads of my gloved fingers rest on the ball, the shape grounding me. I draw in a breath, let my gaze open up until I see the whole picture—my guys, the defense, how they line up.

I call out a play adjustment. My guys hustle, changing positions. And the defense scrambles to follow.

The instant Finn makes his signal, I snap the ball and explode into action. Emmet and I meet like a thunderclap, helmets clacking, bones rattling. My thighs bunch as I push forward, the balls of my feet digging into soft earth as I drive him back. He's hammering his fists at my wrists, sending shards of pain up my arms, straight to my brain. But I hold tight and strong-arm him to the side to clear a path for my guy.

Emmet goes down in a tumble. And, when the play ends, I lean over him. "If you ran your ass half as good as you run your mouth, I just might be afraid, bitch."

Trotting back to the huddle, I give Finn a slap on the helmet. "Let's light 'em up, rook."

He gives me a grin. "You know it."

For the rest of the game, we do just that. We play smart, crafty, and light them up like fireworks on the Fourth of July. My guys play like a well-oiled machine—Finn picking apart the defense with a football sense you can't learn; it's just innate, and a beautiful fucking thing to witness.

But the taunts don't stop, they grow. Doesn't matter if I play my best. It's no longer all about my performance. The world is pulling down the walls I've built to protect myself, exposing me without my consent.

Fiona

I LOVE PARTIES. I love the noise and the chatter and the chance to talk to new people. I love free booze and sampling cute little appetizers. I love dressing up and looking at other women's dresses—I always find myself envying at least one outfit. But this party? Kind of blows.

Oh, the food is stellar. Champagne flows, and the decor is as impeccable as the view. Janice Mark's penthouse is incredible, with views of the entire city spread out beneath us like a sequined dress, glittering and twinkling in the night.

By all accounts, I ought to be loving this. Dozens of top interior designers are here, giving me the chance to network. And the energy in the room is high.

I just don't feel it. Because Ethan isn't here. The sad part is I'm equally sure he'd hate this party. I can imagine him now, tugging at his collar and finding a nice corner to prop up. Now that he holds all my attention, memories of him before we were together come flooding back. He was always in the corner, nursing one of his water bottles, talking to a few guys—or listening, rather, and saying little.

But what he said always seemed to count for more. Ethan chooses his words carefully, never giving up useless spares. I remember that now and how it fascinated me then, because I usually have words enough for two people.

I remember that he used to watch me with those deep-set hazel eyes. It hadn't made much of an impression then because I was loud, and people usually glanced my way when I was in a room. Never really bothered me. I'd assumed Ethan was doing the same—giving crazy Fi Mackenzie a onceover before going back to his life.

Now I know it had been more. Strangely, this makes me warm all over. He saw when I wasn't "on" or trying to impress him, but as myself. And he'd wanted me anyway.

But now he's in New Orleans, and I'm stuck fifty stories over Manhattan, surrounded by the type of people I grew up around. And it all feels foreign and off. Nothing is right anymore.

"Fabulous party, isn't it?" Jackson is resplendent in a shiny, sapphire blue Zegna suit that would look ridiculous on most men but he pulls off with aplomb.

"Yes." It is. Even if I'd rather be somewhere else, I can admit that much. "Makes me wonder why Felix isn't here." My boss should be all over this.

"As I said before, Janice, our lovely hostess, is mortal enemies with his current client, Cecelia. The very notion of letting a potential spy into her nest would enrage Janice. Which reminds me…" He drops his voice. "Let's not tell anyone you're working for Felix, eh?"

My lips quirk. "Don't want to be kicked out on your couture?"

"Don't even jest." He fiddles with the cuffs of his shirt, a silk peacock print that somehow works with the outfit.

"Fine." I set down the glass of champagne I've been holding for the past half hour. It's warm and flat now. "I'll keep quiet."

"What's wrong?" Jackson looks me over with a frown. "Missing your big football player?"

I give him the side eye. "How did you know that?"

"Because Benedict Cumberbatch just walked by, and you didn't even blink."

"What?" I whip my head around, searching the room. "Where?"

"I'm kidding." He laughs when I glare at him. "You should've seen your face."

"You dickweed." I give his side an elbow. "That was beyond low." Jackson knows I have a thing for Cumberbatch—with that deep voice and quiet way of his that you just know hides a total perv in the bedroom.

Jackson fends off my attempt to pull the perfectly folded aqua handkerchief from his coat pocket so I can bat him with it. "Hey now, pixie, easy with the outfit. I give. I give. I was a dick."

"Damn right you were," I say with a sniff. "I'd like to see how you'd handle it if I said I saw Fassy."

He makes a look of mock horror. "You wouldn't. My love of Fassy far exceeds your high-school-girl-crush on Sherlock."

"Actually, I liked him better as Khan."

"Oh, me too. I think if I ever met him I'd have to shout it a la Captain Kirk." Jackson makes a face as if he's silently screaming out, "Khaaahhnn!" and I laugh.

Smiling, I lean my head on his shoulder, and he wraps an arm around me, giving me a squeeze. "So you're missing your man?"

"Seriously, Jax, how did you know?"

"I'm fairly certain I had that look on my face when I first met Hal and he decided he *had* to live in Milan for a summer to learn about textiles. The bastard." Jackson takes a sip of his white wine as he strolls me over to the wall of windows facing downtown. "It was misery. But at least I had the comfort of knowing he was miserable too."

"Cold comfort. I don't want Dex to be unhappy."

Jackson gives the top of my head a kiss. "Sweet girl."

"It hurts, Jax. I actually hurt." I press my fist against my chest where the pain is centered. "I don't like it."

He stares down at me with solemn eyes. "What are you going to do about it?"

With a ragged sigh I stare out the window. The old me would have run, ditched the troublesome baggage and moved on. It hits me that there *is* an old me, because I've changed. I don't think Dex has changed me, but being with him, caring about him, has. And the new me does not run.

Unfortunately the new me did not come with a set of instructions on how to handle a long-distance relationship. Which would have been awesome. So what am I going to do?

"Something drastic," I find myself saying. I take a breath and meet Jackson's eyes. "Something crazy."

Just stating it has my heartbeat speeding up with anticipation. Yes, something risky and daring and right. For the first time in days, I feel like I can breathe.

My old friend starts to grin as if he's been waiting for me to say as much.

"By the way." Jackson reaches into his inner suit pocket and pulls out a slip of paper. "Sold your table the other day."

"You did?" I practically squeal but manage to hold onto my dignity by a thread.

"Yes, ma'am." He hands me the paper. "Your check."

My jaw falls as soon as I read it. "Get the fudgesticks out!" I gape at Jackson, then at the check. "Is this for real?"

"I'm going to assume that's rhetorical."

Well, it is and it isn't. Because I cannot believe what I'm looking at. "I made thirty-thousand dollars on a dining set?"

Jackson gives me a bored look. "Honey, this is Manhattan. You create furniture like that and sell it to the right people, you'd better be making thirty large. At the very least."

My lips feel numb. "I had no idea. I mean, I know how much we pay for our clients' furniture, but I didn't expect I'd make this much. I'm hardly a known name."

"Not yet. But *I* am, and I know how to sell. As for you, this is only the beginning, Fi-da-lee." Jackson's expression goes serious. "Honey, I'm never going to have kids, so you'll have to humor me as my surrogate."

Smiling, I kiss his cheek. "Papa Jackson. Can I fill out my Christmas list now?"

He gives my shoulder a nudge. "I wasn't finished, cheeky. Come work with us, Fiona. Make your furniture, and we'll sell it. When you're established, you can go it on your own."

For a second, I can only stare at him. "You're serious."

"As a personal trainer on New Year's Day." His smile is soft. "Be your own boss, and forge your own path."

Just beyond Jackson's shoulder, the lights of New York glitter. It's as familiar a sight as my own face, and yet it never fails to fascinate me. But I want more.

"Do I have to be here in New York?"

"Setting up camp elsewhere makes it trickier, but honey, we'll make it work." Jackson's smile grows sly. "And there's a certain southern city that's ripe for the picking, especially when one has contacts in the area."

CHAPTER 31

Fiona

SITTING ALONE IN THE OFFICE, I let the quiet ground me. All is still, the sounds of Manhattan a distant hum. I glance out the window toward that gray light. I love this city. Love it with all my heart. But I've been happy other places as well.

And I'm not happy here. Was it Elena's fault? Yes and no. Yes, she made my life misery. But it wouldn't have mattered if I truly loved my job.

I know the world is full of Elenas. I'll meet her time and again. But the question is, what do I want to fight for? Felix's approval? No. I have no respect for him anymore.

Turning in my seat, I slide my hand over my portfolio, the leather smooth under my palm. A small smile pulls at my mouth. It's bittersweet. Maybe I'm doing the wrong thing. I don't know. I thought I'd have a better sense of my life's path when I graduated college, that everything would be clear.

I loved college. Loved it. Life was one big party, peppered with frantic bits of studying in between. I didn't take anything too seriously, and that was just fine. I had time. Because, let's be honest, being in college is safe—a bit like high school but without parental supervision.

But now? Nothing is safe. I'm swinging along without a net. And it feels surprisingly good. Exciting. Yeah, I might fuck up spectacularly. I might never find what I'm looking for in terms of a career. But I do have one thing.

Ethan. He's mine. All mine. It's surprising how completely satisfying that is. And terrifying. If I slip and fall with him, down I'll crash, all broken and damaged. But at least I want to fight for him.

I used to think maybe a guy would make me whole. But that's not really the truth. It's up to me to figure my shit out, but Ethan makes the struggles easier to bear. He's my reward when it's all said and done.

And this place? I'm done with it.

There's only one thing left to do.

"Fiona?" As if summoned, Elena walks around the corner and notices me sitting at her desk. "What are you doing here?"

Reflexively, my palm pushes against the cool leather of my portfolio. "I was waiting for you."

Her steps slow, and I wonder if she's on to me. I give her a bright smile, the same one she's given me for months.

"I wanted to ask your opinion on something." My hand is steady as I flip open the case and pull out a stack of drawings.

She hesitates, her hand hovering and a frown on her brow. "Oh?"

"Yeah. I quit this morning, and I'm thinking of using these for my resume."

"You quit?" There's a weird touch of panic in her voice. "But why?"

"I don't know…" I shrug. "I'm not a good fit here. Felix has a certain vision…" I shrug again.

"Oh, but you'll get there!" She insists. "I'll help you."

I want to laugh at the irony. "So help me now. Quitting is a done deal."

And it is. My resignation letter is sitting on his desk. And I'm not about to give him two weeks notice. Shitty? Yes. But he'll survive. Besides, I don't need his reference; I have other plans.

I push the designs toward her.

Finally she picks them up, her eyes scanning the pages. "These are great. I love them."

So did half of Manhattan's elite when they admired Janice Mark's penthouse. Do I feel guilty about showing Elena what are essentially sketches of the apartment? Maybe I should, but I don't.

I rise and snap my case shut. "Can I leave them with you for the weekend? I don't want to be here when Felix gets in." I give an exaggerated pause. "He hasn't seen these, and I don't want him to, okay?"

There. If she steals these designs, her fall is all on her.

She doesn't even blink when she gives me a solemn nod, her hand already spreading over the pages. "I'll guard them well."

I give a nod of my own. But when she begins to pull them toward her, my hand comes down on the sketches with a slap. "You know what? I can't do this. I was going to give you these, knowing they're bad, knowing you'd take them for your own. But I cannot walk out of here and pretend that what you did, what you've been doing, isn't seriously fucked up."

Her face pales as she gapes at me. Then she's flushing dark red, her gaze narrowing. "This again? Jesus, Fiona, you have to stop. It's pathetic. I didn't copy your designs. I just did them better."

"Whatever you have to tell yourself to get through the day, Elena." I lean forward, the urge to hit her so strong that my fingers actually curl into a fist. "That shit you pulled with the curtains? Pretending we'd talked about them? That's not right. And it's just one of many lies you've told. So don't you dare act like what's gone down is all in my head."

"This is business. You do what you have to do to get ahead."

"I don't want to win that way."

An ugly smile curls her lips. "News flash, Fi. You didn't win."

One punch. Surely one punch would be okay?

I keep it together by a thread. "I'm not the only one who knows."

She flinches. "What?"

"Felix knows. He's always known. He just doesn't care because your mother has the contacts he needs." I take a breath. "Which is why I'm quitting. I can't work for a man who has no morals, or alongside a woman who uses people as her personal creative well."

Elena's hands fist as well. "I have talent—"

"That's the tragic thing. You do. Real, honest-to-God talent. But instead of cultivating it, you waste your time stealing other people's ideas."

Her faces scrunches up, going bright red. "I used to think you were nice. You're nothing but a bitter bitch."

I have to laugh. "If being a bitter bitch means I'm no longer your stepping stone, then I gladly accept the title." With that I stand. "Have a nice life, Elena."

"You don't know what it's like," she says suddenly. "The pressure. My mom. Everyone knows who she is—"

"I don't know what that's like?" I gape down at her. "Are you kidding? My dad was a superstar before I was even born. My mom runs her own business. My sister is fast becoming a regular fixture on ESPN. Hell, I'm swimming in a pool of overachieving family members."

"That's not the same. You aren't in those industries." Her fist hits her chest. "I have to make my mark in this business."

I could understand. Hell, I could almost empathize. Almost. "Our parents don't define us, Elena. Our actions do. And yours suck."

She goes from flushed to bone white. "Fuck you, Fiona."

I shake my head, but I'm smiling now. "You already have fucked me. And yet I'm the one walking out with my head up."

And I do, leaving my sketches, Elena, and all her bullshit behind.

There's a faint fishy smell in the air. I don't want to be around when it grows stronger. Because I left a present for Felix too. Operation Rotten Fish, as Ivy likes to call it.

We did the same prank on our bitchy ex-camp counselor one

summer, smearing fish oil under her bunk and on the inside lining of her trunk. Call it a little *fuck you* for dunking my head underwater when I couldn't swim, and for telling Ivy she looked like a flagpole when she clearly had worries about being the tallest, thinnest girl in the camp.

By the end of the summer, the stench had gotten so bad, they had to fumigate. But the trunk remained, and so did the smell.

And though I'd like to believe I've grown up since then, the thought of all the fish oil I smeared under Felix's desk and the tables in Elena's office gives me a surge of satisfaction. Maybe part of us never grows up. I am surprisingly okay with that.

Dex

"DEXTER, MAN, YOU'RE LIVING THE DREAM!" Shockey, one of my linemen, gives me a hearty slap on the shoulder as we walk to our cars.

"Not my dream," I grouse.

The "dream" Shockey refers to is the swarm of women currently dogging my every step. Panties in my locker. Tweets offering blowjobs, hand jobs, rim jobs, don't-know-what-the-fuck-half-of-this-shit-is jobs. Women showing up outside my townhouse. Waiting for me before practice. It isn't necessarily anything new. All players get this. It's the sheer volume and intensity that's driving me nuts.

"Dex." A pretty brunette saunters up. She's wearing my jersey, or what remains of it, because she's cut the sleeves off and tied it into a knot to bare her midriff. "You look tired. I'd love to give you a massage."

And they wait for me after practice. I shake my head, shrug off her grasping hands, and keep walking. Shockey, on the other hand, slows.

"Aw, honey, don't waste your time on him. Why don't you come and keep me company in my post-workout bath?"

The girl eyes me as if she's trying to figure out if I'll cave. I don't break stride. My keys are out, and I'm in my car. Shockey leads the girl away, and I sit back and just breathe in the scent of fine leather.

I don't care who you are, every guy goes a little crazy when he signs and gets his first big check. You'd have to be inhuman not to. Some go too crazy, buying everything in sight and saving nothing for later. Others get a few big-ticket items and then manage to hold back. Me, I bought a townhouse and a car.

My friends expected me to go in for a truck, maybe an SUV. They were wrong. I fell in love with a sweet little blue Aston Martin Vanquish. Drew instantly wanted one too, but Anna convinced him that he lives in New York City and doesn't need a car. Now he has to admire mine from afar. Sucker.

I'm probably too big for this car, but I don't care. I love her. And right now she's my sanctuary. Okay, she will be as soon as I pluck the numerous perfume-scented notes and scraps of panties that are scattered like snow on the windshield. That people have pawed my car makes my eye twitch.

"Fucking hell…" I take a breath, tossing all of the mess onto the passenger side of my car—because I refuse to fucking litter—and slamming the door shut.

This has to end. Soon. I'm not used to being hounded this badly. I don't like it. At all.

Worse? It's not going away. It's growing. I'm the butt of every damn sex joke in sports right now. Maybe I shouldn't be embarrassed. But I am. My skin feels too tight and my stomach leaden. Every time a woman approaches me, seeking out her opportunity, it feels like high school all over again.

Rubbing the back of my neck, I turn the car on and pull out. I revel in the act of driving, losing myself in the purr of the engine and the way the car responds to my slightest touch. I'm home too soon.

Only to find my street blocked by a few reporters and groups of desperate chicks—a few guys too, who assume maybe I'm just not yet out of the closet. I drive around to the back of my property and park in the small carriage garage.

The engine ticks as I sit there, not wanting to get out.

The team's PR department loves this mess. I'm getting attention—not for drugs or violence, but for being virtuous, which is like a hidden gold mine for them. More ticket sales, more press.

Ivy tells me I should just come out and confess to being with Fi. Or she did until I asked point blank, "And do you honestly believe they'll leave her alone?"

No. Ivy couldn't assure me of that.

I think of Fi, the one perfect thing in my life. I want to keep her safe, shelter her from all this ugliness. Just keep her. Forever. She's mine. Mine to protect. And I really don't give a shit if that makes me sound like a caveman. Because, frankly, Fi drags the caveman out of me and sets him front and center.

But the truth of the matter hits me like a hammer to the chest. Right now, with all of this shit going on, Fi doesn't need protection from anything *but* me.

CHAPTER 32

Fiona

I MEET MY DAD AT our favorite Chinese restaurant on Mott Street. He and I have almost nothing in common, but we do share a deep and abiding love for soup dumplings and have thus hunted down the best of the best. Despite my fluttering nerves, I slide into the cracked red pleather booth with a hum of anticipation.

"What's doing, kid?" Dad asks as he sets down his phone. He already has a bottle of Tsingtao beside him and the menu filled out.

I don't protest because he knows what I like here.

Proof of that, the waitress sets down a Tsingtao for me too. She grabs our order and leaves without a word.

"Lots and lots," I answer before taking a long pull of the beer. It's bordering on lukewarm, but then we don't come here for service.

Dad grunts, focuses on his drink. He's a big guy. Not in the muscular way of Dex, but all long limbs and towering height.

I don't know how long he's been in the city. I never ask. Dad's sort of transient, seems to like it that way. When he's here, he stays at some swanky, members-only hotel downtown. Which is fine by me.

I love my dad. I really do. Only, aside from a mutual love of dim sum, we have always been painfully awkward in each other's presence. I don't even know why, but it hangs over us like a cloud of bad gas no one wants to mention. And there is the fact that he's never approved of me.

To that end, I brace my palms on the worn wooden table and take a breath. "I quit my job today."

Dad sets down his beer. "Why?"

"Does it matter?"

"Of course it does. If you were sexually harassed, I'll get up and hunt the bastard down, make him sorry he ever lived. If you were bored, I'll tell you to get over it, pick a better job next time." He shrugs. "The reason makes all the difference."

I am warmed by the idea of my dad kicking someone's ass for me. "I guess you're right." I tell him why I quit, the whole time shaking deep within the pit of my stomach. I hate admitting failure. But I hated my situation more.

While I talk, the waitress sets down a steaming basket of fresh soup dumplings. Dad picks up a delicate, pale little rose of a dumpling. The fragrance of chicken broth and ginger fills the air as he bites and sucks down the soup hidden within.

"So," he says, "lesson learned. Don't trust sudden friends who are after the same position as you."

I have a mouthful of dumpling, so it takes me a moment to swallow and gape up at him. "You're not going to give me shit?"

"Why would I do that?" His brow scrunches up, making the wrinkles in his face deeper.

"Uhm, because you always give me shit about my…" I hold up my fingers to air quote. "'Flighty nature'."

He frowns as if he can't make out what I've just said.

"Oh, come on, Dad," I say, impatient now. "You've called me Flighty Fi since I was a kid."

"Hey, now. It was a nickname. A term of endearment."

"Your terms of endearment suck, Dad."

His frown grows to a scowl. "Okay, fine. I'm sorry you don't like the term. but…" He shrugs. "You are kind of flighty."

Shit. That shouldn't hurt, but it does. Enough that I have to blink to clear my vision.

I push back my plate. "Do you have any clue what it's done to me to know you think that?"

Dad pauses, dumpling halfway to his mouth. Slowly he lets it settle on his plate. "Honey…" He pauses, his mouth twisting as if he's groping for some platitude to placate me.

I want to get out of here, but I can't run away from this.

"It hurts, Dad. You and Mom, you're both so proud of Ivy. But me? I'm the sad case that keeps letting you down."

For a sick moment, I really do empathize with fuck-face Elena. Which makes my feelings sting that much more. I sure as shit do not want to find common ground with her.

Dad tosses his chopsticks onto the table where they rattle around. "You do not let us down. You're just… You have so much potential. We want to see it come to fruition." He leans forward, the old leather booth creaking beneath him. "Fiona, you're my kid. Every father wants to see his kid settled. Or he ought to, anyway."

A shaking breath gurgles in my throat. "Wanting to see me settled and being dubious of my ability to lead my life are two separate things. I know I'm not like Ivy—"

"No," he cuts in. "You're like me."

"You?"

"Don't look so horrified," he says dryly.

"It's just… You're successful, Dad. People aspire to be like you."

I swear he flushes. He doesn't meet my eye as he rubs the back of his head. "I'm a lucky bastard who happened to be tall and coordinated enough to play the game. The agent gig, well…" He shrugs again, grabbing his chopsticks to poke at a dumpling. "I knew the business by then so I took an opportunity."

I can't believe he's downplaying what he is.

"You are, though," he goes on quietly. "Like me. I too was always searching for something to inspire me, something to get excited about."

I gape. I know I do. Because how the fuck did he know that about me? How, when I thought he never paid any attention. My dad keeps talking.

"My problem is, I did that by screwing around on your mom. By drinking and partying too much. You?" He meets my eyes, though I can tell it's hard for him by the way he winces. "You're more constructive. You're looking for meaning in life. I'm proud of you for that, Fi. Always have been."

"Dad…" A watery laugh escapes me. "Shit, you're going to make me choke up over dumplings."

"Never waste good dumplings, Fiona."

I laugh again, and he gives me a tight smile. Being easy and joking with my dad is a new thing. It occurs to me that maybe he's shy too. I reach over and nudge his bony wrist with my fist. "I'm proud of you too, Dad."

"Remember the dumpling," he says, though he's flushed again. "And never forget this. As much as I want your respect, you never, ever live your life to make someone else happy. You got me?"

He stares me down, he expression as earnest as I've seen it. Lump in my throat, I nod. He nods too.

We eat in silence for a while, ordering a plate of steamed pork buns. Around us, Chinese New Yorkers chatter and slurp up dumplings with a deftness that makes me and Dad look like bumbling amateurs. At the front-window counter, an old guy makes stunning little bundles of food art, occasionally yelling in Mandarin to the hostess by the register.

I soak it in, relish my meal. Four years I spent in the South, playing the part of college party girl. It was fun, but here in New York? I feel at home. I love this city. It hums through my veins and makes my heart beat. And I'm going to leave it. Because I want something more.

I'm about to tell my dad this when he speaks again.

"I'm…ah…seeing someone." Okay, he's definitely pink now. "Genevieve. She does PR for the Hawks."

Just like that, I'm grinning. "It must be serious."

Dad tilts his head in acknowledgement before slurping down a soup dumpling. "She moved into the house," he says after a moment.

"Good. I don't like the idea of you rattling around in that big place alone. Just, please tell me she isn't my age."

Dad rolls his eyes. "Nice, Fi. And you accuse me of giving you shit."

"Sorry." It was a low blow.

"She's only five years younger than me. Is that acceptable?" He's not smiling, but I can tell he wants to.

"Yeah. Of course. I was being a shit."

"Wouldn't be my daughter if you weren't."

It's my turn to duck my head in embarrassment.

"So what are you going to do next?" Dad asks.

"Dex."

Dad rears back. "What?"

"Shit. No. I mean…" I bite on my lower lip before getting it over with. "I'm seeing someone too. Ethan Dexter." Worst segue ever, even if it was probably correct. I really can't wait to do him again. And again. Shit. I'm blushing now.

Dad stares at me for a long moment, his nostrils slightly pinched, then grunts. "Dexter, eh? I kind of thought you'd fall for a chef or some sort of arty type—"

"Thanks, Dad," I say, not bothering to clarify that Dex actually is arty.

Dad doesn't pause. "But he's a good choice."

I blink. "Really? You think so?"

"Why not? You like him, don't you?"

"Of course."

"He's steady, quiet, honest." Dad rubs a hand over his face. "Not too thrilled about the idea of you 'doing' him, but we'll just pretend that was never mentioned."

I bury my head in my hands. "I know. God, I suck at basic conversation with you."

Dad laughs. "No shit."

"Can we move along now?" I ask from the safety of my hands.

"Sure." He falls silent, and I lift my head to find him studying me. "So is he the real deal?"

I'm the one who feels shy now. "Yeah, dad. He really is. So much so that I'm going to claim him."

I cringe again. I meant it figuratively, but it probably isn't something my dad wants to hear. I'm better off stuffing my mouth with dumplings and not talking again.

Fortunately Dad just nods. "One less thing."

I don't know if he's right, because the fact is, there are things I need to tell Dex too, and I have no idea how he's going to take them.

CHAPTER 33

FearTheBeard: Can we Skype?

CherryBomb: On it like a bonnet.

FearTheBeard: Gonna take that as a yes.

CherryBomb: :-*

I CONFESS, I FIX MY HAIR and put on some lip gloss and mascara before I Skype with Dex. Okay, I change my top too. No way am I wearing my frumpy, knee-length t-shirt with *Princess on the Streets, Ogre in the Sheets* across the front. Thank you, Gray, for yet another Fiona-themed birthday gift.

Instead, I wear a casual white tank and leave the bra off. If I can't see Dex every day, I have to make the times we do connect count.

A flutter of anticipation goes through me as I settle down on my bed, my laptop propped on a pillow. Seeing him this way is a treat and a torture. No matter how good it is to talk to Dex, when it's all done, I close my laptop alone.

Even so, I grin like a loon as soon as his face comes into view. Damn, he's fine. Tanned from practicing in the Southern sun, gold highlights streaked through his brown hair. Dex will never be a pretty boy; his features are too strong, his body too big and built. His eyes, however, are devastating and beautiful—and as always, they shine when he sees me. The way he looks at me is addicting. It's everything.

My voice is breathless. "Hey, Big Guy."

The corner of his lush mouth lifts. "Hey, Cherry." His voice is tired and strained, and it hurts not to be with him.

"How are things?" I know full well he's being hounded by the press, stalked by women—the idea of which I hate enough to gnash my teeth. I ask because I want him to unload his problems on me.

He swallows visibly, and his entire body seems to deflate. "Not great, Fi." Slowly he lifts his head, as if it weighs a ton. "My privacy is nil at the moment."

"Baby." I can't help but reach out and touch the edge of my screen, wanting to stroke the soft-rough edge of his jaw instead. "It'll get better."

His nod is vague, his gaze sliding away.

"Hey," I lean in. "I've got loads to tell you."

Again he nods, but it's clear he isn't listening. Then he takes a breath and his shoulders draw back, when he looks directly at the screen, his eyes are wide open and anguished. "Fi...I don't..." His breath hitches. "I don't think we should see each other for a while."

My ears begin to ring as the blood drains from my face, leaving it numb. "What?"

Dex leans forward, his eyes rimmed in red. "They're on me all the time."

"So let's just tell them!" My voice is too high, too frantic. But then again, so is my heart. I can't breathe properly. "Tell them about me and be done with it."

"No." His chin rises. "No, Fi. I told you before, that's not going to happen."

"Why? Because you're protecting me? That's bullshit, Ethan."

A red flush washes over his cheeks. "Look me in the eye and tell me they won't rip you apart. Tell me, Fi, because I know for a fact they will. And so do you."

"So maybe they will." God, my chest hurts. I can't find my breath. "I'll get over it."

But Dex is shaking his head. "I won't. I promised you normalcy. Or as close as I could make it. I won't pull you into this mess."

"So…" I choke back a sob. "So you'd rather dump me?"

He leans close enough that I see his eyes glaze over. "No. Cherry… I just figure we let this settle down for a while, not visit each other until—"

"We barely see each other as it is. What's the point, if we have even less than this?" I have to blink to keep from tearing up. I won't. I will not beg. "Please, Ethan. Don't do this."

"I have to," he rasps. "It's so fucking ugly here, Fi."

My breath hitches. "So that's it? You're just going to push me aside?"

He blanches. "Please don't think of it like that. I'm trying to protect you, Cherry. Even if that means from myself."

"I don't need you to protect me, Ethan. I need you to want me."

"I do want you. You're the most important person in my life."

An ugly sound leaves me. "You've got a funny way of showing it, Dexter."

"You are," he says with feeling, his cheeks flushing dark. "You are everything to me."

"Then don't push me away!"

He sits back in his chair with an audible thud. When his gaze comes back to me, it's filled with pain. "I know you don't believe me, Fiona. But there is no one, *no one*, I care about more than you. I cannot let these fucking vultures go at you. Do you get that? I. Can't. Do. It."

A single tear breaks free from his eye. He doesn't wipe it away but looks at me, pleading.

And suddenly, I'm so angry I can't speak. My nails dig into my thighs as I breathe through my rage.

"Fi." Dex's voice comes from a distance. "Fi?"

My lips press together as I swallow down a scream. Finally I look at him, but all I see is the red haze of my own frustration. "I can't talk to you right now."

Dully he nods. "Okay. I understand. I'll call you later."

And my rage grows.

"Don't…" I suck in a scream. "Don't call me. Don't text. Just…don't."

I slam the lid on my computer and shut off my phone. For a long time, I lie on my bed, stare blindly up at the ceiling, and think.

CHAPTER 34

Dex

ANOTHER DAY. ANOTHER PRACTICE. I don't give a shit about anything. And it shows. My offensive line coach hands me my ass after my shitty footwork and slow reaction time letting yet another defensive end get to my QB.

If it was a game, I'd be riding the bench. As it is, I'm relegated to the sidelines to run ladder drills. I'm thankful for it. Practicing complicated footwork keeps my mind occupied, my body moving. I keep at it until I'm the only one left on the field. Push myself until my body feels like warm Jell-O.

Because there's a void threatening to open up and consume me if I stop to think.

Fi.

I fucked up. I shouldn't have told her all that on Skype like some dumb asshole. I hurt her instead of convincing her it was the safest thing to do for now. I should've waited, told her in person when I could hold her, show her I was only thinking about her happiness.

Only that's all bullshit. I smashed her happiness just as effectively as if I'd taken a fist to her face. I saw her smiling face crumple with pain. I did that. To her. To my girl.

And it guts me. I have to make it right. Only I'm afraid I've done permanent damage.

A groan leaves me as I lean against the shower stall after practice, the water pummeling my skull. I've always wanted a girlfriend. Someone who was mine and mine alone. But the truth is, I have no fucking clue what to do when it comes to relationships.

When I finally trudge out of the showers, the locker room is almost empty, just a few guys left getting dressed, and none of them paying attention to me. Devon, a safety, is bitching about losing his favorite Grinch socks and how it's affecting his mojo. Ryder is explaining to Morgan how to make a proper bread pudding, which apparently involves a dozen eggs and a shitload of cream.

I step away when he starts waxing poetic about types of bread to use.

I don't notice Finn until he gives me a slap on the shoulder. "What's doin', Big D? You played like shit today."

"Master at stating the obvious, aren't you?"

He just grins like a smarmy dick. "So it was obvious to you too? Good. For a second there, I wondered if you had your head totally up your ass."

I rub a towel over my hair and toss it down. I'm tempted to tell him to fuck off, but he's stating the truth, and something worse comes out instead. "Are all men clueless when it comes to handling women? Or am I just gifted at being a spectacular fuckup?"

Finn blinks as if I've told him I have VD. I think I might be wincing too; I do not need the entire locker room knowing my business.

"Well, hell," he says finally. "I don't know. Isn't it our job to fuck up?"

From across the way, Ryder snorts. "First of all, you never 'handle' a woman. She handles you. Your job—" He points at the both of us. "—is to hold on tight, go along for the ride, and pray you don't fuck it up."

"What makes you an expert?" Finn asks. "Last time I checked, you haven't been with the same girl for more than one night for like…ever."

"Four sisters, asshole," Ryder answers as he looks in the little mirror he has attached to his cubby. He runs his hand through his damp hair. "And raised by my mom. I know women." He catches my eye in the mirror. "What did you do?"

Running my fingers through my beard, I debate telling him, but I've already said too much to back out now. "I told Fi we should keep things on the down-low until all of this bullshit blows over."

Every guy in the locker room groans as one. Fuck, I should've known they'd be eavesdropping. Nosy bastards.

"Dude," says Ryder. "Were you aiming for the most bonehead thing to say? Because you fucking nailed it."

"Yeah," says Jones, a defensive end who's pulling on his sweats. "The only thing worse would be if you pulled out the 'it's not you' line."

"I told her it wasn't—"

Another round of groans, even more pained, rumbles though the locker room.

"Bad play, man."

"Way to go, knucklehead."

"Send her flowers."

"Hell, no. That's fucking cliché. Stand outside her window and hold up one of those old time boom boxes."

"As she calls the cops on your ass."

I roll my eyes at them. "Next thing you'll tell me is that you're all single by choice."

I don't know if they get the movie reference, but someone chucks a sweaty sock at me. I think it's Ryder but can't be sure. I glare around the room, as the horrible sinking feeling within grows worse.

"Dex," Finn drawls with a shake of his head. "You're the guy we expect to have all the answers. What the fuck, man?"

With a grunt, I let my forehead slam against the edge of my locker.

The pain feels good. "I don't know." He's right, I'm the one they come to for advice, not some moron who gets it all wrong.

Life lesson that sucks? Giving advice is way easier than living your own life.

Life lesson that sucks worse? Realizing this after you've severely fucked up.

"I just want to protect her." It comes out as feeble as it sounds. And I'm really not talking to the guys anyway. I *was* protecting Fi, but I was also protecting myself. Because I'm embarrassed. This whole situation makes me feel like I'm the butt of a joke, something I've tried to avoid my whole life. And I don't want Fi to see that up close and personal. I don't want her to see me as something less than.

But now I've gone and hurt her.

A nudge at my shoulder has me lifting my head. Finn's expression is neutral. "Ry and I are going out for crawfish and oysters by the lakefront. Come on out with us. Have a beer and forget all this media shit for a while."

Rubbing the back of my neck, I try to perk up, at least give the semblance of a guy who isn't losing it. "Thanks. Maybe next time."

Right now, I've got an airline ticket to buy and a shit-ton of groveling to plan.

It's dark by the time I get home.

I haul my ass upstairs. My left knee throbs and my back feels like a hot iron rod has been shoved up my spine. That's just the top of my list of various aches and pains. I'm twenty-four years old and am hobbling like a senior citizen on his way to a four o'clock dinner. *Old before my time*, I think as I open my front door, toss my keys on the side table, and step into an empty house.

For one dark second, loneliness swamps me and I can't breathe. It takes my air and weighs down my chest. I stare at the floor as my hand fumbles to find my phone in my pocket.

I need to hear Fi's voice. Now. God, I need to see and touch her so badly I grind my teeth with want. But her voice will have to do.

Then it hits me, a certain warmth, the scent of coffee, and the underlying fragrance of fresh flowers. I feel her. Here.

Fi is here.

My bag hits the floor with a thud, and I practically run into the main room. She's pouring herself a cup of coffee, her hair gleaming pale gold under the kitchen light. She looks up at my arrival, a nervous smile drawing tight over her delicate features. "Hey."

I stop on the other side of the massive marble-covered island, pressing my hands against the cold slab to ground me. "Tell me you're really here."

Her smile grows warmer, more real. "You think you're hallucinating, Big Guy?"

"Could be. I dream about this a lot." *Every fucking day.*

She sets the cup down with a clink of porcelain and rounds the island. I watch her approach, her hips swaying beneath one of those flirty little skirts she favors. My chest contracts when her slim hands slide up, drawing little shivers in her wake. Her thumb run over the edge of my beard, then along my lower lip. It's all I can do not to bite that thumb, suck it into my mouth.

"Feel real enough to you?" Her voice is husky.

I breathe in the scent of Fi, lean into her. "Not sure. I think I need more." I need everything. All of her.

She knows this. With a gentle tug, she pulls me down to her. I go willingly. Her sweet, soft mouth finds mine, and everything within me sighs with relief.

I don't know how long I kiss her, but it isn't long enough. Too soon, she's pulling back, but she keeps her arms around my neck, and I hold her close. It's only then that I realize her body is tense, her gaze hesitant.

"I've decided," she says. "You don't get to choose our fate without consulting me."

"Agreed."

My instant answer seems to give her pause, her head cocking back as if she doesn't understand. Her voice comes out unsteady but strong. "Good. You pissed me off, Ethan."

"I know." I should be more contrite, but I'm so fucking happy she's here. I can't keep back my smile, can't stop from touching her cheek.

She bats my hand away. "I'm serious. You…you hurt me. If you don't want me, just say it now. Don't hide behind some ridiculous claim of trying to protect me, because—"

I cup her smooth cheek and kiss her. Fi's mouth moves against mine, shaping words—probably trying to tell me off. I keep kissing her soft and slow until she relaxes with a sigh. My fingers thread through her hair as I look down at her.

"You're right. I was a dumbass. I'm sorry." I nuzzle her cheek. "I was on my way to see you. To apologize." *To beg for another chance.*

Her nose wrinkles in a dubious look. I kiss the tip of it, but she doesn't relent. "I mean, how could you do that? And over Skype, Ethan!"

"I'm an asshole." I keep my eyes steady on hers. "I was embarrassed, Fi. I didn't want you to see me like this."

Her voice is soft. "Like what?"

My skin goes uncomfortably tight, and my insides roll like there's a lead weight falling through me. But I owe her the words. "All these women coming after me for the money. With pity in their eyes and dollar signs dancing in their heads."

She's quiet for a second. "I'm glad they don't know what they're missing," she says low and fierce. "It means I have you all to myself."

Closing my eyes, I press my forehead against the top of her head. "No one else ever stood a chance against you, Cherry." Holding her close eases all the tight spaces inside me. "I panicked, and it hurt you. You have no idea how sorry I am for that."

"Okay, then." Her hand smoothes down my shirt. "I'm glad we had this talk."

I can't help giving her another quick kiss. It feels too good, even if I'm in the doghouse. "Can we get to the make-up sex now?" I ask, wanting to make her laugh. "I've heard good things."

Thankfully, Fi laughs and gives my pec a little punch. "Yeah, I bet." Her smile falls fast. "I need to tell you something first."

Honestly, she could tell me she robbed a bank, and I'd say fine by me. But I keep my expression neutral, trying manfully not to grin like a fool. She's here. She's still mine. That's all that matters.

"All right. Tell me what you did, Cherry."

As soon as she gets whatever it is off her chest, I'm going to fuck her until my dick gives out on me.

CHAPTER 35

Fiona

Ethan is clearly fighting a smug grin, looking as though he's plotting all sorts of nefarious ways to fuck me. Which would be hot if I wasn't so nervous that I might throw up at any second.

Even so, I take the moment to soak him in. God, he feels good. Solid and warm. I'm dying to stick my nose in the center of his chest and just breathe. The ever-thickening bulge growing in his sweats is distracting and delicious. I've missed his gorgeous cock. Without thinking, I press myself against it. He grunts, his hold on me tightening.

But I can't do this when he's touching me. Giving his meaty biceps a kiss, I step out of his embrace. Ethan frowns, but he lets me go.

"All right," he says, running a hand through his hair, sending strands flowing around his face. "Now you're starting to freak me out. What's going on, Fi?"

I love that he doesn't even ask why I'm here, just why I'm worried. I hold on to that fact as I trace a vein in the white marble countertop. "I quit my job."

I love the way he can smile with just his eyes. And I love the tenderness I see in them now.

His big palm comes to rest near mine. "You did something you were afraid of but needed to do. I'm proud of you, Fiona."

A shaky breath flows out of me. "Thanks. I'm proud of me too. It feels good. I'm going to start a furniture-making business, selling my work through my friends' store in New York. And then maybe do a little design consulting on my own."

Ethan blinks, his stoic features never moving, and I can tell he's trying to figure out why I'm freaked if I'm happy. Because I am seriously about to freak out. A slow shake starts in my belly and radiates outward as I search for words.

He sees it and immediately steps closer, his warm, calloused hands rubbing over my upper arms. "Cherry…"

"I know everything is up in the air. I just quit. We haven't been together long. But I just…I don't know. Thing is," I babble on, "I thought I'd visit you for a while. I brought some things and maybe—"

"Stay," he cuts in, his fingers gripping my arm as if he's going to physically hold me here. And then that isn't enough for him because he sweeps me off my feet in that effortless way of his.

I give a little yelp of surprise and wrap my arms around his neck as he carries me into the living room in three long strides. I'm on the couch in his lap the next moment.

His eyes are wide and brilliant as he strokes my cheeks. "Stay with me."

"Well," I say, squeezing the back of his neck. "That was the plan. I want you for more than a sad little weekend. A month or so would be much better."

His lush mouth tilts on a smile, but it doesn't fully bloom. He stares into my eyes, his expression almost shy. "No. Not a month, Cherry." The tip of his thumb touches my lower lip. I don't miss the way he trembles too. "Live with me. Here. Make a life with me."

His words strike us both mute. Ethan looks as if he can't really believe he made the offer. Me? I can't believe it either.

His thighs shift and harden beneath me, and I realize he's holding his breath. Maybe I am too, because I exhale on a long, ragged sigh.

"You mean that?" I whisper.

His throat works on a swallow. "Wouldn't have said it if I didn't."

"Ethan…" I can't speak. My fingers thread through his hair, holding on. This is too much, and yet all I want to do is sink into him, rest against his strength for a good, long while. Never leave his side. "We just started going out. We've only been together a handful of times."

All true and yet, even as I say it, I know I want this. I want to be with him.

"Doesn't change the way I feel," he says. "I'm miserable without you. I need you, Fi."

A little sob bubbles up, and my voice breaks. "I need you too, Ethan."

It feels like we're saying something else. But it doesn't matter because he's kissing me, deep and searching, a little bit frantic as if he's trying to convince himself this is real. And I'm kissing him back, every bit as desperate.

Ethan holds my head, angling his mouth so he can delve deeper, and, God, he tastes good—feels good.

Gently he touches my check, his fingers tracing it. "How is it," he whispers, "that I was just fine being alone until you kissed me in that club?"

I swallow hard, my skin flushed with heat. A lump in my throat makes my voice thick. "I don't know." But it's the same for me. One beard dare, and I was lost.

His fingers run down the side of my throat, then up again. "You've ruined me, Fiona. I'm not sure I know how to live without you anymore."

Before I can answer, he pulls off my shirt. My bra follows as he kisses his way along my neck. His fingers fumble with the zipper of my skirt.

"Take off your shirt first," I tell him, needing to see him too.

He doesn't hesitate, doesn't look away from me, just reaches back and hauls his shirt over his head. All those hard-earned muscles shift and bunch beneath his smooth skin as he flings the shirt away.

Not one to go by half measures, he gently sets me aside and stands to push his sweats down, leaving him gloriously naked, that thick, long cock of his straight and proud and hard, the silver piercings winking in the light.

While I stare, Ethan steps back to look at me, his brow raised in expectation. Waiting.

I rise to face him. The zipper makes a loud hiss as I lower it. I shift my hips, shimmying, and the fabric slithers along my skin, my skirt falling at my feet.

For a long moment, he stares at me, his chest lifting and falling with each breath he takes, his cock quivering, as if impatient. Then he sinks to his knees. I expect a kiss, his mouth exploring my body. But he doesn't do any of that.

Ethan Dexter wraps his arms around my waist and presses his cheek between my breasts. He hugs me close and sighs with his entire body. "I love you."

My breath hitches with an audible sound, and he glances up, his hazel eyes solemn and intent. "I do. So fucking much. Every hour of every day. Don't ever think otherwise."

Relief and happiness are a liquid warmth running through me. My hands tunnel through his silky hair and hold him secure against me. "I love you too, Ethan."

A shudder wracks his body, and he lets go of a long breath. His arms squeeze me tighter. When he speaks, it's a broken rasp, as if he's come to the end of a long journey. "Good. Because I'm not letting you go again, Fi."

I can't help but smile. "We're really doing this? Living together?"

He smiles too, his beard tickling my skin. "Fuck yeah, we are."

For the rest of the night, it's just Ethan and me, every touch an affirmation of all that we've been missing, of all we'll have from this day on.

Living together? We got this. After all, what's the worst that can happen?

CHAPTER 36

Fiona

HAVING NEVER LIVED WITH SOMEONE, I worry how moving in with Ethan will be. Awkward? Stifling? Will we crash and burn?

Because, no matter how much I want Ethan, we've only physically been together a handful of times.

But he doesn't give me time to worry. Every night he's in town and off early, we go out and explore New Orleans—at a jazz club, where I cajole and entice Ethan to dance, or at a restaurant so good, I'm hard pressed not to moan with every bite. I'm a New Yorker at heart, so I'm used to good food. But New Orleans could give New York a run for its money.

We don't hide being together. And a few pictures of us have popped up, along with speculation about Ethan's new girlfriend. But the virgin witch hunt remains. Mainly because Ethan stubbornly refuses to talk about me—even if to confirm or deny a sexual relationship.

"It's none of their fucking business," he grumps. In public, he's more restrained and simply says, "Unless it's about football, no comment."

Despite that ugliness, I'm happy. There are so many things I come to anticipate and love, namely the look on Ethan's face every time he walks through the front door, his expression lit with happiness, his eyes hot with need.

Because the second he's home, he's backing me up against the wall, or bending me over the arm of the couch, fucking me like he's making up for years of lost time.

I can't keep my hands off him either. I catch him doing sit-ups and jump astride his hips before he does another crunch. His chuckle dies in a strangled groan when I kiss and lick my way over his hard body, tugging his shorts down to pull out that glorious, thick cock I crave.

Ethan's often away. It isn't great. But it doesn't hurt the way I thought it would. Because I know that on the nights he is home, we'll fall into his massive bed to cuddle under the covers and talk about anything and everything until a touch or a look triggers the need we have for each other and we come together like a conflagration, burning hot and bright. Only when we're completely worn out will we fall asleep.

More importantly, I know I'm loved. And I love him. Having that security in my life is a joy I only now realize I'd been searching for all along.

I grow inordinately giddy at the sight of Ethan's big shoes—which include a ridiculous amount of sneakers—lumped together with mine, of my body washes and hair products crowding out his lone shampoo and soap.

I get to talk to Ethan's parents, an experience I'd feared would be awkward as fuck, given the circumstances. But they're warm, nice, normal. Ethan's dad thanks me for making his son happy. Ethan's mom assures me her son has impeccable taste, so if he likes me, she will too. I'm left blushing and stammering that, yes, I'd love to meet them when they return to California.

Ethan's little brother is a slightly tougher judge. He asks me if I like Minecraft. When I confess to having had an Enderman figurine on my desk in college, I'm deemed cool.

But I fall irrevocably head over heels for Ethan when he takes my hand one sunny morning and asks me to come out to his studio. I've been there before. It's a bright, airy space. His older work hangs on the walls or sits stacked in the corner. A few pieces are half-done and on easels, waiting for completion.

Ethan specializes in photorealism. He uses lush colors and goes for close-up studies. Most of his subjects are football related, though he's done a few people as well. He's been working on one of Drew, dressed in his uniform, helmet on the ground, his hands low on his narrow hips as he looks off in the distance.

"Anna asked me to do that one," Ethan told me. "It's going to be a wedding present. Though I seriously think she'll enjoy it more than Drew will."

I think he's right.

Today he walks me out to the studio, a secretive smile on his lips.

"Have you finished your portrait?" I ask, though I don't know when he'd have found the time. We've been in each other's pockets this past month.

He shakes his head. "Nope."

"Why do you look so smug?"

His grin grows. "You'll see."

"Tell me." I tug on his hand.

"No."

"Tell me, tell me, tell me." I tug again, wiggling his arm as I smile up at him.

He laughs and swings me up in his arms. "Little pest. So impatient." He kisses my nose and carries me up the stairs. The sharp scents of paint and turpentine mix with the warmer scent of pine and fill my nose as he opens the door.

Ethan sets me down, and I turn around only to gasp, my hand flying to my lips.

The canvases and easels are gone. In their place is a woodworker's fantasy: circular saws, band saws, table saws, routers and lathes, miters, drills, joiners… Everything I need to make furniture.

"I thought maybe you could get started sooner than later," he says, mirroring my thoughts.

"Oh, yes," I murmur, walking around, taking it all in.

Work tables, a dust vacuum, stacks of different types of lumber. Emotion grabs me by the throat as I turn back to Ethan, who leans against the doorway, hands in pockets, a curious, almost anxious expression on his handsome face.

"Where's your painting stuff?" I croak out.

"Moved it to the guest house," he says with a shrug. "I don't need all this room, anyway."

I swallow convulsively. "How—when?"

He pushes off from the doorway. "Found a guy who was retiring. Bought up the whole lot. Had some guys deliver it yesterday." He looks around and then back at me. "You like it?"

"Like it?" A laugh gurgles in my throat. "I love it. I love you."

Without another word, I launch myself at him, and he catches me, holding me secure as I wrap my legs around his waist and kiss his neck. "Thank you, Ethan. It's the best surprise ever."

He kisses the tip of my nose, before nipping it. "I love you too. Happy birthday, Cherry."

His words bring me up short. "How did you know?"

Ethan gives me an exasperated look. "Ivy wouldn't go to our last division championship game because it was your birthday. That was two years ago today."

"You remember that from two years ago?"

"You think I've forgotten a single thing about you?" With a sigh, he leans his forehead against mine. "What I want to know is why you didn't tell me it was your birthday."

My gaze skitters away as I shrug. "I don't know. I'm just not used to waving my own flag about stuff like that."

With a firm but gentle grip, he turns my face back to meet his. I find it totally hot that he can hold me up with one arm. His expression is soft. "You don't have to wave your own flag anymore, Fi. That's my job now. My privilege."

My lips wobble on a smile. "Okay."

He kisses me, lips to lips, then pulls back. "My birthday is June second, by the way."

I laugh and wrap my arms around his neck, bringing myself closer. "Duly noted. Expect furniture. Maybe a console for that monolith you call a TV."

Ethan gives my ass a squeeze, looking smug once again. "Sounds perfect."

Perfect. For the first time in my life, everything *is* perfect.

Dex

ARIZONA IS…FUCKING DRY. I suck down Gatorade as I get into the elevator and push the button for my floor, my suite. Yeah, I upgraded to a suite with the hope that Fi would come with me. But she informed me last night that she was "riding the crimson wave" and there was no way she would be traveling. It took me a moment to figure out what a crimson wave was, then I promptly blocked the image from my mind. Or tried to. Some things can't be unimagined, unfortunately.

And yet I love that she was comfortable enough to tell me so bluntly. I love having bras hanging to dry in my laundry closet, the multiple bottles of shampoo, conditioners, and body wash—sweet Jesus, girls have a lot of fucking body washes—cluttering up my shower. Hell, I even love the boxes of tampons invading the sink cabinet.

And I don't give a shit if that makes me weird. Because all of it affirms that Fi is living with me. That she's claimed my home and me.

So when she looked at me yesterday with pained eyes, I manned up, asked for a list of what she needed, and went to the store to buy her brownies, Midol, and, yes, more tampons and pads—what the fuck "wings" are I don't really want to know.

I did it without one word of complaint, and then I left for my game, a man content.

Now I'm going to sleep and looking forward to getting back home. For the first time in what feels like forever, I think of my townhouse as home, and ain't that a beautiful thing?

I'm smiling as I pull out my phone and check my messages while the elevator takes me up to my floor.

> **CherryBomb:** I ended up working on a piece today. Tired now so I'm going to sleep. Good game, baby. You were great! See you soon. XOXO

I still can't believe she watches my games. Fi has never hidden her dislike of football. Now she not only watches, but she sleeps in my jersey—when I don't strip it off her.

I let myself into my room and am greeted with light instead of darkness. Did the maids turn on the lights? For some reason, the little hairs at the back of my neck rise.

I hear a noise, and I realize I'm not alone.

Instantly, every muscle tenses, my senses going on high alert. Then I see the bra on the floor. Lacy and pale purple, it lays like a heap of discarded flower petals, and my heart stops. I've seen a bra like that before.

Fi? Is she here? Was she trying to surprise me? I set my phone down on the table and move across the room toward the bedroom door. A tiny pair of underwear dangles from the door knob.

I cross the small living room in two steps, a smile blooming.

The smile dies a swift death when I reach the bedroom.

"What the fuck?" My shout echoes through the suite.

The naked girl in my bed winces but puts on a brave face. "Hey there. I…ah…"

"How the fuck did you get in here?"

I'm trying real hard not to shout again or lose my shit; I'm a big dude, and there's a very naked chick alone with me. I'm aware of her vulnerability and her sheer stupidity, even if she isn't. I could be into beating women for all she knows.

And I'm also aware that she could spin this any way she wanted. Suddenly I'm afraid of her. Of what she represents.

I back up, my shoulders hitting the wall. "You need to get out. Now."

The girl rises to her knees, her tits pointing straight at me. The sight does nothing but send a rush of frustrated outrage through my chest.

"But, Dex, honey, it's okay. I want to be here! I want help you."

I laugh without humor. "I don't think you're getting it. I don't want you here, and the only way you can help is to get dressed and go."

"I'll split the money with you," she says, parting her thighs.

I look over her head. "I'm going to go out on a limb and suggest that earning money on your back will eventually eat at your soul."

"Are you calling me a whore?" she screeches.

Oh, I want to laugh. I really do. Only I want to punch the wall more. I take a breath and relax my fists. "Out. Before I call the police."

I hear her huff, and she launches off the bed, gathering her clothes.

"Are you gay? Is that it?"

And there it is, the cheap shot. I don't even answer. When she stomps past, I look down. Thankfully she's dressed—if you call the band of pink spandex that barely stretches over her ass a dress. "Come anywhere near me again, and I will call the cops."

Her face flushes red. "I wouldn't fuck you now if you begged me on your knees, asshole."

Right. That's why she's hovering in front of me, her eyes wild and desperate. I gesture to the door, and she snarls again before rushing off.

The slam of the suite door tells me I'm alone.

I want to sink into my bed and sleep. But I'm not touching it now. Instead, I reach for the phone and prepare to hand hotel security their ass.

It isn't until I'm in a new suite—comped after profuse apologies from the management—and crawling under fresh sheets, ready to drift off, that my eyes snap open with dread as I realize something. The little witch stole my phone.

CHAPTER 37

Fiona

EXPECT THE UNEXPECTED HAS GOT to be the most annoying phrase ever. I mean, if you're expecting it, how can it possibly be unexpected? And yet that stupid phrase runs like a taunt through my head when in the kitchen for my morning coffee, I open my browser—as I always do—and see my own face smiling back at me.

It's weird. I stand there looking at myself, the same face I see every day in the mirror, but I can't quite accept that it's me. Why is a picture of me front and center in my Twitter feed? And then the shape of me takes more meaning. It's not just my face. Not by a long shot.

Hot prickles of sheer horror explode over my face, my arms, my entire body. Bile surges up my throat as I stare at the picture—multiple images of the same picture—that's been splashed all over social media.

It's me, managing to grin as my tongue reaches out to flick a familiar, pierced nipple. Jesus. It's the picture I took in bed with Dex, me in all my naked glory draped over his chest as I playfully lick his nipple. We'd been laughing as we took the selfie. Having fun.

"Here's one for my wallet."

"Shit," I whisper now, though there's no one here to hear it. "Shit."

Because somehow that picture, complete with my bare tits pointing straight at the camera, is now out in the world.

I DON'T WANT TO EXIST ANYMORE. Not die, just stop existing. Ugliness is a taint that seeps through my skin, as heavy and itchy as a hair blanket. It claws at my chest, digging deeper, tugging on the center of my sternum.

Curling in on myself doesn't help. It doesn't matter how tight a ball I squeeze my body into, it still feels violated, on display.

Another picture released: the one I sent to Ethan of me wearing nothing but a bra. I'd posed like a pinup girl, teased him about not giving me my undies back. I'd felt safe giving that pic to Ethan, felt sexy and wanted. Not so much now.

So much ugliness. Endless tweets, Facebook messages, Instagram messages—telling me I'm a whore, asking if I'd like to fuck, picking apart my body, leering at it. I tried not to look, but it was nearly impossible to hide from, not when a tidal wave of disgusting hate and judgment washed over me in one swoop.

I've turned off my phone and crawled into a corner in the bedroom. I know I should talk to Dex at least. But I can't. I can't move.

Vaguely, I hear the front door of open. Everything in me tenses.

Dex is in Arizona. Even if he managed to get the first plane out, I doubt he'd be here by now. Dex I can handle. I think. I don't know for certain because the picture was definitely from his phone. How did it get out? I'm afraid if I ask him, I'll rage. I know he didn't do it. But still. How?

Swift footsteps give a dull echo as someone strides across the living room downstairs. *Don't let it be Dad. Not him.* Just the thought of my parents seeing those pictures makes me want to throw up. And I know Dad will see. It's as inevitable as the sun setting. Dad shouldn't have the code to Dex's house, but who knows with that man. For all I know, he might kick the door in.

"Fi? Fi, honey?" Ivy's voice.

I turn away, facing the wall. Maybe she won't notice me.

But then the bedroom door opens, and her tall, slim form is silhouetted in the ambient light. That's all it takes for sobs to break free.

"Oh, Fi." Ivy is instantly by my side.

Her strong arms pull me close as I cry, clinging to her like a raft.

"Honey." She pets me, murmuring nonsense words the way our mom did when we were little.

I don't know how long I cry. I'm sick with it, my stomach aching and writhing.

I feel someone else come into the room, and then a big hand strokes the back of my head. It's Gray. "Fi-Fi, we'll get you through this."

He talks so low, it's barely audible. But the anger under his words is fierce. I appreciate it, but he's wrong. No one can help me through this. The world has labeled me a grasping whore who fucked Ethan Dexter for a prize and took pictures of it. God, they've made what we are so ugly and foul.

Ivy backs away, and Gray bends down to pick me up. For some reason, this makes me cry more. I love Gray for his care. But I want Ethan here to carry me.

Gray sets me down on my bed, and Ivy pulls the covers high before climbing in with me. Their soft murmurs go over my head as I burrow down, but Gray soon leaves the room.

"I'm so embarrassed," I whisper.

"I know. We'll find out what happened. Then I'm going to kick some serious ass." There's a hard note of accusation in her voice I don't like.

"Ethan didn't do this."

Her body tenses. "I know. But it's out there now, and we have to think of damage control."

That squirming feeling goes through my insides again. "The damage is done, Ivy."

She gives me a light kiss on my shoulder. "Get some sleep. We're here for you."

The idea gives me little comfort. For the first time in my life, I feel truly helpless.

CHAPTER 38

Dex

H AS A FLIGHT EVER BEEN so fucking slow? By the time I land, I'm nearly out of my mind. Usually I'm careful of my size, wary of accidentally bumping into someone and sending them flying. Today, I use it in my favor, shouldering my way past slow-moving people.

My insides are rolling so hard I have to swallow several times to avoid being sick. It didn't matter that I contacted my phone provider and reported my phone stolen. The damage was already done. Because I'm the stupid, lazy ass who didn't use password protection. I'm the one who let some spiteful, desperate girl slip out of my room with my phone, and she sold the pictures on there to the tabloids.

And it isn't just pictures she sold, but text messages between Fi and me. Personal thoughts are now fodder for the world. But those pictures. Fi, my girl, the person I care about most, displayed as if she's nothing more than a thing.

It makes me so insane I can't see straight. It doesn't matter that I have lawyers on my side, threatening to sue, ordering take downs. The pictures are out, and the Internet is forever.

The world has seen Fiona exposed. I fucking hate that. I cannot stand the idea of guys looking at her that way. Not without her permission, without her consent.

A snarling noise comes from deep inside of me. And it's all I can do not to start screaming or fucking crying. Because it's my fault. All my fault.

The taxi drive is even worse. The motherfucker recognizes me.

"Hey, man! You're Ethan Dexter!"

Like I don't know my own fucking name. I ball my fists and push them hard into my thighs. Hard enough to stress the muscles there. *Go. Just Go. Get me to Fi.*

"You really a virgin, man?" Clueless fuck who's about to get pummeled chuckles. "Well, not anymore, eh? That's some sweet piece—"

"Say another word and you'll lose your tongue," I snap.

The cabbie blanches, his eyes bugging out. Hell. He might throw me out of the cab, and I'll be stuck on the side of the fucking highway while Fi suffers. I force myself to breathe.

"That's my lady you're talking about, all right?"

The cabbie nods, his gaze darting between me and the road in front of him. "Yeah, man. That's cool. Uh…no disrespect meant."

I grind my teeth, trying to calm. "If you could just get me home as quickly as possible."

"Sure, man. Sure. No problem."

With that, my talkative cabbie speeds up.

———————

I EXPECTED IVY AND GRAY to be at my house; I gave Gray the passcode. They'd been closer to Fi. Gray was playing a game in Atlanta, and Ivy had been visiting her Dad with the baby. What I did not expect, though I probably should have, was Fi and Ivy's dad, Sean Mackenzie—my co-agent with Ivy—to be here.

Shit.

He does not look pleased.

Sean, or Big Mac, as a lot of us call him, used to play point in the NBA. Six-foot-seven if an inch, he's long-limbed and gaunt like some sort of modern day Abe Lincoln. He also has a fierce glare that says he'll gladly tear me a new one. At this moment, I might not give a shit, but he's Fi's dad. If I have it my way, he'll be in my life for as long as we're alive, which means I'd rather be on his good side.

He doesn't wait for me to set my bag down before launching an attack. "What the fuck did you do, Dexter?" He takes a step forward as if he might throw a punch.

Gray steps in too. "Easy there, Sean."

Sean glares and swings his gaze back to me. "I asked you a question."

"I fucked up." And it guts me.

"No shit, Sherlock."

My gaze slides past him to Ivy, who is pale and unusually quiet. "Fi? She here? Is she…" Shit. I can't get the words out. Regret is an agony crushing my chest.

She gives me a nod and gestures toward the stairs. "She's sleeping."

My bag hits the ground and I move.

"Where the fuck do you think you're going?" Sean snaps.

"Where I'm needed most." I don't look back. "You can bawl me out later."

CHAPTER 39

Fi

THE BEDROOM IS DIM AND COOL, the covers heavy and warm. I love this bed. It's big, the mattress firm yet plush on top, the bedding soft and brilliant white. Ethan's bed. Our bed. But it smells of him, spice and warm.

I hug a pillow close and sigh. But the snick of the door opening has me tense. Light angles across the bed then fades as the door gently shuts. I hug the pillow closer, trying to keep it together as Ethan walks in. I don't have to see him to know. He's in my blood now. I'm as aware of him as my own breathing.

The bed creaks and he sinks into it, pulling the pillow free and gathering me into his arms. I flow into his embrace, a sob breaking free despite my best effort.

"Ethan." I wrap myself around him, clinging tight.

"Cherry, baby." His hold is so hard it aches. I love it. He holds me like he's trying to make me part of his body—strong, capable, a sentinel against all the shit the world has thrown at us. His hands stroke my hair, my back, everywhere he can touch.

"Darlin'," he whispers. "Cherry...I..." A ragged breath tears out of him and he shakes. "Fuck. I'm so sorry. I'm so fucking sorry."

I cling to him, fisting his hair. "It's okay."

"It's not," he snaps, low and angry. He takes a deep breath that ruffles my hair. "It was my fault. I let you down."

He sounds so broken that I turn my head and kiss the sweaty crook of his neck, feeling his throat move as he swallows.

"What happened?" I ask.

Ethan swallows again, another tremor running through him. His lips press against my head as he takes deep, hard breaths. And I'm afraid. What has he done?

When he begins to tell me what happened, I'm no longer afraid. I'm enraged. It runs through me like wildfire, heating my blood and setting my heart racing.

He finishes on a garbled sigh, his head sinking as if he can no longer hold it up.

I lean back to face him, touching his cheek so he lifts his head. His bleak expression hurts to see. "You want to hear the fucked up thing?" I ask.

He frowns. "What?"

"My brain stalled out at the naked woman in your bed."

A sad smile drifts across his face. "That was the least important part of the whole story, Cherry."

"I know. But I have this mad urge to hunt her down and punch her in the tit."

Ethan laughs as if he can't help it. "Her tit? That's...oddly specific."

I shrug. "I'm not thinking very rationally at the moment." My eyes begin to water again. "I guess I have tits on the brain."

As if the word *tit* flips a switch, I start to cry, an outright bawl that has my chest heaving. Ethan curses and pulls me tight against his body once more. "Fi...angel, baby..." He murmurs endearments as he strokes my back, runs his fingers through my hair.

Gently he rocks me as we lie in bed and I cry.

"You're killing me, Fi," he whispers brokenly.

"I know." My breath hitches. "I just can't seem to stop."

I want to pull it together, get on with life, and forget all of the shit. But it doesn't work that way. I have an endless supply of tears and rage.

His embrace goes tighter, near the point of pain, but I welcome it, want him to hold me this way forever. He nuzzles my temple. "Then cry all you want. I'm not going anywhere."

Strange thing is, the moment he gives me permission to let loose, I calm. After a while, my body stops shaking and feels heavy with fatigue.

Ethan never stops caressing me. My nose is pressed into the center of his chest. I breathe in his scent and clutch his shirt.

When he speaks again, his voice rough and cracked as if he too has been crying. "Gray texted me a joke the other day. Want to hear it?"

"Knowing Gray's terrible jokes, probably not. But okay."

He rubs the back of his neck. "What do you call a cow with no legs?"

I caress his waist where muscles ripple. "What?"

"Ground beef."

We're both silent for a moment, then I burst out laughing. "God, that's just wrong."

"It's terrible." Ethan turns to his side and touches my cheek. "But it made you laugh. That's all I care about." Pain and regret darken his eyes. "I want to fix this, Fi. But I don't know how. I don't know what to do."

For a guy like Ethan, being helpless must burn. I can feel it in the way his muscles keep bunching and releasing, as if his entire body wants to act, lash out.

My gaze drifts past him, focusing on a distant point, and my voice comes out hollow. "Thing is, Ethan, you can't."

I know it doesn't sit well with him. He's scowling like he wants to punch something. I empathize. But for the first time, I really don't care. I've lost the ability, it seems.

Dex

As SOON AS I TELL Fi her dad is here, she sits up like a shot, her eyes wide, and her hair sticking up at odd angles. She looks heartbreakingly beautiful and completely freaked out.

"Mother fuck." Hauling her little ass out of bed, she pads to the bathroom and starts washing her face. "Just fuck it all. I do not want to face Dad right now."

I get up and follow as she starts to put makeup on with a deft hand. I have no idea how she doesn't poke herself in the eye with that mascara wand thing. Regardless of the situation, watching Fi make herself up is fascinating. It's such a private thing, and I get to witness it.

"Well, he's here, and I don't think he plans on going anywhere," I say as she dabs some sort of ivory cream under her eyes. "Why are you putting on makeup, anyway? You look perfect."

She huffs. "I'm a freaking mess. I'm not facing my dad looking like I've been crying."

A heavy weight sits on my heart. "But you have. There's no shame in that." Fuck, I want to cry too. And that's the truth. It took all I had not to sob right along with her. I feel so fucking helpless right now, I want to punch a hole in the wall.

I cross my arms over my chest and clench my fists so I don't do just that.

Fi flits past me, going to the dresser to pull out a clean shirt. "Well, I am ashamed." Her face twists. "He probably saw pictures of me naked, Ethan."

I duck my head and follow her out.

As expected, Sean is waiting in the living room. He bolts up as soon as we enter, his attention solely on his daughter. "Fiona, honey…" He takes two steps, as if he wants to hug her, but Fi's body language is stiff, and she backs up, bumping into me.

I let her rest against my chest, but I don't put a hand on her either. It's clear that physical comfort is the last thing she wants right now.

"Hey, Dad." Her pained gaze goes to Ivy and Gray, who are also standing—baby Leo secured in his sling against Gray's chest. "Hey."

Ivy glances around. "I'm going to make some coffee. Gray's going to help."

"I made soup for later," Gray tells us, then clears his throat and abruptly turns to follow Ivy into the kitchen. More like runs out of the room. I can't blame him.

Fi looks like she wants the floor to swallow her whole, and Sean has turned his attention to me. I'm pretty sure I'd be dead on the floor if he had his way.

"I want to know what the fuck happened, Dexter," he demands. "Why did some bimbo have your phone?"

From the kitchen I hear Gray say, "Bimbo?" and then grunt. I'm pretty sure Ivy elbowed him. Resisting the urge to run my hand over my beard, I tell Sean what happened.

Even though she's already heard the story, Fi's body grows stiffer and stiffer as I speak. I know I'm causing her more embarrassment, and I mentally curse the little gold-digger who stole my phone and sold our privacy.

Sean glances as Fi again. "I'm sorry, baby girl. I've already sent out a cease and desist order."

"Which is utterly useless," she says in a dead voice. "The damage is done."

"Damn right it is," Sean snaps, glaring at me. "Of all the fucking moronic, idiotic, stupid, fucking, brainless—"

"Dad, stop," Fi cuts in with a hard tone. "Yelling at Ethan won't change anything."

"It'll make me feel a hell of a lot better." He doesn't take his eyes off me. "I trusted you to protect her."

"I know," I manage past the lump in my throat. "You aren't saying anything I'm not saying to myself."

"It wasn't his fault," Fi says. She sounds remote, her gaze lackluster. "It was that opportunistic *bimbo's* doing. Let it go."

Sean runs a hand through his hair. "Look, why don't you pack a bag? Come back to New York while this blows over."

At that, my hands grasp Fi's shoulders. "Like hell."

"You don't get a say anymore, Dexter. Not after you fucked up her life."

The truth of his words is an ugly blow but not enough to keep me quiet. "I appreciate that you are upset, Sean, but there's no way I'm letting you take Fi out of here. I'm not letting her face this alone."

He growls in disgust. "Because you've done such a fine job of caring for her so far?"

Fi shrugs out of my grip, stepping away from me. She might as well have ripped my hands off. She doesn't even look my way as she moves closer to her dad. Away from me. I want to snatch her back, haul her out of this room and back to our bed.

"Dad," she says with a soft sigh. "I need you to go home."

He blinks at her like she's not speaking his language.

Ivy and Gray slowly walk out of the kitchen as if they can't keep hidden for this. Sean doesn't notice. "Fiona—"

"I'm sorry," she cuts in. "I know you want to help. But you being here, saying these things to Ethan. It just makes everything more real. More...humiliating." Her small hand shakes as she runs it through her hair in a gesture just like her dad's. "I can't handle real now, okay? I want to be left alone."

Her dull gaze slides to Ivy and Gray. "You too. I'm so grateful that you guys came here for me, but now I want you to go."

Ivy nods, her expression broken. "Okay, Fi. We'll give you space."

"Now wait just a minute," Sean starts, only to be cut off by Fi again.

"Please, Daddy. I can't." Her chin quivers, but she stays firm. "I need this. Please go now."

I feel sorry for the guy; he looks gutted. For a second we all stand there, no one making a sound. And then Sean sighs. "All right, Fiona. I'll go."

He moves like the walking wounded, slowly gathering his phone from the table. Gray clears his throat. "We'll go with you, Sean."

Ivy looks around as if she suddenly doesn't know which way is out. "I'll just… There's coffee, and I baked you a pecan pie, and…right." Her gaze goes to Fi, but she doesn't make any move to hug her as if she knows Fi won't want it now. "Call me, okay?"

"Okay." Fi stares at the floor, her body stiff, her arms clutching her middle. She looks so small and defeated, I'm crushed all over again. I murmur my goodbyes but keep my eyes on Fi.

It isn't until we're alone in the silent house that I move to hold her. But her hand swipes up, coming between us. "I meant it," she says. "I want to be alone for a while."

Leaving her alone goes against every instinct I have. But I do it. Because whatever Fi wants, I'll give to her.

CHAPTER 40

Dex

WALKING DOWN THE DARK TUNNEL from the locker room toward the bright light of the field beyond is an activity I've always paid attention to. I think a lot of guys do. And it sounds crazy, but the imagery is unavoidable—the dawn of a new game, a new opportunity to change your fate, to win.

It's different at halftime. You can be on top of the world, kicking ass, or lower than sludge, down by horrific numbers, or somewhere in between. In those minutes, those steps between cool darkness and harsh brightness, you make a decision within yourself—quit or to keep fighting.

All the inspirational speeches, tongue lashings, or hand clapping can't do it for you. It's something every man has to find in himself. Sure, we're a team. But no matter how you cut it, a team is made up of individuals, and is only as strong as its weakest link.

I'm almost at the end of the tunnel when it comes to Fi. I can see the light and the possibilities of us. But right now, it's fucking dark. I'm afraid for her. She's been battered by this shit, and I don't know how to fix it.

God, I want to fix it. I want to keep her safe, shelter her from all this ugliness. Just keep her. Forever. She's mine. Mine to protect.

But I give her the space she asks for. Fucking hate that word now.

Space just means I'm alone in my courtyard, and Fi is holed up in our room, napping. That's all she does now: nap.

And I can't snap her out of it. She doesn't want to go out—not that I can blame her. Far too many people recognize her now for all the wrong reasons. It probably isn't a good idea anyway, considering I'm likely to beat the shit out of someone if they make the wrong remark.

I try to entice her to at least come out of the room, watch a movie, work out with me, anything. Sex is out of the question. She changes in the bathroom and crawls under the covers before I can get near her. She always cuddles close in at night, but if I try to touch her in any way that's sexual, she freezes.

When I ask what's wrong, she shakes her head and says the same thing. "I just keep thinking of all those people looking at me naked. It turns my skin, Ethan."

What can I say to that?

Sitting on my tractor tire, I stare up at the window to our room. I ache for Fi.

It's fairly cool outside, the air laden with humidity. I feel it in all my joints and along my shins. My phone buzzes in my back pocket. It's Drew calling.

"Hey, man," I say as I answer.

"Hey. How's Fi?"

I pinch the bridge of my nose. "Not great. She's listless, not interested in anything. It's like she's just…slipping away, you know?"

"Sounds like she's depressed."

"I know that, Battle," I snap, then sigh. "I just don't know what to do about it."

I gave a press statement, saying Fi was my serious girlfriend and someone I admired and cared for. The implication being that all the Fi-haters needed to fuck off. It did precisely dick.

Drew's voice is low. "You need to get her out of the house."

"She won't go."

"Tough love, Dex. Be the guy who kicked my ass every time I moped. You're the anchor, our Big Daddy, and so on."

I laugh without much humor. "I really don't want to play Big Daddy for Fi."

He laughs too. "Yeah, okay, *not* that. But the other shit."

I glance up at the window again. "She's fragile right now. I don't want to hurt her anymore."

"You won't. But that's kind of the point of tough love, isn't it? You do what has to be done no matter what."

No matter what. I push off from my seat on the tire. "I gotta take care of some things," I tell Drew. "Call you later."

"Good luck, man."

I'll probably need it. I hang up and head into the house.

Fiona

FOR THE MOST PART, I avoid the phone. I answer Violet's call because I know she won't give up until we talk, and it's rude to leave her worried.

"I am going to fucking rip this fucking company wide open," she promises, her voice shooting through the phone like street justice.

"No, you aren't," I tell her sternly. "I won't have you risking jail time for me. Revenge doesn't get my pride back."

"It's a start."

"No, Violet. No," I repeat again because I need her to hear me. "Promise me you won't touch them. I'll just worry and be upset if I think you're breaking the law."

She huffs, loud and sharp. "Okay. Fine. But I have to do something." I can hear her nails clack on her desk. "I know! I'm sending you a kickass bag."

"A bag?"

"A new handbag always makes me feel better. Oh, Prada has the cutest little turquoise clutch. I'm sending you that. My cousin works at Vogue. She can get anything."

We chat for a while but it exhausts me. I beg off by saying Ethan is home. A lie. But it sounds better than telling her I just don't have it in me to talk anymore.

A text follows a short time later, one that I can't ignore. It's from my old co-worker Alice.

AliceW: Thought this might cheer you up. Elena's out. Felix gave her the boot this morning.

Me: Get the Papa Smurf out! Why?

AliceW: Apparently her designs for Cecelia Robertson's apartment ended up being an exact copy of Janice Mark's new penthouse. Cecelia was humiliated. Which means Felix was too. He's in the shit now.

I blink at the phone, my mouth hanging open. Holy fuck. Elena used the designs anyway. I'd told her they were bad. Then again, I hadn't exactly explained why they were bad. Maybe she took my words to mean bad quality.

I wait for the guilt to hit but it doesn't come. I can only shake my head. Part of me hopes she's learned her lesson. The other half of me doesn't give a good ripe grape what happens to her. Once a thief always a thief, I guess.

I answer Alice.

Me: I am agog.

AliceW: Take care of yourself, kid. We (and by that I mean all of us lowly workers) are giving Bloom the finger on your behalf.

Me: Thx. Give everyone (and by that I mean all of you lowly workers) a big hug.

After that revelation, I drift off for a while. Then I call my mother. I can't help it. All I want to do is sleep, hide under the soft protection of the covers, and I know it isn't healthy. I know this, and yet I can't stop doing it. I've pushed Ethan away, ignoring the pain in his eyes. Ignoring everything, even the thoughts in my head.

My eyes are gritty from too much crying, and my skin feels swollen, as if I'll soon split down the middle. I know I'm being maudlin and dramatic. I can't keep on like this. So I call my mother.

Even as the line rings, I sweat and wonder why I had to turn to Mom. She answers before I can gather the courage to hang up.

"Fiona, darling girl," she says by way of greeting.

"Hey, Mom." My voice wobbles, and my eyes smart.

"I was going to call to tell you I've booked a flight to see you."

I clutch my phone. "No. Don't do that. Please." I suck in a breath. "It's harder when I have to face you guys."

Silence ticks for a beat. "Sean told me you gave him his walking orders. He was quite put out."

"I didn't mean to hurt his feelings, Mom. I just couldn't deal with…anything."

"You don't want to be coddled," she says. "I understand. More than you know."

An ugly memory stirs, of Mom taking to her room after dad's numerous affairs became public. Which was kind of a joke because his cheating surprised absolutely no one, including her. But the public humiliation was too much.

"I don't know how to get past this," I tell her, my eyes welling up.

"You just do." Her voice is soft, soothing. "Time goes on, and things get easier."

"I tried to go out, but people looked at me…" My stomach clenches, remembering the way the delivery guy seemed to leer at my chest when I'd gone to pay for the carryout Ethan had ordered.

Ethan had stepped in a second later, gently putting me behind him and paying the guy. He didn't say a word. Didn't have to. It was obvious to the terrified delivery guy that he was a few seconds away from breathing out of a tube. He took his money and practically sprinted away.

It might feel good to have Ethan to stand over me like a protective bear, but he can't be there all the time. And he can't keep people from thinking what they want.

Some jackhole reporter pulled up pictures of me kissing Jaden—that silly stunt that feels like an eternity ago—and now they're calling me a money chaser, the same type as the woman who made my mom cry and my dad stray. I shouldn't care what strangers think. It's a horrifying realization to know that I do.

Mom is talking again, drawing my attention back to the present. "Why don't you come to London instead?"

"I don't know…"

"No one here gives a fig about American football. You can relax. We can go Christmas shopping, have hot toddies, perhaps attend a musical."

It sounds so perfectly lovely that I tear up again and sniffle. I miss my mom. I miss being a kid under her care, when the biggest worry I had was doing my homework on time and whether she'd let me have cookies after school.

Mom's voice is coaxing, working over me like spun sugar. "Think about it, darling girl."

I close my eyes and take a breath. "Okay."

CHAPTER 41

Dex

I FIND FI IN THE KITCHEN. She isn't drinking or eating or preparing anything. Which worries me. It isn't like her to stand around, staring off at nothing.

Fi is light and love. Happiness and laughter. Even when she's peaceful she has a radiance. But it's gone now. She's pale and quiet. Her hair has lost its shine, hanging limp around her pretty face.

I want to go to her, hold her close. But lately she flinches when I touch her. And it hurts too much for me to risk it right now. "Hey, Cherry."

Fi blinks as if pulling out of a fog. "Hey. Were you working out?"

"No. Just sitting outside for a while."

My naturally curious girl doesn't ask why. Drew is right; I need to snap her out of this. Even if I have to haul her out over my shoulder.

"I was talking to Drew."

She winces, her shoulders hunching in. "Let me guess, about me."

"He wanted to see how you were doing. He cares about you, Fi."

She shakes her head. "You know you're fucked up when you'd rather no one cared."

"You don't mean that."

"But I do," she snaps, her eyes hard and cold. "I'd be perfectly happy if I never got asked how I'm doing again."

It's my turn to wince. Because I ask her every day. I'm hovering, annoying her with my concern. Her expression tells me that's exactly what she's thinking.

My head begins to pound along with my heart. I run a tired hand over my brow, not knowing what the fuck to say anymore.

Fi runs a finger along the grain in the marble countertop. "I was on the phone too. Talking to my mom."

I've met Fi's mom twice. Fi has her coloring, but Ivy has her features. I'm looking forward to meeting her as Fiona's man, but I don't think that's what this conversation is about. Instinct has me bracing for impact.

Fi's gaze flicks to mine. "She asked me to come to London."

"London. Now?" The pounding in my heart gets harder, faster.

Fi shrugs, studies the marble. "I could go out there. Do things. Not be trapped."

Trapped like she is here with me.

I run a hand through my beard and discover my fingers are trembling. "I can't go with you right now, Fi."

She doesn't look up. "I know."

I've been hit by three-hundred-pound men intent on mowing me down—that hurts less than those two flat words. She doesn't want me to come.

Her voice is soft when she speaks, as if she's trying to spare my feelings. "You once said we should take a step back until things blow over."

"And you told me I was wrong." *Tell me I'm wrong again. Fight for us.*

"Maybe you were right."

My throat clogs, and I have to clear it. "You said you didn't want to be apart."

"I didn't—don't. But this…" She gestures to the windows and the world outside of it. "Is no way to live."

"So stop hiding. Let's go out there, and fuck what anyone thinks."

Her eyes flash, deep green and angry. "Easy for you to say."

"It isn't easy at all, Fi. This whole thing fucking kills me."

"Then help me," she says, leaning toward me, her slim body tight and tense. "I can't stand this, Ethan."

I can't look at her. Not without losing it.

"It's not forever," she says.

She's right. It's just a trip, not the end. But it feels like it. I have a sickening fear that the second she walks out my door, she'll be lost to me.

I want to fight for her. Insist that she be with me. But I can't be selfish. If I force her to stay, I'll lose her anyway. Fi isn't an object. She's the woman I love. And if she needs her mother right now, that's what she'll get.

I swallow hard, and it feels like I'm drinking down chunks of glass. When I talk, my stomach turns over.

"Let me know when you want to go, and I'll book you a flight."

CHAPTER 42

Dex

I GO TO BED FIRST and wait in the dark for Fi to finish up in the bathroom. I used to sleep sprawled out, dead center in my bed. No more. I have a side now—the left, which is closest to the door. I chose it because of some deep instinctual need to place myself between Fi and any possible harm that might come into the room.

Won't matter much when she goes to London. I know I should suck it up. It's just a trip. But it feels like failure. She's going because I fucked up.

I run a hand over the center of my chest. It's constricted, not letting me breathe properly. I hear the sounds of running water stop and then Fi flicking off the bathroom light of as she comes into the room.

I stare up at the ceiling. I used to love watching her walk toward the bed, her hips swaying, a smile touching her lips. God, I loved that sight, loved seeing the heat in her eyes. Most nights, we couldn't keep our hands off each other. It's too hard looking at her these days, knowing she doesn't want me to touch her anymore.

The covers lift, and I steel myself for that inevitable moment when she whispers "Goodnight" and curls in on herself.

But she doesn't do that. She moves across the bed, toward me, the action so surprising that I turn her way to question it just as she snuggles up against me. I automatically wrap her in my arms, my body reacting before my brain can catch up. But then I feel her smooth, warm skin against mine and realize she's naked.

Hell.

She hasn't come to bed naked in what feels like forever. A tremor goes through me as my hand runs down the small of her back. I've missed this. Just holding her. I want to roll her over and push into her, but I keep still, afraid to break this spell that finally has her back in my arms. Her face burrows into my neck as her hands grip my shoulders.

"Thank you, Ethan."

I frown down at the crown of her head, her wild hair shining silver in the darkened room. "For what?"

Fi leans back a little, lifting her face to mine. "For letting me go."

It's hard, looking her in the eye. I don't want her to see my grimace. Having her stay because of guilt is absolutely out of the question. So I distract her, and myself, by caressing her arm. "You'll go…" I clear my throat. "You'll go and have some quality time with your mom. It will be good."

That's about as much as I can say without caving and begging her not to leave me.

Fi's bright eyes shine in the lantern light streaming through the windows. Her expression is thoughtful. "I know you're unhappy," she murmurs, running her fingers through my beard.

"I'm happy when you're happy." It's as simple as that.

She sighs and leans close, pressing her forehead to mine. I close my eyes and just breathe, soaking in as much of her as I can. And she does the same, breathing deep and slow, her touch roaming over me, petting and stroking.

Before Fi, I had no idea how much I needed to be touched. It isn't something you can fully understand until you have it. Fi's hands on my skin eases me in an elemental way, down to my very core. I crave it now, want it always.

And she's leaving me. Maybe not tomorrow, but soon. I don't

know if she'll come back, because I wonder. She's told me she loves me. I've told her too. But is that enough? I want to tell her again, now, but the words get stuck in my throat. To say them at this moment feels like it would be another plea. I can't do that. Not when agreeing she should go to London has her more relaxed and herself than she's been since the pictures were released.

But it doesn't stop the aching weight that's settled in my chest.

Fi threads her hands through my hair, and little shivers run down my spine. It feels so good, I lean into the touch. She does it again and again. "The first time we met," she says, "you were wearing faded jeans and a white button-down shirt."

I exhale in a ragged rush. "You remember that?"

Soft lips brush over my cheekbone. Scooting closer, she kisses my temple, the spot right before my ear. "Your hair was shorter then, but you had that thick beard and kind, knowing eyes. You sat next to me at dinner, staring at me."

A half-laugh lifts my chest, even as I stroke along the curve of her waist. "Jesus, you must have thought I was a total creeper."

I can feel her smile against my skin. "No. It turned me on."

"It did?" Shit, did that sound like a squeak? No. I *don't* squeak.

Her smile grows as she nuzzles my neck. "Of course it did. You were this big, solemn guy looking at me like you'd rather have *me* for dinner. How could it not make me hot?"

I had wanted her for dinner. I'd wanted to place her on the table and sink my tongue into her pussy and discover her taste. Had I any idea at the time how sweet she'd truly be, I'd probably have had to excuse myself from the table.

Fi keeps talking, even as she pets and kisses me everywhere she can find. "But I had a boyfriend…"—Fucker. If he let Fi go he had to be one—"…And I was too young for you."

I have to chuckle. "I'm only three years older, Cherry."

She lifts her head. Hair mussed, cheeks flushed, she's perfection.

Her gaze is soft and tender, and it kicks me right in the heart. "I was a child then, spoiled and not ready to grow up. You were a man. You've always been a man, Ethan. Strong and steady, watching over everyone. I knew that just by looking at you."

She's killing me, bit by bit. I tuck a lock of her hair back, use the gesture as an excuse to stroke her cheek. But she isn't finished talking.

Pressing her cheek into my palm, she smiles a little. "At graduation, you wore a robe, of course, and a dark red tie. Nothing special, but you stood next to me while I took pictures of Ivy and Gray. A guy running by almost knocked right into me, but you stepped between us at the last second and took the impact."

I can't speak. She doesn't seem to need that. Fi leans down and kisses the hollow of my neck. I feel it in my heart, in my toes.

"Draft day, you wore a dark gray suit and a sky blue tie. It made your eyes look more blue than hazel. Everyone around you was nervous. Gray was practically jumping in place, sweating and pulling at his collar. But you simply sat at the table and drank your water."

She chuckles, the sound a purr that makes my skin go tight. "I asked if you were nervous, and you winked at me, told me—"

"Nerves won't get me drafted any sooner," I finish for her, my voice husky and thick.

Her smile blooms wide. "Exactly."

She presses her lips to my sternum before lifting her head again. "I remember everything about you, Ethan. It just took me a while to do it."

I take a breath. Then another. Pressure builds at the bridge of my nose and behind my eyelids. "Cherry."

I kiss her softly, gently, just because I can. And she threads her fingers through my hair, playing with it as if she loves the feel of me.

But she doesn't linger. Instead she moves on, kissing my brows. My eyes close, and she kisses the lids. Her voice comes at me like a dream. "I'm no one special, just a girl who tries to do the right thing when she can."

My eyes snap open. "You are everything," I protest with a fierce whisper. "You are perfect—"

She gives me a quick kiss. "To you, I am. But I guess that's the point. No one has ever looked at me as though they want me—all of me just as I am—until you, Ethan."

"Because I do," I tell her. "I always have."

"And I don't want anyone but you. It doesn't matter if we're a thousand miles apart or right next to each other, I will always want you. Because that's how it is when you find your forever."

My nostrils flare on a sharp breath. I haul her close, wrapping my arms around her so tight, I'm probably crushing her. But I can't let go. My face burrows in her hair. On the next breath, I'm rolling over her and pushing inside of her with a mindless need to feel the tight clasp of her body.

She makes a little sound—half-whimper, half-groan—and I freeze, realizing that, in my desperation, I didn't check to see if she was ready. She's slick, but not enough. I move to draw away, maybe kiss between her legs and make it better.

But her hand slides down my back and grasps my ass. "Don't stop," she whispers. Please don't stop."

A groan tears out of me, and I thrust again, find her mouth with mine. Her body yields to me, soft and luscious, slick and tight.

Awareness ripples over my body. I feel the clench of my ass when I thrust, the tight pull of my abs as I drag back out. My skin prickles with heat, and my panting breaths mix with hers.

I get lost in the act of loving Fi, moving in and out of her with strong, steady strokes that have my cock pulsing and my balls drawing tight. I kiss her until my lips are swollen and sensitive.

Beneath me, Fi's slim body trembles, little gasps leaving her as she lifts her hips to meet mine every time.

"You like that, darlin'?" I murmur into her mouth. "Like my cock moving inside you?"

She grips my ass harder, urging me deeper. "Yes. Yes."

"Good, because it's yours, Cherry. You're the only one who will ever own this cock." I rock into her, the bed creaking beneath us. "The only one who ever has."

She whimpers, her back arching, her sweat-slicked skin pearlescent in the dim light. "Ethan…" The stiff tips of her nipples brush my chest as she writhes. "Ethan…"

She's close. So close. The knowledge sends a punch of hot pleasure up my inner thighs. "Let go, Cherry love." I thrust, working that spot within her that I know she loves. "Let go. I've got you."

Fi's entire body locks up on a wordless cry. Her head presses into the pillow, her nails digging into my flesh as she comes. Slick wetness coats my thighs as the walls of her sex milk my cock with rhythmic tugs.

It sends me over the edge, and I come with her, shouting so loud it echoes through the room. Panting, I roll to my side, pull her close. My body is limp with release. Fi lies quiet, and I can feel the pounding of her heart against her ribs.

A lone tear trickles down her cheek, but she's softly smiling, her expression relaxed. "I needed that."

I'm pretty sure I needed it more.

I brush away the tear with the tip of my thumb and kiss the corner of her eye. "Whatever you need, Fi, I'll give to you."

Even if it breaks my heart to do it.

CHAPTER 43

Fiona

TRUDGING TO THE BATHROOM, I feel hollow, yet calmer. Last night with Ethan made me remember how good it can be between us, how necessary. Nothing is perfect, but I feel grounded now. A little more myself.

In the shower, I turn the water to as hot as I can stand it. Ethan's shower is a glorious thing with multiple heads, designed to shoot out water at different speeds and strengths. The first time I used it, they were all adjusted to his height, and I got a face full of water.

Hearing my shouts of ire, Ethan had run into the bathroom—and promptly laughed his ass off. A wet washcloth to the face ended his glee. He'd retaliated by fucking me up against the shower tiles until I cried for mercy.

I smile at the memory, my thighs tightening with a luscious pull that makes me want Ethan here now, loving me hard and deep all over again. But he's already gone to the stadium to prepare for his game today.

I know he doesn't want me to go to London. While he's excellent at hiding his thoughts from the rest of the world, I can read him like a favorite story. I know the idea of me going away hurts him. But he agreed to it anyway. Because I wanted it.

For so long I thought I needed a man who was always there. One who'd cling to me and tell me he couldn't bear to leave my sight. Which makes me wonder what the hell I was thinking. I like my space, those quiet times when I'm in my own world, creating a design or working on a piece.

A clinger would annoy the shit out of me. Ethan doesn't do that. He has his own life, and while it sucks when he's at an away game, when we're together it's perfection. Being apart and having those times to myself only makes me crave him more, makes me treasure our time together.

I tell myself it will be the same when I go to London, that our eventual reunion will be awesome. But it all feels off, wrong in some way. I think about leaving, and I'm not happy; I'm sad, desperate to hold onto Ethan and not let go. Does that make me the clinger now?

Frowning, I turn off the taps and reach for a towel. Only I make the mistake of turning on my phone as I brush my teeth. It's habit, checking for messages, trolling the Internet. Stupid habit.

Because they've found me again. Doesn't matter that I've changed all accounts. Ugly messages find their way to me.

U Suk cum slut

You dnt deserve him whore!

I wanna fuk U good.

With a shaking hand I delete it all, set the phone down, and close my eyes. I didn't sign up for this, never wanted attention. But it's my world now.

The reality of it threatens to break me. Even now, I can feel all that judgment pushing into my flesh and expanding outward, filling me with hate and self-loathing.

It makes me want to run. Far away. London seems like the answer. But even as I cling to the thought, I think of Ethan. I fear running will break us. He blames himself for this. If I leave, I'm confirming that it's true.

They claim love conquers all. I used to believe that. Used to think that if someone just loved me enough, it would make everything better.

Now I know the truth. Ethan's love won't fix me. I have to do that myself. So, no, his love isn't the cure. But it is something to live for. Without him, I might not want to fix myself. Ethan Dexter makes me want to be a better person. To be brave.

With a hard swipe, I clear the condensation away from the mirror. A version of myself stares back, her eyes ringed with fatigue and stress, her cheeks hollow. I rake my fingers through my wet hair, and Mirror Fi's face comes into sharper relief.

I take her in, study her with unblinking eyes. She looks like shit. Ragged. Defeated.

Before he left, Ethan kissed this face, raining soft gifts of love over cheeks, nose, chin, mouth. Ethan worshiped this face, whispering, "You're beautiful" with each reverent touch. Thing is, I knew he wasn't talking about the way I look, but about how he saw the whole of me.

Who is the real me? I'm not sure I've ever really known. Despite what I project to people, I've never taken the time to get comfortable with myself as a person.

Truth is, we all project a false front to the world, peppering our social media pages with witty words and silly emoticons. Life narrowed down to 140 characters, staged selfies, and tirades over opinion posts. Life lived for the approval of the masses, all while tearing strangers down for the slightest misstep.

And when you turn away from that electric glow, when you no longer see those silent, pixelated opinions, who are you, really?

Who do you see in the mirror? When did the regard of those unknown masses become your existence? Those who will never be there for you except to judge.

If I run, I'm saying that every ugly word thrown my way is true. Worse, if I run, I'm taking the easy way out. I'm letting those people define me.

Staring in the mirror now, a surge of potent rage hits me. It's all bullshit, these pictures I've let tear me down. I let myself feel the rage. And it gives me power. It fills me up and breaks free with a scream. Because I'm over feeling ashamed, and I'm never running away from life again.

Ethan once told me I'd been searching for my joy. I've found it. Now I need to reclaim it.

The edges of my phone bite into my palm as I clench it and dial.

"You've reached Bloom," a woman's voice purrs. "What is your pleasure?"

I grit my teeth, clutch the phone hard enough to feel it creak. "My name is Fiona Mackenzie. I took Ethan Dexter's virginity. I want my million-dollar prize."

Dex

I HAVE ABSOLUTELY NO DESIRE to play the game today. But there's no such thing as taking a personal day in the NFL. Certainly not because you want to watch over your girlfriend. And sure as shit not on a game day.

Fi had shoved me out the door with the assurance that she'd be fine. Right. As if I don't see the shadows under her eyes, the tight lines around her usually soft mouth.

I'm in a bad mood when I enter the locker room. But the familiar reek of sweat, body wash, and equipment soothes me a bit.

No one makes eye contact. It's fucking awkward, and I spot more than one wince as I walk by. The idea that these fuckers have seen Fi's naked body makes me want to break teeth.

I'm almost to my spot when Darren, a safety, mutters "titties" under his breath. He doesn't get to take another. With a snarl, I grab hold of his throat, slam him into the wall. Guys explode into action around me, pulling at my arms to get me to let the little shit go. I brush them off, step into Darren's face.

"You got something to say, motherfucker?"

Darren is wiggling like a worm, punching at my arms, his face darkening and sweaty under my grip. "Get the fuck off me."

I don't think so. No even when hard hands are jerking me back. Not when all the guys are shouting at me to take it easy. Fuck easy. I give Darren another slam before letting him drop. He stumbles but rights himself and takes a step toward me, murder in his eye. Good. Bring it.

"Dexter!" At my head coach's shout, everyone goes still.

I give Darren one last glare as I turn around. No one will look at me.

Coach's expression is tight. "In my office."

I don't say a word as I follow coach. There isn't any needed. I'd do the same thing again, and everyone in the room knows it.

Getting called in to Coach's office is never a good feeling. You remember training camp and the utter terror that hung over your head waiting to be called in to be cut or kept on. It permeates your bones until even walking by Coach's office doors can give you the willies.

Inside, Coach stares me down from the opposite side of his glossy desk. "You going to be able to hold it together, Dexter?"

"Yes." *No. Maybe. I don't fucking know.* But he doesn't want to hear any of that noise. So I stare back calmly, collected.

He temples his fingers—resting them under his chin in the annoying way of all coaches—and continues to stare like it's a high-noon showdown.

Unfortunately for him, that shit has never worked on me. Something he clearly realizes when he sighs and his hands fall to his lap. "You're one of the smartest guys on the team, Dexter. You've always played well. But that extra bit of intensity was missing. It's there now. Focused. You're playing better than I've ever seen."

Great. So my rage is a bonus. It's not like I haven't realized this as well. But I don't like it. Maybe Coach knows that too because he leans forward, bracing his hands on the desk.

"This media circus will die down soon enough. In the meantime, take this as the opportunity it is. Channel that rage, Dex." His expression goes brutal and dead serious. "But keep it on the fucking field."

"Sure thing, Coach." Because what else can I say?

I'm no less angry once I'm on the field and playing. Not by a long fucking shot. Oh, but I channel that rage, pushing it through my lungs until they burn, forcing it into my muscles until they twitch with the need to punish. I use it to break apart the defense, and I soak it up when the crowd roars it approval.

It feels good. All of it so fucking good—an adrenaline rush, the likes of which I've only come close to while thrusting into Fi.

I love football. Always have. Lived and breathed it. But it's never been like this. This rage, the way it suddenly flows through me without hindrance, is something different. Something inside has finally broken free. No more holding back. No more fear.

But my logical brain can't switch off entirely. Because I still know it's Fi's pain that has set this part of me free. How fucked up is that?

At the line, the defense scrambles around, and I sense a zone blitz coming. You can see it, if you pay attention, not just in the way the defense positions themselves, but in their eyes, the tension around their mouths.

I know they think Finn is too inexperienced to deal with them. They're wrong.

I signal the play, and my guys adjust quickly. I get the snap off and we're countering with an offensive blitz before the defense knows what's happening.

It's a beautiful play, and it clearly pisses them off. Norris, a nose tackle, and the fuck-nugget who outed me to the tabloids, whistles long and low. "Feeling good, Dexter? Yeah, I would too if my girl had them perky titties."

Red fogs my vision. "The fuck?" I lunge forward, only to bump into Rolondo, who braces a palm against my gut.

His eyes are dead serious. "Let it the fuck go, man. He's only trying to get to you."

From behind him, I hear a laugh. "Sucking on those titties…"

My teeth gnash. But my guys are surrounding me.

"Save it for the play," Ryder says at my side. "We will fuck them up."

Someone gives me an encouraging slap to the helmet. I move back to the huddle, trying to concentrate. Finn gives me a quick look, but he's calling the next play.

Breathe. Focus. Get it together.

I try. I really do. But I miss a beat, and when I snap the ball, a defensive end blows by me and sacks Finn.

"Shit."

Norris is at my elbow again, snickering. "Fiona Mackenzie, eh? Sweet little honey, D. Looks like she's a natural blonde—"

I don't see anything but a haze and the whites of Norris's eyes as I grab hold of his helmet and rip it from his head. Mine is off too. Not sure how. Don't care. My fist connects with his face, smashing into it so hard I feel it in my spine.

Whistles blow. Yellow flags fly.

Guys pile on top of us. Mine. His. Blows hit my head, back. I don't feel them. I'm pounding Norris, who is stuck beneath me.

And then I'm thrown on my back with a jarring thud. It clears my head enough for me to pop up. A ref struggles to step into my path. I duck around him as other guys scuffle.

"Cool it," shouts a ref.

Finn is at my arm, pulling me back. "Easy, Dex."

But then Norris is coming at me, blood pouring down his nose and in his teeth. "That's why your girl took the money, cuz you're a fucking pussy!"

I'm two steps into coming at him again, when his words hit me and I go ice cold.

Took the money?

Guys are getting into smaller fights again. Rolondo is now up in Norris's face, calling him a punk-ass bitch—refs are plucking them apart.

Someone is walking me backward, pushing me toward the sidelines as shouts continue. But I'm numb, my ears ringing and all available blood rushing to the pit of my stomach.

Took the money?

The ref ejects me and Norris from the game, and the stadium erupts into a chorus of boos.

On the sidelines, my offensive coach is shouting at me that I fucked up while slapping my shoulder to say it's okay I nearly tore Norris's head off. My head coach is bellowing in my ear about being a dumbass. But I'm barely listening.

I find an assistant coordinator. "You got a phone?"

He glances around as if trying to find an escape.

"Give me your fucking phone," I snap. Blood trickles in my eye, and a medic is trying to press a cloth to the cut on my forehead. I wave him off, grab the phone that's offered to me with a shaking hand.

One glance around confirms that everyone's been keeping something from me. I find out soon enough when the headlines pop up.

Fiona Mackenzie claims her million dollars

There's a picture of Fi and me, fuzzy and taken from a distance.

We're laughing, my arm slung around her slim shoulders as we stroll through Jackson Square.

And under that, the confirmation that Fi called Bloom this morning, demanding her prize.

CHAPTER 44

Dex

I DON'T GO HOME. I can't.

Rolondo takes me to his apartment. I head straight to his guest room and into the shower. I hadn't bothered washing up at the stadium, just sat on a flimsy chair in front of my spot until the guys came back in and Rolondo hustled me out of there.

Now I stand beneath cold water, letting it pummel me. Images flash through my mind: Fi's smile. Fi crying. Norris's ugly grin, blood running down his nose. Fi arching beneath me as I take her. Fi and me laughing in a grainy picture. Fi telling me she wants to go to London.

She asked for the money.

Black rage, thick, hot, and choking, surges up my throat. My shout shatters the air as my fist smashes into the tiles. Pain explodes in my hand, but it takes me a moment to stop.

Slumping against the stall, I stare down at my split knuckles, the blood thin and pale as it mixes with the water beating down on it. Tentatively, I make a fist. The skin stings, but nothing else.

Stupid. Fucking stupid to risk a busted hand. I ought to be horrified. I'm not. My mind's on that picture of Fi, a once-beautiful private moment reduced to something ugly and cheap. Does she hate me for giving that chick the opportunity to steal my phone? Was that why?

It makes no sense. Nothing does. I think of Fi and everything she told me last night. She wouldn't do this. There has to be more.

Chest tight, I run my uninjured hand over my wet face, and my fingers tangle in my beard. Again comes the rage, sticky and thick, as if it's coated my insides like hot tar. Pushing away from the wall, I wrench off the shower.

When I emerge, Rolondo has stepped out, probably thinking I need to be alone. He's right.

The pain in my busted knuckles keeps me focused. For so long, pain was the one real thing in my life. Taste the pain, ignore the rest.

By the time I find what I'm looking for under his bathroom sink, the room is a mess. I don't give a ripe fuck. My chest heaves as I stand and look in the mirror. For so long, I didn't know who the fuck I was. Only with Fi did I feel right, at ease within my flesh. The world has tainted that too.

To hell with it.

Grimly, I lift the razor and press it to my skin.

———————

Fi

WITH AN EXCESS OF NERVOUS ENERGY zinging through me, I decide to bake some biscuits. Ivy was right; I do know how to bake. I just tend to do it for emergency purposes only. Right now, baking is the only thing I can think of to calm my shaking hands and reaffirm that Ethan's home is my home too.

It's been a weird day between demanding my money from Bloom and setting up an interview with the press to explain why I did it. Ivy helped me with that, choosing a sympathetic sports reporter—a woman so I would feel more comfortable.

We held the interview through Skype. Ivy had joined from her home in San Francisco, acting as Dex's agent and my moral support.

I was so nervous I feared I might throw up just seconds before we went on air. But then a strange sort of cool calm came over me as I told the reporter of my plans for the money. I didn't speak about the pictures or how it felt to be exposed, and Ivy shut down those questions every time they were asked. The truth is, none of that mattered.

What matters is that Bloom's dirty money will be put to good use. One million dollars to help stop childhood hunger and homelessness.

I went as far as throwing down a gauntlet to Bloom, daring them to double their money and do good for once. I don't expect them to, but it was satisfying to make them squirm.

Ivy thought it was a most excellent *fuck you* to Bloom and all the haters. I'm just happy it's over. I want to get back to my life, to focus on my furniture making, and most importantly, on Ethan.

There hadn't been time to tell him what I was doing and why. He was at his game, and I was too anxious to wait, afraid I'd chicken out.

But it's done now. I feel lighter, free. All that remains is to explain it to Ethan and tell him I'm staying right here where I belong.

The joy I feel in knowing he's mine, in being with him, is so strong it scares me. I want to guard it with my entire soul. I want to tuck big, strong, capable Ethan Dexter to my side and protect him from the world.

It makes absolutely no sense; he doesn't need my protection. But the desire is there just the same. I don't want him to be unhappy or vulnerable to the vultures out there. I want—need—him to know how much he's loved.

I know he feels the same about me. It's in his every touch, every word, look, and smile he gives me. With him, here in this home he's made, I feel that safety.

Only now I'm afraid I might have fucked up by not warning him. Highlights from the game show him being ejected for starting a brawl. I've watched the footage over and over, my mouth gaping. Ethan never fights, never really loses his temper at all.

God, but he looked so angry, blood and sweat running down his face as he pummeled the shit out of a player on the other team.

At first I thought maybe he was fighting because of a disparaging remark the guy made about me. But now I'm not so sure. Because the game is long over, and Ethan still isn't home.

When I tried to call him, I found his phone sitting on his dresser, forgotten in his haste to be on time today.

Short of roaming the city for him, I can only stay here and bake and wait.

I'm pulling a tray of biscuits out of the oven when I hear him come in. "Ethan?"

The sound of his car keys falling into the bowl on the front console fills the silence. Then he speaks, his voice deep. "Yep."

One word. I shouldn't read anything into it, but he sounds off.

"I hope you're hungry," I say in a bright voice, trying to sound upbeat. "I'm making biscuits and was thinking about getting some gumbo from down the street."

Footsteps thud across the floorboards, and Ethan appears.

A biscuit drops from my fingers to the floor as I behold the man standing at the threshold of the kitchen. He's tall, broad, and muscular, his eyes jewel bright. The line of his jaw is a clean sweep, his smooth chin stubborn, firm, and unfamiliar to me. This man doesn't have a beard. Or much hair. All that glorious, sun-streaked brown hair has been shorn off close to his skull.

And he stands there—hands shoved in his pockets, a gray cotton button-down shirt straining at his shoulders—looking so different I hardly recognize him. Younger, more vulnerable. Exposed.

"Why?" I warble, my heartbeat thudding in my throat.

He shrugs, his gaze sliding away. "Felt the need for a change."

In a daze, I walk to him. He keeps his head down, the squared-off hinge of his jaw bunching as if he's grinding his teeth.

"Ethan." My hand touches his smooth cheek. God. His beard. His thick, lustrous beard is gone. A deep pang of mourning rips through me. "Why?"

He shakes his head. Once, as if to say, *don't ask me. Don't make me say it.*

But I know. With a cry, I fling myself on him. And he gathers me up, holds me against him as I press my face into the warm hollow of his throat. He smells the same. Exactly the same. Like birthdays, Christmas morning, and pancakes at midnight.

I've needed to feel his solid strength and hear his steady breath, more than I realized. Tears well hot and heavy in my eyes as my fingers find the back of his shorn head.

I must be choking him, my arms are wrapped around his neck so tightly. But I can't stop. I want to be closer, under his skin, or maybe tuck him under mine where I can keep him as safe as I can. Sobs burst out of me, rapid fire.

Ethan's arm wraps more snuggly around my waist, his big, warm hand on the back of my head. "You're crying over the loss of my beard." He doesn't sound upset but as if he's confirming a long-suspected belief.

And it breaks my heart. Somehow I manage to let him go enough to look up at his face. His eyes are solemn, sad, as if he hates seeing me cry but doesn't know what to do about it.

His thumb brushes my wet cheeks, but he doesn't say anything, just lets me look at his now-smooth face.

I cup one of his cheeks, press my palm against skin that's warm and tight. "I'm crying because you thought this outer shell meant more to me than what's inside of you."

His big body jerks in surprise, but I cling, not letting him go. As if he's too tired to keep his head up, he bends down and buries his face in the crook of my neck.

Gently, I stroke his head, his close-cropped hair bristly yet soft.

"You think I kissed you that first time—that I wanted you—because of a beard? You couldn't be more wrong. It was because you were a sexy-as-fuck, sly-as-all-hell charmer who grabbed my attention and held it."

A muffled grunt blows into my hair.

"I mean, look at you," I say, even though we're still clutching each other and I can't see anything. But my memory is just fine. I think of his solemn eyes and that mouth of his, that soft, wide, pouty mouth. "I'm in serious danger of having a young Marlon Brando *Street-Car-Named-Desire* moment here. I kind of want you to tear at your shirt and shout '*Stella!*' Or I guess it should be '*Fiona!*'"

Ethan snorts, but it sounds like he's trying not to laugh. Still, tension vibrates along his strong body, and I know he remains upset.

When he finally answers, his voice is raw. "Rather hear you shout *my* name, Cherry."

"So make me."

He doesn't move, only grows stiffer.

"Ethan, I loved your beard, but I love you more."

He blinks down at me, then he swallows hard as if trying to clear his throat. "I love you too, Cherry." He presses his forehead to mine. "Feels like I've loved you forever. I thought you knew that."

There's an accusation in his voice—soft but there all the same.

"I do, Ethan. You've been so good to me."

His grip flexes on my hips. "Then why did you do it? Why did you take the money?"

Surprise freezes me to the spot. He stares down at me, no longer soft but completely hard, stark devastation and cold anger in his eyes.

CHAPTER 45

Fiona

E THAN HAS NEVER LOOKED AT me in anger. It's a horrible thing to see it now. "I can explain," I say.

He scoffs. "Just the words a guy wants to hear after he's been metaphorically kicked in the teeth by his woman."

My breath pushes out in an anxious rush. "I'm not going to London."

Not the best opener. Based on the sidelong look he gives me, Ethan clearly thinks so too.

"Okay. And that has to do with taking Bloom's fuck-money how?"

Wincing, I try to touch his chest, but he backs away, shoving his hands deep in his pockets as he goes. The fact that he no longer wants to touch me, that he's putting physical distance between us, has my insides tumbling.

"I realized that going to London was just me running away—"

"No shit," he cuts in, his voice flat, his gaze blazing with tamped anger. But it's slowly starting to simmer. He looks so different without his beard, his head shaved close to his skull. His features are stern and unforgiving.

I clutch my skirt with cold fingers. "Right, so…thing is, I didn't want to run any more. I demanded the money from Bloom because I knew that would end it."

Another ugly snort leaves him, and he shakes his head. "Well, it certainly does end things—"

"No, Ethan," I say, stepping forward. "Not like that. I'm giving the money to your charity. All one million. Ivy and I had a press conference. I said I was donating it on your behalf, because Bloom getting sleazy PR by exploiting your personal life should come to some good."

He stills, his eyes narrowing. "You gave it to charity?"

"Of course. Did you really think I'd claim that disgusting prize for myself?" I swallow hard, trying not to be offended at the idea. I ought to have warned him.

Ethan's shoulders bunch with tension. "No. But I didn't know what to think, Fiona. I had some fucking linebacker laughing in my face, telling me my girl went for the money."

"Baby…I'm so sorry." I take a step forward.

But he backs away, his face closed off. Regret punches through me.

"Do you have any idea what it did to me," he grinds out. "To hear it from someone else? Because, let me tell you, not a single fucking person on that field knew about you giving the money to charity. They looked at me like I was a massive dupe, a fucking joke."

Shit. I didn't consider the lag time between asking for the money and my interview, which should be airing right about now.

"I'm so sorry, Ethan. You're right. I should have warned you. I wasn't thinking. I just… I wanted to set us free. I needed to take the wind from their sails. Taking that money and giving it to your charity? What can anyone say about us now?"

He expels a breath. "Okay, fine. But we should have done it together."

I give a jerky nod, misery spreading. "I'm sorry."

Ethan laughs without humor, tilting his head back to blink up at the ceiling. "God. You cut me off at the knees out there, Fi. I walked into that blind."

"Ethan—"

"I know," he says with a terse snarl. "You're sorry. You didn't mean it." He glances at me, and there's no joy in the look. "Believe me, I'm trying to get over it. But you were my safe harbor, Fi. The one person I've never had to worry about…"

He spits out a curse and turns away, as if he can't look at me.

"You're my safe harbor too," I say, holding back a sob. "I messed up. I never wanted to hurt you. I didn't think—"

"No," he shouts, "you didn't."

Emotion punches into my chest, and I snap. "Damn it, Ethan. I've been hurting here too! It wasn't your naked picture spread all over the Internet. You're not the one being called a whore or having fucking creepers comment on your body!"

"You think I don't know that?" He takes a step toward me as a deep flush works its way up his neck. "You think it doesn't fucking gut me that I caused it? You know it does."

"Then don't rip into me for finally taking control of the situation! Because your whole 'no comment' stance wasn't doing the fucking job."

He freezes and frowns at me as if seeing me for the first time. "Shit, did you do it this way because you were pissed at me?"

All the air leaves my lungs. I practically choke as I stumble back. "Did you just say that? Did you just fucking accuse me? Fuck you, Ethan!"

His face twists. "Don't get all righteous on me. I'm allowed to question this."

"Then don't *you* go getting all righteous on me," I snap back, stabbing my finger in the air. "I get that I fucked up. I get that you're mad. But you have no right to—"

"I've no right?" His expression is feral now, teeth bared, muscles bulging. "Because I'm calm, sensible Dex? The guy who takes a beating and gets back up without complaint? Well, too fucking bad. I *am* mad. And I'm sorry if that offends you, but I'm not going to suck this up.

Not yet. Not fucking yet, Fiona!"

I hate the sound of my name on his lips—no longer reverent but a curse. "I didn't mean to hurt you," I whisper.

His chin tilts up. "I know that. I know you didn't mean it, but...shit." He begins to pace, his hands going to his head to pull at his hair, which is no longer there. Agitation makes his steps jerky, his arms restless. "I know. I'm just. Fuck, it. I can't—" He takes a deep breath and then another.

I see the moment he totally loses his shit, like a dam that can no longer hold back the flood. He cracks with a long, ragged cry. "Fuck!" He slams the side of his fist against the aged brick wall. "Fuck, fuck, fuck!" Every curse punctuated by a punch.

"Ethan. Calm down—"

"No!" he shouts over me, his eyes on the wall. A sheen of sweat covers his skin, glistening over his biceps. "No. I'm so fucking sick of always being the rational one! Well, guess what? I'm done."

His voice rises with every word, going to full-on bellow. "I'm pissed. At everything. I'm just...fucking pissed, Fi!"

Noted.

I bite my lip, tears smarting. This isn't just about today. It's everything that's come before. It's Ethan never allowing himself to fully let go until now.

With a guttural cry, he turns, tearing one of his paintings from the wall. It flies through the air, spinning like a pizza box before crashing into the far wall, the frame snapping.

I can only stand silent as he shouts, his voice filled with pain and rage. He punches the edge of the heavy wooden bookcase that divides the living room and a small reading nook. "Just—motherfucking shit!"

Books soar across the room as he hurls them in rapid succession.

I've always wondered how it would be for Ethan to totally lose it. Now I know. And it breaks my heart. Because I know his rage right now is pain, a soul deeply hurt that has no other outlet but to burn, hot and violent.

A sob of frustration rips from his chest, and he braces himself against the bookcase. For a second, I think he's calmed.

An ungodly roar tears from him, and his muscles bulge as he pushes against the bookcase, which is bolted to the floor. The whole structure creaks, threatening to topple.

"Ethan," I shout. "Careful—"

But I'm too late. The massive case tips too far and smashes to the floor with such force that the house shakes. I jump back, plastering myself to the wall as broken pottery shards, knickknacks, and books fly everywhere.

It scares the shit out of me. I know he'd ever hurt me, but the base violence of the act rattles my bones.

He stands there, his muscles straining, his chest heaving. He blinks rapidly as if to clear his thoughts, but that crazed look is still there.

"Okay," I say through a breath. "That's it."

I turn, grabbing my bag and coat off the hook.

"Fi!" Ethan's shout blasts over my skin. "You walk out that door—"

I don't hear the rest because I've already slammed it shut.

Dex

THE RED HAZE THAT CLOUDS my vision blows away with the slam of the door. For too long, I simply stare at the empty space Fiona used to occupy, trying to figure out what the fuck just happened. And then what I've done hits me like a blindside tackle. My breath leaves in a whoosh, and I struggle to find it again.

"Fi!" I stumble forward, tripping over the stupid bookshelf. "Shit. Shit!"

Hopping over the case and picking my way through the mess slows me down.

Shit, I'm such an asshole. I had a total mantrum, and now I've scared the hell out of her. The expression in her eyes was terrorized. And that's all on me.

I wrench open the door and race down the stairs.

"Fi!" I don't see her, but she can't have gone far.

Outside, rain is coming down in hard sheets. I'm instantly drenched, my vision obscured as water runs into my eyes. I wipe my face, scan the gloomy courtyard. Empty.

Shouting her name, I run toward the garage. She isn't there. Isn't in the studio.

My heart pounds, fear and regret squeezing at my chest. I knew the moment I saw her anguished look that she hadn't meant to hurt me, hurt us. And still I lost it. I said horrible things, made her afraid. I think of the room I wrecked in front of her and feel sick.

Bracing my hands on my wet knees, I try to breathe, to think of where she might be. It occurs to me that she might have gone out the front entrance. But the street is dark and empty, except for the lone, hunched vagrant in the distance, picking his way through garbage bins, his shape a black blob beneath the hazy streetlight.

With a sigh, I sink down to sit on my doorstep, unwilling to go back inside. Rivers of dirty water rush along the gutter. Rain comes down so hard it bounces off the pavement. I sit with my knees up, holding my head in my hands as if it can stop the ache. I sit until I'm soaked to the skin. But I'm not going to move. Not until Fi returns.

Hell, she might not return. Have I lost her?

The idea that she might think I don't want her any more closes my throat.

"Hey there, fella." The old homeless man stands in front of me. His tattered overcoat seems to be keeping him fairly dry, though water beads in his gray hair and runs down his ruddy face.

"Take this." He hands me what used to be an umbrella, the spines broken and hanging higgledy-piggledy. It wouldn't protect against a mist, much less this. But it's his, and he's offering.

I blink up at him, shocked and feeling like shit, but find my voice. "That's okay, man. Can't get much wetter."

He lets out a raspy laugh, tucking the umbrella back into the basket-cart at his side. "Ain't that the truth." He nods toward the night sky. "Bad weather will blow past. Always does."

I want to laugh until I cry, but I nod and reach into my pocket for my wallet. He sees me and holds up a hand. "No need for that. No need at all. I'm getting on home now."

I've seen him around and know this is a lie. But pride is a powerful thing, and so I push my wallet back. "Have a good evening, mister."

He leaves me to silence and the sound of the rain pattering against the pavement. And I sit back, my head thumping against my front door and close my eyes.

Pride. I thought I was so fucking humble, above it all. But my pride kept me from going after Fi when I first saw her. It's kept me from demanding the things I want in life until it was easy. And it had me lashing out when I should have listened.

Fucking pride.

"Ethan?"

My eyes spring open. Fi stands a few feet away, holding a grocery bag in her hands. Illuminated by the gas lantern hanging over our door, her little frame is dwarfed by her big yellow raincoat. I scramble to my feet, my sneakers squeaking on the pavers.

"Fi." I take a step forward, my chest heaving. "Cherry, I... I'm sorry. I didn't mean to scare you."

"I know."

"All that stupid shit I said, I was just—"

She takes a step too. "You don't have to explain. Everyone deserves to howl at the moon at some point. And you've had a shitty day. A shitty month, really."

We've both had a shitty time of it, yet she wasn't the one who went into Hulk-Smash mode. "I shouldn't have trashed the room. I scared you."

She frowns, and rainwater trickles down her cheeks like tears. "What scares me more is that you believe you need to hide your emotions."

My throat works on a noisy swallow, and I have to blink away the rain drops that blind me.

"What's really bothering you?" she asks when I don't speak.

"I liked it," I confess in a tight voice, my eyes finding hers. "Allowing myself to let go." It had relieved a pressure I'd felt building for what seems like forever.

She gives me a small smile. "It's okay to get angry or upset, you know. If all this has taught me anything, it's that we can't plan life. It just happens. If you hold on too tight, you might break. And I don't ever want to see you broken, Ethan."

I don't have it in me to explain the stark, gray terror I felt when I realized she was gone. If losing my temper meant losing her, I'd hold onto it as tight as I could. Because without her, I'd be broken anyway. "Being with you. Loving you—You make me feel everything."

Another step and she's within touching distance. "And that's a bad thing?"

"No. I was numb before you. I want to feel. I just… I don't want to scare you. I got angry, and you left. I thought…." My breath hitches. "You left."

Green eyes stare up at me through clumped, wet lashes. "I needed air. You needed to cool down."

"You didn't let me finish back there. If you leave, I'll follow. I'll always follow."

"I know that. In fact, I'm counting on it. But I'm done running. You're stuck with me, Big Guy." She raises her hand a little, showing me the bag she's holding. "I just thought I'd get you some gumbo. It's cold and raining, and you love it—"

I grab hold of her and haul her close, wrapping her up in my arms. My lips find hers, cold and wet but perfect. I slip my tongue into her warm mouth where she tastes of rain and Fi. I cup her cheeks, try to warm her skin, and kiss her until I can't breathe.

She leans into me, her raincoat squeaking, her soft breasts plump against my chest. Somehow we're both apologizing in the kiss, breaking apart and coming back together again and again, soft, deep, finding new angles.

With every touch of her mouth to mine, the tight knot inside my chest eases. I've made a habit of locking up my emotions and hiding them from the world. But this girl—the one who inspired me to sing my ass off on a stage, who brings me gumbo when I've shown her my worst—she makes me whole. She helped me find myself.

Fi is done running, and I am over hiding. It's as simple as that.

Our lips drift apart. Rain turns the world into a blur, but my mind is clear. "I love you. I don't say that enough. Just know that whatever I do, wherever I am, it is a constant refrain in my heart. You color my world, Fi."

She smiles up at me, her skin glistening and her eyes bright. Gently she touches my cheek with her free hand. "Ethan, I might not be perfect, but no one will ever love you more than I do."

I don't think I knew how much I needed to hear those words until she says them. I rest my forehead against hers. I'm freezing, but my heart is finally warm again. I snuggle her closer.

"You *are* perfect, Cherry. You're my kind of perfect."

"You're my kind of perfect too, Ethan Dexter."

That's all I've ever needed.

EPILOGUE

Fiona

One year later…

THE HOUSE LOOKS PERFECT. Garlands of evergreen—entwined with twinkling white lights—grace the doorways, window frames, and the big fireplace mantel. Ivory pillar candles are set up in clusters, paired with clove-dotted oranges and sprigs of holly. In the corner by one of the big windows that overlooks the street stands a twelve-foot tree. I kind of love the fact that even Ethan has to pull out the stepladder to decorate the top of it.

But he does the job with a smile on his face. He hangs little football helmets covered in glitter, deep red crystal cherries, die-cast commercial jet planes, even a blown-glass ornament shaped like the Golden Gate Bridge.

"Fi sure likes her themes," Gray observes, helping out too.

Ethan grins, his concentration on hanging a tiny mic. There's a flush on his cheeks that I know is from happiness. This year, our tree tells the story of us, and he knows the significance of each and every item I've picked.

"What's with this one?" Ivy asks, holding up an ornament shaped like a stack of pancakes.

Ethan glances at it and catches my eye. His brows rise with humor even as his gaze goes hot. My cheeks flush warm in response. We've had plenty of pancakes at midnight since our first attempt. After all, a girl needs to keep up her strength.

"Inside-joke ornament," Anna guesses, her nose wrinkling. "Quick, put it on the tree and move on before they feel compelled to explain."

At her side, Drew kisses the top of her head before saying, "I'm pretty sure Dex would have to be threatened with grievous bodily harm before he talked."

I hand Drew a mug of hot cider before giving one to Anna. She isn't drinking any alcohol: three guesses why. I give them both a big, sweet smile. "I'm happy to tell you all about those pancakes—"

"No!" the room shouts as a collective whole. Well, all but Ethan who snickers as he hops off the stepladder and comes to me.

He wraps me in his arms, bringing my back against his hard chest. His breath stirs my hair. "You're so bad, Cherry."

I relax against him. "Suckers. As if I would talk about our midnight *lurve*."

His chuckle is a rumble I feel through my body. With a quick, affectionate kiss to my cheek, he walks off to collect the stepladder and put it away.

"How's the shop going, Fi?" Anna asks.

Last April, I'd picked up my first client in New Orleans, Ethan's teammate Rolondo Smith.

Rolondo had me redecorate his condo and then his beach house in Florida. When he found out I'd planned to open my own business, he offered to back me financially. And while Ethan had insisted that he wanted to help me with funds, I finally made him realize that I needed to do this without my boyfriend's help. In October, I opened a furniture-design shop on Royal St.

"Really well," I tell Anna now. "I'm at the point where I need to hire an assistant."

"More like two," Ethan says. "So my girl can spend more time in her workshop."

I love that he knows how cathartic it is for me to spend time working on my pieces, and how much attention he pays to my work.

"This is true," I say to Anna. "Definitely two assistants."

I'm still working with Jackson and Hal, selling furniture to their New York clients, who pay top dollar. To say business is booming is an understatement.

When Ivy goes to check on Leo, who is napping in the bedroom, Drew and Ethan help me set the table. Anna and Gray fuss in the kitchen. Apparently they're picking up an argument they started this morning about brining versus basting the turkey.

Gray had argued with a complicated mathematical defense, complete with statistics and water-retention ratios, that had our eyes glazing over. Though he'd gotten his way in choosing the method of cooking—mainly because no one could stand hearing him talk nerd any longer—he and Anna are back at it again. Because Anna still thinks brining is better.

Ethan ends the argument by pointing out that the damn bird is done and could we please just eat it now?

"You'll see," Gray promises as he carries out a golden brown turkey worthy of a Norman Rockwell painting. "Simple butter basting produces a superior tasting bird."

"A dry bird," Anna retorts.

Despite their bickering, we're all looking forward to our meal as we sit down at the table—one of the first pieces created in my new workshop. Made of reclaimed cypress wood, it's wide and long enough to seat twelve. With six of us here, we have room to spread out, which is good since the table is laden with food.

Football players eat. A lot. But I'm not complaining. Especially when I have Ethan's big, strong body to play with on a daily basis.

I watch him as he leans over to light the candles. He's dressed in jeans and a dusky blue button-down that hugs his broad chest. His sleeves are rolled up to the elbows, exposing the colorful tats on his forearms. Those arms can toss around tractor tires without breaking a sweat and hold me as gently as if I'm made of blown glass.

A beard—not as full as it used to be but no less sexy—shadows his jaw. His hair is growing out too, still super short on the sides and sticking up in thick, dark brown spikes at the top.

He's so damn hot, he leaves me breathless every time I look at him. I honestly don't know how I didn't jump on him at that first Christmas party.

Catching my gaze, he winks and sits at my side. One hand slips under the table to settle warmly on my knee while the other lifts his wine glass high.

At his salute, we all pick up our glasses.

"So then," he says. "Merry Christmas."

Even though it's technically Christmas Eve, we all toast.

Gray sets his glass down. "Shouldn't Fi be saying, 'And God bless us, every one'?"

"Are you implying I'm Tiny Tim in this scenario, dickface?"

"Dickface?" Gray gives an expression of mock outrage. "If I didn't happen to have an awesome dick, I might be offended."

"So you're saying you're on board with your face resembling your dick?" Drew asks with a laugh.

"I'm saying that if my face has to resemble a dick, it might as well be the stunning sight that is my own," Gray retorts with a waggle of his brows.

I lean in. "If you want to talk about stunning dicks—"

"No!" everyone shouts again.

I shrug and hide my smile as I take a sip of wine.

"I'm so glad sausage is on the menu," Ethan deadpans before slicing into his banger. Drew and Gray wince, but Anna, Ivy, and I laugh.

Happiness is infectious and fills me with warmth. I'm no longer that restless girl I'd been for so long. I'd finally found my place. I give Ethan's shoulder a kiss, and he winks at me as if he knows exactly how I feel.

MUCH LATER, it's just me and Ethan, kneeling on our big bed, the golden glow of lamplight casting shadows over his bold features. With infinite tenderness, he cradles the sides of my neck as he slowly peppers my face with kisses. His soft lips and prickly beard send little tickles along my skin, and I sigh, leaning into his touch.

His voice is a low rumble. "So your stance on beards is?"

I smile, remembering how he first got me to kiss him. "Total fangirl. You might even call me a groupie."

He grins against the corner of my mouth before giving my upper lip a little suck. "And football players?"

"I'm completely gone on one in particular."

He hums in approval. "Good thing. He loves you, heart and soul."

This time, I capture his lips and kiss him with enough heat that his chest hitches. I smile at that. "I love you too."

Warm breath gusts along my mouth as he speaks again. "So tell me," he murmurs, still mapping my face with kisses, "what's your stance on marriage?"

My heart stops, and I utter a small gasp. Ethan pulls away just enough to meet my eyes. He looks at me with that solemn, steady gaze I've come to love so much—the one that sees my soul and wants to keep it in his care.

Tears clog my throat, make my voice thick, but my lips quiver with a smile. "Is this your way of getting me to marry you?" I tease, even as my heart pounds against my ribs.

His thumbs stroke my cheeks as his quiet eyes stare into mine. "Will you?"

I laugh, the sound getting caught on a gurgle of happy tears. "Yes, Ethan Dexter. Hell fucking yes." I launch myself into his arms.

Laughing, he falls back on the bed, taking me with him. "Hold up," he says, as I cover his face with kisses. "You didn't let me give you the ring."

"The ring! I forgot about that. Gimme, gimme."

He laughs again. "Then give me some room to get it."

As soon as I lean back, he grins and reaches into his pocket to pull out the ring.

It's a large, round, pink diamond in a rose gold bezel setting. Simple, elegant, yet wonderfully girly. He slips it on my finger, and I'm in instant love.

"You made this, didn't you?" I ask, my gaze going to his and then back to my ring.

"Not made," he says a little gruffly. "But designed it, yeah. How did you know?"

"Because I know you." Ethan would plan everything out, down to the exact way the ring should look.

"Do you like it?" He's frowning at the ring as though checking for flaws in the design.

I cup his cheek and lean against his solid warmth. "It is utterly perfect. Just like you."

He blushes at that. So I kiss him some more until he forgets to be embarrassed and gets caught up in kissing me back. He's completely mine now. He put a ring on it, and I'm going to do the same.

"Let's do it in San Francisco," I say, resting my chin on his chest and admiring the way the pink diamond glitters in the low light.

He nods as if this makes perfect sense. "At the scene of the crime."

I tickle his ribs, and he grabs my hand to nip my fingers.

"Be warned," I tell him. "I might get the urge to take off my dress and jump in the pool. But if I do, I'm taking you with me this time."

His smile holds the promise of forever. "Sounds like a plan, Cherry."

Thank You!

Thank you for reading THE GAME PLAN! I hope you enjoyed it!

Would you like to receive sneak peaks before anyone else? Or know when my next book is available? Sign up at www.thehookup. kristencallihan.com for my newsletter and receive exclusive excerpts, news, and release information.

Reviews help other readers find books. I appreciate all reviews, whether positive or negative or somewhere in between.

Author's Note

One of the first lines I wrote about Dex appears in THE HOOK UP, when Drew wonders if Dex is "pulling a Tebow", which was Drew's way of saying he suspected that Dex was a virgin. Until then, I hadn't considered writing a virgin hero, but the idea stuck and fit with Dex's quiet, reserved nature.

Later, when I was doing research for THE GAME PLAN, I came across a story about the infamous cheating site, Ashley Madison, offering a reward of one million dollars to anyone who could claim they'd taken Tebow's virginity. It was too fantastical to pass up, and it fit with Dex's underlying fear of his private life being publicly exposed.

It was in my head to have a spinoff featuring Violet, Fi's hacker friend, threatening to destroy the site by releasing the client roster to the public. Because that really would be a meaty tale. And then the Ashley Madison hacker scandal ended up happening in real life about a month before I finished the book.

All of which is to say that THE GAME PLAN is my "ripped from the headlines" homage.

Hope you enjoyed!

Acknowledgments

A huge thank you to the awesome people who gave me feedback, sent me NFL/football factoids, and basically held my hand throughout the writing process: Jen, Elyssa, Sarina, Tessa, Monica, Carolyn, and Jill. Thank you, most excellent beta readers, Katie and Sahara. Thank you, Nina, for your on point PR skills and advice.

Gray's terrible joke comes to you via one drunken night with my sisters, Liz and Karina. I believe it was Karina's joke. Thank you for that.

To my husband who held down the fort while I was writing, and to my kids who gave me encouragement along the way.

Thank you awesome readers and bloggers—without you this book would not exist.

And a special thanks to the members of The Locker Room, the best place to hang out and talk sports romance (heck, ALL romance) that I know.

About the Author

Kristen Callihan is an author because there is nothing else she'd rather be. She is a RITA award winner, and winner of two RT Reviewer's Choice awards. Her novels have garnered starred reviews from Publisher's Weekly and the Library Journal, as well as making the USA Today bestseller list. Her debut book FIRELIGHT received RT Magazine's Seal of Excellence, was named a best book of the year by Library Journal, best book of Spring 2012 by Publisher's Weekly, and was named the best romance book of 2012 by ALA RUSA.

Made in the USA
Coppell, TX
13 April 2020